I0762265

TO WIELD A CROWN

CURSE OF THE CYREN QUEEN BOOK IV

HELEN SCHEUERER

www.helenscheuerer.com

First printing, 2022

Print paperback ISBN 978-1-922903-00-6

Print hardcover ISBN 978-1-922903-01-3

Ebook ISBN 978-0-6452216-6-4

Cover design by Deranged Doctor Design

For Aleesha and Claire,
who championed this series from beginning to end.

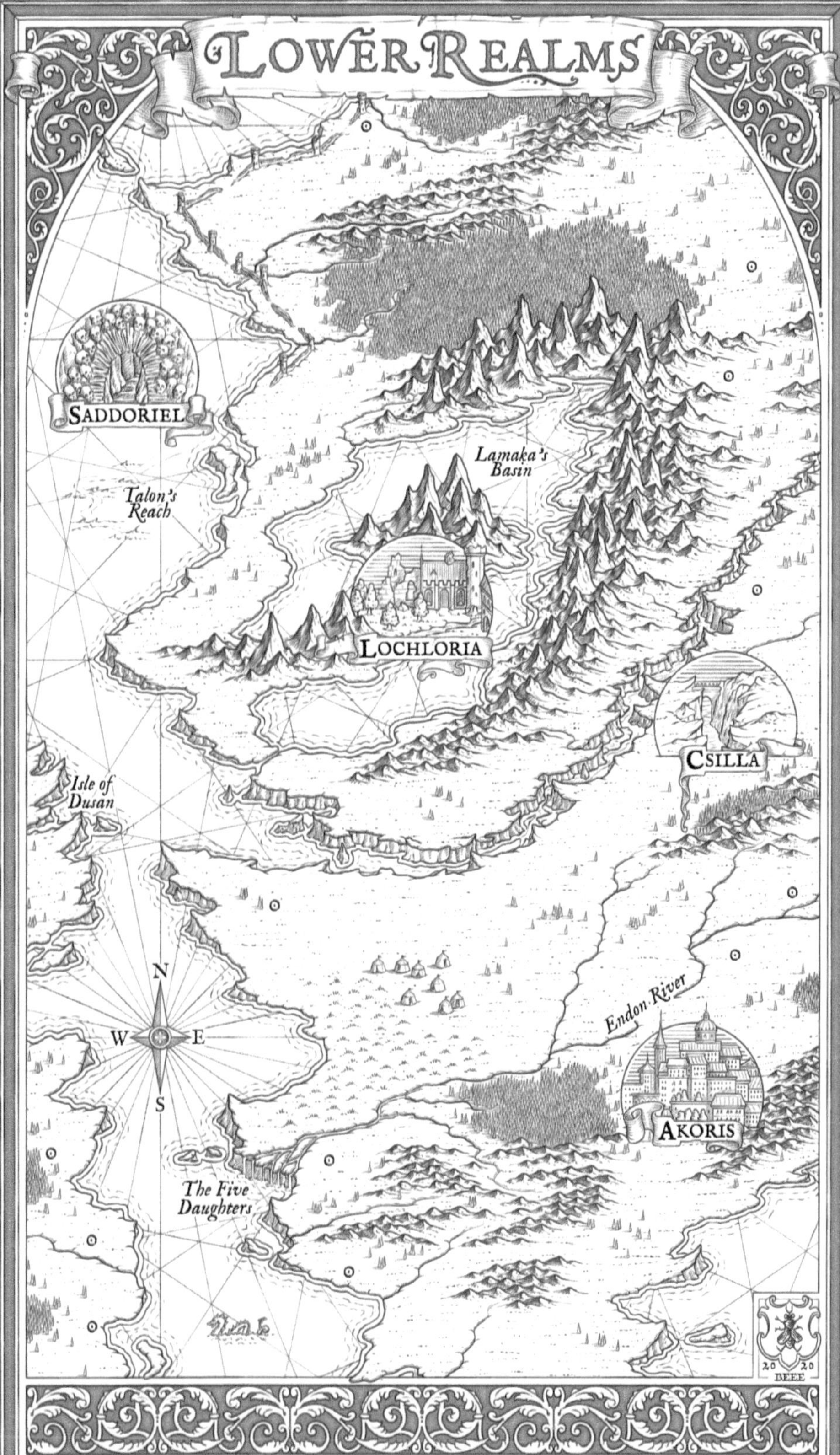
LOWER REALMS
SADDORIEL
Talon's Reach
Lamaka's Basin
LOCHLORIA
CSILLA
Isle of Dusan
N
W
E
S
Endon River
AKORIS
The Five Daughters
20 20
BEEE

PROLOGUE

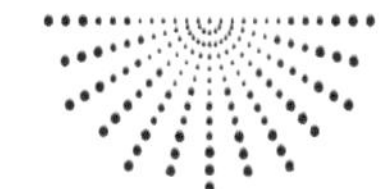

In the waning torchlight of her cell, Cerys sliced through her matted curls with a jagged, bloodstained talon. Severed midnight tendrils fanned out around her on the algae-slick stone and she moved slowly to the next lock, pretending to carefully consider it before she sawed through it, letting it float to the ground. She knew Rohesia was watching her from beyond the bars of bone, and so she kept cutting, playing the part of the mad cyren, maintaining the mask she'd worn for centuries.

Curiosity won out in the end, though, and not only because she was dying to gaze upon her daughter, but because for the first time in seventeen years of visits, her daughter had *brought someone with her.*

Cerys lifted her gaze, noting her daughter's talons shoot out. It was a testament to the mask Cerys had worn for so long, that Rohesia didn't know how deeply loved she was. After a moment, Rohesia's talons retracted and Cerys saw the lifetime of questions in those moss-green eyes, the longing for answers. She watched as Rohesia surveyed her hacked hair and the carvings of supposed madness behind her in horror, her thoughts as plain as day on her face.

The scrape of shoes sounded behind Rohesia, and squinting into the darkness, Cerys spotted him … A young human man, his half-gloved hand reaching for the brooch pinned to Eadric's cloak.

A *human* … In *Saddoriel's Prison*. With *her* daughter. Of all the things Cerys had imagined over the centuries, the scene before her was not one of them. She gazed upon him keenly, all long-limbed and wide-eyed, a mop of dark hair swinging about his brow. There was something about him, she realised, straightening; a quiet strength to him … He reminded her of a human she'd known long ago.

Rohesia too was watching the human, clearly biting back an objection to him touching the warlocks, seeming to think better of it. Instead, she licked her lips and shoved her hands in her pockets, facing the cell once more.

Cerys drew a sharp breath as her daughter's voice broke the long-held silence.

'It has begun,' Rohesia said slowly, her voice echoing down the passageway. 'The Queen's Tournament, it has started. I'm a participant.'

That had been several months ago, though it felt like a lifetime. Cerys had only seen her daughter once more after that, where she had allowed Rohesia to see a glimmer of the truth behind the madness, a glimmer, but nothing more, then Rohesia was gone. Since then, alone with her black thoughts, Cerys had fretted that she had revealed too much; someone was always listening, always watching the bone cells of the prison. Should Rohesia or anyone else discover the truth too soon, it would jeopardise the future Cerys had given everything for, and her daughter would pay with her life.

Marlow sent news when he deemed it safe, which wasn't often. His water birds always startled the life out of Cerys when they arrived, but once the initial shock wore off, she revelled in the long-forgotten artform of warlock magic. As a child she had envied her brother for the drop of skill he'd inherited from their father, but now, in the dark depths of the prison, they offered her something she rarely experienced: joy.

But now, time passed in long stretches without any word from Marlow. Dread crept into her bones with every day, every hour that disappeared, and Cerys started to suspect that it wasn't merely precaution that kept news of her daughter at bay. Something had gone wrong. There would be no other reason for her brother's silence. Cerys was no fool, she knew the perils Rohesia faced in the extension of Deelie's godsforsaken tournament, but she had never allowed herself to imagine the unthinkable … That harm or worse had befallen her daughter.

Cerys' fears were confirmed when Delja appeared at her cell. The queen was as regal and immaculate as ever, even without the crown of coral atop her head.

Cerys clung desperately to that detail, as though it might mean that very crown was in question. But when Delja smiled, Cerys knew there would be nothing good to come from this visit.

'What brings you to my humble abode this time, Deelie?' Cerys asked, fighting to keep her voice even.

Delja gave a dramatic sigh. 'I'm not sure if I should be the bearer of this news.'

Despite the enchanted manacles at her wrists and ankles, Cerys felt her magic flare in tandem with her fury. 'Why else would you be here?'

If Deelie felt any flicker of power, she didn't acknowledge it. Instead, she paced the span of the bars. 'I tried to help her, you know,' she said quietly.

The words were like a blow to Cerys' gut. Her rage dissipated beneath an icy blanket of fear. 'What happened?' she breathed, approaching the door to her cell and trying to catch Deelie's gaze. 'Deelie?'

'I have told you not to call me that,' Delja snapped, without looking up.

'I'm sorry,' Cerys said instantly. 'Your Majesty, please ... Tell me of my daughter.'

At last Delja stopped pacing, her eyes meeting Cerys' between the bars of bone. 'She failed to obtain the second birthstone. Things went wrong.'

Cerys gasped. 'Is she alive?'

Delja pinched the bridge of her nose and it took every ounce of Cerys' fading willpower to keep from throttling her, cell or no cell.

'For now,' Delja replied at last.

'What do you mean?'

'Rohesia made a sacrifice of the highest order.'

Cerys' heart all but stopped. 'She *what*?'

'She made a sacrifice of the highest order, a requirement of being reinstated in the tournament.'

'And what did she give?' The words came out slow and slurred.

The triumph in Delja's eyes was undeniable. 'Her deathsong.'

Cerys fell to her knees, feeling no pain as bone cracked against hard stone.

'To think,' Delja was saying. 'She could have inherited your or Sedna's power ... She could have been unstoppable.'

Cerys' chest constricted and she struggled for air. A cyren without a song was like the sea without a current, still and lost to the darkness. What would happen to Rohesia now, with her power torn away from her?

'A fool's choice,' Delja was saying, shaking her head. 'To sacrifice a deathsong rather than a human or warlock ... All that magic, snuffed out like a candle. What a waste.' She gave Cerys a pointed look. 'I thought you should know.'

With that, the queen left.

It wasn't until Delja's footsteps had faded that her words sank in.

'To sacrifice a deathsong rather than a human or warlock ...' Those were the exact words Delja had spoken, weren't they?

A small, breathless sound escaped Cerys and then she did something she hadn't done in decades. She threw her head back and laughed. The sound rumbled from deep within her, warming her cold heart.

Rohesia had sacrificed her deathsong for the lives of a warlock and a human.

She was her father's daughter.

And all was not lost.

CHAPTER ONE

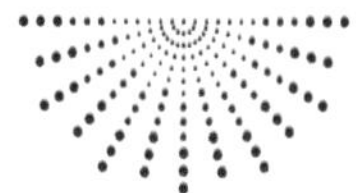

The sails billowed in the cool breeze that swept through the ravine, urging the river boat onwards across the surging turquoise waters. Jagged white cliffs towered on either side, close enough for Roh to reach out and touch with her fingertips if she so wished. The chasm between the northern and southern lands was a marvel: an abyss carved by the talons of the gods themselves. The sun's buttery rays were an upside-down stream of gold between the two edges of the gorge, but light and warmth did not reach Roh and her companions down in the shade of the cliffs; there, the air was crisp even in the midst of day.

'Hold on,' the Csillan Arch General, Kezra, called loudly, as she directed the narrow boat, which sat low and long in the water.

Roh heeded the Csillan's warning, gripping the wooden side before dipping her hand into the icy water and manipulating the drag of the current to ease the strain of the rapids on their small vessel. Kezra shot her a grateful look before returning her focus to the rudder and the waters ahead, guiding them around another bend.

There was a loud retching sound from what Kezra called *the starboard side*, as Odi threw up into the river.

Narrowly dodging the splashback, Harlyn cursed in disgust. 'I thought you were a well-travelled musician? You've been sick for hours.'

Odi, his face tinged green, could only muster a groan.

They had boarded Kezra's river boat that morning, after a week's travel through the Csillan gorges. After Roh's *sacrifice of the highest order* on the Bridge of Csilla and her reinstatement to the tournament, Kezra had insisted on joining their quest for the final birthstone of Saddoriel – the Gauntlet Ruby. Leaving her sister, Floralin, in charge of the territory, the clan leader who had once been known as The Carver seemed to revel in her newfound freedom, and with her guidance, Roh and her companions had crossed over Csillan lands in record time. Navigating the cliffs and moors had been much easier with Kezra at their side.

'Port side turn, coming up!' Deodan's voice sounded from the crow's nest, bringing Roh back to the present with a jolt. The warrior warlock had charged himself with directing from above after they'd set off earlier that morning. Since Roh had sacrificed her deathsong, Deodan had been different. Gone was the solemn demeanour and short temper that had kept them company for so many weeks. In the wake of Roh's acceptance of his alliance, the warlock had been himself once again and was the most eager of all her companions to keep moving forward with their quest. He had also taken on Roh's request about researching the terror tempests with a fevered passion, determined to provide her with answers about the storms that threatened to breach her homeland. He had spent long hours with Floralin, who oversaw the monitoring of the tempests and had sent queries around the world to distant scholars who might know more.

Roh glanced at her final two comrades. The Jaktaren were taking turns with the pulley system for the sails. Both Yrsa and

Finn looked at ease, as they often did with adventuresome tasks; Roh had no doubt they'd sailed boats before. To her, it seemed there wasn't much they *hadn't* done. Yrsa's sling swung at her hip as she held the mainsail in place and there was no sign of the tears she had shed upon leaving her partner, Piri, in Csilla. As a disgraced former soldier of the Saddorien Army, Piri was on parole, and thus was restricted from travel between the territories. She had tried to insist to Yrsa that she would be of more use sending frequent reports of the terror tempests back to Saddoriel, but it was of little comfort to the Jaktaren. Still, they persisted. Roh herself had sent several warnings addressed to Isomene Sigra, the council elder in charge of the lair's security and defence. Yrsa had suggested that Sigra had the ability to put aside her misgivings of Roh for the good of cyrenkind. Roh wasn't entirely convinced, but took Yrsa at her word and wrote the letters.

Finn's linen shirt was damp with sweat at the back, his hair swept from the nape of his neck in a messy bun. Roh watched him intently for a second, reliving the hungry kisses in the hallway back in Csilla. Her face burned at the memory.

'I don't want this to be a balm for an open wound,' he had said.

There had been no stolen, secret moments between them since, only a taut tension of awareness, that the thing between them was alive, and unfinished.

Roh dragged her attention from the Jaktaren and surveyed the whole group with a swelling sense of pride; they had come a long way since they had first left the lair of bones.

At Deodan's instruction, Kezra guided the boat around another turn and Roh continued to assist with what little of her cyren magic remained. It was different to manipulating the currents of the sea, but the river understood her. Parts of it were calmer, curving gently around the pattern of the cliffs, while other parts flowed rapidly, foaming white over moss-covered boulders, but under Roh's influence, the water didn't smash their boat to pieces upon the rocks.

'Deodan,' Kezra shouted. 'Have we passed the blue boulders yet?'

'Just then,' came the reply.

Kezra nodded and gestured to the two Jaktaren at the ropes. 'Keep the mainsail up, raise the smaller two as well. We've reached the straightest part of the ravine now. We can increase our speed.'

'Thank the gods,' muttered Odi, wiping the sweat from his brow, his top half practically hanging over the side of the boat.

Overhead, a dark shape blocked out the sun. Giant wings spanned the width of the ravine and something enormous took a dive, hurtling towards them and plummeting into the water ahead of the boat, sending a wave crashing onto the small deck.

Roh was instantly on her feet, rushing to the front of the boat, peering over the edge.

A golden head emerged from the water, molten eyes blinking innocently at her.

'You damn menace!' Roh hissed at the sea drake, who ducked under the water again and swam ahead beneath the surface, flicking his barbed tail in her direction.

'You need to get him under control,' Harlyn said.

'Under control?' Roh scoffed. 'You try *controlling* a teenage sea drake, Har. Let me know how that works out for you.'

Finn laughed, the rich sound warming Roh from within. She glanced up, only to find Harlyn grinning at her, pointedly looking between the Jaktaren and Roh as she toyed with the bronze key she wore around her neck.

'What?' Roh asked.

'Oh you know *exactly* what.'

'I'll take that back if you don't behave yourself,' Roh warned, nodding to the key she'd gifted to Harlyn after they'd freed the teerah panther in Csilla. Roh had insisted that it belonged to

Harlyn, a reminder of the beast she'd conquered after its kin had changed the course of her life with a swipe of its claws.

'No, you won't,' Harlyn said, tucking the key into her shirt. 'You'll forget about it in a moment anyway, your focus is elsewhere.'

'No idea what you're talking about,' Roh muttered.

Harlyn didn't stop grinning.

As the river boat settled into the steady pull of the current, they watched Valli shoot out of the water and into the sky again, his great wings cutting through the air, majestic and powerful.

'That might be you one day,' Harlyn said quietly, with an appreciative nod towards the creature in the near distance.

Roh snorted. 'What?'

But Harlyn eyed her seriously. 'You know … if what you saw in the mirror pool comes true.'

'I doubt I'd show off as much, flapping into the sky like him,' Roh replied. 'Besides, we don't know what it meant.'

Harlyn shrugged, clearly unconvinced.

Roh had told her friends about the vision the gems and the mirror pool had shared – an older version of her, with great wings at her back – and there had been a new seriousness to the group ever since. While they didn't exactly treat her differently, Roh had noticed them exchanging looks when they thought she wasn't paying attention, or their gazes lingering a little longer on the crown of bones she now wore permanently atop her head, the Mercy's Topaz and Willow's Sapphire shining in their rightful places.

They had always been taught that a cyren who bore wings was a powerful descendant of the goddesses, rare and chosen, a deity incarnate, someone to be revered and feared, just as the former queen, Delja, was throughout the realms.

Roh ran a hand through her hair, realising it had grown in the weeks past. Perhaps that was just as well; she wasn't sure cyrenkind could cope with a queen who had sliced all her hair off *and* was songless.

Songless. The word reverberated through Roh like an echo through the gorge. It was the thing she had always feared, fully come to pass. With Odi and Deodan still whole and healthy at her side, she didn't regret her decision, and yet she mourned for what she had lost, for all that she could have been and now would never be. And then the damn pool had shown her the wings. Roh supposed if one of the others had told her the same story, she might look a little differently at them, too.

'You alright?' Harlyn asked, watching her warily. She had an unnerving knack for sensing exactly when Roh was about to spiral into the dark abyss of her thoughts.

'Yes,' Roh reassured her.

Harlyn raised a brow.

'Absolutely,' Roh insisted, mustering up her brightest voice.

Harlyn rolled her eyes. 'You're not fooling anyone.'

The truth was, Roh didn't know if she was alright. Ever since her sacrifice on the bridge, she felt as though a part of her was missing, as though a vital piece of her had been carved out and now floated in some desolate place far away in the realms, completely untethered from her being. But how could she explain that to the others? How could they understand what it was like to have one's deathsong ripped from their very soul?

'I'm trying,' Roh said quietly.

Harlyn reached across and squeezed her shoulder. 'That's all I ask.'

Roh found herself nodding.

Harlyn's face split into a grin again and she elbowed Roh in the ribs. 'Now, when are you going to tell me about you and Haertel?'

Roh flushed. 'Har! *Shhh!*'

At that, both Finn and Yrsa looked up from where they'd sat on the far bench. Yrsa's eyes twinkled in a way that told Roh she suspected the topic of conversation, while Finn merely frowned in their direction as he removed the wooden prosthetic from his leg, sitting back with a grimace.

'Remind me again why you won't just take your tonic?' Odi said, watching him from the other side of the boat, his face still an unsightly shade of green.

Roh tensed instantly, waiting for Finn to bite the human's head off. She knew they had all wondered it over the last few weeks, but no one had dared ask the Jaktaren, knowing how private he'd been about it before.

'Not that it's *any* of your business,' Finn replied tersely. 'But I don't like relying on it. I've had to go through withdrawal twice in the last few weeks and it's not pretty.' He sighed, scanning the rest of the group, clearly understanding that he was addressing all of them now. 'Plus, the main reason I took it was to keep this hidden …' He gestured at his stump. 'But the secret's out. I'm not hiding anymore.'

Roh watched Finn, realising how different he looked from when they'd first met. He was still all sharp lines and fierce eyes, but he'd also kept the shadow of the beard he'd grown on his trek from Csilla to Serratega and his complexion had darkened in the sun. His face was more relaxed and even his movements weren't completely rigid with discipline. Roh was glad for him. It was about time he was free of the shame he'd been burdened with under his parents' rule.

'Good for you,' Odi said with an appreciative nod, echoing Roh's thoughts.

There was a thud nearby as Deodan dropped down to the deck from the crow's nest. 'You don't think that decision will hinder you should you need to fight?'

Roh stiffened, the blunt words settling between the two warriors.

Finn eyed the warlock evenly. 'No.'

Deodan simply shrugged. 'Glad to hear it.'

Yrsa clicked her tongue in frustration. 'The male ego truly knows no bounds, does it?'

Roh's whole body sagged as the tension broke with Kezra's answering laugh.

'Why do you think Floralin and I never sought partners?' Kezra called.

'Why do you think I'm with a female?' Yrsa countered, returning her smirk.

'Well, for starters, Piri's prettier than either of those two lumps,' Harlyn offered, with a casual wave towards Finn and Deodan, who were now exchanging baffled looks.

'True,' Yrsa agreed. 'Better personality, too.'

'Also true,' Finn admitted.

A smile tugged at the corner of Roh's mouth. It was these small moments that she loved best, in which familiarity flowed between them easily, in which she could pretend, for the briefest of seconds, that they were ordinary friends. Roh wished it had been like this all along, but there was nothing ordinary about her companions, or their journey. Reluctantly, she withdrew from her daydreams of normalcy and went to Kezra.

'How are we faring?' she asked, gazing at the river ahead, the giant cliffs still looming on either side.

'Won't be long before we reach the open seas. We'll all need to work the waters together to reach the entrance of Lamaka's Basin. The tide will be against us.'

Roh glanced up at Valli, who was still flying closely. She wondered if he could smell the sea already, if she'd imagined that flicker of restlessness within him …

'How many times have you taken this route? Why not just take to the waters yourself?' Roh asked Kezra.

'A handful,' the Csillan replied. 'Sometimes a cyren needs to feel the wind on her face. Surely, a Saddorien would understand that?'

Roh recalled the dark depths of the lair of bones, her home, and how she'd longed to feel the sun's rays on her skin and the sea's current in her heart. 'More than you know,' Roh told her.

Kezra nodded knowingly. 'It's been some adventure for you.'

'It has,' Roh murmured. 'And now we're almost at the end ... After all this, we're so close to the final gem, I can almost taste it, Kezra.'

It was the first time she'd said those words aloud. She'd been dreaming of the Gauntlet Ruby, of the gleaming blood-red gem being placed in her crown of bones, completing the trio of birthstones, completing her quest for the cyren throne. In her dreams, it didn't matter that she was a songless cyren, all that mattered was the crown atop her head and the *Tome of Kyeos* in her hands. The tome would right all wrongs, it would tell her everything she needed to know, song or no song, and a better Saddoriel awaited them.

'It's close alright,' Kezra allowed. 'But time is not on your side, Roh. You whittled away too many weeks in Serratega. And you still need to get from Lochloria back to Saddoriel, with your entire company, Odi and Deodan included. Which means you won't be able to use the waters as you would, you'll have to go by ship, or find a passageway from one of the mainlands that takes us all beneath the seas.'

'I know.' Roh had been waiting for one of her companions to address that simple fact. Of the seven moons she'd been given to complete her quest, six moons and one week had passed, leaving her with three measly weeks to obtain the Gauntlet Ruby and return to Talon's Reach to claim the cyren throne. Alongside her lack of song, the brevity of the task ahead had haunted her every waking second. Roh knew all too well how deeply the council schemed against her and what horrors they were capable of putting between her and the gems. And she knew all too well how long these obstacles took to dismantle and overcome. In her darker moments, she wondered if it would all amount to nothing, if she and her companions would be defeated not by savage sea drakes, poisonous Arch Generals or an underhanded trial by combat, but by time itself … And so she had read, tirelessly poring over the one thing that had kept her in this godsforsaken tournament.

Roh went to her pack, stowed away beneath the deck, and rummaged through its contents before returning to Kezra with *The Law of the Lair*.

Kezra's head tilted with curiosity as she eyed the book. 'Another nugget of wisdom from the council elders past?' It had been the Csillan who'd found the clause that had enabled Roh to re-enter the tournament after her exile.

'We can use the mirror pool,' Roh explained, turning to the page she'd discovered a few nights after they'd retrieved the Willow's Sapphire from the teerah panther's collar. 'Here.' She pointed to the passage she'd marked and Kezra peered over her shoulder to read aloud:

'Clause eight hundred and seventy-three: Once the three birthstones of Saddoriel have been obtained and placed within the crown, access to the Pool of Weeping via the mirror pools throughout the cyren territories will be granted.'

'See?' Roh smiled. 'That solves our timing issue. And any obstacles we'd face trying to travel through the seas with Odi and Deodan. Humans can travel through it, we've seen the Council of Elders bring the Eery Brothers to Csilla just recently, so it works.'

Slowly, Kezra smiled at Roh and clapped her heartily on the back. 'That is good news indeed.'

'I'll take good news wherever I can get it,' Roh replied. She returned the book to her pack and surveyed her companions, who were now sprawled out on the deck. The waters had calmed and the boat now passed gracefully and steadily through the ravine, allowing them to pause for a momentary rest.

'You look better,' Roh told Odi, taking the seat to his left.

'I feel like my insides have been purged,' he retorted, picking at the loose threads on his fingerless gloves. 'But Deodan's given me something to ease the churning in my stomach.'

'Could he not have done that earlier?'

'That's what I said.'

Roh huffed a laugh. 'Unlucky.'

'Story of my life, Roh.'

The bench creaked beneath them as Deodan sat down near Odi, casually resting one of Killian's journals in his lap. 'Is the Prince of Melodies complaining about my remedies?'

Roh nodded. 'Yes, he's whingeing.'

'No!' Odi frowned. 'I'm *not*. Only suggesting that perhaps you could have generously eased my suffering *before* I turned such a nasty shade of green.'

Deodan shrugged. 'How was I to know you wouldn't ever find your sea legs?'

Odi shook his head in disbelief and muttered something about helping Harlyn with her arm exercises before leaving them.

'He makes it too easy.' Deodan smirked.

Roh was about to agree, but her gaze caught on the end of the ravine up ahead, its meaning not lost on her in the slightest. The ravine led to the open sea, but just north of there, the entrance to Lamaka's Basin awaited them. Without thinking, Roh's hand went to the bone-hilted dagger strapped to her thigh, the blade made of quartz; her father's weapon. She inhaled the chilled air deeply. It was to *his* homeland they travelled now: Lochloria – the scholar's city.

She turned to Deodan. 'I've been meaning to ask you something …' she started, her stomach rolling uneasily.

'Oh?'

'Do you think … Do you think I'd be able to learn warlock magic?'

Deodan stared at her for a moment, as though he couldn't believe the words leaving her mouth.

Roh rushed on. 'I mean, my father was a warlock. And the mountain pass recognised me as one of its own … And I gave up my deathsong … Does that not make me …' She lowered her voice. 'More warlock than cyren?'

Deodan exhaled heavily through his nostrils and fished out his pipe. He packed the bowl tightly with his favoured herbs and lit it, taking a long, deliberate drag. He seemed to mull over her question as he blew a stream of smoke out over the water.

'You're truly asking me if you can do warlock magic?'

'Yes,' Roh answered. 'We were going to find someone … to train my cyren magic, remember? But now … well, I just wondered if it was an option.'

Deodan considered her thoughtfully. 'I imagine it's possible. Birthed by a cyren, fathered by a water warlock …'

Those words had belonged to her mentor, Ames, whom she now knew to be her uncle, Marlow, and Roh sighed upon hearing them again. Marlow would know the answer, but he was far away, as he always was when she needed him, wrapped in his cloak of secrets.

'We can try to teach you warlock magic,' Deodan was saying. 'Though, I should warn you, it usually takes years.'

'But –'

'We can try,' Deodan repeated. 'Once we get to Lochloria … I suppose there's no better place.'

At the mention of Lochloria, Roh's stomach swooped.

'Are you nervous?' Deodan asked, following her line of sight.

Roh took another deep breath, the cold air hitting her lungs. 'Yes. Are you?'

'To see the place my ancestors called home? To see where they were slaughtered? Yes, I'm nervous, among other things.' The warrior warlock's shoulders sagged at Roh's side. 'I know it is in ruin, but … I dream of it as you drew it.' He pulled a weathered piece of parchment from his pocket and unfolded it.

Roh stared at the sketch – a design she'd drawn after her horrific experience during the Rite of Strothos. According to Deodan, the poison had shown her the scholar's city in its days of glory, not as it existed today; in pieces.

Roh tore her gaze from her drawing, gently pushing it away, quietly surprised Deodan had kept it for all this time. She didn't like to dwell on what she'd gone through at the hands of Adriel, the Arch General of Akoris.

'Why is it still in ruin?' she asked. 'Surely cyrens tried to rebuild? Strategically speaking, it's the most valuable of all the cyren territories, isn't it?'

'The warlocks cursed the land,' Kezra's voice cut in, drawing the others' attention towards them. 'It was all the punishment their kind could muster as they fled the Scouring.'

'What kind of curse?'

'One that makes it hard to yield any prosperity from the land,' Kezra replied.

Roh frowned, recalling an entry from one of Killian's journals: *The territory itself seems to be affected by the despair; the buildings have begun to crumble and the land wilts around us. The crops no longer flourish and the livestock weakens each day.*

'There were rumours of a prophecy,' Kezra was saying.

Roh's gaze shot back to the Csillan's. 'About what?'

Kezra's eyes shone with dark amusement, glancing from Roh to the others, who had got to their feet and gathered around.

'Stone will crumble and land will fester, until the winged one flies forth,' she recited.

Goosebumps rushed across Roh's arms, Kezra's words sinking

in deep. Around her, Finn, Harlyn, Odi, Yrsa and Deodan were all exchanging meaningful looks.

'Everyone thought it referred to Delja,' Kezra told her with an infuriating shrug. 'But apparently, that's not who it meant.'

Roh's head snapped back to Deodan. 'You didn't think to tell me this?'

But Deodan threw up his hands in surrender. 'I didn't know, I swear.'

'Well, even if it wasn't Delja, it doesn't mean it's me. I haven't got wings,' Roh protested.

'Not *yet*,' Deodan said.

Roh got to her feet, shaking her head in frustration as she paced. 'This is ridiculous.'

'Which part, specifically?' Finn asked.

Roh shot him a glare. 'All of it. Kezra, what else do you know about Lochloria as it is now? Who guards it?'

Kezra was making her way back to the rudder. 'From what I've heard over the years, it's an even smaller clan than Csilla. A single family residing in the last of the academic buildings.'

'That's all you know?'

'It is. Csilla has kept to itself over the centuries. And there hasn't been much call for uniting the territories throughout the years. We have reported to the council and the queen, not to each other.' Kezra motioned to the Jaktaren. 'Back in your positions, we're about to hit the sea.'

Roh could see the open expanse of water drawing closer and closer, its dark surface stretching on to the horizon. Briny wind whipped through her hair, and all at once, she felt the all-consuming power of the currents wrap around her, welcoming her home. She breathed in deeply, tasting the salt on her lips and the magic of the tides in her heart as the river boat surged forward. She wondered if Valli felt the same. The sea drake had stayed close to her since their separation, and to her knowledge had not yet graced the tides with his presence. The thought prompted Roh to think about the mother drake who lurked in the ancient deep, somewhere out there. Did she still seek him? Did she still hunt Roh? Was that a flash of gold on the horizon?

'Cyrens,' Kezra called. 'At the ready! We need to veer to the starboard side and head north as we leave the ravine!'

Roh reluctantly left the bow and took up her post by Kezra, reaching into the waves, ready to shape the current, just as the others had done. Together, they could take the river boat all the way to Lamaka's Basin.

As the water kissed her fingertips, Roh felt the great sea greet her with its call and she sighed in relief. The water did not forget its kin, song or no song. Roh relished the pull of the tide and the cold against her skin –

A dark shape graced the sky and Roh glanced up, ready to chastise Valli for whatever mischievous thing he was no doubt about to do.

'That's not Valli …' She squinted into the afternoon sun at the winged creature soaring ahead of them. It wasn't big enough to be the sea drake, but it carved powerfully through the air nonetheless, a predator of the sky.

'I know that bird,' Deodan murmured.

Roh's gaze snapped to his, recognition prickling across her skin. 'It's not …?'

Deodan's expression was grim. 'The Warlock Supreme's eagle, yes.'

'What in the realms is it doing out here?' Harlyn exclaimed, gripping the side of the boat as it hit a set of waves.

Roh's hand drifted to the hilt of her father's dagger. 'I believe we're about to find out.'

CHAPTER TWO

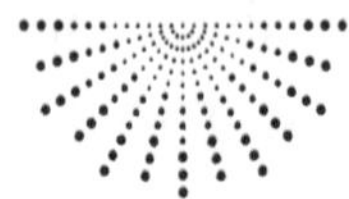

Roh's whole body tensed as she watched the eagle beat its giant wings and ascend into the clouds.

'Maybe it's looking for me? Perhaps it's got a message,' Deodan murmured with a frown.

'Seems to be going the wrong way for that,' Roh retorted, watching the bird of prey circle the skies before disappearing to the north.

Deodan stared after it. 'This isn't good.'

Roh locked eyes with him. 'We're in agreement there. But we've got a bigger problem.' Roh had felt a shift in the water swirling at her fingertips as they'd turned into the sea, and now, as they followed the coast towards Lamaka's Basin, something pressed against her magic.

'What now?' Frustration lined Kezra's face, her cheeks tipped pink from her exertions at the rudder.

'There's conflict in the waters,' Roh mused. 'Two opposing forces ... Like ... like the water from Lamaka's Basin wants to keep the sea, or us, at bay.'

'That makes no sense,' Harlyn said.

'Doesn't it?' Finn argued. 'The waters that were stained with warlock blood are at odds with cyren magic? It makes perfect sense to me.'

'You know I usually hate to agree with the Jaktaren,' Deodan allowed. 'But he's right.'

As they followed the jagged cliffs of the coast, drawing closer to the entrance of the sacred lake, Roh felt the resistance to her cyren magic grow stronger, pushing back against the river boat. They were almost at a standstill.

'We won't make it like this,' she declared, scanning the skies for her sea drake. 'Where is that nuisance when you need him?'

'What do you suggest, then?' Kezra asked impatiently, her arms straining to keep the rudder in position.

Roh put her two index fingers to her mouth and whistled loudly, the sound piercing even the nearby crash of waves.

Her companions jumped as Valli shot out of the water ahead of them, sending a foaming tide towards them. He spread his golden wings and dived gracefully through the air, having grown out of his clumsy flying stage a few weeks before, though his landings still left much to be desired.

'He'd better not land on this boat, Queen of Bones,' Kezra warned. 'Not if you want the human and the warlock to remain safe and dry.'

Roh waved Kezra away and snatched up a thick coil of rope, securing it to the bow. There, she leaned down and splashed the water in front of her, hoping that Valli would understand what she was asking.

The sea drake took a dramatic dive towards her, creating another massive spray of water, soaking them through before popping his head above the surface, blinking expectantly at her.

'I need you to pull us,' she told him, holding out the length of rope. 'Into the basin.'

The sea drake seemed to consider her and the task warily, as though deciding if it was beneath him, his gold eyes transfixed on her. At last, he snatched up the rope between his fangs and ducked beneath the waves.

'Hold on,' Roh called out to her friends just as the boat surged forward.

Valli pulled them through the opposing currents with ease, cutting through both kinds of magic with his own great power. Roh clutched the side as the river boat bounced off the waves, picking up speed.

Kezra let out a gleeful cry. 'Not just a pretty face, are you, Queen of Bones?'

A laugh bubbled from Roh, until the boat began to turn towards the cliffs. A narrow fissure greeted them; the gateway to Lamaka's Basin. The smile died on Roh's lips as they approached, a chill washing over her skin. The gap between the cliffs was even tighter than it had been in the ravine, and Roh grimaced as the sides of the boat grazed the rocks as Valli pulled them through the entrance.

As soon as they passed the rocks, Roh gasped. For the mouth had opened up onto an immeasurable lake of ice-blue water. White-stoned shores hugged its banks and forests of deep-green pine stood tall behind them. Beyond the trees, snow-capped mountains towered all around them, many of their peaks disappearing into the clouds above.

'Gods …' Roh breathed in awe.

'You're shivering,' a soft voice said into her ear, before a cloak was draped around her shoulders, calloused fingers brushing the bare skin of her arms.

Finn Haertel stood behind her, his gaze following hers to the surrounding beauty. 'It's something else, isn't it?'

The pair had kept their distance since Roh's little meltdown back in Csilla; her face heated with embarrassment at the very thought of it. She'd practically thrown herself at him. Now, her words got stuck in her throat and so she simply nodded as Valli pulled them further into the great lake.

An icy wind swept down from the mountains, causing the waters to swell around them and whisper ancient magic against Roh's skin as they reached its heart.

Something is different here, Roh realised. *Or is it me? Am* I *different here …?* By the grace of the gods or whatever warlock power lingered in these parts, Roh could feel the presence of her ancestors from both sides in the water. They called to her, and though she knew she had no deathsong, she felt something unlock within her.

She felt Deodan's eyes on her and she met his gaze from across the deck. 'You feel it, too?' she asked.

But the warlock stared at her in awe. 'I feel *you,*' he said. 'I feel *your* magic.'

'That's not me,' she tried to explain, as the others looked to her as well. 'It's … them … All of them …' She knew it made no sense, but she didn't know how else to –

A flicker of movement on the shore caught her eye. She narrowed her gaze, trying to determine what exactly she'd seen as Valli brought them closer to the stony bank.

Roh's breath caught in her throat. 'Are you all seeing this?' she asked, leaning over the side of the boat.

'Are those …?' Finn trailed off.

Greying tents lined the shores, strung up between the dark trunks of pine trees. Roh could make out the tattered, open-backed robes of the Akorian cyrens as they crowded around small drums of fire amidst the white stones, warming their hands.

'What are they doing here?' she murmured, as Valli dragged them through the lake towards the shore.

A high-pitched scream sounded from the banks as the sea drake emerged from the waters and shook his wings. A mad scramble ensued. Cyrens tripped over one another, running from the shores, shouting in terror.

Roh leaped from the boat into the shallows, water surging around her boots and slapping against her shins as she lurched towards the cyrens with her hands up. 'It's alright, it's alright,' she told them hurriedly, gesturing towards Valli. 'He won't harm you!'

But the Akorians shoved their nestlings and fledglings behind them, eyeing the great creature with terror-filled gazes, screams still punctuating the air. Several of the male cyrens gripped rusty spears, but Roh could see their knees quaking.

'Truly, he won't hurt anyone,' she implored, moving to Valli and reaching up to touch his golden scales.

But the fear in their eyes wasn't just for the mighty sea drake at her side. It was for *her*, she realised with a jolt.

'*I* won't hurt you,' she rasped, hearing the others drag the river boat onto the banks behind her.

'You already have,' a strong, clear voice cut through the quiet and a female cyren came to the front of the ranks. Roh recognised her, sort of. She recognised the costume she wore, even though it was in tatters.

'You're one of Adriel's oracles,' Roh said, taking a step towards her.

'I belong to no one,' the Akorian told her, crossing her arms over her chest, a muscle twitching in her jaw as she kept one eye on the sea drake.

'Of course.' Roh offered her hand. 'I'm Roh. What's your name?'

She ignored the gesture. 'We know who you are, *Queen of Bones*. You're the cyren who burned down our fields, who threw our city into chaos and despair.'

Murmurs of agreement sounded behind the cyren and Roh's stomach roiled uneasily.

'I'm sorry,' she said, forcing herself to remain still. 'I didn't know what would happen —'

'Sorry? Because of *you*, our home descended into ruin. Because of *you*, a *warlock* took hold of our monastery. *Because of you*, all of these poor Akorians have nowhere to go.'

Roh opened her mouth, but she had no words of comfort to offer these people. They were right, it *was* her fault. Her rash actions, however well intended, *had* caused the fall and destruction of an entire cyren territory. She scanned the faces before her. Fear had leached away to reveal gaunt, hollow expressions: sunken eyes, too-sharp cheekbones and chapped, pale lips. The clothes they wore were dirty and torn and the shoes at their feet in near pieces. Roh heard Harlyn's intake of breath from behind her.

'How long have you been here?' Roh asked.

'Weeks. Those of us who made it, anyway.'

The added comment was a barb to Roh's heart. She didn't want to know the answer to the next question, but she had to ask it nonetheless. 'How many have you lost?'

The cyren surveyed her people. 'Too many to count, Queen of Bones.'

'Can you tell me your name?'

That muscle moved in the cyren's jaw again, but she said, 'Seraphine.'

'And you are the leader here?'

'There is no such thing here.'

'Your actions say otherwise,' Deodan's voice was a deep boom in the quiet.

Seraphine's eyes widened and she looked in disbelief from Deodan to Roh. 'You brought one of them *here*? You welcomed one of *them* into your ranks?'

Roh pushed her shoulders back and met the cyren's stare. 'He has sworn fealty to me. He's part of my court. He means to see me sit upon the cyren throne.'

'And at what cost?' Seraphine hissed.

Again, the murmurs of agreement sounded behind her, more confident than before. Roh stopped herself shifting from foot to foot in discomfort, sensing the dissent brewing amongst the refugees.

'Can we go somewhere?' Roh changed tact. 'To talk? To see what can be done about this?'

Seraphine laughed darkly. 'Nothing can be done.'

'That's not true. We can find you temporary accommodations: food and shelter for you and your nestlings.'

'You are not queen yet,' Seraphine said. 'Nor will you ever be, after what you have done to your own kind.'

Roh clenched her jaw. 'Can we go somewhere to talk?' she repeated, this time lacing her voice with an edge. Valli heard it immediately and approached her, tilting his head to study the Akorian with a menacing glint in his molten-gold eyes.

Seraphine flinched at his attentions, but curled her lip into a sneer nonetheless. 'You see? You're just like the rest of them. One second of not getting what you want and you resort to threats.'

'I didn't say a word,' Roh argued.

'You don't have to, not with that beast at your back.'

A sharp yelp sounded from nearby and Roh's head whipped around, trying to locate the source. It didn't take long.

Her blood ran cold as she spotted the figure strung up between two trees. The healer's body hung limp between her bonds, a larger cyren standing at her back, meaty hands holding a club.

'Incana,' Deodan breathed, rushing to her. 'What is the meaning of this?' he demanded of Seraphine, unsheathing his cutlass and carving through the healer's restraints.

No one stopped him, for there were no warriors here. But each Akorian watched on, full of loathing, their fists clenched at their sides.

Incana fell into Deodan's arms, only semi-conscious. Even from where Roh stood several feet away, she could see the mottled bruising on the healer's skin. She had taken beatings at the hands of several assailants, by the looks of things.

'He asked you a question, Seraphine,' Roh ground out, not realising that her own hand was at her dagger.

There was no empathy in the Akorian's eyes as she shrugged. 'She was the one who gave you the information about the fields. A healer from our own monastery turned against us ... She knew what would happen to us. She deserves her punishment.'

In a wild blur of movement, Roh's dagger was in her hand and pressed against Seraphine's throat.

'See?' the Akorian taunted, a gleam of triumph in her eyes even as the quartz blade threatened to break the soft skin below her jaw. Her hands gripped the front of Roh's shirt, pulling her closer. 'You are indeed like the rest of them.'

'Perhaps I am,' Roh said, her voice low as she leaned in. 'Or perhaps I will not stand for such behaviour. No one deserves to be treated like an animal,' she spat. 'Surely as one of Adriel's former oracles, you know that better than most.'

Seraphine's grip loosened at those words.

Seizing the moment, Roh shoved her back, letting her stumble across the stones and gape at her.

Roh didn't look at Incana, who had indeed betrayed her, or at the very least, misled her about the consequences of burning those fields. Instead, she turned to the faces that peered back at her from the tattered tents. 'I am sorry for my actions in Akoris. I know those words change nothing – that I cannot bring back those you lost, nor can I undo all that brought you to these shores. But you are cyrens of Akoris, you are *my* people, and I will do all that I can to help you, whether you like it or not.'

Roh didn't wait for a response. She motioned to her companions behind her and started for the edge of the forest, where Deodan was cradling Incana in his lap.

. . .

In the late-afternoon light by the great lake, everything was tinged with blue. Roh found herself sitting on a damp log next to Yrsa, who was counting the clay balls for her sling, while the others warmed their hands over a small campfire. Valli monitored the waters, his head snapping to every sound around them, setting Roh's teeth on edge.

'I would offer you something to eat, but we have nothing to give,' Seraphine said, her voice still laced with anger.

'Why have you not sought the help of the Lochlorian clan?' Yrsa asked, not looking up from the projectiles in her palm.

Seraphine scoffed. 'You will find out for yourself soon enough. And the land outside doesn't prosper, with the exception of these ancient giants.' She gestured to the towering trees around them. 'There is no game to be hunted, no plant life to forage.'

'So it's true,' Kezra ventured. 'The land is cursed.'

'Yes.'

Roh listened without comment, watching as across the fire, Deodan tended to Incana with his warlock enchantments, pouring vials of sacred water into his palms and bringing remedies to life before their eyes. Roh had always been able to feel the presence of his magic – it had drawn her to him from the moment they had met in the gilded plains all that time ago – but now ... Now it was stronger than ever. It whispered to her, stirring up long-forgotten power in her veins, but she said nothing of it. For the brief time she'd had it, she'd taken her deathsong for granted, and now that had been stripped away, she was wary of any magic that moved within her.

'Roh ...' Harlyn said her name quietly, as to not draw attention from the others.

'What is it?' Roh asked, noting the crease between Harlyn's brows and the stiffness of her body.

'I can hear her again ...'

An icy shiver snaked down Roh's spine. She knew exactly to whom Harlyn referred. 'Orson.'

Harlyn nodded, her gaze darting around at their companions and shifting suspiciously to the forest. 'She calls out to me.'

Roh rubbed the scales at her temples, an ache starting to bloom there. 'What does she say?'

'Nothing. She just calls my name, like she's looking for me, like she's lost.'

'Gods,' Roh muttered. 'I don't hear anything.'

'I know. But I swear, Roh, I'm not going mad. I can hear her clear as day.'

'I don't doubt you, Har. I just don't know what to do. The only thing I can think of is if you try to ingest the same flower that cured me. We still have some in one of our packs.'

'I'll try anything at this point,' Harlyn said. 'She's driving me mad. Perhaps that's her goal.'

'Is it malicious, then? The voice?'

Harlyn shook her head with a heavy sigh. 'No. I don't think so, anyway. I just … I want to try the plant cure.'

Roh hated the idea of her friend suffering. She herself had been through a similar experience after she'd emerged from the Rite of Strothos. It hadn't been until she'd ingested that flower that she'd felt like herself again, albeit for the briefest of times.

'Let's do that, then,' she said, and went to find the right pack.

After Roh had given Harlyn the antidote, she found herself pacing the shores of Lamaka's Basin alone, breathing in the strange and eerie atmosphere of her ancestral homeland. It was beyond beautiful, but sadness blanketed the exquisite terrain. The place throbbed with tragedy and the feeling latched onto Roh, sinking into her bones, making her feel heavy. It didn't help that the Akorians tracked her every movement, their angry gazes following her up and down the water's edge. She glanced back to her companions, who still sat by the fire, trying to keep the damp at bay, waiting for her next instructions. They had to press on, they had to get to Lochloria and to the Gauntlet Ruby; only then would she have the power to help the Akorian refugees.

A lilac gaze locked onto hers from across the way, fierce and unyielding, full of unspoken promises.

Finn.

Roh had nearly stripped the Jaktaren naked out in the open by the ravine in Serratega, and she flushed at the memory of his mouth, hot and insistent on hers.

'I don't give a damn where you undress me, as long as you do.' Roh had relived those words numerous times since then, each time causing her toes to curl in her boots.

Roh dragged her eyes away from Finn to find Seraphine approaching, her hardened expression now more haunted than before.

'What is it?' Roh asked her.

'One of your companions mentioned the Arch General Adriel,' Seraphine said.

'What of the slimy bastard?' Roh snapped, an oily feeling snaking in her gut at the sound of his name.

Seraphine stood with her feet in a wide stance and held her chin high. 'Have you seen him?'

Roh's gaze snapped to hers. 'Once since Akoris. He was in Csilla, for a … ceremony of sorts. I don't know what happened to him after that.'

'He fled,' Seraphine said quietly. 'When the Warlock Supreme attacked Akoris, the snake fled, without so much as a word of instruction to the remaining guards, without a thought for those who had … served him for years.'

'Did you expect otherwise?' Roh asked, realising too late how harsh her words sounded.

The cyren simply pulled her tattered cloak tightly around her. 'No.'

Roh resisted the urge to offer words of comfort and condolences. Instead, she faced Seraphine with her fists balled at her sides. 'He will pay,' she vowed. 'I promise he will pay for what he has done.'

Seraphine began to reply, but she suddenly darted to the water's edge and scanned the sky, shielding her eyes from the sun. Roh was at her side at once, finding the Warlock Supreme's bird soaring above higher ground nearby.

'They've been hunting us since we fled Akoris,' Seraphine told her, a tremor clear in her voice.

Roh's stomach dropped and she bit the inside of her cheek. But her eyes didn't leave the eagle as she started towards the camp.

It was circling Lamaka's Basin, as though it had at last found its prey.

CHAPTER THREE

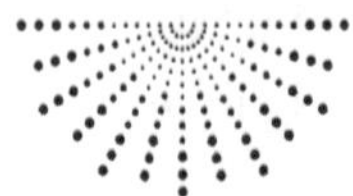

The others were already on their feet, weapons unsheathed and gripped in anticipation as Roh reached them, her own sling loaded in her hands, Valli close behind her.

'We saw,' Finn said by way of greeting.

'I want to go up there.' Roh gestured to the higher ground. 'I want to know how many there are and their intentions.' She turned to Deodan. 'They can't mean to attack a refugee camp, surely?'

Deodan's expression was grim. 'I wouldn't put anything past my mother. Her thirst for revenge knows no limits.'

Seraphine and the rest of the Akorians sensed the commotion and gathered around, all of their anger suddenly dissipated; instead, their faces were tight with anxiety and they looked to Roh for instruction.

'What's happening?' a male cyren demanded, a nestling tucked behind his legs.

'We're going to find out,' Roh told him. 'Stay here, all of you.' She looked around, adding, 'And arm yourselves with what you can.'

Seraphine began herding lone nestlings and fledglings into the cover of the woods, her jaw set in a grim line of determination. Roh said no parting words to her, only nodded to Finn and their companions before they set off towards the hillside.

No one spoke as they started the ascent to higher ground, the giant eagle still circling. Roh wanted to insist that Valli remain behind, that she wasn't ready for the warlocks to know of him yet, but there was no excuse, no reason for him to stay hidden. They had likely already spotted him from their vantage point anyway. Besides, Valli was part of their team and a powerful part at that; to leave him behind would mean weakening their group as a whole. Roh stole a glance at the great drakeling as they trudged upwards, his gold wings tucked behind his back, his claws leaving deep imprints in the damp earth.

For a moment, Roh wondered if he knew how much he meant to her, if he knew what gratitude was and how much of it she felt for him. But those abstract thoughts weren't for now. She fixed her gaze ahead as they wove through the dense tree line, her calves burning at the incline in the terrain and her gut roiling uneasily. Whatever lay ahead wouldn't be something she welcomed, that much she was sure of. She didn't like walking into the unknown. Everything she knew about the Warlock Supreme told her it could be a trap, but there was no other option. Anticipation hung thick in the air and the Akorian refugees below were helpless. She needed to know what was happening, one way or another.

A whistle sounded from above as Roh and her companions reached the crest of the hill, and a hurried rustle of movement sounded from the woods.

'Don't attack,' Roh said loudly, though she kept her grip on her sling tight and at the ready as a small unit of water warlocks appeared from the trees and surrounded them, swords pointed at their throats.

'Deodan,' someone said, their voice laced with shock. A female warlock stepped forward, her mouth agape. Roh didn't recognise her as one of the warlocks who'd attended the meeting back in Akoris, the one where she and Finn had been held captive. She glanced at Deodan, whose expression seemed pained.

'What are you doing here?' the woman asked, slowly lowering her sword.

'Didn't you hear, Yenvis? He defected,' one of her comrades sneered, making a point of *not* lowering his weapon. 'He'd rather see Lochloria in the hands of a bone-loving cyren.'

Valli stepped out of the shadows and growled viciously, baring his fangs.

The warlock's sword wobbled, but he didn't retreat.

Valli growled again, the sound reverberating through the trees. Roh raised a palm, a signal for him to stand down.

However, Deodan stepped towards the blade of his challenger, seeming to almost welcome the press of it against his skin. 'I didn't *defect*, Barrow.' He spat the word in disgust. 'I stood for a better realm, a better life for our kind. Less bloodshed.'

'The only bloodshed we seek is that of the monsters who slaughtered our ancestors.'

'They're all dead,' Deodan hissed. 'Why do you insist on reviving a war long past?'

'You think it's over? You —'

'What are you all doing here?' Roh cut in before blood was spilled.

Barrow turned to her and laughed, despite the sea drake at her side. 'What are *we* doing here?!' he parroted, his beady eyes latching onto the crown atop her head. 'This is our homeland. And *you* must be the bone-lover that our heir has attached himself to.'

'I'm Rohesia of Saddoriel, future Queen of Cyrens,' Roh informed him, using every bit of her willpower to keep her talons sheathed. 'Now tell me, what business do you have here?'

'We're scouting,' Barrow said, a nasty smile on his face.

Roh tried not to recoil at the sight of him; he and Adriel would make quite the pair together.

'Scouting for *what* exactly?' Yrsa interjected, rolling one of her projectiles between her thumb and index finger and eyeing his head as though she'd like to slam her sling into it.

'That's between us and the Warlock Supreme.'

'Take us to her, then,' Roh ordered. 'She's here. We've seen her eagle flying overhead.'

'Deodan,' Yenvis implored. 'Stay out of this. If what Barrow said about you is true ... Your mother let you go once, she won't do it again. You're free to leave now, keep going with your journey.'

'When have you ever known me to turn a blind eye, Yenvis?'

There was a long pause. 'Never,' she said at last. 'And it'll be the death of you.'

Roh cleared her throat. 'Take us to her.'

With a final seething look at Deodan, Barrow gave a reluctant nod and motioned for them to follow. He led them to a winding path that wove through the pine trees and then back towards the edge of the hill, revealing a small clearing just beyond that overlooked the entire basin.

Roh stopped in her tracks at the majestic sight before her. The great still lake stretched on farther than she had imagined, to a distant, golden horizon. The surrounding pine forests were like a dark carpet that swept across the dips and rises of the terrain, and the hazy mountains, with their jagged cliffs and plummeting valleys, were mirrored perfectly in the ice-blue lake.

'Do you see why we fought so hard to keep it?' Deodan said quietly, so only Roh could hear.

'I do,' Roh murmured, goosebumps chilling her skin. 'And I gave you my word, Deodan. It will be —'

'We can see everyone who comes and goes from here,' said a cold voice.

Roh's head snapped up, her eyes immediately finding the Warlock Supreme in their midst, her eagle perched on her shoulder. The thick, ridged scar across her throat was starker than ever, and Roh found herself wondering what exactly had come to pass to result in such a wound, and how the Warlock Supreme had survived.

'Lamaka's Basin and Lochloria are the best-positioned territories in all the lower realms,' the Warlock Supreme said as she came to stand alongside Roh, looking out onto the landscape. 'Defended by the mountains, with access to the seas, and at the heart of all other cyren territories ... You think I would just let the Akorians take it?'

'They're not taking it,' Roh argued. 'They're seeking asylum, from the turmoil you helped create in their homeland.'

'Oh, you'd very much like to blame me for that, wouldn't you?'

'You attacked Akoris when it was defenceless. Where's the honour in that?'

'I never claimed to have honour. And that word coming from your mouth seems high and mighty. Your kind certainly isn't known for the trait. It was *your* actions that put the Akorians in danger.'

'My actions?' The words suddenly bubbled out of Roh, along with the anger she'd kept leashed. 'What about the actions of their regent? What about how Adriel *drugged his people into submission* for gods know how long?! I may have gone about it the wrong way, but I was trying to help them, to free them from his influence and then *you* —'

'Good intentions mean nothing if the consequences pummel an entire territory into the ground, wouldn't you agree?'

Roh looked hard at the Warlock Supreme, her blue-grey eyes so unnervingly similar to Deodan's, her silvery hair pulled back in a warrior's braid, a longsword strapped across her shoulders.

The warlock's words about the tactical advantage of Lamaka's Basin stuck out to Roh then.

'You mean to take this territory before waging war,' she realised, her gaze flicking to where Deodan stood quietly, his hands resting on the grips of his cutlasses.

The Warlock Supreme's lip curled in disgust as she studied her son. 'You have been the biggest disappointment of all,' she said, her words sharp enough to cut. 'Bowing to a cyren would-be queen after everything that was done to your ancestors.'

'She is not just a cyren queen,' Deodan argued. 'She is of warlock descent, too. The mountain pass recognised her as one of its own. The basin whispers to her as it does to me. She sacrificed her deathsong *to save my life*. To save a human's life. She means to return Lamaka's Basin and the scholar's city to the warlocks.'

Surprise flickered across the Warlock Supreme's face, but not enough to change her firm stance, poised for battle. 'Then her own kind won't accept her and she'll never sit upon the throne,' she countered. 'She will never have the power to give us what we want. She will make no difference to our cause.'

'You don't know that,' Roh said quietly, determination rising within.

'I know as much about the future as I need to,' the Warlock Supreme snapped. 'That it means *nothing* unless we take it into our own hands.'

'But that's exactly what I'm doing,' Roh argued. 'Lochloria will be the home of the water warlocks once more. You have my word. You do not need to wage war —'

'You mean to give back what you stole from us? How generous. Regardless of whatever intentions you sprout here and now, I will *never* trust a cyren.' Her withered fingers went to the pouch at her belt and withdrew a vial, similar to those Deodan used.

Roh's hands shot out, a gesture to stop the warlock. 'What are you doing?' she exclaimed, panic latching around her heart.

'Listen,' she implored. 'I know that your kind has suffered, more than I can possibly ever imagine. I know you are owed a home, that you have done whatever you could to survive and that you have earned your place in Lamaka's Basin and Lochloria. But —' Her voice broke as Deodan's mother began whispering enchantments to the liquid spilling out into her palms.

'But you don't have to do this. Those are innocents down there. Helpless cyrens. *Nestlings.* They won't stand in your way —'

Roh gasped as the water took the form of eagles, spreading their wings and diving straight off the hillside towards the heart of the lake. Soon, the water rippled at their approach.

The Warlock Supreme smiled. 'Sometimes, it's not about what you're owed or what you've earned ... It's about what you dare to take for yourself.'

The warlock magic dived into the vast body of water. The great lake stirred as gurgling bubbles rose to the surface, along with shoals of fish darting away from its centre.

Roh couldn't tear her eyes away as a giant reef dweller emerged from the waters and lurched to shore, its tentacles shooting out towards the helpless Akorians.

CHAPTER FOUR

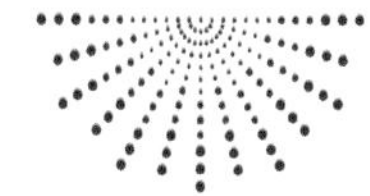

'Roh!'

She heard the shout sound from behind her, but Roh was already charging back down the hill towards the cyrens, towards the giant monster on the attack.

The colossal squid was singularly the most disgusting thing Roh had ever seen. As she ran towards it, she could see the mottled dark purple of its skin that shifted to various spectral shades as it moved. Its bulbous head overshadowed its arms, giant eyes boring into the poor souls still on the shore.

'Roh! Don't get involved,' Harlyn shrieked, barrelling through the undergrowth after her.

'You want to stand back and let the Akorians be slaughtered?' Roh yelled back, darting through the trees.

Around the reef dweller, the lake surged, causing waves to crash upon the shore and sweep away parts of the refugee camp.

'Do *you* want to be slaughtered by that *thing*?' Harlyn countered breathlessly.

The giant squid's tentacles lashed out, powerful enough to snap trees in two, with what looked like poison dripping from its suckers.

More footsteps pounded behind Roh, but she didn't chance a glance back, lest she lose her footing. She only hoped that Deodan, Yrsa, Finn, Odi and Kezra were with her.

'Valli!' she shouted, praying that her sea drake had understood her intentions.

An ear-piercing shriek curdled her blood and she looked through the trees to see Valli diving towards the massive creature. With her heart in her throat, Roh kept running, the screams from the Akorians below hitting her as hard as blows.

'We have to help them,' she shouted.

Yrsa was at her side, lassoing her sling with precision. 'Our projectiles won't cause much trauma to the body,' she assessed. 'So aim for the eyes. I believe it has several.'

As soon as they reached the white stone shores, Roh did exactly that, loading her sling with a larger clay ball and taking aim at the shining black eyes on the creature's head.

Valli's fangs gnashed around one of its tentacles, causing it to reel back and lash out violently.

Finn leaped forward, his prosthetic leg not hindering his movements in the slightest as he took the opportunity with his two swords to hack off one of its arms in a bloody spray.

'Attack!' Seraphine yelled. She had gathered what little fighting cyrens remained in their ranks and equipped them with makeshift weapons. They charged across the shores, throwing themselves at the beast to defend their young.

'Where's Deodan?' Roh shouted, scanning the fray for the warlock.

'Can't see him.' Finn swung at another tentacle that shot towards the unit.

'What of Odi?' Roh released another projectile, hitting the reef dweller with a wet thud in the eye. It recoiled slightly, only to launch itself at them with more might than before.

A crossbow bolt shot through the air and the screech from the beast that followed had Roh nearly covering her ears.

Finn pointed to a nearby tree, a grin wide on his face. 'Must have had a good teacher.'

Odi was perched on a precarious branch of a pine tree, loading a new bolt into the crossbow Finn had gifted him. But there was no time to watch him take aim again. The reef dweller's tentacles were crashing onto the shore, swiping at anything in its path.

'Watch out!' Roh cried, as its elongated arm swept towards Kezra, and in that moment she remembered how poisonous its arms were.

The image of Toril Ainsley's scars flashed before Roh.

'The reef dweller had wrapped its tentacles around me as well, and its poison was eating through my skin ...' The former competitor had told them as she rotated her arms before the group to reveal the depth and breadth of her burns. *'It even damaged my scales,'* she had said, gesturing to the gruesome burn on her temple. *'I can no longer communicate with other cyrens under water because of it ... I nearly died.'*

'None of us die today,' Roh muttered through clenched teeth, launching another projectile at the vile creature's eyes with her sling and her free hand moving to her dagger. But Kezra beat her to the closest writhing tentacle with a loud warrior's cry, and all at once, Roh understood why the towering Csillan Arch General had been dubbed The Carver. She was nothing short of wicked with a blade, slicing through rubbery flesh with a single swing of her sword, causing black blood to spatter the white stones of the shore.

A wild screech filled the air as Valli shot into the sky. But a man's shout snatched Roh's attention and she looked across the struggle to see the Warlock Supreme's unit charging towards them from the foot of the hill.

'They're attacking *us*?' Harlyn exclaimed in disbelief as she herded a group of nestlings into the cover of the forest.

'Bastards,' Finn spat. 'At least they'll be easier to kill.'

'Don't kill them!' Deodan shouted from where he fended off another tentacle's assault with his cutlasses.

Finn gaped at him. 'What?!'

'Please, they're my people —'

Roh started towards the warrior warlock, rage surging through her. 'And they're trying to kill *us*, Deodan!'

An ear-piercing scream echoed through the basin as the reef dweller took advantage of the diversion and surged forward onto the banks, its poisonous arms latching around several Akorians before tossing them brutally aside like toys.

Roh flinched as their burnt, broken bodies hit the rocks. And still the warrior warlocks attacked, wielding their blades not only against Roh and her companions, but against the unarmed refugees as well.

'Deodan!' Roh shouted. 'If you don't take care of them, I'll let Finn finish them!' She didn't stop to make sure he followed her orders. Instead, she turned to Kezra, Odi and her fellow Saddoriens, who were still trying to bring down the reef dweller.

'We can't get close enough to its body!' Kezra called out, her blade slick with black blood.

Roh readied her sling again, but a vat of something caught her eye. Without hesitating, she brought her fingers to her lips and whistled.

Valli swept in, not quite as gracefully as he had done before; one of his wings was slightly lopsided.

'Gods,' Roh murmured as she took in the burn blistering there. But the sea drake nudged her firmly, as if to say, *What do you need me to do?*

Pushing her concern for him aside, Roh pointed to the drum she'd spotted. 'Can you carry it? Drop it on him?' She nodded towards the reef dweller still wreaking havoc on the shore, the screams of the Akorians echoing between the mountains.

She didn't need to say any more. Valli snatched the vat by the handle in his mouth and took flight. Roh couldn't hesitate now. She raced towards Odi, grabbing one of his bolts and dipping its head in the nearby campfire. She offered it to the human, just as Valli dropped the drum of oil on top of the reef dweller.

'Light it up,' she said, and watched as Odi shot an arrow of fire straight for the sea monster's oil-covered heart.

CHAPTER FIVE

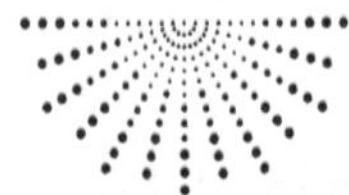

Flame erupted and the reef dweller screeched in agony, reeling back from the shore, its remaining tentacles flailing and smashing into the trees and white-stoned banks. The creature recoiled from the land, strange screams omitting from its huge body before it slipped beneath the surface of the lake.

The ear-ringing clang of steel on steel had Roh whirling her sling as she started towards Deodan, who was fighting three warlocks at once. Finn and Yrsa surged towards the fray, sliding seamlessly into the battle, driving the warlocks back from their friend.

'I don't want to hurt you,' Deodan was saying to Barrow, advancing on the warlock with his cutlasses gripped tightly in his hands.

'Your abandonment hurt us more than any blade could,' Barrow spat at him, side-stepping a half-hearted blow.

But Deodan's hesitation stopped none of the others. They attacked with ferocity filled with hatred, their strikes and swings suddenly all the more desperate in the absence of the brutal reef dweller. Finn, Yrsa and Kezra didn't hold back, and nor did Roh.

She joined them as they pushed their way into the heart of the skirmish, loading her sling and pummelling it into the gut of the nearest warlock. They were outnumbered, Roh realised, but not out-skilled. She had two Jaktaren and The Carver at her side.

When she ran out of projectiles for her sling, at last she unsheathed her dagger. She knew the basics by now, and it felt familiar in her grip as she used it to block a fatal sword blow to her chest. In the face of death, however, she couldn't help but lament the fact that she hadn't trained more. She dodged another swipe of her opponent's blade and vowed to change that in the immediate future. With Jaktaren and warriors in her midst, she had no excuse for being unprepared.

'Where's the human when you need him?' Finn scanned the trees for Odi and his crossbow as he fought off a warlock with ease.

'I don't think he wants to kill them,' Roh replied, dodging another attack.

'Well, I'm pretty sure we've established that *they* want to kill *us*,' Finn retorted, thrusting his sword into a man's stomach and then swiftly kicking him off the blade. Blood spattered across the pale stones, a cry of agony on the man's lips.

Roh sought Deodan, shooting him a questioning look. This couldn't go on.

Deodan was duelling Barrow, their boots crunching atop the rocks, their weapons gleaming in the fading light of dusk. He blocked a blow and took a step back. 'Please,' he implored his fellow warlock. 'It doesn't have to be like this.'

'Yes. It. Does.' His opponent struck again, straining against the force of Deodan's weight pressing his blade back.

Pain exploded and Roh went sprawling across the stones. The air was knocked from her lungs and a ragged gasp escaped her. Her stinging hand went instantly to the spot at her lower back, but it came away clean – no sign of blood. Still wheezing, she scrambled painfully to her feet, scooping up a fistful of stones and setting them to the pouch of her sling.

Her attacker held a thick club and Roh's side ached at the sight of it, an image of it caving in her head flashing before her. *Not a pretty way to go,* she thought and started to whirl her sling.

'To think, I'll be the one to end the bone-lover,' the warlock said, a violent gleam in his eye as he came towards her, drawing the club back.

But that was the thing about weapons like that. In the brief moment it took to ready them, they exposed their master. Roh launched her sling at the warlock's face with a sickening crunch. A second later, he slumped to the ground.

A thud sounded behind Roh and she felt the impact of Valli hitting the ground. She didn't look at him, though, knowing she might come undone at the sight of the burn on his wing. Instead, she turned to the waning battle, wincing at the pain blooming in her side.

'Enough!' she yelled, her commanding voice causing everyone to falter and pause mid-blow.

At her back, Valli reared up and roared, sending a hot gust of wind rippling through the trees and across the lake.

'You've lost,' she said to the warlocks, taking in their bloodied faces and fallen comrades. 'Walk away while you still can.'

'We're warriors, we don't walk away from a fight,' Barrow shouted, brandishing his sword.

'This is no fight,' Roh argued. 'Not anymore.' She looked around, failing to see the silver hair of the Warlock Supreme. *Has she been here at all?* 'Where is your beloved leader? Too good to get her hands dirty alongside the rest of you?' Roh called, forcing herself not to limp as she approached the warlocks, now held at sword-point.

'Do not speak ill of her,' Barrow hissed.

'She left you,' Roh told him. 'She unleashed her monster on us all and then left you here to die.'

'She did no—'

'You've done enough talking,' Roh cut him off. 'Surrender and leave these shores. We do not wish to spill more warlock blood upon the banks of this place.'

Barrow laughed darkly, red staining his teeth. 'These lands have had their fill of warlock blood, bone cleaner. It's cyren blood they thirst for now.'

Roh stared hard at the man before her, at the unadulterated loathing in his eyes. It was a hatred that had been taught, passed down from one generation to the next, festering year upon year.

'Kill us,' Barrow dared. 'You know you want to. It's in your nature.'

Roh looked across to Finn and Yrsa. Each had two warlocks on their knees at sword-point. 'Take their vials,' she ordered. 'And tie them up.'

Night had well and truly fallen. Darkness blanketed the bloodied shores and muted the moans of pain from the wounded. Only small campfires illuminated the burns and broken bones of the injured; both cyrens and warlocks alike had suffered at the poisoned, swiping tentacles of the reef dweller; monsters did not discern between races.

A sharp, icy wind funnelled down through the mountains, chilling Roh's skin as she wandered the lake's edge, her mind churning through the events of the day. She had long ago taught herself to expect the unexpected, but this? A host of Akorian refugees and an attacking force of warlocks, with a reef dweller at their backs? They hadn't even made it to Lochloria yet. There was still the Gauntlet Ruby to obtain, and in all likelihood, a challenge to win.

Pain bloomed at Roh's right kidney with each step, exactly where the warlock had struck her with his club. Rubbing it with a wince, she realised in frustration that it would be sore for days to come.

'Gods,' Roh cursed, tentatively testing the injury with her fingers. Her breath whistled between her teeth at the pain and she kicked a stone, swearing angrily. She had wanted to arrive at Lochloria ready for anything, at her strongest, but this … She reeled herself back in, recognising that she was about to start catastrophising.

It could be worse, she allowed, starting back towards her companions. None of them were seriously injured and she'd managed to convince the Akorians *not* to kill the warlock prisoners, for the time being, anyway. Valli had flown out to sea, with a definite lean in his flight, before she could get a decent look at his wing. She knew one of the reef dweller's tentacles had got him, she just didn't know how badly. But there was nothing she could do for him right now. She only hoped the magic of the currents would cleanse the wound.

Roh needed another moment alone to gather herself, to assess her level of pain. *I'll manage,* she told herself as she reached the others.

Deodan was sitting by one of the fires, his pipe stuck between his teeth.

'Why haven't you started healing them?' Roh asked him with a nod towards the injured Akorians.

Deodan's expression was incredulous. 'Why haven't I healed *them*?' he repeated, dumbfounded.

Roh looked around, confused. When she'd left, she'd asked that the wounded be tended to. Everything had seemed in order, well, as in order as it could be after an attack like that. And yet now, tension was thick in the air between her companions and the refugees, and their gazes kept darting towards the warlocks who were tied at the foot of a massive pine tree.

'What's happened?' Roh's chest was suddenly tight.

It was Odi who came to her side and said in a low voice, 'The Akorians … they're insisting on stringing up the dead warlocks, hanging them from the trees … as a warning to any other warlocks who wish to attack.'

Roh shuddered as rage curdled in her veins. 'What? That's insane.' She searched the group for Seraphine. 'You can't be serious. After everything that's just happened, *that's* your answer?'

To her credit, Seraphine looked ashamed. 'It's not my idea.'

'Now, tell me again why I should be healing them?' With that, Deodan got to his feet and stormed off into the dark.

Roh made to follow him, but a hand closed around her arm. 'Let him go,' Finn said quietly. 'I think he needs to work through some things on his own.'

Roh stared at the point of contact between them before looking up at Finn's face, illuminated by the orange glow of the fires. A scratch had scabbed over across his left cheek and his lip was swollen and bloody, but otherwise he seemed unharmed.

'You worried about me, Roh?' he asked, his dimple showing.

'You wish.' But Roh couldn't help the smile that tugged at the corner of her lips, or the way her stomach dipped as his gaze flicked to her mouth and lingered there.

Someone cleared their throat and Roh reluctantly pulled away from the Jaktaren.

Kezra stood waiting for them back by the fire with Harlyn and Odi, her eyes intense. 'What's the plan now, Queen of Bones?'

Roh tried to hide her wince as she moved. 'We stay the night here, rest up and push on to Lochloria at dawn.'

'Right. I'll go find the warlock, then,' Kezra told them, touching a torch to the fire before heading towards the water's edge.

'We should take turns at watch,' Finn said. 'I don't trust these Akorians.'

Yrsa snorted. 'You don't trust anyone.'

'Likely why you're still alive, Yrs.'

Yrsa merely shook her head.

'I'll do the first watch,' Roh volunteered, taking up a spot on a nearby fallen tree, damp seeping into the seat of her pants already. 'I don't think I could sleep if my life depended on it.'

The others were too exhausted to argue, they merely gave her resigned nods and unpacked their bedrolls, fanning out around the fire. Roh cupped her hands to her mouth, trying to blow some warmth onto her cold fingers, her foot tapping erratically against the ground.

A blanket fell across her shoulders, followed by a firm kiss to the top of her head. Roh looked up to find Harlyn standing over her.

'Probably the only kiss you'll get tonight,' she teased. 'Thought you might need it.'

Roh couldn't help it, she laughed, the joy spreading in her chest warming her more than a blanket ever could. Gods, she was grateful her friend was here, that she still had the ability to make her laugh.

'Har?' Roh called after her.

'Hmm?'

I love you. The words were on the tip of her tongue, so why were they so hard to say? Harlyn was her best friend, her sister ... They had been through so much together, those three words should have been easy.

Harlyn gave a soft chuckle. 'Don't worry, Roh. I know.'

'You do?' Roh blinked at her.

'Yep. Same to you.' Harlyn winked before dropping down to her bedroll and settling in to sleep.

In spite of everything, Roh sat there smiling to herself for a time. She knew she had to cling to these quiet moments of happiness as they were all too few and far between. It was hard to comprehend just how much had come to pass since she'd left the passages of Talon's Reach all those months ago, and yet she sat there, pondering as the fire crackled into the cold night's air.

There's so much I would change, were it in my power ... If I could go back and do it again, she thought. She had hurt so many people. Not just the Akorians, but her companions as well, Harlyn in particular. But there was also a lot she wouldn't change, not for the world. The lessons learned, the truths uncovered, the friendships forged ...

'You're looking contemplative,' a warm voice said as the log shifted beneath an additional weight.

'It comes with the territory,' Roh replied, her eyes meeting Finn's lilac gaze.

'I imagine it does.'

Roh nodded, all too aware of the press of his thigh against hers and the fact that the others were so close. 'You couldn't sleep?'

'No. I never can after a battle.'

They were quiet for a time, and in spite of everything that had just happened, all the churning thoughts emptied from Roh's head. All she could think of was his mouth on hers, the taste of him, and the brush of his fingertips across her ribs.

Roh couldn't stand the silence, nor the tension that seemed to cling to the air between them. 'I used my dagger today,' she said.

'And?'

Roh gave him a grim smile. 'I could be better.'

Finn laughed softly. 'Is that a request?'

'Is that an offer?' she countered.

The Jaktaren got to his feet and offered her his hand. 'Come on. We'll go over there, so we don't wake the others.'

Roh's heart stuttered, but she took his hand and her cold fingers warmed instantly in his grip. He led her to a small clearing a few yards away from their campsite, where they could still keep watch, but any minor commotion from them wouldn't disturb their sleeping friends.

Dropping her hand, Finn stood opposite her. 'You've only got the one, right?' he asked.

Roh nodded, unsheathing her dagger. 'I blocked several blows with it today. It served me well enough, but … I don't know how to wield it, to attack.'

'Well, defence is the first thing we're always taught. There's no sense in being able to stab someone if they stab you first. I'm guessing you remember the defensive stances and moves we taught you in Akoris?'

'I do.'

'Good.' Finn unsheathed his own dagger from his boot. 'So, let's focus on slicing the enemy to pieces, then.' He flicked the weapon over in his hand, catching it by the tip of the blade and offering it to Roh, handle first.

'What are you doing?' Roh asked.

'Daggers work best if you use them in pairs.' Finn motioned for her to take his.

Someone else's words filled her mind then. *'This belonged to your father.'* Ames had pressed the quartz dagger into her palm. *'It is one of two. A pair forged at the very beginning of our kinds …'*

'Where is the other?' she had asked. *'Please don't tell me it's another object I have to find.'*

'It will find you.'

Roh looked down at the quartz dagger, the weapon her father had once held and pictured its twin, wondering where it had ended up and how it was supposed to find her amidst all this chaos.

'Roh?' Finn was still holding out his blade.

'Sorry.' Forcing the memory to the back of her mind, Roh took it, the weapon feeling strange in comparison to her own.

'Not ideal, I know.' Finn glanced from one blade to the other. 'They're different weights and lengths, but better than nothing. Now, take up your attacking stance, feet apart.'

The training sessions he and Yrsa had led in the gardens of Akoris came back to Roh and she found herself moving into position without thinking, her muscle memory taking over.

'This type of fighting is called dual wielding,' Finn told her. 'A lot of people think daggers are more defensive weapons, but when used effectively, they can be just as deadly as any sword or cutlass. And they have the added benefit of being lighter, making them ideal for someone of your size, who's already using speed and agility to their advantage.'

Roh weighed the daggers in her grip. 'Makes sense.'

'You're already using your sling to get up close and personal with your attackers, so the manoeuvres I'm about to show you shouldn't worry you.'

'I worry about everything,' Roh muttered.

To her surprise, Finn didn't brush off her retort. 'That's good,' he said. 'It means you care. But the beauty of combat is that it narrows your focus. It's just you and your opponent, none of those churning fears in your mind. It's just the blades between you: life and death. There's an exquisite simplicity to it.'

There was something oddly calming about the thought that with her daggers, Roh could peel away all the superfluous layers and settle a single truth. She shifted from foot to foot and waited for Finn to continue.

'Your stance is strong,' he noted, his gaze trailing down her legs.

Roh forced herself to concentrate, holding up her daggers.

Finn picked up a branch from the ground. 'Let's assume that your attacker will strike first. Perhaps they have knowledge of who you are, and as such they'll likely assume you've got no experience. Always use their assumptions against them. So when they strike, block the blow with one of your daggers.' He struck at Roh with the branch, but she was ready and knocked it aside with her quartz blade.

'Good,' he said. 'Then don't hesitate to go in with an immediate stab. Usually when an opponent strikes, their midsection or at least part of their side is left vulnerable. Use that to your advantage.' He pointed to his side, which was exposed as he'd raised his arm.

'Again.' He struck, Roh blocked and thrust her other dagger at him. Finn jumped back with a grin. 'Good.'

Roh's cheeks warmed at his encouragement.

'It'll be a lot faster when it's happening, but with practice, it should become like second nature. Once you've blocked and struck once, you want to keep your attacks brief and swift to maximise the power of your weapons, as well as keep yourself out of striking range when you're exposed. Understand?'

Roh bowed her head, keen to try again.

'Then let's spar.'

In the faint glow of the campfires, they trained. While it wasn't a matter of life and death, Roh forgot the pain pulsing at her back and the jumble of decisions and worries roiling in her head. Her mind quietened and the rest of the world faded into the background. It was just her and Finn, and the impact of her daggers against the stick he wielded against her. Her focus was on his attack and the scrape of their boots through the damp leaf litter. He moved slower than usual for her, not using the full force of his strength, nor his Jaktaren tricks, but he made her sweat nonetheless.

'Good,' he murmured as she made to thrust her dagger up into his ribs. 'Very good. Again.'

And so they continued. Roh improved with each round, her movements growing more confident, her decisions more instinctual. She came to relish the strange weight of the daggers in her palms and the kiss of the wind against her skin as she struck and parried. Until she realised Finn was smiling.

'What?' she snapped, recognising a joke she wasn't in on.

A laugh bubbled from his lips. 'It's just ...'

'What?' she ground out.

'Well, you have this look.'

Roh's hands went to her hips, which was difficult when she held daggers. 'Spit it out, Haertel. What look?'

'You have a *concentration* look. You frown really deeply and then when you're about to slash, you bite your lip. You do it every time. It's a good thing you'll be fighting strangers.'

Roh narrowed her eyes and laced her voice with a warning. 'You keep this up, it might not be a stranger I fight.'

'Is that so?' Finn's smile grew wider as he took a measured step towards her.

'Possibly.'

'I may only have a stick, Roh, but I can still best you in seconds. You forgetting who I am?'

'As if I could forget who you are with all that arrogance rolling off you in waves —'

But Roh's words were cut off. Finn didn't even raise the branch, he merely swept her legs out from under her, sending her falling clumsily to the ground. Roh tried to scramble to her feet, but a sharp point grazed her neck and Finn crouched at her side.

'Seemed like you needed reminding,' he said.

Roh let out a stream of curses and Finn laughed, tossing the branch away and offering her a hand.

Shaking her head at her own stupidity, Roh took it and Finn pulled her to her feet, only to find her own dagger pressed to her breast. 'Thought you knew never to trust a cyren,' he murmured.

Roh's breathing hitched, her chest rising to meet the tip of the blade, her gaze flicking to Finn's mouth. She bit her lip, dragging her eyes up to his, hoping he was thinking the same thing she was.

Finn watched her, a glint of hunger in his stare as his grip faltered and he leaned in.

In a blur of movement, Roh had her other dagger between them, disarming him of the quartz weapon and violently shoving him up against a nearby tree, his own blade to his throat.

Eyes wide, he blinked at her.

Roh smiled. 'I *do* know,' she said, 'better than most.'

A grin that mirrored her own broke across Finn's face. 'Impressive,' he allowed.

Roh suddenly became all too aware of the heat between their bodies and the intensity of Finn's stare. He didn't move beneath her hold, though she knew he could have her on the ground in seconds. Instead, he didn't move, as if waiting for her to make up her mind.

Slowly, Roh took the dagger from his throat and let it drop to the ground. She leaned in, kissing the same spot where the blade had been. Finn's skin was hot against her lips and she swore she could feel his pulse rising beneath it. She heard his sharp intake of breath and the twitch of his body as he refrained from touching her, from taking control. Her stomach swooped, her hand finding the side of his head, her fingers weaving through his hair as she kissed his neck again, tasting the salt in his sweat.

'Gods, Roh ...' Her name was said between clenched teeth.

Roh drew back, just enough to peer at Finn's face. The fire that blazed in his eyes was enough to snap the last of her restraint. She kissed him, hard.

Instantly, his hands were on her, tight around her waist, pressing her into him at the small of her back. A low noise escaped him and Roh smiled against his lips. She liked that she could elicit such sounds from him. But as his mouth opened on hers, she nearly let out a noise of her own. Heat pooled within her as Finn kissed her deeply and her hands went to the hem of his shirt. She let her fingers trail up beneath it, finding his skin just as heated as her own must have been. He shifted from the tree in one swift movement, turning them around so he was pushing her back against it instead, his body covering hers.

Roh kissed him hungrily – she couldn't get enough of his taste or the feel of his hands on her. He toyed with the hem of her shirt and she clicked her tongue in frustration, guiding his hands up beneath the fabric and underneath the thin camisole she wore. But Finn wouldn't be rushed. His touch trailed along the curve of her ribs and brushed against the soft underside of her breast.

She arched into his touch, pushing her body closer to his.

'Roh,' he murmured against her lips, stroking her skin.

How had she waited so long for this? In spite of all the obstacles and dangers they'd faced, in spite of her lack of song and her constant inner battles, her thoughts had always come back to him, to that moment between them in Serratega. And now that he was here kissing her, touching her, she couldn't let it end here, she couldn't wonder *what if* any longer.

'Don't stop,' she breathed, desperate for more of him.

He kissed her fiercely, his hand cupping her breast, his palm like a brand on her bare skin. That heat within intensified, throbbing between her legs and tingling at the base of her spine. Finn rolled her nipple between his fingers and she moaned, the sound stifled by another kiss.

Her hands went to his belt and Finn drew back, panting. 'Roh … we can't.'

Roh's fingers stilled at the buckle, and she looked up at him. Even in the dim light, she could see the flush on his cheeks, his dishevelled hair and the quick rise and fall of his chest.

His hands closed around hers. 'This isn't right … The others … Anyone could see us.'

'Not if we're quick.' The words were out of Roh's mouth before she could think.

Finn gazed thoughtfully at her. 'Have you done this before?' he asked quietly.

Roh's mouth was suddenly dry. 'I've … I've done *some* things.'

'But not all?' he pressed.

Roh's cheeks burned as she shook her head.

Finn brought his mouth to hers again, kissing her thoroughly. 'Then I don't want to be quick,' he told her. 'I don't want to worry about being discovered, or being in a hurry. If we're going to do this …' He kissed her again, gripping her hips firmly. 'Then I want to do it right.'

Roh's heart was still racing, that need still roiling within her, but Finn was right. With their companions mere yards away and a band of hostile Akorians nearby, now was not the time.

'But make no mistake, Roh,' Finn added, adjusting his shirt to hang over the front of his pants. 'I want you. Have done for a long while now.'

Roh's toes curled in her boots, but she nodded. 'Right,' she said. 'We should get some rest, wake one of the others to take watch.'

'Good idea.'

CHAPTER SIX

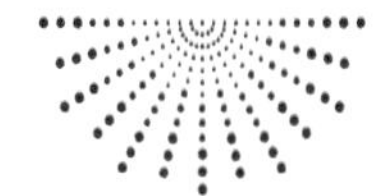

Watery golden light and a throbbing pain woke Roh. Her whole body was sore and stiff, and the spot where the warlock had clubbed her on her back was tender. She winced as she pushed herself from the ground, gritting her teeth through the discomfort. He hadn't hit her that hard, had he? Perhaps she had overdone it with the training last night.

At the thought of last night, Roh's cheeks heated and her fingertips went to her near-bruised lips as she scanned the campsite. Finn and Deodan were nowhere to be seen, Harlyn was still snoring lightly by the glowing embers of the fire, while Kezra, Odi and Yrsa sat on a nearby log, talking quietly.

'Morning,' Roh said, her voice scratchy and raw. Approaching them, she tugged her cloak tightly around her against the chill of the mountain air.

'Morning, Queen of Bones,' Kezra said, smiling. She'd long since adopted Deodan's title for her. Once, it had bothered Roh, but now she recognised it for what it was: a term of endearment.

Yrsa gave her a wave and went back to rolling clay balls between her palms, forever stocking up on projectiles for her beloved sling. Odi, Roh realised, was polishing the crossbow Finn had given him.

'For someone who was opposed to learning how to use that thing, you've certainly got the hang of it now,' Roh told him, lifting a canteen to her lips.

Odi shrugged. 'It's proved useful in our last few … skirmishes.'

'I can't argue with you there,' Roh said, surveying their campsite, their packs and spare blankets in disarray. The disorder grated on her, but there were more pressing matters at hand. 'Where are the others?' she asked.

'Fishing,' Kezra supplied.

'Fishing?' In light of everything that had happened the previous day, the simple act of *fishing* seemed surreal.

'Finn was adamant we should have a decent meal before we head for Lochloria. Can't say I was opposed to the idea. I don't remember the last time I had something other than stale flatbread,' Yrsa said, at last looking up from her task. She frowned at Roh. 'Are you alright? You're looking … pale.'

'Just sore from sleeping in the dirt,' Roh replied. 'Have you seen Valli?'

Odi pointed through the trees. 'By the lake. I think he's been guarding it in case that thing comes back.'

Roh's gaze found the mass of gold scales and wings by the water's edge. Valli was sprawled on his belly, staring out onto the ice-blue surface of the lake. She needed to check the burn on his wing, perhaps get Deodan to work his magic on it.

Odi cleared his throat. 'I heard that if you defeat a reef dweller, it grants you a wish.'

Roh snorted, and the others laughed quietly around them. 'Well, where is it, then? I've got plenty of wishes to be granted,' Roh quipped. 'Where'd you hear such nonsense?'

Odi shrugged. 'Townsfolk of a coastal village up north. Plenty of myths and legends about the sea up there.'

'You've travelled that far?' Kezra asked, her eyes wide.

A groan sounded from near the campfire. 'Some of us are *trying* to sleep,' Harlyn muttered.

'Well, the *rest of us* are awake and getting ready for the day ahead,' Roh shot back at her.

Harlyn made another disgruntled noise before promptly pulling her blanket over her head and ignoring them.

Odi had a fond smile on his face when he turned back to Kezra. 'I travelled all over for my music,' he told her. 'So did my stepbrothers. We went on a tour of sorts around the Upper Realms.'

'Would you like to do that again?'

Odi sighed. 'I think I would like to see the Isle of Dusan again and stay in one place for a while.'

'Well, your people will be lucky to have you back,' Kezra said kindly.

He gave her a nod of thanks but spoke no more of his homeland.

A wet thud interrupted the quiet. Roh looked to the ground to see a large trout flapping in the dirt.

'Breakfast is served,' Deodan announced, wiping his hands on his jerkin.

Roh eyed the silver scales and bulging eyes of the fish. 'Not quite like that, I hope.'

The warlock shrugged. 'I thought that part would be a job for The Carver.'

Kezra already had her blade out, grinning.

The morning sun was high when they finished eating their fill, though its warmth didn't quite reach them in the shade of the forest. Roh instructed the others to gather their things. They had done all they could for the Akorian refugees here, and their best move would be to continue on to Lochloria as planned and return to help once Roh had the throne. She didn't like to leave the warlock prisoners in their hands, but there was no other choice. She couldn't bring injured captives into the scholar's city with her. Seraphine begrudgingly gave Roh her word that the prisoners would remain unharmed and that would simply have to do.

Roh went to Valli, who was sitting by the great lake's edge. The aftermath of the reef dweller's attack had created a strange tide that lapped at the shore, refusing to still.

'How are you my friend?' she asked quietly, running her hand over Valli's scaled side.

He let out a low noise and extended his wing for her to see. Roh winced at the sight of it. A patch of scales roughly the size of her palm was blistered over, pus oozing from the wound.

'Valli … You should have shown me sooner. We don't leave until this has been treated.'

Roh found Deodan back at the campsite and all but dragged him to the subdued sea drake. 'He was burned by one of the tentacles,' she explained. 'Please, heal him.'

Deodan's brows furrowed as he examined the wound. 'I don't know if I can,' he said. 'This is not as simple as a flesh wound. The tentacles are laced with a powerful, magical poison.'

'Please, Deodan.' Roh gripped his arm. He had to know how important Valli was to her, that he had been hurt *defending them,* after all.

'I'll see what I can do,' Deodan allowed, reaching for one of his vials. 'But I can't make any promises, you understand that?'

Roh nodded, not acknowledging the possibility that Deodan's magic might not work. She wouldn't accept that as an option. She watched quietly as the warlock poured a vial of sacred water into his palm, cupping it close to his face. He whispered an enchantment in a language she didn't understand, the words sounding like a song of old, with their own rhythm. The water took form, moulding into the shape of what looked like sea grass from the ancient deep, the fronds fluttering in the air before dancing around Roh and drifting to Valli's injured wing.

The sea drake let out a hiss of pain as the water magic settled across his burn, but he didn't move, clearly understanding that Roh and Deodan were there to help.

The sea grass seemed to meld to Valli's damaged scales, becoming a second skin of sorts. It shimmered and Deodan murmured his enchantment again, as though he was encouraging the magic, coaxing it to fulfil its purpose. The water sank into Valli's wing and Roh peered over Deodan's shoulder.

'Thank the gods,' she muttered. While the scales there were a slightly different shade of gold to the rest, the blistered patch was gone. Valli stretched out his wing experimentally and gave a short sharp shriek, nuzzling Deodan with his snout.

'I think that means it's better?' Deodan said, a soft smile on his lips.

Roh studied the movement of the sea drake's wing. It was ever so slightly restricted ... But Valli shot into the air and beat those glorious wings, causing more waves in the lake, a cold wind whipping through Roh's hair and she exhaled a deep sigh of relief.

'Thank you,' she told Deodan.

The warlock merely strode back to camp.

There were no farewells between Roh and the Akorians, only angry, accusing stares. It didn't sit well with her, but there was nothing more to be done.

'I'll hold you to your word,' she told Seraphine as she shouldered her pack.

The former oracle nodded, her jaw clenched. 'And I'll hold you to yours.'

And that was that. Roh put her fingers to her mouth and whistled. Valli dived from the sky and landed deftly on the shore, stretching out his wings before tucking them behind his back. He approached the group, eyeing Seraphine suspiciously, and waited.

'You know what we have to do,' Roh told the others. 'We reach Lochloria, we get the gem and we return to Saddoriel via the mirror pool.'

'Simple as that, eh?' Harlyn said, brows raised.

'As simple and as hard as that, yes,' Roh replied, adjusting the straps on her shoulders. She turned to Finn, who held the weathered map in his hands. 'Lead us to the scholar's city.'

The pine forest was dense, the terrain uneven beneath their boots as they left the great lake behind and forged ahead, aiming to reach Lochloria before dark. Roh wished they had started their journey sooner, but Finn had been right about needing a decent meal to begin the day; they would need their strength before long.

The group chatted quietly amongst themselves, but Roh lingered towards the rear of the company, where Valli was trudging through the forest, his wings tucked away protectively. It was an odd sight: a creature of the ancient deep surrounded by trees, padding across the land rather than soaring through the skies or carving through the currents.

Roh's pack knocked against her sore back as she walked, sending dizzying jolts of pain through her whole body, making her feel queasy.

Valli nudged her with his snout, and sniffing her, he made an unhappy sound.

'I don't smell *that* bad,' she muttered, though she realised with a start that it had been days since she'd bathed properly. *To think I wanted Finn to peel away these grotty clothes last night ...* She flushed, suddenly glad for the restraint they'd shown, but all the same, her gaze sought him out.

Finn led the group through the forest, consulting the map

they'd copied from a book in Csilla. It provided far more detail on the territory than the original chart they'd brought from Saddoriel and had argued over, a lifetime ago. Lamaka's Basin had long ago vanished behind the trees and the canopy of the pines blocked out any view of the surrounding mountains. There was an eeriness to this territory and a coldness Roh hadn't imagined when she had dreamed of stepping foot on her father's homeland. She knew deep in her bones that no deathsong stirred within her – she had watched it leave her very being back in Csilla – and yet … she felt different here. There was a flicker of magic in her veins, what exactly it was, she didn't know, but it whispered against her skin all the same, as though Lochloria itself was calling to her.

Roh was brought out of her reverie by Harlyn suddenly trudging alongside her.

'How do you feel?' Roh asked her. 'Has the antidote changed anything?'

Harlyn gave an uneasy shrug. 'It's too soon to tell. I haven't heard Orson since I ate that horrible flower.'

Roh grimaced in sympathy. She remembered the disgusting bitter taste of the antidote.

'But sometimes I go days without hearing her, then she's the loudest voice I hear for hours,' Harlyn continued. 'I guess we'll have to wait and see.'

Roh nodded. 'I guess so.'

'Are you alright?' Harlyn frowned at her.

'Of course, I'm fine.'

'You look … You just look a bit off.'

'Thanks,' Roh said sarcastically.

Harlyn rolled her eyes. 'You know that's not what I meant.'

Roh waved her away. 'I know, I know.'

Satisfied, Harlyn looked ahead. 'You really think we'll be there by nightfall?'

'If we keep up this pace, I hope so.'

'We've come a long way, you and I,' Harlyn said slowly. 'Can you believe we're about to visit the *scholar's city*?'

Roh laughed, ignoring the pain in her side. 'Not really. Can you believe my father is *from* the scholar's city?'

'Definitely not. What do you think it'll be like?'

'I haven't got a clue,' Roh admitted, still trying to shake the strange feeling from her body. The eeriness clung to her as though she'd walked through a web of spider's silk.

Her eye caught on something. A wilted flower at the foot of a pine tree. And another, and another.

Harlyn followed her pointed finger. 'So it really is true ... The curse is true?'

Roh's eyes narrowed as she looked closer, where the earth itself looked scorched. 'Perhaps it is. What was that part of the supposed prophecy ...?'

'Land will fester,' Kezra answered, approaching them with a thoughtful expression. 'Deodan,' she called, 'what do you make of this?'

The warlock paused mid-conversation with Odi and he went to them. He crouched at the base of the tree, leaning over the wilting petals. 'I don't know what to make of it, Kezra.' He plucked one of the greying flowers from its roots and it disintegrated between his fingers. 'But it doesn't look good, does it?'

'Roh, can't you use the gems?' Odi asked, his gaze resting upon Roh's crown. 'They've given you guidance before, haven't they?'

Finn shifted, still holding the map. 'That's not a bad idea.'

'Was that a compliment?' Odi gaped at him.

'I wouldn't go that far,' Finn retorted. 'Well?' He looked to Roh. 'What do the gems tell you?'

'It's not as though they constantly whisper in my ear,' Roh said, but she focused on the weight of her crown all the same, and the energy of the gems in its apexes. When she had sought the truth about Ames, she had merely stated a fact and the warmth of the stones had told her where sincerity lay. But this seemed more complex somehow.

Suddenly feeling faint, Roh swayed on her feet, peering at the dust in Deodan's hand and touching her fingers to it.

Valli nudged her again, more roughly this time, causing her to stumble over a fallen branch. She went sprawling, her palms stinging as she hit the dirt, her face inches from the wilted flowers.

She shot Valli a glare over her shoulder. 'What was that for?'

'Roh, are you alright?' Yrsa helped her up.

'I'm fine,' Roh told her, getting to her feet with a grimace. She pointed a finger towards her sea drake. 'He was being pushy.'

'What was that about?' Finn ran a critical eye over Roh.

'Roh fell,' Yrsa replied.

'I didn't *fall*.' But as the words left Roh's mouth, she was hit by a wave of dizziness and she staggered again, and this time Yrsa caught her. Black spots swam before Roh's vision. She felt Yrsa take her whole weight.

'What's happening? Roh? Roh?' Finn's voice sounded far away.

She could feel Valli nudging at the painful spot on her back, but she was slipping. Someone was fumbling with her shirt and she felt the kiss of icy air against her skin.

'Gods,' someone cursed. 'Deodan! Deodan, we need help!'

Roh heard the panic in the voices around her but did not feel its familiar tightening grip herself. Instead, she was calm, calmer than she had been in a long while. A sense of serenity wrapped itself around her and the pain disappeared. So she let go, of all the worries churning in her head, of all the fear of what was to come, and then she was floating, far, far away from everything and everyone.

'Stone will crumble and land will fester, until the winged one flies forth …' The so-called prophecy echoed in Roh's mind like a melody on

loop until a voice she recognised dragged her from beneath the dark surface.

'She's been bleeding internally this whole time?' Raw fear laced Harlyn's voice.

Roh's eyes opened to slits. 'I'm bleeding?' she croaked.

'You *were*,' Deodan said. 'Internally. But you're not anymore, thanks to Valli.'

'You had something to do with her healing as well, warlock,' Finn added with an edge to his tone.

Roh blinked slowly, her vision coming back into focus. She was lying on her side in the dirt, the others all gathered around her. 'What happened?' she asked.

'At some point, you were hit in the kidney. I don't know how long you've been injured for, but … You passed out and Valli pointed us to the wound.'

'It wasn't that bad, a bit sore,' Roh muttered, trying to sit up.

Harlyn helped her get half upright, saying, 'Deodan healed you.'

'If he hadn't been here, you would have died,' Kezra offered, casually sharpening one of her knives from where she sat on a nearby log. 'You didn't know you were hurt?'

Roh shook her head. 'Well, not badly.'

'I've never seen something so horrible,' Harlyn declared, clearly trying to keep her voice light. 'That bruise was the deepest purple, spread all over your lower back.'

Roh didn't know what to say to that, so instead she met Deodan's gaze. 'Thank you.'

'Don't mention it, Queen of Bones. Can't have you dying on us now. We've still got a gem to find and a throne to win.' He offered her a hand up.

She took it. 'That we do.'

'We should let you rest a little longer,' Finn said, frowning in her direction.

'I feel alright, better than alright,' Roh reassured him. 'The pain is completely gone.'

A muscle twitched in his jaw, but he didn't argue. Instead, he turned to the rest of the group. 'Does anyone else have any hidden injuries we need to worry about?'

There was a general murmur of 'no', and seemingly satisfied, Finn turned back to his map. 'We're not far,' he told them and started off once more.

Roh shouldered her pack with ease, Valli monitoring her closely. 'Thank you, my friend.' She reached up to stroke his snout, wondering how in the realms he'd detected her injury.

'Come on,' Finn called.

Roh's skin bristled. *Am I imagining things or is there a note of anger in his voice?*

The Jaktaren didn't say much else as he led them through the forest, setting a gruelling pace. Roh felt the tension rolling off him in heavy waves. She wanted to talk to him, to ask him what was wrong, but with the others there, it didn't feel right. Roh knew she had a lot to learn about Finn Haertel, but she knew enough to recognise that he wouldn't want everyone involved in a conversation about his feelings. So she said nothing.

That same tension seemed to seep into the rest of the group. There was no more quiet chatter amongst them, only the crunch of leaves beneath their boots and the trickle of a nearby stream.

Hours passed and no one asked to stop, so they didn't. The sound of rushing water grew louder, and soon they found themselves at a river, the same ice-blue water as the lake coursing over the moss-covered boulders, carving through the earth. Around them, the trees began to thin and suddenly Roh found herself staring at a pair of iron gates that towered over the river, and beyond it giant crumbling sandstone buildings.

'Lochloria,' Deodan breathed, as though he couldn't believe he stood before it.

Goosebumps rushed across Roh's skin as they approached the gates, finding a doorway through one of the watchtowers. It swung open at Roh's touch, the rusted hinges squeaking loudly. On the other side, the late-afternoon sun illuminated an open space with a line of pavers leading down its centre.

'The Scholar's Green,' Finn told them with a glance at the map.

'Nothing green about this place,' Harlyn muttered as they crossed the strange, empty courtyard. The little grass remaining was yellow and brittle.

But Roh's focus went to the building just beyond the so-called green. It ran the length of the dead grass, and despite its state of disrepair, the sandstone at the edges falling away revealed a strong framework beneath, with a pair of intimidating gates reinforced with steel towering through the middle. Roh's skin prickled. There was a reason the Akorians had not migrated this far into the territory and she suspected they were about to discover that reason ... When she reached the entrance, Roh placed a hand on the rough timber and steel, and to her surprise, the heavy gates lurched inwards with a groan.

It was the quadrangle from the vision she'd had during the Rite of Strothos. The place where she'd watched her grandmother, Sedna Irons, comfort her sickly infant by the babbling stream. The quadrangle which had once been a glorious feat of architecture, a bright space, full of life, was now in complete ruin. But it was not the recognition of the place, nor its destruction, that snatched a gasp of shock from Roh's lungs.

It was the battalion of Saddorien soldiers standing in wait, blades gleaming.

This was why neither the Akorians nor the warlocks had ventured closer to the scholar's city.

Roh heard the slide of weapons leaving their sheaths behind her, her companions ready to fight, to claw their way out of the council's grasp once more, but it was unnecessary.

Even the most stoic of soldiers flinched as a dark, long shadow cast across the formation of cyrens. Valli prowled through the gates, snarling, his barbed tail slicing menacingly through the air.

'Well, if the council hadn't heard about him yet ... They will now,' Harlyn muttered.

'Perhaps it's time they knew the extent of the alliances we have formed,' Roh replied, ensuring her voice carried across to the army before her.

But the threat of death by drake did not cause the battalion to scream or flee. The Saddorien soldiers held their ground, the sun glancing off their coral armour. It was an impressive sight, one that only fuelled the sinking sensation of dread now coiled low in Roh's gut.

What percentage of the entire Saddorien Army did this battalion make up? How vulnerable had their presence here left the lair?

'Sometimes, it's not about what you're owed or what you've earned ... It's about what you dare to take for yourself.'

With the Warlock Supreme's words still echoing in her ears, Roh's sense of urgency flared to life. 'Where is your commander?' she called out, her voice strong as she scanned the rows. 'Where is the Arch General of Lochloria?'

A soft breeze danced around them and Roh swore she heard the delicate chimes of music from somewhere.

Suddenly, Valli hissed viciously, the wind stilling around them as Roh heard what he had: the soft tap of footsteps on pavers. The battalion did not answer, did not move while she searched the grounds for the source of the noise.

Roh was surprised to find that despite the general decay of Lochloria, the buildings running parallel to the ruins were intact, as though untouched by the Scouring that had descended upon the territory, untouched by any supposed warlock curse and untouched by the trials of time itself. They were long structures of golden sandstone, bright in comparison to the crumbling, decrepit buildings elsewhere. The sound of footsteps continued.

Roh felt her companions band closer together, their backs to one another, gripping their weapons tightly as they readied themselves to face whoever came next.

From the building marked with a sign that read *Resident Halls*, a cyren emerged. A warrior, there was no doubt about it, not with the hardened nature of her beauty, the worn coral breastplate strapped to her chest and the steel trident clutched in her grip.

The cyren seemed to sense Roh's focus and locked eyes with her as she reached them, ignoring the silent battalion completely. Her gaze didn't falter, not even when she saw the sea drake at Roh's back. When at last the cyren spoke, her voice was like steel.

'And so …' she said. 'The warlock-loving bone queen has come to Lochloria.'

CHAPTER SEVEN

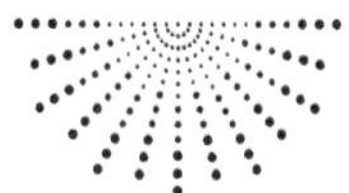

The cyren was standing close, too close for Roh's comfort, but as desperately as she wanted to, Roh did not move, she did not yield a step back. Instead, she stared back at the female, her free hand clenched at her side to stop her talons sliding free.

It was Deodan who spoke. 'This is Rohesia Irons, future queen of cyrenkind.'

Roh's stomach rolled. She hadn't yet claimed the name for herself aloud, the name her mother bore, the name her grandmother had borne before her ... And yet here it had now been claimed, in front of the very army they had once fought for.

Something flickered across the cyren's gaze. 'Irons?'

Roh ground her teeth. 'My name is Rohesia,' she said coldly. 'You would do well to address me as such.'

She seemed to sense the challenge in Roh's tone and gave a stiff nod, easing out of Roh's immediate space.

'Who are you?' Roh demanded, taking advantage of the small reprieve.

'I'm Elna,' the warrior said, 'I am the keeper of Lochloria.'

'The Arch General, then?'

'I have always preferred the title of keeper.'

'Tell me, *keeper*, how long has this battalion been stationed here?'

A smirk tugged at Elna's mouth. 'Since you became a traitor to your own kind in Csilla.'

Roh suppressed the urge to roll her eyes. It was not the first time she had been referred to as such, nor would it be the last.

A hot gust of air hit the back of Roh's neck, a huff of frustration from Valli. She turned to see him staring down at two young nestlings, no older than ten, who were openly gaping up at him.

Where did they come from? Roh stared. *What are a pair of nestlings doing running around a battalion base?*

'Nym! Maiella! Get away from that thing!' Elna darted forward to drag the youngsters away from the sea drake, her mask of composure slipping momentarily.

'He won't hurt them,' Kezra assured her, the memory of her own nestlings playing with Valli clearly fresh in her mind.

But Elna hauled the nestlings away, shoving them behind her. Roh watched curiously. The little ones were almost identical, their features mirroring their mother's ... But their wild curiosity had the innocence and abandon of youth, their bright gazes lacking the sharp harshness their mother's eyes held. Roh went to Valli and he leaned down, allowing her to stroke his forehead.

'He won't harm anyone,' she told the keeper of Lochloria, though she hoped the implication was clear enough: *yet*. 'He's part of our – my – court.'

Dark amusement flashed across Elna's face as she took in the sight of Roh's unlikely companions, her icy gaze lingering on Odi and Deodan. 'Your *court* ...' She said the word as though it soured in her mouth. 'So there was no mistake, no rumours gone astray? You truly are the songless bone queen we've heard of.' Her eyes scanned Roh's shorter hair, her nose wrinkling. 'You don't look like much of a Saddorien.'

'And this doesn't look like a territory that needs a "keeper".' Roh looked pointedly at the crumbling buildings. 'Yet here we are.'

Ignoring her daughters' tugs at her trousers, Elna seemed to draw herself up. 'I am the cousin of Elder Colter, and I have been charged with holding Lochloria for the past century and a half.'

'Nepotism … Figures,' Harlyn muttered.

'Tradition,' Elna corrected with a sneer. 'I don't expect a bunch of bone cleaners and their *other companions*,' she added, jutting her chin towards Odi and Deodan, 'to understand that. Especially after I heard that you want to return this territory to the warlocks.'

Roh took a deep breath. From the moment Elna had emerged from the building, she should have known that she was going to make things difficult. 'I do,' Roh told her evenly.

'You don't even deny it?'

'No. But before you harp on about cyren loyalty, why don't you tell me why you haven't helped the Akorians on your shores? You know they're there. And you have an entire force at your disposal.'

Elna laughed darkly. '*Help them?* A cyren should not *need* help, a cyren's cunning should see them through all challenges. The Akorians have no cunning, only addictions to substances that leave them without mind or will. They are weak.'

Fury bubbled to the surface at the ugliness of Elna's words. 'So, you would leave them to die on the shores of Lamaka's Basin?' Roh challenged. 'And at the hands of the warrior warlocks? Don't tell me you don't know what goes on in your own territory. They'll be back.'

Elna waved to the formation of soldiers behind her. 'And we'll be ready when they return.'

'But not in the defence of the Akorians?'

'As I said, they are weak. And not our responsibility.'

Roh could hardly believe what she was hearing. 'They are *cyrens*, just like you.'

'A frail link in the armour wounds us all,' she replied. 'Do you know who coined that phrase?'

'Should I?'

'The great Sedna Irons.'

At the mention of the name, the army battalion shifted.

Elna pressed on. 'She said it many times while defending the homeland you seek to ruin. Wisdom passed down through generations of Saddoriens.'

'Somehow I doubt that's how she meant it.'

'What would you know about it?' Elna snapped.

Roh's cheeks burned. She hated that Elna was right. She had never known her grandmother, she hadn't even known who she was until recently. She was the last person who could claim what Sedna Irons had meant hundreds of years ago.

But she seemed to have ignited a fury within Elna, for she carried on, her voice an octave higher in anger. 'What responsibilities do you understand? None. I am the *keeper of the scholar's city*, it is my duty to survive and hold the territory, not to pander to the needs of foolish Akorians who find themselves hungry on our shores. I am bound by my duty to the lair, to the *rightful* queen, by the vow I have made.'

'As am I,' Roh said, pushing aside her initial embarrassment and remaining as calm as the eye of a terror tempest. 'So, let me clarify things for you. You asked if I intended to give Lochloria back to the warlocks. I will say it again, so there's no confusion: I do. It's their home by right.'

'By right?' Elna scoffed. 'It belongs to the cyrens. We took it, therefore it is ours.'

'By that ruling, then it is also mine to give to whom I wish,' Roh countered. She could practically feel Deodan holding his breath nearby. She also noticed that the two nestlings were peering at her in wonder. It was clear they had never seen anyone stand up to their fierce mother.

Elna sneered. 'You're not queen yet, warlock-lover.'

'You're right, I'm not,' Roh said. 'But let's get to that, shall we? I don't wish to stand out here on these rotting grounds all day. Where is the Gauntlet Ruby?'

Elna adjusted her grip on her trident and eyed Valli warily. It was clear she was weighing up the battalion's odds against such a beast. Apparently, Valli didn't like her attitude. The great creature snapped his fangs in her direction, causing the nestlings to shriek.

Elna's expression hardened further. 'First, tell your beast to be gone,' she said, her throat bobbing. 'He is a threat and I don't comply well under those.'

Roh hesitated, eyeing the battalion again. *Their* very presence was a threat, but was she really willing to use Valli's might against her own kind? Especially when Saddoriel might need defending before long?

Elna watched her coldly. 'Without me, you'll never find the stone.'

Roh knew there was truth to Elna's words and they would get nowhere in this stalemate. She and her companions were still only at the entrance to the scholar's city and she had no desire for bloodshed so soon. Grinding her teeth, Roh went to her sea drake. It was clear that any attempt to intimidate Elna would be ineffective, and that to do so in front of the nestlings would not be wise.

'Roh …' Harlyn warned in a low voice. 'Don't.'

But Roh spoke quietly to Valli. 'You should go find yourself a meal, my friend, there'll be nothing large enough here for your greedy guts.'

With an impatient huff, Valli nudged Roh's shoulder, before launching himself skyward, not deigning to glance again at the keeper of Lochloria or the battalion at her back.

Harlyn clicked her tongue in objection, but the youngsters stared after the sea drake.

'He'll be back,' Roh told the little ones, knowing that at some point, curiosity would override their fear. Then, her sense of purpose firing up once again, she looked at Elna, preparing for a fight. 'Well?' she prompted. 'I have done as you asked. Now, tell me, where is the Gauntlet Ruby?'

To her surprise, Elna seemed to relax slightly. 'Perhaps it's best if I show you.'

It was not the answer Roh was expecting, but she certainly wasn't going to object. She gave Elna a nod.

'You can leave your supplies by the Archives,' Elna told her with a wave at a building. 'We'll organise your accommodations after.'

Roh left her bag, but kept her weapons close, motioning for the others to do the same when she noticed that Elna still clung to her trident. She needn't have worried though, it seemed they were to leave the battalion behind and she was with two Jaktaren, The Carver and a warrior warlock.

Elna whispered something to her daughters, who ran off in the direction of the Resident Halls. Roh watched them go, wondering where their father was, wondering if it was safe for them to be in this place unattended.

'This way,' Elna barked, leading them alongside the stream running at the heart of the quadrangle and through a gate at the far end.

Roh felt the Saddorien soldiers' eyes on her, but they didn't move from their formations. She realised she was clenching her jaw and her chest tightened at the thought of what might await her now. Every time she had attempted to obtain one of the gems, it had cost her dearly. That moment would soon be upon her again. Elna's smug expression told her that whatever scheme the council had come up with this time, would be just as bad, if not worse than the previous.

And Elna had sent her nestlings away, which meant she didn't want them seeing it. Roh shook the thought from her head. Inhaling the crisp air, she forced her attention elsewhere, towards the structures around them. It certainly wasn't much of a scholar's city, not with only two functioning buildings remaining, but it was still Lochloria. It was still her father's homeland, where her mother had grown up and where the warlock Killian had written many of his journals. Whether she liked it or not, this territory was a part of her and she wanted to see it for herself.

As they left the buildings behind, the wind picked up again, dancing in the loose fabric of Finn's shirt and swirling dead leaves at Roh's boots. This time, there was no mistaking it. Roh heard the gentle notes of timber wind chimes, the music of chance laced in the breeze, threading between them. She found herself at a standstill as the sweet sound washed over her and sank into her very being, nature's own melody. When was the last time she had heard music? It had been weeks, and her whole body yearned for it, craving the salve to that inherently cyren part of her, even without her song.

'There are not as many as there once were,' Deodan said quietly, directing her gaze to the wooden chimes hanging from various stone archways. 'Supposedly, there used to be hundreds.'

'They took them down?' she asked, her voice raw.

Elna turned sharply, bringing the group to a halt. 'Take them down? Never. It is their beautiful chaos that keeps any shred of magic in this place. But like the rest of Lochloria, they have fallen over the years, weathered and worn by time and ...'

'The curse?'

Elna nodded reluctantly. 'Yes. The curse. Your warlock friends brought ruin upon this territory.'

Roh gaped at her. 'You can't be serious. Is that truly what you believe?'

Elna sent Roh an icy glare. '*We* didn't spoil the land.'

'No, you only slaughtered hundreds of warlocks.' Deodan's voice was venomous.

'They were a threat to cyrenkind. It had to be done,' Elna stated, as though from a rule book.

Roh could feel the rage rippling off Deodan in waves from behind her, merging with her own fury.

'We were never a threat, we were your *allies*,' Deodan spat, his knuckles white on the grip of his cutlass. 'Were it not for us, that lair of yours wouldn't exist. The gems in Roh's crown wouldn't exist. All the enchantments you —'

'Enough,' Elna cut him off, her nostrils flaring. 'I will not be lectured by the likes of you. Not in my own home.'

An almost manic laugh escaped Deodan. '*Your* home? You really are deluded, aren't you?'

In a blur of movement, Elna's trident was poised at Deodan's throat, her face inches from his as she spat, 'Say that again.'

Deodan leaned into the teeth of the weapon. 'You. Really. Are —'

But Elna was suddenly shoved back, not by the warlock, but by Kezra. She towered above them both, and gripping Elna by the sides of her breastplate, she lifted her from the ground entirely, leaving her feet dangling.

Elna's eyes bulged at the effortless nature of Kezra's strength. 'You're the one they call The Carver.'

'I am,' Kezra told her, her voice low. 'Though you'll notice I don't need my blades to inflict damage.'

'That's enough,' Roh snapped, her own blood boiling. As tempted as she was to let Kezra throw the keeper of Lochloria across the grounds, the ruby was close. 'Put her down.'

Kezra unceremoniously dropped Elna, whose legs buckled

beneath her, and in that moment Roh could see the family resemblance between Elna and the Council Elder, Erdites Colter; they shared the same rage-filled glare.

'You were showing us the ruby, Elna. So, show us and keep your ignorant notions to yourself, or I'll let Deodan and Kezra bury you.'

The cyren seemed to pause, weighing up her options before giving Deodan a final filthy look and leading them out into the open again.

Roh could hear the rush of water in the distance and noted a line of pine trees at the base of an almighty mountain range, its slopes and jagged terrain a dusky violet hue leading to a snow-capped peak that disappeared into the clouds. It wasn't long before they reached a dense forest and plunged into the thickets. Goosebumps rushed across Roh's arms at the silence within. There were no birds chirping or creatures rustling in the undergrowth; instead, eeriness blanketed the place, thick and heavy, like the damp that closed in around them.

Elna spoke no more as they headed deeper into the trees, but Roh noticed that she was careful where she stepped. Roh could feel the wary glances her friends exchanged around her, but they too remained quiet.

The air became colder and Roh gathered that they were growing closer to the mountain range she had spotted earlier. They must have walked for thirty minutes before Elna broke the silence.

'It's just ahead,' she told them.

Roh's stomach churned with unease. Had this been a foolish idea? To follow the keeper of Lochloria unquestioningly into the cursed forest? She placed her hand on her sling and readied herself, feeling the others tense around her.

'There.' Elna drew to a stop and pointed.

In front of them, covered in vines and forest debris, was the stone entrance to a tomb. Roh could see the steps that led down beneath the earth into darkness.

She drew a sharp breath, the icy air stinging her throat. 'The ruby is in there?'

'Yes,' Elna said simply. 'The council have declared that should you succeed in becoming the next ruler of Saddoriel, it's only fitting that you confront your split heritage. You're half warlock ... You will find your ancestors within the tomb. And the task will demonstrate your worthiness of the final stone.'

Roh took a step forward only to halt before the cavernous entrance, hearing hammering within. 'What's that noise?'

'Oh, that will be the council's workers,' Elna replied casually. 'You see, the test is not yet ready. We didn't expect you so soon.'

It took all of Roh's willpower to remain upright on her watery legs. 'It's not ready?' she echoed.

'That's what I said.'

'Well, that's not Roh's problem, is it?' Harlyn snapped. 'We're here. It's their fault for being unprepared. We'll go in and retrieve it now.'

'And risk disqualification?' Elna smirked. 'Go ahead.'

'This is horseshit,' Odi muttered.

Roh stared into the dark depths of the tomb, feeling a whisper of magic against her skin. She could feel something within calling to her, but whether it was the birthstone or the spirits of her ancestors, she couldn't say. She turned to Deodan. 'Do you know of this place? I can't recall Killian mentioning it in his journals.'

Deodan's face was tight with worry. He rummaged for his pipe as he spoke. 'Nor can I. But warlocks are known to create memorials to their dead like this one.'

'Are they always so creepy?' Harlyn interjected, eyeing the structure apprehensively.

It was Yrsa who tugged gently on Roh's arm. 'What do you want to do?'

Roh tore her eyes away from the tomb and turned to Elna. 'How long until this so-called test is ready?'

'The day after next, I'm told.'

'I have your word?'

'I have no control over the workers, they do the council's bidding. But yes, you have my word, that's what I've been told.'

'What are you thinking, Roh?' Finn asked.

Roh chewed her lower lip, her mind racing. 'I do not know what repercussions we'd face if we stormed in there now. My gut tells me that this quest has gone on far longer than the council ever anticipated and that it's now in their best interests to finish it quickly. Surely, the Saddoriens must be questioning their strength ... I say we wait until the day after next. Should the test not be ready by then, we go in.'

The gems in her crown gave a pulse of reassurance as her words fell, and Roh knew she was making the right decision in this moment. But the thought of whatever horrors the council had waiting for her in the tomb left her uneasy.

At the sight of her friends nodding, Roh felt the familiar swell of gratitude in her chest. They trusted her completely and so she had to trust herself.

'Very well,' Elna said, her expression unreadable. 'Shall we return to the grounds?'

'Lead the way,' Finn said.

Elna studied him for the first time, her gaze lingering on the foot of his wooden prosthetic. 'You're the defected Jaktaren.'

Finn gave a mock bow. 'The one and only.'

Elna's nostrils flared in distaste, but she said no more and started back towards the scholar's city.

The company followed Elna through the forest, the rhythmic flow of the forked stream sounding nearby. The air was cold between the trees, the late-afternoon sun unable to reach the forest floor, making Roh's nose run and her fingertips numb. With her mind full and her stomach empty, she was looking forward to cooking over the fire. She was about to ask Elna regarding the arrangements when she noticed a faint purple hue between the thinning trees to her left.

Roh found herself moving towards it, her steps hurried. Leaving the others behind, she wove through the last of the trees, the air icy on her face as the forest opened up into a great clearing at the foot of several towering mountains.

There, the willow trees were different to those she had seen framing the other mirror pools. These were gnarled and knotted, the branches reaching out across the pool, coming together in a canopy, like the roof of a cave. Several unlit beacons dotted the rocky shore, beacons that matched those she'd seen in Akoris and that Finn had described in Csilla … War beacons, as Deodan had told her.

But Roh's gaze was snatched elsewhere, to the heart of the space, her breath catching in her throat as she stopped in her tracks.

For the water did not ripple, it did not reflect the leaves above it. It was still, too still. Its surface was a hard sheen. Not water, but *ice,* tinged not blue, but a shade of violet.

Roh fell to her knees.

'Gods …' she heard Harlyn murmur from somewhere behind her.

The mirror pool of Lochloria was frozen over.

CHAPTER EIGHT

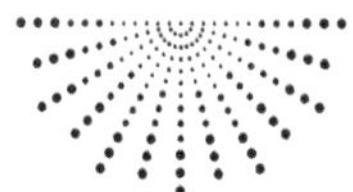

Roh stared at the frozen pool as her plans shattered like a sheet of ice beneath a hammer.

'How long has it been like this?' she asked, a cloud of air forming before her face.

'For centuries,' Elna told her. 'Since the Scouring. It's cursed, like the rest of this territory. A warlock did it as he fled. It cannot be used like its counterparts in Csilla and Akoris. It offers no link to Saddoriel.'

Roh was still on her knees in damp, frosted earth. *No link to Saddoriel ...* Gods, even if she managed to obtain the Gauntlet Ruby from the tomb, how in the realms was she supposed to get back to Saddoriel in time? Any method of travel that would see both Deodan and Odi kept safe would take weeks, longer even. She did not have that kind of time up her sleeve, the deadline was looming.

'How did the battalion get here?' she heard herself ask weakly.

'By the seas,' Elna replied tersely. 'As I said, no one has passed through the mirror pool in a very long time.'

Someone knelt beside her. 'This is a *good* thing, Roh,' Yrsa said.

'It means you can't be challenged, not here anyway. The council always arrives via the pool.'

Roh shook her head. 'It means *we* can't use the pool to get back.'

'We'll figure it out.' Yrsa placed a reassuring hand on her arm. 'Where there's a will, there's a way.'

Roh stared at the violet-coloured sheet of ice, her chest tight with more worries than she had ever known. 'Gods I hope you're right.'

If their way of returning to Saddoriel was no longer feasible, it meant one thing: she needed to get the birthstone as soon as possible, to buy them enough time to get back to the lair before the rise of the seventh moon.

Roh barely noticed the cold trek back to the scholar's city in the fading dusk light as her mind whirred to the point of dizziness. Abstractly, she knew she was in shock about the mirror pool and its irreparable state, and yet she did not stop scheming and calculating and weighing up every single option she could possibly think of. Did the state of the mirror pool change her decision about entering the tomb? Not yet. She had to have faith in Yrsa's words: *where there's a will, there's a way*. She just had to find it.

Roh was surprised when Elna led them towards what she called the Admissions Building. From the outside, it was in a state of utter disrepair: its windows missing, its walls almost crumbling before their very eyes. Roh had thought they'd at least be taken into one of the structures that remained intact.

Roh exchanged a look with Kezra, who was no doubt raging internally at the poor hospitality. Although Kezra had had her fun with Roh when she'd first arrived in Csilla by hiding her true identity, she'd still taken great pride in the meal she'd prepared and the accommodations they'd been given, and there certainly hadn't been the open hostility that Elna currently directed their way.

The warrior cyren led them through a windowless antechamber, and as they entered the main hall Roh wasn't the only one who gasped. Jars of valo beetles on the floor revealed what had once been a grand building with floor-to-ceiling windows, and a towering domed roof that was now a skeletal space, empty but for a long oak table running down its centre. Roh imagined that in another time, that table had belonged elsewhere, perhaps pushed up against one of the walls where a banquet could be laid out, or rows of warlocks could sit, documenting a new intake of students. But now, the Admissions Building was just a shell. Roh could see dust motes floating in the air above, through the weakened rays of sun stretching through the broken windows.

'Maiella, Nym!' Elna commanded. 'Show yourselves.'

Giggling sounded from a nearby corner and Roh turned to spot the two nestlings hidden beneath a smaller table.

'I hope you haven't been harassing the soldiers,' Elna muttered, more to herself than to her daughters, who approached the main table, exchanging excited glances and staring at Roh.

Roh slid onto one of the benches at the oak table and the sisters started to whisper. Elna clicked her tongue in frustration, apparently torn between her parental duties and her desire to be cold to Roh and her companions.

'Why don't you ask her yourself, Nym?' she snapped.

Unsure of what to make of the strange situation, Roh looked to the smaller of the two nestlings. 'Do you have a question for me?' she asked, trying to sound as non-threatening as she could.

The girl blinked at her, wide-eyed, before burying her face in the folds of her sister's cloak.

'She wanted to ask the name of your dragon,' the older sister blurted.

Roh smiled. 'Well, he's not a dragon. He's a sea drake. And his name is Valli.'

'Actually, it's Vallius,' Finn interjected, taking up the seat beside Roh. 'But Valli for short.'

Roh raised a brow. 'Did you deliberately name him to match you, Finnicus?'

Finn winced at his full name. 'No.'

'Bet you did,' Harlyn said from across the table.

'Absolutely,' Yrsa agreed. 'Needed to have someone to suffer with him.'

Finn merely rolled his eyes.

There was a tug on Roh's sleeve and she nearly jumped, turning to find Elna's smaller daughter, Nym, now standing behind her.

'Is he coming back?' Nym whispered.

'Yes, he is,' Roh told her, plastering her best smile on her face. 'I can introduce you to him, if you'd like?'

Nym nodded enthusiastically. 'Maiella too?' she asked.

Roh glanced across to Elna, who had gone to the entrance to talk to one of the Saddorien soldiers. 'Maiella too.' Roh winked at Nym. Then, a realisation hit her. The mirror pool had been frozen for centuries, which meant ...

'So, Nym and Maiella haven't completed their First Cry?' she asked upon Elna's return to the table.

Elna looked immediately uncomfortable. After a moment's hesitation, she answered. 'No, they haven't. They're likely the only cyrens in recent history who haven't.' Regret laced her words. 'In both cases, we sent word to the council before the nestlings were born, by other means of course, but by the time their reply reached us, it was too late. The opportunity for the First Cry had been missed.'

Roh had to hide the dark streak of her amusement. *The only cyrens in recent history who hadn't completed the First Cry ...* The two nestlings and Roh herself, according to what Marlow had told her in Akoris. *Gods,* Roh thought, adding the oddity to her list of concerns. Would there be no end to the mysteries and secrets of her kind?

'And there's been nothing of note because they missed it?' she pressed.

'Of course not,' Elna hissed, now looking up from where she was braiding Maiella's long hair tightly. 'Besides, it hardly matters out here. We are not connected to the rest of the cyrens of the realm.'

Before Roh could ask more, the door banged open and a soldier strode through, carrying a basket and a large flask. Without ceremony, he tipped the basket upside down on the table. Three loaves of hard bread tumbled out, along with several raw vegetables and a few dozen dirt-speckled mushrooms. 'Enjoy,' he said.

So much for cooking by the fire, Roh thought, suddenly immensely grateful for the delicious fish they'd feasted upon that morning at Finn's insistence. There was nothing appetising about the spread before them now, though she supposed she could stomach some bread, if only to keep the hunger pains at bay later on so she could focus on the problems at hand. As she reached for the food, she couldn't help glancing at Kezra, whose face was pinched with disgust.

'This is what "dining" means in Lochloria?' the Arch General and *chef* of Csilla said. 'This is the sort of fare you greet your guests with? Your future queen?'

'As you've no doubt gathered from the cursed lands upon which you've journeyed, we are short on supplies here,' Elna practically snarled.

Kezra slammed her hands down on the table, the whole thing shuddering beneath them. 'Doesn't look like you're starving to me.' She was on her feet, towering over Elna once more. 'You clearly only have limited supplies when it comes to visitors and refugees. And to receive us here, in this decrepit place rather than your own residences … You clearly mean not only to sap our future queen of her time, but her stamina as well. I have lived a long and varied life, Elna, but *never* have I been so insulted. You'd best remember we will not forget this. And when Roh is queen, you will have some explaining to do, and some amends to make, if you're lucky.'

While a thrill shot through Roh, fully enjoying Kezra threatening their host on her behalf, she knew the night was young. 'We'll make do,' she said quietly, taking a piece of bread.

But Elna did not take the peace offering. Instead, while she shrank away from Kezra, she still sneered at Roh. 'You're the daughter of a murderess, and who knows what manner of warlock miscreant your father was. Bad blood flows through your veins —'

Roh shot out of her seat, her talons unsheathed, a strange magic searing beneath her skin. 'And you're the relation of a council elder, do you think your hands are clean? Whatever you think to say to me, believe me, I've heard it before, not once but one hundred times, and I will be queen regardless. So save your breath, Elna. If you mean to host us, then host us. Otherwise, show us to our rooms, or our patch of dirt, and we'll retire. It's been a long day.'

Roh noted the flash of shock across Elna's face, as though she hadn't expected an *isruhe* to have a backbone. A small sense of satisfaction swelled in Roh. Yes, she had made mistakes since she'd entered the Queen's Tournament, many mistakes, if she was honest with herself. But standing up for herself had never been one of them. She could never regret speaking her mind in such instances, in putting her fellow cyrens in their place when it came to who she was and what she stood for.

She stared expectantly at Elna.

The warrior's nostrils flared yet again. 'Fine,' she snapped. 'Soldier! Fetch the wine.'

The male cyren hesitated, just for a moment, as though he couldn't quite believe what he was hearing, but he hurried away before Elna could reprimand him, as she looked poised to do.

'Thank you,' Roh said, taking her seat once more. 'Now tell us, what do you know of this curse? What have you observed in your time here as keeper of Lochloria? How did you come to hold that position?'

Roh felt her companions tense around her, but she was done with holding back. She wanted to know as much as possible, as soon as possible. She wanted to learn everything about this place and its guardian. If there was one thing she'd learned over the moons past, it was that knowledge was power.

Elna clasped her hands before her, her gaze flicking to her daughters before settling on Roh. 'Our family had conflicting roles during the Scouring of Lochloria. My family were part of the Saddorien Army.' She said this with an obvious note of pride. 'Whereas my late husband's kin resided in the scholar's city, tended to the books and the lessons of the cyrens here. We were stationed here together, to keep the peace, and of course, to keep Lochloria in rightful cyren hands.'

Roh ignored the barb. 'What happened to your husband?'

'And the peace?' Deodan muttered.

'The cursed land did not agree with him,' Elna replied curtly. 'He fell ill. It went on for years. He passed away shortly after Nym was born.' Though she spoke matter-of-factly, Roh could see the pain in Elna's eyes.

'I'm sorry,' Roh told her. She herself had experienced a fleeting taste of loss and she wished it upon no one, especially not someone with two nestlings, no matter how foul her outlook.

Elna gave a stiff nod. 'You've seen it for yourself, the land will grow nothing new, the mirror pool hasn't melted a single drop and the buildings decay around us as we speak. We suspect he came across something that poisoned him slowly.'

Odi cleared his throat. 'And what do you make of the supposed prophecy? That *stone will crumble, land will fester, until the winged one flies forth*?'

The soldier from before reappeared with two large jugs of wine and several cups.

Elna motioned for him to pour. 'The winged one *did* fly forth,' she said. 'Delja arrived and nothing happened. There was no change, the curse was not broken. Here we are still, sitting in the midst of rubble and festering lands … The curse will not be broken until the death of the last water warlock.' She gave Deodan a meaningful stare.

'And that is based on what, exactly?' he challenged.

'Instinct.'

Deodan merely rolled his eyes.

'That's not what Papa said,' Maiella's voice sounded from beneath the table.

Elna closed her eyes and inhaled deeply, seeming to muster up every ounce of patience. 'What have I told you about spreading your father's silly ideas?'

But Maiella's head popped up, her face alight with a cheeky grin. 'He told me that the curse will lift when warlocks and cyrens share the lands again, as they once did. Once balance is restored, the land will prosper, the buildings will find their foundations —'

'Utter nonsense,' Elna said quietly. 'Go back to your games.'

The child's words sank into Roh like a brand, adding to the utter chaos churning in her mind. She knew she shouldn't drink on an empty stomach, but she needed something to take the edge off this gods-awful day. She took the cup offered and swallowed several large gulps, not even cringing at the sour taste as both wine and dread swirled uncomfortably in her gut.

She leaned in and whispered to Finn, 'A test in an ancient

warlock tomb. A frozen mirror pool. A cursed territory. The Akorian refugees … Am I missing anything?'

Finn gave a quiet laugh. 'Only the revenge-seeking Warlock Supreme and the terror tempests in Csilla.'

'Of course,' Roh muttered, drinking again before meeting Elna's gaze. 'If you know of my plans for Lochloria, I also assume word has reached you about the terror tempests in Csilla?'

'I am a relation of Council Elder Colter,' Elna answered dismissively. 'Of course I know of the terror tempests. What about them?'

Roh's eyes sought Finn, whose expression was hardened. He was the *son* of two council elders, their *direct heir*, and he had been told *nothing* of the terror tempests. The knowledge had been kept from him. Roh knew why, she knew that Finn had come to terms with it long ago, and yet it made her blood sing with rage.

She calmed herself. 'I'll need you to send word to Saddoriel. Tell Elder Sigra that they're worsening and that the lair becomes more vulnerable by the day.'

'You wish for me to threaten a council elder on your behalf?' Elna asked incredulously.

'For Lamaka's sake,' Roh snapped. 'I am asking you to *warn* her. To prepare. They are doing all they can in Csilla, but the terror tempests worsen by the day. Talon's Reach is at risk. Elder Sigra needs to be on alert, she needs to put defences in place.'

Elna regarded Roh with suspicion.

Roh threw up her hands. 'I cannot say it more plainly than that. I am trying to protect the territory I wish to rule. If you believe nothing else, believe that.'

At last, Elna nodded. 'Fine.'

'Right,' Roh said, a note of finality in her tone, despite the fact that much of the fare offered remained untouched on the table. 'Perhaps it's time we got some rest.'

The scrape of the bench on either side of Roh told her that her companions were in agreement. The presence of the abrasive keeper of Lochloria was draining, and the sooner they were rid of her, the better.

'Maiella will show you to your quarters. Some of the soldiers already moved your belongings there.'

While Roh didn't like the idea that their possessions had been left in the hands of the Saddoriel battalion, there was nothing to be done. She tried to offer Nym a reassuring smile as she passed, but there was no doubt she had sensed the hostility pulsing around the table. The nestling clung to her mother's legs and hid her face.

With young Maiella in the lead, they left through the rear exit of the Admissions Building and the icy night air hit Roh's face with full force, and she shoved her hands under her arms in a futile attempt to keep warm. Darkness had fallen in a heavy blanket over Lochloria and the grounds were wet with dew. Millions of stars littered the inky sky, though they did nothing to ease the eeriness of the empty scholar's city.

It must be a powerful *curse,* Roh thought as she took in the rotting exposed beams of the building, wondering how the ancient magic had clung so steadfastly to the territory for all this time. She imagined students flocking to the halls after their lessons, full of knowledge and laughter and hope. *How wrong they all had been ...*

Maiella stopped in front of a series of four smaller dwellings, clapping her hands together excitedly. 'My papa called this the *arts sector*,' she said. 'There is the old theatre, he told me there used to be stories acted out there, like how me and Nym play queens and councils.' She pointed to the structure beside it. 'That is what he called the gallery, where Mama said you'll be staying. The one next to it was the music hall—'

Roh heard Odi's intake of breath. She couldn't tell if it was excitement or fear that he might be forced to play piano at sword-point again.

Maiella continued, as though reciting her late father's words verbatim. 'And that last one there was the *lecture auditorium*. Which is a very hard word. He said I was very smart for learning it.'

'He was right,' Roh heard Yrsa praise the nestling.

But Roh stared at the buildings. *An entire sector dedicated to arts?* 'Were classes for architects held here?' she heard herself ask, her fingers suddenly itching to drag a stick of charcoal across parchment and capture the likeness of Lochloria.

'What is an ... archi ... What you said?'

'Someone who designs buildings,' Roh told her, not taking her eyes off the sandstone tinged with the blue of the night's sky.

Maiella frowned. 'I don't know.'

It was Finn who answered. 'Some of the most renowned designers in our history came here to study. Icus Sothra himself came here to learn from the masters. Estin Ruhne told me during the Queen's Tournament.'

'Who's that?' Odi said, his arms folded over his chest now, trembling from the cold.

'He's the architect who designed the entrance to Saddoriel,' Roh told him, pained that she was the one to share the knowledge with him.

Odi's gaze shot to hers. 'You mean the archway of bones?'

'Yes,' she said sombrely.

But Maiella was growing impatient. 'This way,' she demanded. 'Up here.' She led them along a set of stairs and pushed open a pair of grand double doors.

Inside, a roaring fire burned in the hearth and someone had lit dozens of candles, illuminating the space with a lovely warm glow. The condition of the gallery wasn't as bad as the rest of the buildings. It was dusty and old, a few windows broken in, but the walls seemed to be holding strong, with framed paintings still hanging proudly from them. Exposed timber beams ran across a high arched ceiling, and ivy from outside had crept in and wrapped itself around the foundations there. Across the hardwood floor, dozens of easels stood at the ready, as though waiting for artists to flood through the doors at any moment and take a brush to canvas.

The nestling pointed to a door in one of the far corners. 'There's a bathing chamber with hot water through there. Mama said you all smell.'

Odi laughed. 'Gee, thanks.'

And with that, the nestling left them to the crackle of the fire and the enormity of the tasks ahead.

CHAPTER NINE

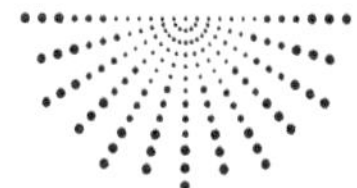

Upon the nestling's departure, Roh felt a half-delirious laugh bubble out of her, the tight tension she'd been carrying since their arrival easing slightly from her shoulders.

'Well, on that, at least, we can agree,' she said, rubbing the back of her neck and grimacing at the grime she felt beneath her fingers. Surveying her companions, she noticed their dirt-smudged skin and travel-worn, dishevelled clothes. The luxuries of Csilla felt far away indeed.

The group seemed to be watching her, too, as though they thought she was about to crack under the pressure of all they had learned. She could hardly stand it.

'I'm going to see about this bathing chamber,' Roh announced, striding towards where Maiella had pointed.

It was a large, square room with a freestanding screen of woven grass separating two round wooden tubs on either side. A small stove sat in one of the far corners, where a large cauldron of water bubbled away. There were several other buckets of water of varying temperatures lining the wall and a small crate of fresh towels and soaps; lavender, if Roh wasn't mistaken. She supposed it made up for the less-than-welcoming dining experience, though perhaps Elna just couldn't stand the smell of them.

Harlyn poked her head around the door. 'You alright?' she asked.

'Fine,' Roh told her. She was itching to submerge her tired body in clean, hot water. 'Who's going first, then?'

Harlyn snorted and said loudly as she strode from the chamber, 'Well, you and Haertel are undoubtedly the filthiest.'

Roh could have cuffed her over the head, especially when Harlyn followed her comment with a mischievous wink.

Roh caught up with her in front of the fire. 'What are you playing at?' she hissed.

Harlyn merely shrugged. 'There's a privacy screen, what's the issue?'

If the others knew what Harlyn was getting at, they didn't let on. They simply waved her towards the bathing chamber. But Roh knew her friend better than that. She was using Finn to take Roh's mind off everything, so she didn't spiral, and Roh didn't know whether to be grateful or furious.

'Take a proper soak, Roh,' Deodan called after her. 'My magic likely didn't heal all of that injury from this morning. You need to take care of yourself.'

Gods, was that only this morning? Roh wondered. In a blur, her mind took her through the events of the day and she felt suddenly heavy again. Part of her felt she was so close to the finish line of her quest she could almost taste it, and the other part of her baulked at all there was still to do, still to face. She felt Harlyn's eyes on her; her oldest friend never missed a beat, and she jutted her chin in the direction of the bathing chamber.

'Whoever wants their clothes washed, leave them in a pile by the door,' Odi was saying. 'I can't stand another day of wearing the same stinking shirt.'

Kezra clapped him on the shoulder. 'Now there's a true friend. I'll be sure to include my ripest pair of socks for you.'

Odi groaned in disgust, but the rest of them laughed. Over the past few weeks, Kezra had gained the esteemed reputation of having the feet with the strongest odour. In any case, Roh took the opportunity to duck into the bathing chamber, not looking back to see if Finn would be joining her.

Roh's chest tightened with anticipation as she swiped a fresh towel from the pile. *Why?* she asked herself, frustrated. She needed to regain some semblance of control over herself. Why in the realms was she worrying about something so small in the face of such enormous challenges?

The door creaked open and Finn entered the bathing chamber. 'Do you mind?' he asked, with a nod to one of the tubs.

Stomach roiling, Roh shook her head but didn't move.

'Are you using your friend as a ploy to get me naked, Roh?' Finn said quietly, closing the door behind him with a deliberate push.

'N-no,' Roh stammered. 'And I haven't told her, not that there's much to tell ... I –' Roh cut herself off before she could make any more of a fool of herself, stopping short of putting her head in her hands.

Amusement gleamed in Finn's lilac eyes. 'I'm only teasing,' he told her. Then he grew serious. 'I was upset with you, you know.'

'What? When?'

'When you didn't tell me you were hurt. Then you asked me to train you ... You could have died. When I first saw that bruise, I thought I had done that to you and I ...'

'I'm sorry,' Roh said, painfully aware of his anguish.

Finn gave a stiff nod. 'It's alright now. I ... I was just worried.' The look he gave her seemed to pierce her to the core.

Roh felt suddenly self-conscious, aware of every inch of her skin and every fleck of dirt that marred it. She didn't know what to do with her hands, she didn't know if she was supposed to talk, and if she was, what she was meant to say. But Finn seemed to sense her uneasiness and simply moved about the room, filling his tub, and hers, with hot water, testing the temperature with his fingertips.

'Are you alright?' he said finally.

With the question posed for the second time, Roh found she couldn't lie as easily. She still hadn't moved. She watched him from across the room, biting her lip as her thoughts warred with one another. She pushed her hair back from her brow, sighing deeply. 'It's ... it's a lot to take in.'

Finn quirked a brow, his mouth tugging into a suggestive smile as he placed an empty bucket on the floor. 'Is it?'

Suddenly, irritation crashed through any self-consciousness and Roh clicked her tongue in frustration, waving the Jaktaren away with a flick of her hand. 'Forget it.'

Her words didn't dim the smile on his face, nor the tug of the dimple in his cheek as his hands went to the top buttons of his shirt. As the fabric fell away from his muscular body, her attention snagged on the scar on his bicep; the letter C that had been carved viciously into his skin.

Finn followed her gaze to it. 'What is it?'

Roh chewed the inside of her cheek. 'I'm ... I'm sorry that was done to you. Sorry for the violence that links our families.' She had tried not to think of the death debt between the Haertels and the Ironses, but the proof was carved into Finn's flesh.

'The *Tome of Kyeos* will tell us the truth of the matter. Your promise means we will finally know and we can put it behind us.'

Roh's eyes didn't leave the scar. 'How ... how can you ... *want* me ... when you have *that* because of my family?'

Finn's gaze turned steely and his next words were heated. 'I can't *not* want you.'

It took every fibre of willpower for Roh to move herself to the other side of the privacy screen. Through the woven structure, she could see the outline of Finn's body and the shadow of the rest of his clothes falling away.

'Are you just going to stand there all evening?' he called softly.

Trying to shake the thoughts from her head, Roh's hands went to her own shirt, her fingers trembling slightly at the buttons. Her skin tingled, feeling Finn's attention through the screen.

'Are you watching me?' she asked, in a near whisper.

His voice was low when he spoke. 'Yes.'

With her heart pounding against her chest, Roh removed her shirt and the camisole beneath it, her breasts suddenly bare, with Finn only mere steps away from her.

'You'd best get in that tub,' he said, his words seeming to vibrate in her chest.

'Or what?' she asked.

She heard his breath whistle between his teeth. 'You know what,' he replied.

Her nipples hardened at the implication and she experimentally ran her hands over her curves, arching into her own touch, wondering just how much he could see through the screen.

Finn swore loudly.

He can see enough, then. Roh smiled to herself, peeling her pants down her legs and stepping out of them.

A curse and a splash of water sounded from the other side. Finn had submerged himself in the tub.

With a soft laugh, Roh stepped into the tub, the hot water instantly flushing her skin. She nearly moaned as she sank into it, the heat surging around her body, already easing any aches it held. As she sat back, for a moment, she forgot where she was and just savoured the feel of clean water, resting her head against the edge of the tub. But conscious of the others outside waiting their turn, she reached for the fresh bar of soap, inhaling the rich lavender scent. Ducking beneath the surface, she wet her hair and scrubbed at the dirt coating her skin, lathering up and cleaning herself thoroughly, feeling more and more like herself with every rinse and repeat.

A pained groan sounded from the other side of the screen. 'I thought Harlyn was starting to like me.'

Roh frowned, tipping a jug of water over her soaped hair and wringing out the ends. 'She is.'

'Then why did she send me in here to be tortured?' Finn muttered. 'My imagination is going wild, knowing that you're an arm's length away, running your hands over your naked, wet body …'

Roh's stomach tightened. 'Oh.'

'Exactly.' There was a pause. 'I want to see you.'

'You don't *just* want to see me,' Roh ventured, reaching for her towel on the side. Water sluiced down her body as she stood, inhaling deeply as cool air kissed her flushed skin.

Splashing on the other side of the screen sounded and Roh glanced across to see Finn's silhouette rising from the tub, as well. Biting her lip, she wrapped her towel across her chest and heard the shaky exhale from Finn.

She stepped out of the tub. 'Are you decent?'

Quiet followed before Finn answered, 'Yes.'

Slowly, Roh stepped out from behind the screen, the ends of her hair dripping, her face flushed and droplets of water still clinging to her skin. Her eyes found Finn instantly. He was sitting on a stool in the far corner, a towel slung low around his waist, his prosthetic leg resting against the wall. His hair was wet, dripping onto his broad shoulders and chest as he gazed intensely back at her, his posture rigid, as though he was holding his breath.

'Roh …' he murmured in warning as she walked towards him, the tiled floor cold beneath her feet.

Clutching her towel to her chest, she closed the gap and

lowered her weight onto him, straddling him on the stool, the fabric of their towels the only barrier between them.

'I know that now is not the time and place for … everything,' she heard herself say, surprised to find that she sounded confident as a strange ache began to build inside her. 'But … I need to feel you … just for a moment, before …'

'Before what?'

'Before we enter that tomb, before everything changes.'

'Roh,' Finn's voice rumbled. 'We will have time, after all of this, for us.'

Touching her forehead to his, she closed her eyes. 'Do you really believe that?'

'I do.'

'Despite the tomb, and the battalion, and the frozen mirror pool? And everything else?'

'Despite all that.'

Roh wanted to believe him, with every piece of her battered soul. 'Please,' she said as she opened her eyes. 'I need to feel —'

Finn's large hands gripped her hips and he drew her in even closer, the rough fabric of the towel scraping against her sensitive skin, a hardness pushing against her from beneath.

Finn's determined gaze met hers. 'Can you feel me now?'

Roh's breathing hitched and she brought her lips to Finn's, kissing him hungrily. 'Yes,' she murmured.

They kissed deeply, thoroughly, their heated skin pressing against one another. Finn's hands were in her hair, trailing across her collarbone, gripping the back of her neck while his tongue brushed against hers. Roh's towel slipped, revealing the tops of her breasts, rising and falling with each desperate breath.

Finn's throat bobbed as he stopped kissing her to gaze upon her.

There had been others before him, those who fumbled on the outside of her clothes in the shadowy corners of the Lower Sector.

She could count on one hand a select few who'd sought her attention rather than Harlyn's, but their pawing had always left Roh hollow and disinterested. A disdainful boredom surrounding that form of intimacy had developed and she'd dismissed it almost entirely, favouring ambition and friendship over all.

But no one had looked at her like Finn looked at her now.

Roh met his stare, her hand moving to her towel, not to cover herself, but to pull the fabric away, baring herself to the waist.

Finn's lips parted as he drank in the sight of her, the swell of her breasts and the shiver of goosebumps across her naked skin. With an appreciative noise sounding at the back of his throat, he lowered his head and began kissing the soft skin of her breasts, trailing down.

Roh gasped, her whole body singing for him, begging to be touched, needing more. His teeth grazed her sensitive skin and his hand slid down from her neck to cup her other breast. She arched into his touch, a quiet moan escaping her.

'Gods,' he murmured against her skin. 'This was a very bad idea …'

'I know,' Roh breathed, her chest heaving.

Finn groaned, pushing himself against her for emphasis. 'We should stop, before this gets …'

Roh pressed her forehead to his. She knew he was right. She should never have started things up, she had just been so … She didn't have a word for what she felt. Slowly, she pulled her towel up under her arms and pushed off him gently, still aching for him.

Finn subtly rearranged his towel and pointed across the chamber. 'I think I saw some fresh nightshirts by the shelf over there.'

Her face still flushed, Roh went to the stack of linens and sorted through them, finding one for her and one for Finn. She ducked behind the screen again to pull one over her head. It fell to her knees and was thick enough that she didn't feel completely naked. When she returned to him, Finn was grimacing as he fitted his prosthetic to his stump.

'Does it hurt?' Roh asked, handing him the clean shirt.

'A bit.' But his expression changed when he looked up, smiling at her in her nightshirt. 'Do you remember what I told you in Akoris, when you had to wear that other shift?'

Roh swallowed the lump in her throat. 'You told me that Saddorien cyrens used to wear them into battle ... That they needed no armour, no weapons to shield themselves against the realms ... They were magic, cunning and power incarnate. And they answered to no one ...'

Still only wearing his towel, Finn stood, leaning in close, with a different sort of intensity in his gaze. 'Now, nor do you ...' With that, he gently took the spare shirt from her, pressed a firm, heated kiss to her lips and left.

Roh stared after him, stunned, her skin still burning, before busying herself with emptying the tubs for the next person.

When she finally emerged from the bathing chamber, Roh avoided Harlyn's gaze at all costs. She knew her friend would be able to sense the secrets on her and would be relentless in trying to uncover them. Instead, Roh found herself staring at a large scaled mass lying in front of the fire.

'How did he get in here?' she asked no one in particular.

Odi laughed, nodding to the entrance. 'He barged through the doors.'

Roh smiled. 'Good.'

While the others took turns in the bathing chamber, Roh made herself comfortable next to Valli in front of the fire on one of the thick blankets that had been left out for them. She glanced at the sea drake, quietly amused at the fact that for a water creature, he seemed to love fire quite a lot. With the warm glow of the flames settling around her, Roh savoured the feeling of her clean hair and skin, vowing never to take hot water for granted again. She felt herself eventually relax, the tension of the day melting away as the fire crackled before her. Roh took in the gallery. It was easy enough to imagine it as a place of learning and art, and for a second, she pictured herself at one of the easels. She had never tried painting; there had only ever been the time and resources for a stick of charcoal and a sketchpad back in Saddoriel. Had her father sat at one of these artist stations? Had he walked these very halls? Had her mother? And grandmother? If Roh closed her eyes, she could envision the hall restored to its former glory, busy with students, like her parents had once been.

Valli made a low noise beside her, as though frustrated her attention had strayed from him.

'I hope you had a better meal than us, my friend.' She patted him on the head and glanced at his bloated belly sticking out from beneath him.

He huffed a heavy, contented sigh.

'I suppose that's a yes.' Roh smiled.

'Could have brought some back for us,' Harlyn muttered as she tended to the fire. 'I'm starving.'

'I took some bread with me?' Roh offered, motioning vaguely to where she'd left it.

Harlyn made a face, sitting down beside Roh. 'I've had enough stale bread to last a lifetime. Give me pies filled with gravy, roast potatoes and a giant cake for dessert.'

Roh laughed. 'When have you *ever* eaten like that?'

'I'll eat like that *every* night when you're queen,' Harlyn retorted, frowning at Valli's belly. 'Gods, I hope he didn't eat anything he shouldn't have.'

'Like what?'

'I don't know ... A horse? Or five?'

'I haven't seen any horses around here,' Kezra interjected from where she sat on a stool by one of the many easels. 'They would come in handy tomorrow, that's for sure.'

Roh nodded. 'You're thinking the same as me, then?'

Kezra shrugged. 'I don't presume to know what rattles around in that busy mind of yours, so you'd best tell us.'

Deodan and Odi were taking their turns with the baths, but a few feet away, Finn and Yrsa, who sat cross-legged before the fire, poring over one of Killian's journals, looked up with interest.

'Well ...' Roh straightened, mulling over her words. 'My feeling is that we should use the day to scope the place out, learn all we can about this territory and its supposed keeper. I suspect Elna will have more than one surprise up her sleeve, especially now that I've made my stance on warlocks clear.'

The others were nodding in agreement.

That encouraged Roh. 'Which means we'll have to spread out across Lochloria tomorrow, explore the city, find out what we can about this tomb before we enter it. With the mirror pool being frozen over, we need to get the Gauntlet Ruby as soon as possible, so we have as much time up our sleeves to return to Saddoriel another way. I can't afford to lose any more time.'

Kezra unsheathed one of her blades and began to sharpen it on a whetstone. 'So, we'll split up tomorrow and search as far as we can. Finn, can we take a look at the map? Let's figure out who will cover what ground.'

'It's in the front pocket of my pack,' Finn said without looking up from something he was fiddling with in his hands.

'What are you doing over there?' Harlyn frowned in his direction.

Finn looked up, pink tinging his cheeks. 'Mending Odi's gloves.'

Quiet fell.

Finn looked around, scowling. 'What?' he demanded hotly. 'He's always picking at the holes and it was driving me mad. Can't a cyren fix a man's gloves without the rest of you making a scene about it?'

Roh held back a laugh. 'We didn't say anything.'

'You didn't have to,' he muttered, returning to his task, clearly intent on ignoring them.

'Where'd you learn how to sew?' Harlyn asked.

Finn scoffed, as though the answer was the most obvious in the world. 'All Jaktaren are taught how to sew.'

'Really?' Harlyn's brows shot up.

'Yep,' Yrsa interjected, getting up to rummage through Finn's pack. 'But I was never any good myself. Finn always mends my clothes for me.'

Her fellow Jaktaren shot her a dirty look and continued to scowl as he sewed Odi's gloves.

'Well,' Harlyn said, with no small note of satisfaction. 'You learn something new every day, eh?'

Roh laughed. 'I suppose you do.'

Kezra sighed heavily. 'Was I the only one who thought it was incredibly sad?' she asked, lines of concern deepening on her face.

'There's a lot of sadness lingering in this place,' Roh said. 'You'll have to be a bit more specific.'

Kezra grimaced. 'That the two little nestlings are growing up in this place? So tainted by hatred and prejudice? That their only company is their sour mother and a battalion of armed cyrens? My heart breaks for them. What manner of selfishness isolates children in such a way?' The note of melancholy in her voice told Roh that Kezra was thinking of her own two nestlings back in Csilla, little Sol and Mora, who ran amuck all over the bridge.

'Perhaps it won't always be like this,' Roh ventured.

'I hope you're right.'

A few moments of silence passed before Harlyn clicked her tongue impatiently. 'For Thera's sake,' she snapped. She got to her feet and went to pound on the door of the bathing chamber. 'There are still *three of us* who need to bathe,' she yelled. 'Only so much clean water can fix those faces of yours, now hurry up!'

While Harlyn harassed Deodan and Odi, Yrsa brought Roh the map, and together they spread it out across the floor, flattening the curling parchment beneath their palms.

'That's a lot of ground to cover,' Roh murmured, trying to commit the landmarks of Lochloria to memory. 'We have one day. *One*. We need to make the most of it.'

Yrsa was nodding as she pointed. 'The tomb is roughly there.'

Roh found her stick of charcoal and marked it on the map. 'A pair of us should be stationed there tomorrow, to see if we can find any clues as to what awaits us within.'

'Agreed,' Yrsa said. 'I also thought perhaps we could search the Archives? There might be information there about the structure of one of these things?'

Roh nodded. 'I thought the same.'

'Good. And another pair could do a head count on the battalion? See where they're staying and if we can gain a better idea of their purpose and motives?'

The plan came together quickly and Roh was suddenly glad for the extra day between their arrival and the task. The council had inadvertently given her a pocket of time to prepare, to gather herself and the information she might need.

'We can do this, Roh,' Yrsa said, determined, her lilac eyes scanning the map. 'Who do you want to pair with tomorrow?'

Roh made a snap decision. As much as she wanted time alone with Finn, she knew if she went with him, she wouldn't be able to think clearly. And she'd be just as distracted with Harlyn, talking about Finn. Whereas Yrsa … Yrsa was always so logical and methodical, her sense of duty was unparalleled, and well, there were things Roh needed to think about, and Yrsa was a part of that.

'You,' Roh said. 'I'll team up with you.'

CHAPTER TEN

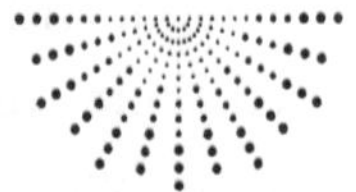

The next morning, Roh and the others awoke to a grey and wet scholar's city. Outside, the rain fell in a constant, heavy sheet, leaking through the holes in the ceiling and blowing indoors through the broken windows. The damp made everyone miserable, as did their growling, empty stomachs. But they soon discovered that a basket of eggs and fresh bread had been left for them on the doorstep of the gallery, so they made quick work of frying food over the still roaring fire.

However, as much as Roh wanted to stay dry and warm indoors, the opportunities the day presented called to her and she rallied the others after breakfast. 'The weather changes nothing,' she told them apologetically. 'Our goals remain the same. We meet back here at sundown and share what we've learned. Keep your weapons on you, stay alert. I think we all know there is much we have not been told about Lochloria.'

With that, Roh donned her waxed coat, pulling the hood up over her head and strapped her father's dagger to her thigh. She straightened her crown before sticking her sling in her belt and shouldering a small satchel containing fresh water and a lump of leftover bread before turning to Yrsa. 'Ready?'

The Jaktaren nodded. 'Always.'

Leaving Valli basking by the fire and with a final wave to the others, Roh and Yrsa exited the gallery, heading out into the rain, straight for the western ground of the scholar's city. Neither cyren complained as they trudged past the rest of the Arts buildings and past the old Resident Halls through the downpour, a grey fog settling around their ankles.

'Finn told me of the Lochlorian Archives back in Akoris, at least, I think that's what he was talking about.' Roh glanced around at the decaying buildings, all the more eerie in the pouring rain. 'He said that this place used to be famous for its books.'

Yrsa was nodding, following Roh's gaze around the campus. 'It was. Hopefully, if the building is still intact, so are the texts it contains.' She sighed. 'This must have been some place in its day.'

'It was beautiful when I saw it during the Rite of Strothos,' Roh confided. 'Hard to imagine how it came to all of this. That it was our kind that saw its ruin, its fall from glory.'

'Well, you will be the one to restore it.' Yrsa offered a reassuring smile.

'*We* will,' Roh corrected as she pulled her cloak tighter around her against the chill.

Yrsa ignored this. 'Have you had any more visions? Since the rite? The cure you took from the pass truly did the trick?'

'I think so. I haven't had any other visions, no.' Roh shook her head. 'Apart from the one the Csillan mirror pool showed me.'

They continued walking across the muddy grounds, avoiding deep puddles as they crossed into the quadrangle.

'And you've not seen the wings since? There's been no sign of them?' Yrsa pressed.

'No. Perhaps it was simply a daydream? A trick of the mind. Wishful thinking even ...'

Yrsa laughed quietly. 'We both know that's not the case.'

'Do we?' Roh challenged. 'I have no idea what it means.'

'It means you're a descendant of Dresmis and Thera.'

'It means nothing of the sort.'

Yrsa came to an abrupt halt in the mud. 'I don't understand why you'd deny something like that.'

'It's not a fact, Yrsa.'

'Everyone knows it's the truth, Roh. Are you scared to admit it? What does it change for you?'

Roh wiped the rain from her eyes and shoved her hands into her relatively dry pockets. 'Change? Everything is changing all the time. I can't keep up with it all.'

'Do you still *want* to be queen?'

No one had dared to ask her that since they'd left Saddoriel all those months ago. Roh had hardly dared to ask herself. After all that she had been through to achieve that very goal, it seemed too big a question.

Yrsa pulled her under the shelter of the west side of the quadrangle and waited patiently.

'I think so,' Roh said softly. 'But … I don't think my reasons for wanting it are the same as they were.'

Roh didn't know what she'd been expecting from Yrsa, anger, perhaps, that she'd been dragged all around the realms on a quest for a potential ruler who wasn't even sure of herself. But to Roh's surprise, Yrsa was smiling.

'You can always change your mind, Roh,' she said. 'Ambitions can change, motivations can change. It doesn't make anything less valid or less worthwhile. Perhaps it makes them even more so.'

'I suppose.'

'Do you not think it's *good* that your goals have changed? That to want for an entire people is a far mightier ambition than to want for one's self?'

Roh watched the rain hit the yellowed grass of the quadrangle, the brimming stream bubbling through its heart. 'Is that what's happened?'

'Yes, Roh. I don't doubt it for a moment. That's why I *know* that vision is true, that your wings will manifest sooner or later, and that you'll be the one, as your uncle said, to bring us all together.'

'Do you not think that this tournament, this quest will simply take and take from me until I have nothing left?' Roh had hardly dared to think it, let alone say it aloud, but she trusted Yrsa with her life, with her darkest fears, too, it seemed.

'Only you decide how much to give,' Yrsa told her.

'I wish that was true.' Roh shuddered in the cold.

Yrsa gripped her by the shoulders suddenly, her stare hard. 'You are not alone in this, Roh. Nor will you be when the realms call you Cyren Queen. You have us. Not just for this part of the journey, but for the next, and the next.'

Yrsa's words sparked a memory in Roh. The exchange between two young cyrens before The Dawning came to her, their shared dreams unhindered by the rotting world around them –

'Roh? What is it?'

Roh smiled. 'I'll tell you later,' she said. 'Come on, let's get out of this godsforsaken rain.'

Yrsa didn't argue with her, but that was part of the Jaktaren's power – she never needed to, her stance was always abundantly clear.

The two cyrens finished crossing the quadrangle and found the entrance to the Archives on the other side easily enough. Two heavy wooden doors reinforced with flourishes of black steel greeted them, but Roh didn't bother with the knocker, which took the shape of a roaring teerah panther. Instead, she put her palm flat to the door and pushed, finding it unlocked.

'You don't think we should announce ourselves?' Yrsa asked as they stepped inside.

'No. There will be someone watching.' Roh was sure of it.

Lit candles lined the sandstone walls, illuminating tapestries framed in gold filigree and a coat rack by the door. Roh shrugged off her sodden cloak and hung it as she continued to scan her surroundings. A faded narrow rug ran the length of the chamber, crinkled in the middle as though someone had hurried across it. An identical pair of doors led straight out the back of the room onto the grounds beyond, while smaller timber doors beneath paved archways of stone were positioned on each side.

'Which way?' Yrsa ran her hand over the pavers.

Roh shrugged. 'Your guess is as good as mine. It's not like there's a sign.'

Yrsa went to the door on their right and pushed it open for Roh. 'After you, Queen of Bones.'

Roh rolled her eyes. 'I can't say I care for that term catching on.'

Yrsa merely smiled and waited.

Roh passed through the narrow doorway. The grey daylight outside filtered through the opulent curved windows, revealing a high ceiling and rows and rows of shelves, much like the library Roh had seen in Akoris, only grander.

'Bring one of those candles,' she whispered to Yrsa. It felt right to whisper here, as though anything louder might disturb the history that slumbered around them. Thousands of tomes lined the shelves, covered in a thick layer of dust. Roh could see it floating in the air around them, too.

Yrsa found a torch and lit it with her candle, turning expectantly to Roh. 'What exactly are we hoping to find here?'

Roh touched her crown. She knew the Mercy's Topaz and the Willow's Sapphire gleamed; she could see their coloured reflections dancing across the floor in the candlelight.

'The topaz led me to *The Law of the Lair* containing the clause that saw me back on this quest,' Roh explained. 'Perhaps together, the topaz and the sapphire can lead us to something even more useful ... Something that tells us about warlock tombs and what to expect inside them ...' She took a measured step towards the closest shelf, hoping to feel that familiar tug from the birthstones.

'Anything?' Yrsa asked.

'No.' The quiet of the gems seemed all too loud. 'Let's walk around.'

They started at the far end, walking the length of the whole building between the shelves, where various ladders on wheels stood, reaching up to the books at the highest points. Little plaques of numbers and letters were stuck to each row, some sort of warlock system that Roh didn't understand but intrigued her. The pair moved through the Archives, breathing in the musty air and the smell of weathered parchment. Roh had never seen so many books in all her life, in so many different languages, too, judging from the lettering on their spines. She was hesitant to touch them, though, wondering when exactly they had been disturbed last, not in decades at least, by the looks of things. She had a vision of them crumbling apart at her fingertips.

They passed another towering shelf of volumes, the gems still lying dormant in Roh's crown.

'Look!' Yrsa pointed to a spiral staircase in the far corner. 'It looks like there are other levels, too.'

Roh was already starting towards the stairs when she heard a young voice from the doorway.

'Mama said she wants you to stick to the ground levels.' Maiella stood there, straight-backed, watching them, her younger sister peeking from behind her.

'How long have you been there?' Roh demanded.

Maiella didn't look bothered by her harsh tone. She approached them, her cloak swishing behind her. 'Only a little while. We heard your voices.'

'So, you're not spying on us?'

'Oh, yes, we are. Mama said to keep a close eye on the bone queen. Why does she call you that?'

Roh sighed. 'I used to be a bone cleaner in Saddoriel.'

Maiella's eyes bulged and she nudged her sister. 'Really?'

'Really,' Roh told her. 'And Yrsa here is a Jaktaren.'

'She is?' blurted Nym.

Yrsa smiled. 'Yes, I am.'

This news seemed to render the nestlings speechless and Roh took the opportunity to inch closer to the stairs.

But Maiella was sharper than Roh gave her credit for, and she folded her arms over her chest. 'You're not allowed up there.'

Roh raised a brow. 'You're telling me that you never do things you're told you're not allowed to?'

Maiella's cheeks flushed. 'No.'

Nym pushed past her sister and blinked up at Roh. 'Can I see your dragon?' she asked boldly.

Roh laughed quietly. 'Perhaps this evening.'

That seemed to satisfy the nestling and she darted off.

But Maiella remained, seemingly intent on carrying out her mother's orders. 'What are you looking for?' she asked.

Roh exchanged a wary look with Yrsa. 'Books on the warlock tombs,' Roh replied truthfully, not sure what there was to gain by lying to a nestling.

'Mama took all those books last week,' Maiella replied matter-of-factly.

'Oh?'

'She said there are whispers that important volumes go missing when the bone queen is around.'

It was Yrsa who laughed this time. 'Well, she's not wrong, is she?'

Roh raked her fingers through her hair, the tightness in her chest returning tenfold. She should have known Elna would have more sense than to leave a bunch of answer-filled books around for her to find. She turned to Yrsa, trying not to let the despair show on her face. 'What now?'

Yrsa looked around. 'Well ...'

'Mama said you're an Irons,' Maiella stated, as though waiting for Roh to contradict her.

Roh straightened. 'That's right ... I'm Rohesia Irons, daughter to Cerys Irons. Granddaughter to Sedna Irons ... They —'

'I know who they are,' Maiella told her. 'Mama told us all about them. Do you want to see something? It's not a book.'

Curiosity piqued, Roh found herself nodding. 'Alright ...'

The pair followed the nestling as she led them from the Archives out into the rain with the confidence of a much older cyren. They crossed the grounds hurriedly, clenching their teeth against the wind that whipped their cold, wet skin. They came to another near-decrepit building and Maiella kicked the door open, the timber swollen in its frame from the weather. Inside, the entrance hall was eerily quiet, with leaves and dust covering the once-tiled floor, while spider silk webs and birds' nests filled the corners. What was once a grand staircase greeted them, its carpet brown and sodden, littered with filth.

'This is the Old Teacher's College,' Maiella told them proudly, starting up the steps, the timber groaning despite her light weight.

'Is it safe?' Roh asked with a pointed look at the floor that was visibly bowing under her boots.

'It holds me and Nym,' Maiella reassured them, as though they weren't double her size. 'Come.'

Frowning, Roh followed carefully. 'What exactly are you showing us?' she asked once they'd reached the landing safely.

Maiella ignored her. 'This way,' she commanded, clearly used to being in charge. She turned down a hallway.

Roh shot Yrsa a questioning look, but the Jaktaren merely shrugged.

At last, they came to an ordinary-looking door.

'Here we are,' Maiella said, reaching for the handle.

'What exactly are you showing us?' Roh demanded, her patience finally wearing thin.

The door swung inwards and a wave of goosebumps rushed across Roh's skin instantly. Her scalp prickled, as though there was someone else with them. A large, circular dining table stood to one side, four chairs around it. Empty bed frames stood at the far end of the chamber, a curtain tied back there. Wind chimes hung from the ceiling beams, still and silent in the breathless air.

Roh found herself stepping deeper into the room, an old private residence, by the looks of things. 'Why did you ask me if I was an Irons?' Roh said.

But this time, Maiella didn't answer, she pointed.

Following the gesture, Roh spotted something hanging on the wall.

A coral breastplate.

She reached out, her fingers grazing its rough surface, whispers of conversations long past filling her head.

'How were your lessons today?'

'Killian showed us more warlock magic.'

'Are we winning?'

'It's not that simple.'

'Why not? A war is a fight, isn't it? There's always a winner.'

'Maiella ...' Roh croaked. 'Is this place what I think it is?'

Their young host nodded eagerly. 'It's the home of Sedna Irons. Me and Nym come here sometimes to play.'

Roh turned. 'It's where she and her fledglings resided while they stayed in Lochloria ...' she realised, a shaky breath escaping her. She walked tentatively, taking in every inch of what should have been an ordinary room. But it was far from ordinary, at least to her. This was where *her family* had lived. Her mother and her grandmother ... Ames, or as he'd gone by back then, Marlow, all had sat at that table, had slept in those beds ... Delja, too, she realised with a start. This was where she'd grown up amongst the Irons family. *Roh's family.*

She could feel Maiella and Yrsa watching her as she paced the apartments, but they felt far away. Roh ran her hands over the surfaces, paused over the scratches on the floorboards and the small discoloured patch above one of the beds, as though a picture or artwork had once been pinned there. She drank in the sight of the meagre remaining belongings – a mug on the shelf, an empty woven bag on a hook and a pair of small boots discarded by the door, all of it untouched for centuries. All the while, Roh couldn't help her gaze flicking to the coral breastplate that hung on the wall, imagining it strapped to the chest of the great Sedna Irons ...

Roh's skin prickled, an echo of the past coming to her again.

'Such is the price of war ...' the voice said.

Roh shivered before the birthstones in her crown sent a pulse of warmth into her body, telling her that those words had once been spoken by the owner of that armour. Part of her wanted to wrench it from the wall and strap it to her own chest ... But the other part of her wanted to leave it undisturbed, as the room mostly was – a memory of her family intact and whole, before it had been torn apart.

'Roh?' Yrsa was saying. 'Roh? Are you alright?'

'Yes,' Roh managed, tearing her eyes away from the breastplate and doing her best to gather herself.

Maiella was watching her curiously. 'Do you like it?' she asked.

'I ... uh ... yes,' she managed. 'Thank you for showing me.'

Maiella beamed. 'It's our favourite place. There are even toys —'

'We should go,' Roh said quickly, unsure that she could handle seeing the toys her mother had played with as a nestling before she'd become the Elder Slayer. She didn't wait for a response. She pulled Yrsa from the room and led them straight back out into the rain.

Yrsa pulled her to a stop and peered into her face, concerned. 'What's going on?' she demanded.

Roh wiped the rain from her eyes. 'I could … I could hear them, my family … I could feel them there … Or at least, an echo of them, as they once were in this place.'

Yrsa nodded, glancing at the birthstones in Roh's crown. 'Do you think it was the gems?'

'I don't know …' Roh went to say more, but something in the sky caught her attention.

Overhead, a great eagle circled.

'Gods …' she murmured, not taking her eyes off it.

'Is that the Warlock Supreme's bird again?' Yrsa said, following her gaze.

'Yes.' Roh squinted up into the downpour, dread solidifying in her gut. 'We have to find the others. Outside the city the Akorians are dying and the warlocks are gathering once more. We're running out of time, Yrsa.'

It was late afternoon by the time Roh and Yrsa found the others taking shelter in the porter's lodge by the great gate.

Deodan's gaze was on the circling eagle outside. 'She's getting ready.'

'To do what?' Roh asked, wringing the rain from her hair. 'Attack here?'

'I don't know … But this is what she does. She bides her time, gathers information … She waits for the opportune moment and strikes.'

'What would be the point in taking Lochloria as it is now? The Saddoriens would simply retaliate and retake the territory,' Harlyn said.

'Perhaps it's not her plan to attack Lochloria. Perhaps she

simply wants to know our whereabouts,' Yrsa replied, peering out the window into the downpour.

'We can stand here guessing all day,' Roh interjected. 'What did you find?' she asked the others.

Much to Odi's displeasure, they had stumbled across a herd of wild backahast, magic water horses. Kezra explained how the creatures had followed them for a time.

'After my first experience with those things, I was hardly thrilled,' Odi muttered to Roh, disgruntled.

Roh remembered the encounter all too well; how during the very first trial of the Queen's Tournament, the backahast had galloped towards Odi and wrapped its form around him, encasing him with water, filling his lungs.

'Well, you were fine this time, weren't you?' Finn clapped Odi on the shoulder, devoid of any sympathies.

'No thanks to you.'

Roh glanced between them. 'What does that mean?'

Finn rolled his eyes. 'The backahast seemed to take a liking to me. Our human friend objected to their close proximity, that's all.'

'You were practically goading them towards me!'

'I'd never.'

Roh was sure she saw a glint of mischief in the Jaktaren's lilac eyes. Odi swore and pinched the bridge of his nose.

Roh waved them away. The presence of a backahast herd was hardly news; they were native to Lochloria. 'Now's not the time. What about the rest of you?'

Kezra cleared her throat. 'There were a number of guards stationed outside the tomb. Harlyn created a diversion and I was able to slip inside the entrance – it was pitch black, I couldn't see a thing. But there is work still being done down in its depths. I could hear hammering and workers' voices. Whatever awaits us is no warlock contraption ... The council has made something down there.'

Roh cursed silently. *Of course*. 'Anything else?'

Deodan tore his gaze away from the eagle and turned to Roh. 'I didn't have much luck getting information from the battalion.'

'Figures,' Roh muttered.

'But I did.' Harlyn smirked.

Roh couldn't help grinning at her friend. 'Your charm's not too rusty, then?'

'Who said anything about being rusty?' Harlyn quipped. 'Their force is perhaps a sixth of the overall Saddorien Army, according to the numbers Finn told us. They were sent here weeks ago, but don't know why, at least the three I spoke to didn't. I couldn't get to the higher ranks, they were hidden away in the heart of the camp, which is far beyond the arts buildings, in a sort of valley below.'

Roh nodded. 'Thank you.'

'For what it's worth, the cyrens I spoke to weren't necessarily against having a bone cleaner as a queen.'

'They weren't?'

'Well, they said if she's anything like me, she'd be a sight for sore eyes,' Harlyn said, wiggling her brows.

Roh rolled her eyes, but couldn't help returning Harlyn's smile. The others chuckled as well.

Yrsa turned to Roh. 'What do you want to do, then?'

It was Deodan Roh turned to next, fixing him with a determined look. 'I want to learn warlock magic.'

CHAPTER ELEVEN

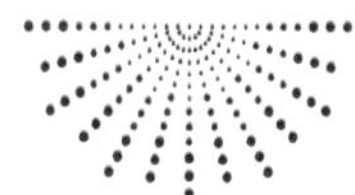

'You said there's no better place to learn than here ...' Roh ventured, noting Deodan's stunned expression. 'I am vulnerable without my deathsong. If there's the slightest chance I can wield a fraction of your power, it's better than nothing, don't you agree?'

Around her, the others were silent, their own shock rippling outwards.

The warlock's brow furrowed. 'It's not that I don't agree, Roh, but I'm no teacher.'

'You can try,' she pressed. The urge to learn had grown more insistent, and wandering her father's native home made her all the surer that this was right. It made sense, to find strength elsewhere when she'd lost what she had. 'Teach me what you were taught at the beginning.'

'Now?'

'Is there a better time?' she challenged.

He huffed a quiet laugh. 'I suppose not. But we can't do it here.'

'Good. The rest of you go back to our quarters and dry off, have something to eat. We'll join you there later.'

Deodan sighed. 'As you say, Queen of Bones.'

Finn's hand closed over Roh's arm in a warm, gentle grip. 'Are you sure?'

Heat flushed Roh's cheeks as she looked from his hand to his face, his brows knitted together in concern. Her skin prickled as she felt everyone else's eyes on them.

'I'm sure,' she said, pulling away.

Drawing their hoods up over their heads, Roh and Deodan stepped out into the wind, before anyone could insist on accompanying them.

At least it has stopped raining, Roh thought.

Moments later, she found herself trudging through the forest with Deodan, the chilly air sharp against their skin.

'I've been meaning to tell you,' Deodan said as they walked. 'I've been thinking about the tempests.'

'And?'

'Remember what Floralin said: *A gathering of power that no longer exists in the realms as we know them today.*'

'How does that help us?' Roh failed to keep the impatience from her voice.

Deodan gave her a sympathetic look as he led them further into the woods. 'Well, as we've seen for ourselves, while cyrens and warlocks are not unified, there is other magic in the world.'

'Like?' Roh pressed.

'Your scaly gold friend.'

'What does Valli have to do with this?'

'The beast has shown several signs of great power, Roh. Especially when he is linked to you in some way. Kezra agrees.'

'But he is no longer linked to me,' Roh argued. 'He hasn't glowed since my deathsong was taken from me, has he?'

Deodan scratched the stubble at his chin. 'No, but your deathsong isn't the only thing that connects you. You have *raised him*, Roh. You converse with him in your own way.'

'Only because I *stole him*! And just because I have a basic understanding of him doesn't mean he is mine to command.'

'I realise that, Roh,' Deodan said calmly.

Roh sighed. 'What makes you think Valli can help defend Saddoriel anyway? I know he is powerful, but … *that* powerful? The poor beast still can't land without felling a few trees!'

'I don't know,' Deodan muttered, seeming lost in his thoughts. 'It's just a feeling.'

Roh huffed her annoyance. 'Well, forgive me if I don't base any sort of strategy on your hunches.'

Deodan didn't look fazed. 'I was hoping to get to the Archives myself, there might be answers in the texts there, but I'm not sure we'll have time. For now, let's get back to this warlock training of yours.'

Roh controlled the urge to stop in her tracks and throw her hands up in frustration.

'You need to learn how to quieten your mind first,' Deodan was saying as he held back a branch for her.

'You may as well ask me to drain the seas,' Roh muttered. If there was one thing she failed at dismally it was silencing the whirring thoughts in her head, especially after the warlock had put terror tempests back on her mind.

Deodan smiled. 'No easy feat, I know. But it's the first thing all warlocks learn. If we are to tap into the magic of water, we need to be able to hear it, above all else.'

'Hear it? Does it speak to you, then?'

'In its own way, yes. It has its own music, its own spirit. Cyrens can manipulate bodies of water, but warlocks can harness it in a much more complex way. We can convey messages, memories, images … We can shape water into a remedy or a weapon, as you've seen many times by now.' Deodan paused and scanned the clearing they'd reached. 'This should do. We just needed somewhere quiet and where we wouldn't be disturbed.'

Without ceremony, he moved his cutlasses aside and sat on the wet forest floor. Frowning, Roh did the same, sitting opposite her friend, the seat of her pants becoming instantly soaked. 'Well, you've got me intrigued.'

'I don't expect that to last,' Deodan said. 'We'll be trying a form of warlock meditation.' He raised a brow at Roh's sceptical expression. 'You wanted to learn.'

'Alright, alright,' she said. 'Show me.'

After another stern look, Deodan straightened. 'Put your hands on your knees, and sit up straight, like this.'

Roh did as he bid and waited.

'Close your eyes. First, you need to try to rid yourself of your inner voice – the one that drags you from thought to thought.'

'The spiral,' Roh said quietly.

'That's the one. Take a deep breath.'

Roh did.

'Start by focusing on the small sensations – the dampness of the earth, the rustling of the leaves in the wind ... If you're bombarded by a thought, accept it and then let it float onwards. Imagine a river if you have to, set the thought down in the current and let it wash away.'

Feeling increasingly foolish, Roh tried to do as Deodan instructed. She concentrated on the physical: the chill of the air on the tips of her ears, the tightening of the muscles in her back and shoulders at the rigid position, the distant call of a lone lost bird. But her thoughts were a current of their own, forceful like the sea, not the comparatively gentle rush of a river.

'It's not working,' she ground out, keeping her eyes closed.

'It's barely been a few minutes, Roh,' Deodan chastised gently. 'You think a warlock learns this skill in a single afternoon? Stop talking and try again.'

Roh clamped her mouth shut, trying to bat away thoughts of wasted time and inadequacy.

'When you have quietened your mind, or acknowledged all the physical things around you, whatever comes first, then, you can listen for water. Send your senses outwards. Is there a stream nearby? The drip of dew from a leaf? Puddles on the ground from this morning's downpour? Let them call to you.'

Roh had felt the call of the sea all her life, but drops of dew and puddles? The idea was almost laughable were it not for the seriousness in Deodan's tone. She doubted that she'd ever achieve complete silence of her inner voice, so instead she focused on the world around her, pushing aside the questions and the lure of the spiral as best she could. She reached out with her mind and senses, trying to find a similar song to the sea in the forest around them.

Behind her lids, Roh's eyes grew heavy, as did her torso, but she kept throwing her senses out, desperate to feel just a flicker of warlock magic in her veins. If she could master this, then she wouldn't be powerless, she would have some form of strength against the council and their plans. She shook the notion from her head; she was letting her thoughts back in.

'What do you do once you hear the water?' she asked Deodan.

'You draw from its power,' he replied. 'Draw it together. You try to shape it into what you need it to be.'

'But I need a vial of sacred water, don't I? For anything to actually take shape?'

Deodan seemed to consider this. 'Most likely. But the exercise is one and the same. Trying to will the water into a specific form, just as you cyrens manipulate the currents of the sea.'

'Like your water birds?'

Deodan nodded. 'Yes, like them, although anything that takes on the shape and mannerisms of a living being is very complex magic.'

'What about the flowers you manifest, to heal people?'

'Still a living thing ... Still complicated.'

Roh gave a huff of frustration. 'Then what's a good starting point?'

'Something simple. A shape. A shield. A symbol.'

'Helpful,' Roh muttered.

'I told you, no warlock masters this sort of magic in a day. I know it's not your best strength, but try to be patient.'

Roh had to laugh at that. She certainly wasn't known for her patience.

They practised until dusk fell, and though Roh felt no closer to mastering her water warlock magic, she at least felt as though she had done something, taken some sort of action. Her mind buzzed with Deodan's instructions as they trudged back towards the gallery. Even as they walked, she tried to silence her inner voice and hear the call of the water, desperately hoping the way would become clear to her, that the warlock blood in her veins would guide her to a new kind of magic she could control. But the power of water remained quiet and out of reach.

'It's only been a few hours,' Deodan said quietly as they reached the steps of the gallery. 'You expect too much of yourself.'

'Or … perhaps it doesn't matter who my father is. Maybe I don't have warlock magic.'

'That's possible,' Deodan allowed. 'Or it might be that it's dormant within you, stifled by your cyren nature for all these years. As we discovered upon entering Lamaka's Basin, cyren and warlock magic can be opposing forces.'

Roh's head was suddenly tight, and she rubbed her eyes.

Seeming to sense her weariness, Deodan reached out, clasping Roh's cold hands in his warm grip. 'You are working to bring those magics together,' he said, his voice full of meaning. 'Do not let one brief training session derail your confidence.'

Gently, he unfurled her fingers so her hand was facing up. On her palm, he traced the first half of a pair of wings; the symbol of the ancient alliance between the warring races.

Roh smiled wistfully and drew the other half of the wings, her skin tingling. 'I hope you're right.' Straightening, she took her hand back and gestured to the gallery, waving him away. 'I'll be in shortly,' she said, having spotted Valli by one of the buildings.

Deodan looked as though he wanted to protest, but in the end he let her be.

Roh's mind swam as she went to her sea drake; the gap between her and the Gauntlet Ruby only seemed to widen; the hours whittling away, minute by minute, causing her chest to constrict; the echoes of her family in her mother and uncle's childhood home, and her grandmother's coral breastplate on the wall …

Roh reached up and stroked Valli, who sighed contently and leaned into her touch. Affection entwined with guilt bloomed in her chest. She'd spent hardly any proper time with him over the past few weeks and yet he was always there when she needed him. She gazed at him in wonder, recalling how tiny he had been when he'd hatched from that egg along the banks of the Endon River, how he'd spent the first few weeks of his life curled up in the pocket of her shirt. She ran her hand along his spine where vicious spikes stood out from hardened gold scales. Since her sacrifice on the Bridge of Csilla, he hadn't glowed, not how the others had described it in the past. Roh wished she could have seen it for herself back then. She didn't understand the link between them, but she knew an element of that connection had been severed the moment her deathsong had been torn from her.

She rested against Valli's sturdy weight, and stayed with him until the sun disappeared below the horizon.

Dark had descended in the decaying scholar's city, but in the warmth and shelter of the gallery, Harlyn approached Roh with a broad grin on her face and something hidden behind her back.

'You thought I'd forgotten, didn't you?' she said.

Roh blinked at her friend, stumped. 'Forgotten what?'

'You're telling me that *you've* forgotten?' Harlyn asked, incredulous.

'Forgotten *what*, Har?'

Harlyn produced a wreath from behind her back and presented it to Roh, as was tradition on a cyren's —

'It's my name day,' Roh recalled then.

Harlyn gaped at her in disbelief. 'You truly *did* forget.'

Roh took the wreath, slightly bewildered, and turned it over in her hands. It was largely made of dried leaves and grass fronds, unlike the colourful creations she'd seen and made herself back in the lair.

'Obviously everything's barren here, so it's a rather lacklustre gift, I'm afraid,' Harlyn explained. '*But*,' she motioned to the others with a flourish, who came forward, their arms laden with dark bottles and packages wrapped in parchment, 'Finn found Elna's secret stores …'

Finn gave a casual shrug. 'Thought I'd put those tracking skills to use,' he quipped, his dimple showing.

'And we thought we'd have ourselves a little name-day feast at dear Elna's expense.' Yrsa brandished a fancy-looking bottle.

The exhaustion of the day fell away from Roh, a smile tugging at her lips. Her eighteenth name day had been the furthest thing from her mind, but now … Now she was glad for it, and grateful that she would spend it here, that she would come of age with her friends by her side.

They settled around her on blankets by the fire and set about unpacking the various goods. Odi saw to the generous pours of wine, while Kezra appreciatively inspected the food.

'That wench,' she muttered. 'She had all this, likely sent from Saddoriel, and didn't offer us more than stale bread?'

'Well, that hardly matters now, does it?' Harlyn snorted,

drinking straight from the bottle of something sweet smelling and greedily eyeing a jar of preserved fruit.

When they all had cups in hand, Odi took it upon himself to stand, raising his own in the air. 'To our beloved Queen of Bones, whose determination and bravery know no bounds ... Happy name day!'

'Happy name day!' the others echoed.

'To our Queen of Bones,' Deodan toasted.

Roh's cheeks flushed with pleasure. Her previous name days had passed with no great fanfare. Usually, Harlyn and Orson made her a wreath and saved her an extra serving of dinner. If time permitted, they would sneak off to find a veil to the sea and dive through, relishing the kiss of the water, but as they grew older, the opportunity presented itself less and less.

'I've never had a party before,' Roh said.

Kezra snorted. 'This is no party. We'll endeavour to give you a proper one for your next name day.'

Roh just smiled. 'This is the perfect party to me.'

The intensity of the last few days fell away as Roh ate and drank with her friends, laughter echoing through the gallery. Finn sat at her side, his knee brushing hers, and Roh revelled in the subtle touch, in the energy and connection between them. Though, she did wonder if he ever planned to give her that sketchbook he'd bought back in Thornhill, the one he'd told her he'd intended for this very name day. But she didn't bring it up. The joy was thick in the air for once and there was no need to dilute it.

Harlyn gave the gift of music, strumming at her lute as best she could, while the sight of Odi trying to dance with Kezra's towering form sent the rest of them into fits of laughter. The poor human was on his tiptoes and Kezra was all but lifting him off the ground.

The hour was late when one by one, they made their excuses to retire. It was a rare occasion that Roh felt such contentedness, a feeling that only bloomed further as Finn pulled his bed roll beside hers. He lay down next to her and without any trace of self-consciousness, pulled her body close to his, fitting her back to his chest.

'Happy name day, Roh,' he murmured into her hair, just before sleep claimed him.

At last, the wine and food blanketed Roh in drowsiness. Smiling, she nestled into Finn's warmth, savouring the weight of his arm around her, and drifted into dream herself.

Roh woke suddenly, a ragged gasp on her lips, knowing that something was wrong. She felt it in her chest, that strange, uncomfortable instinct that screamed *danger*. But what was it? She scanned the space around her. The fire had died out and her companions slept in the darkness, the steady rhythm of their breathing filling the quiet of the gallery. She could hear each and every one of them, with one exception.

Harlyn.

Roh salt bolt upright then, wildly scanning the gallery for her friend, disturbing Finn at her side.

'What is it?' he murmured sleepily.

But Roh was on her feet, checking the empty bathing chamber, checking every corner of the space. Harlyn wouldn't leave, not without telling her, Roh knew that in her bones.

'Roh?' Yrsa's voice sounded far away, as did the sounds of the others waking up.

But only one thing halted Roh's panicked antics. She watched as the first rays of dawn filtered through the broken windows and realised in horror what they meant …

Today she would enter the tomb of her ancestors to find the Gauntlet Ruby.

And the council had taken Harlyn as a hostage.

CHAPTER TWELVE

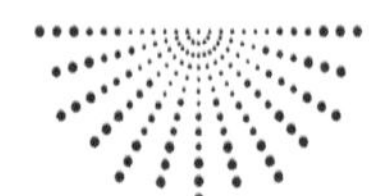

There was no doubt in Roh's mind that the council had taken Harlyn. How, she did not know, but the gems in her crown offered all the dread-filled confirmation she needed. Around her, the others dressed and armed themselves in silence, while Roh checked her own dagger and sling. This was it. The test for the Gauntlet Ruby was upon her, and Harlyn's life hung in the balance. Roh would waste no time. With Valli at her back and the others by her side, she led them deep into the festering forest, ignoring the numerous cyren soldiers stationed throughout.

It seemed mere moments later that they stood before the warlock tomb, the dawn light breaking upon the pale stone entrance marked with carvings she didn't understand. Roh wasn't surprised to see Elna waiting for them, her expression as smug as ever.

'The council's not here,' Odi whispered.

Scanning the forest, Roh realised he was right. It was only Elna and a unit of the battalion.

'They don't expect me to win,' Roh murmured. 'Why bother?'

'Surely, they'd want to witness your downfall if that was the case?' Yrsa replied.

'I've long since stopped trying to guess.'

Elna seemed to listen to this exchange with deep interest. She leaned casually against the frame of the tomb and met Roh's gaze. 'It appears you've lost something you value, warlock-lover,' she said, folding her arms over her chest.

Roh took a deliberate step forward, fury crackling in her veins. 'If Harlyn does not emerge from this ordeal whole and healthy, I'll set my drake upon you,' she said, her voice low. 'And I will revel in the melody of your screams.'

Now standing in Valli's shadow, Elna's face paled. 'You —'

'You'll think wisely before you speak again.' Finn's voice was as sharp as a blade. He closed the gap between him and Roh, his grip tight on the sword at his belt.

Elna opened her mouth to say something but then seemed to think better of it.

'Are there any instructions?' Roh demanded.

'Retrieve the birthstone,' Elna replied, motioning for Roh to enter.

'Nothing else?' Odi insisted. 'No other conditions? Rules?'

Elna eyed the human with renewed interest. 'You know our kind well, Prince of Melodies.'

'You have no idea,' Odi all but growled. 'Well?'

'No,' Elna allowed. 'All I was told was that you are to retrieve the Gauntlet Ruby from the tomb.'

'So be it,' Roh said curtly. In previous trials, she had been required to give up her crown and guidance of the gems. Elna made no such demand and so Roh started for the entrance with her teeth clenched, determined to take advantage of what she imagined was an oversight. She heard the crashing of branches around her as Valli made to follow. She halted, eyeing the narrow entrance and the size of her protector.

'Stand guard,' Roh told him, running her hand across the scales of his neck. She gave Elna a pointed look. 'Make sure this one doesn't move.'

Valli growled in the keeper's direction.

But Roh drew his focus back to her. 'You understand?' she asked quietly. 'You're a noble guardian, my friend. But I cannot risk the tomb collapsing while Harlyn is in there.'

Valli huffed but seemed to accept her decision.

Roh turned to her companions. 'Are we ready?'

'As we'll ever be,' Deodan replied, his mouth set in a grim line as he used a piece of flint to light a torch.

The others nodded, bodies tense.

With a final warning glance at Elna, Roh unsheathed her father's quartz dagger and took the torch from Deodan, crossing the threshold into the warlock tomb.

Her eyes adjusted to the dark passage, the flames of the torch flickering across the walls. She was only a few yards in before she was greeted by a path of shallow stone steps, leading down into the belly of the tomb. There was no other option, and so, with her heart in her throat, Roh started the descent, unable to see where the stairs stopped.

Down, down, down, they went.

Roh concentrated hard, paranoid she'd miss a step and go tumbling forward into the black abyss. She hoped that the others behind her were being just as careful, lest they let off a chain reaction of falls.

The air around them became damp and musty; it seemed to bear down on them more heavily the deeper into the tomb they descended. No one spoke and Roh was glad for the silence. Workers had been down here for days; there was no doubt that there would be obstacles ahead, and she needed every ounce of focus.

Just when she thought the stairs would never end, her torch cast flickering light across a flat surface before her.

'Stop where you are,' she called back to her friends.

Their steps ceased.

'What is it?' Kezra called from the rear.

Roh wasn't sure, but her skin prickled. She sniffed the air – there was a different scent down here. Sawdust, if she wasn't mistaken.

'No one move,' she ordered, still on the final step herself.

I need more light, she thought, squinting as she tried to scan the ground in front of them.

'There are sconces,' Finn said, as though reading her mind.

Roh's gaze went to the walls on either side of them, and sure enough, Finn was right. 'It could be some sort of trap ... To light them, I mean.'

'It could be. But whatever work was done down here, they needed to see, too.'

Finding it hard to swallow, Roh nodded. Slowly, she touched her torch to the sconce on her right.

A quiet hiss sounded and flame rushed across the wall, lighting several torches along it. The tomb was suddenly bathed in a golden glow and Roh shielded her eyes, blinking hard to adjust her vision.

'Roh ...' Yrsa came to stand on the same step.

But Roh's attention was on the freshly laid wooden floor before them. She crouched on her step, biting her lip as she surveyed the path, the only way forward into the tomb. 'It's new,' she murmured, noting the hum from the gems in her bone crown. She scanned the steps for something, anything she could use.

'Here,' Finn took the torch she held and handed her a rock.

Giving a nod of thanks, she accepted it and launched it across the floor.

Nothing happened.

When the echoes of the stone's impact ceased, Roh loosed a breath.

'Well, it's good to check,' Deodan said, starting forward.

'Wait!' Roh half shouted, flinging an arm out to stop him. She was eager to get to Harlyn, eager to find the birthstone, but ...

'What?' Deodan asked impatiently.

Finn handed Roh another rock, and she threw it at a different section of the floor.

A loud snap sounded.

Deadly spikes shot up through the floor.

Deodan swore. So did Odi and Kezra.

'There you are,' Roh muttered, grinding her teeth.

'How did you know?' Deodan asked, noticeably paler than before.

'Floor's been freshly laid,' Roh said, not taking her eyes off the spikes. 'And can you smell the sawdust? I didn't think they'd be renovating for our comfort ... Gather anything you can from the steps, and *do not* step anywhere else,' Roh ordered. 'We'll test each patch of floor before we move. We'll cross onto the safe areas one at a time. I'll go first —'

'Not a chance,' Finn said, squaring his shoulders.

Roh raised a brow. 'If I said I'll go first, then that's what's happening, Haertel. Deal with it.'

'You're too —'

'I go first,' she repeated, gathering an armful of rocks from the edge of the stairs. 'We check everywhere we intend to step twice. It's a pressure system,' she told her friends. 'The first rock might not weigh enough to set off the trap, or it might hit it at a strange angle. I don't want us taking any chances. Got it?'

Murmurs of agreement sounded and Roh decided that that would have to do. Harlyn couldn't wait forever. Although Elna had given no indicator, Roh knew there would be some sort of time limit, just as there had been when Odi had been taken hostage in the third trial all those months ago. This time, though, she had no token of Harlyn's to determine how quickly the sand in the hourglass was falling.

Roh threw another rock, setting off another square of spikes. It took several goes before she felt confident stepping out onto the floor.

'One at a time,' she called out to her friends. But she didn't look back. She didn't need to see the terror etched on their faces. She needed to concentrate.

It was a painfully slow process to cross the trap-covered floor, and every time the spikes shot up, Roh's heart stopped and she heard the collective sigh from the others. On they went, fists and jaws clenched. There was no pattern to the madness, not that Roh could determine anyway. The workers had selected the traps' placement at random, which meant there was no way to predict where the spikes would eject and impale someone.

Kezra cursed loudly as a set released inches to her left.

'Are you alright?' Roh called.

'Fine,' Kezra replied through gritted teeth.

'Remember, step only where I have stepped.'

'You might remember that I'm a tad heavier than you, Rohesia,' Kezra ground out.

Roh *had* realised that at about the halfway mark; that her weight might not set off a trap that another's might. But by then, it had been too late, and so they had continued to cross.

By the time Roh reached the secure tiled floor on the other side, she was drenched in sweat and her whole body remained tense as she watched her companions inch their way closer to her.

'Nearly there,' she said, as much for her reassurance as her friends'.

Finn was the first to reach Roh and she lunged for him, hugging him to her tightly.

'Two down,' he said, giving her a one-armed squeeze and turning to watch the others.

One by one, they all made it to safety, all significantly sweatier and more shaken than they had been at the start. It didn't stop Roh releasing a trembling sigh of relief. They were all across at last.

A smear of red caught Roh's attention. She snatched Kezra's arm. 'You're hurt,' she said, studying the deep gash on her friend's forearm. Blood trickled down to her fingertips, making a tapping noise as it hit the tiles.

'Just a scratch, Queen of Bones, I'll live.'

'You'd better,' Roh replied, releasing her.

'Resorting to threats again, are we?'

'If they keep you alive.'

Satisfied that Kezra's life wasn't in danger at present, Roh turned to what lay ahead. A narrow corridor.

'We're out of rocks to throw,' Odi muttered.

'Helpful,' Finn retorted, scanning the ceiling and the walls of the passage before turning to Roh. 'You're expecting more traps?'

'I'd say the opener was just a warm-up, wouldn't you?'

Finn nodded. 'Agreed.'

'Deodan!' Kezra shouted, causing Roh and Finn to both jump. Roh whirled around to find that the warlock had stepped several paces into the next part of the tomb.

'It's alright,' he said.

'You didn't know that when you kept walking,' Kezra barked.

'Well … no. But now we do.'

Roh shook her head in disbelief and adjusted her grip on her dagger. 'We move together,' she told the others. 'And slowly. Or not at all.'

They caught up with Deodan, crammed in the small space, and inched forward. To move at such a pace pained Roh as the worry for Harlyn well and truly set in. Who knew how many more traps they were to face and how maimed they might emerge from the tomb, if they managed to emerge at all? But there was no going back now.

They made their way down the tiled corridor, step by careful step, towards a door at the end. None of them spoke, all of them concentrating hard on their surroundings, lest something jump out at them, or –

Something clicked beneath Roh's weight.

A gasp of horror was ripped from her as the whole floor vanished from underneath them, and suddenly, they were falling.

The surprised shouts of her companions echoed through the chamber as they flailed in the air. For a brief moment, Roh imagined the spikes that would greet them at the bottom – a violent and bloody impaling to end them all. And it would be her fault.

She hardly had a second to scream. She landed hard on her backside in soft, damp earth. The thuds and curses of the others sounded around her.

'Is everyone alright?' she managed, her bones jarring as she clumsily got to her feet.

There was a moan of pain from Deodan. 'Nothing broken … I don't think.'

'Thought you were meant to be a *warrior* warlock,' Kezra grunted as she helped him up.

Roh scanned Yrsa, Finn and Odi as well, while they were wincing and brushing the dirt off their clothes; they all seemed to be in one piece. Her heart still hammering wildly, Roh inhaled deeply and studied their new location: another passageway framed by stone pillars with roots creeping through the earth, its walls also lined with lit sconces. Apparently, the council wanted her to witness the carnage it intended to rain upon them.

Roh supposed the tomb was not unlike Saddoriel in a way, a network of winding tunnels, full of traps and secrets. Abstractly, she wondered how much of it was original and how much the workers had altered at the council's bidding.

Roh's back twinged as she surveyed the passageway and she hoped she hadn't aggravated the injury Deodan had healed, not that it mattered now. Shaking the thoughts from her head, she forced herself to focus.

'Both traps have used some form of pressure system,' she said. 'Not overly original, but effective nonetheless. I think we can expect more like them.'

'Or perhaps something a little more familiar …' Finn was crouched, studying the ground in front of them almost at eye level.

'What do you mean?'

'Look from here,' he beckoned.

Her back protesting, Roh knelt beside Finn and followed his gaze. Wire glinted in the torchlight, running from one wall to the next. Roh's hand went to the faint second scar on her face where a piece of jagged coral had sliced her.

It was Odi Roh looked at then, for the human had wrenched her from the coral's path, saving her face from a mangled fate.

His mouth quirked in amusement as he too recognised the design. 'Suppose you've forgiven him, haven't you? You've stopped calling him *the Haertel bastard …*'

Finn didn't hide his surprise.

Roh huffed a dark laugh, not taking her eyes off the trip wires, wondering what exactly would come flying out at them. 'And you've stopped calling him a highborn prick.'

'So it would seem.'

A shriek jolted them out of their musings.

Roh's blood ran cold. 'Harlyn,' she breathed. There was no mistaking her scream, it was drenched in the same terror that had sliced through the air when the teerah panther had attacked her on the gilded plains.

Two sets of hands gripped Roh's arms, Finn and Yrsa pulling her back from the trip wires.

She clawed against them. 'We have to —'

'Of course we have to find her,' Yrsa said through clenched teeth. 'But you'll be no use to anyone if you charge headfirst into a trap. Calm yourself.'

Roh met the Jaktaren's gaze, her chest painfully tight. 'I'm calm.'

Yrsa examined her critically. 'You're not. But you'll do.'

They released her and Roh forced herself to take steadying breaths, despite the shrieks echoing off the walls around them. She couldn't let herself imagine what they might be doing to Harlyn. She had to stay strong.

She turned to Finn, motioning to the wires. 'This is your domain,' she said, fighting to keep her voice steady. 'How do we disable them?'

Finn was already pulling Odi towards him and pointing to the various wires. 'I hope you've been practising,' he said, patting the crossbow across the human's back.

'You want me to shoot the wires?' Odi asked, incredulous.

'I want you to shoot the wires.'

'I'm ... I'm not that good a shot.' Odi paled at the echo of Harlyn's screams.

'Yes, you are.'

'You don't know that.'

'I do. You had the best teacher. Now hurry. Aim for the centre of each wire. You can do this.'

Roh chewed the inside of her cheek raw as she watched Odi fit a bolt to his weapon and take aim. The mechanism loosed and the arrow shot through the air.

The wire snapped and two giant blades came swinging down, shaving the fletching from the end of the bolt. They swung like deadly pendulums, the steel gleaming in the torchlight.

'Again,' Finn said, pointing to another wire.

Odi didn't hesitate this time. He loaded the crossbow and fired, releasing two more hidden blades from the crevices in the stone wall.

Roh wrung her hands as she watched him, dread bubbling up inside her. What was happening to Harlyn? Was she part of another trap? Was she hurt?

Another bolt went flying from Odi's crossbow, this time releasing a container of liquid from above.

'What is that?' Kezra peered across the battlefield, sniffing.

'Not water,' Yrsa replied. 'Look ...' She pointed to a star-shaped leaf that was drifting towards them in a river of clear liquid.

'Leaves from the vine of Strothos ...' Roh breathed. She'd know that foul plant anywhere. 'Nobody touch it. We have some of the antidote left, but trust me when I tell you that the effects will haunt you forever.'

'I think that's the last one,' Odi said, swinging his crossbow back over his shoulders. 'Did you mean what you said before, Roh?'

'What?'

Odi's amber eyes were determined. 'That you'd set Valli upon Elna if Harlyn wasn't alright?'

Roh met his gaze. 'Yes. Every word.'

'Good. Let's get her back.'

Roh couldn't agree more. With the field cleared of traps, they crossed, avoiding the puddles of poisoned water, and rounded a corner. They were greeted by five doorways. And Harlyn's screams seemed to echo from them all.

Panicked, Odi rushed from one to the next, leaning in, his eyes wide. 'Roh ...' he croaked, throwing himself at another doorway. 'Roh, she's in all of them ... What do we do? She's scared.'

'I know,' Roh replied, schooling her features into a mirror of calm, though her talons unsheathed at her sides and cut into her palms. Odi's erratic movements weren't helping – what if he were to set off another contraption? But she didn't want to alarm him further, so she kept her mask of calm as she moved towards the first door, the stale air within tickling her skin.

Harlyn's shouts were distant and her words indistinct. Roh couldn't tell if her friend was in pain or if she was trying to warn them of what lay ahead, but the sound fuelled the urgency within Roh and she moved from door to door, lingering between the frames and adjusting her crown of bones atop her head.

'Do not fail me now,' she murmured to the Mercy's Topaz and Willow's Sapphire. The former could guide its bearer when lost and the latter could provide endurance and faith … And she needed all the help she could get now.

In the fourth doorway, Roh felt it. A tug at her naval and the pulse of confirmation from the gems in her crown.

'This way,' she told the others, starting into the tunnel.

'Be careful,' Deodan warned.

'I think that's a given,' Roh muttered, trying to ignore her heart thumping in her throat, making it hard to swallow.

Harlyn's shouts grew louder.

'We're coming, Har!' Odi shouted. 'Hold on!'

Roh heard someone cuff him over the back of the head. 'Did you really feel it necessary to announce our presence?' Kezra growled. 'Who knows what is lying in wait for us next.'

'She's panicking,' Odi argued, pushing up alongside Roh.

Roh reached across and squeezed his arm as the gems pulsed more strongly in her crown. 'We're getting closer.'

The reassurance from the gems told Roh that the passage hadn't been tampered with. She also knew that the council had anticipated her getting this far; they would want her to actually witness the cruellest part of their ploy, which risked her oldest friend.

Brighter light appeared at the end of the tunnel and Roh broke into a run. Harlyn was somewhere just beyond this passage and she had to get to her and the gem before whatever horrors the council had planned befell them all.

'Roh!' Harlyn shouted.

As Roh burst into what opened up into a grand cavern of pillars and statues and towering walls, she gasped at what she saw. On a plinth, Harlyn was trapped in a glass tank, one that was eerily similar to the one that had caged Odi as Roh had sought the scale of a sea serpent in her third trial of the Queen's Tournament. Only, Harlyn's tank was not filling with water, but with grain.

They couldn't drown a cyren.

No. They meant to suffocate her.

Roh rushed to her friend, Odi close behind, pressing her palms to the glass. 'We'll get you out, Har, we'll break it —'

'No!' Harlyn screamed. 'Don't!'

Roh looked from the grains inching up her friend's legs to Harlyn's terrified stare. 'What have they done?'

'They learned from your antics last time, Roh,' Harlyn murmured, as Finn, Yrsa, Kezra and Deodan caught up. 'If you break the glass … we'll all die.'

Odi started. 'What?'

'They treated it with some sort of airborne poison from the grounds. Whole, the glass is harmless, but smashed, it fills the air with toxic mist and we'll be dead in minutes. They …' Harlyn's voice broke as she pointed to something in the far corner of the cavern. 'They demonstrated.'

In a glass tank similar to Harlyn's, a body was slumped lifeless on the floor, a shattered vial at his feet. Roh took a step towards the transparent cage and her heart caught in her throat as she spotted another detail. The cyren within wore a gold circlet across his brow. A fellow *isruhe* … A warning to her.

'Roh …' Finn's voice was low.

'We'll find some other way to get Har out.'

'That's just it,' Harlyn said, her voice trembling. 'There's only one way …'

Roh was at Harlyn's tank again. 'They told you? What is it?'

Her expression grim, Harlyn jutted her chin from a strange latch at the side of her tank to the opposite side of the tomb. A high dark wall towered above them, and embedded in its rocks were hundreds of gleaming red stones – rubies.

'The Gauntlet Ruby is somewhere there, Roh. And it's the only thing that will unlock this tank.'

'There are hundreds …' Deodan was saying, scanning the precious stones and then the rising grain in Harlyn's cage.

'I know that,' Harlyn snapped. 'The ultimate joke, isn't it?' she said bitterly. 'In the quest for the ruby, you'll lose me. And once you lose me, you won't care about the ruby. They've been watching you, Roh, learning bit by bit how to break you.'

'I won't let them have you, Har,' Roh told her friend and started towards the wall of rubies. 'I won't.'

'It's not just about me, Roh,' Harlyn called out, desperate. 'Whatever happens, *do not* smash the glass. That goes for the rest of you, too.'

Roh blocked out her words, refusing to acknowledge any option except the one where she placed the Gauntlet Ruby in the latch that released Harlyn from the death tank. Standing at the foot of the wall, she looked up, fighting back the waves of her own panic with the ferocity and determination of the teerah panther they'd freed back in Csilla. Deodan had told them tales of a legend, a girl in the northern lands who rode on the back of one of those great beasts, a girl who led an entire pride of them. Now faced with a hundred wrong choices and the death of her oldest friend, Roh decided then and there that one day, if they lived, Harlyn might like to meet this supposed panther whisperer, and if she did, Roh would take her.

The rubies glinted in the orange glow of the torches.

'I have to climb,' she realised as she took in the near-vertical wall.

'We all can,' Kezra said. 'We can cover more ground.'

Roh hadn't noticed her companions had come to stand by her, all of them but Odi, who remained with Harlyn, surveying the gleam of the gems in the black, rocky surface.

'No, we can't,' Roh replied, reaching for her crown. 'With this many red gems, there's only one way we'll be able to tell which is the *true* Gauntlet Ruby.'

There was an intake of breath as Roh took her father's dagger and prised the sapphire from its inset in her crown. She held it out to Yrsa. 'You and I make the climb,' she said. 'We split the wall between the two of us, each of us with a birthstone. They'll pulse when we grow near it.'

Roh could hear Harlyn's panicked gasps growing more frequent, but she did not turn back. She couldn't turn back.

Odi's whispered words drifted towards her. 'She can do this, Har. You're not going to die.'

Roh was determined not to make a liar out of him.

Yrsa was still looking at the sapphire in Roh's outstretched palm. 'You're sure?'

Roh pushed it into Yrsa's hands. 'Yes.'

'Roh —'

'There's no time, Yrs. Climb.' Roh's fingertips were already searching for purchase. And so they climbed. It wasn't long before every muscle in Roh's body was screaming in protest, before her heart was a constant thud against her chest as she struggled to find sturdy footholds to push herself up. But she ignored all that. Clinging on for dear life with one hand as she gained more height, she ran her palm across the numerous blood-red stones embedded in the rockface, desperate to feel that pulse of warmth, that recognition from the topaz in her crown as she came into contact with the Gauntlet Ruby. But there was only cold.

She could hear the others pacing below, could hear the steady rush of the grain as it fell into Harlyn's tank, closing in around her. But Roh did not look down. She kept climbing, kept feeling for the true birthstone of Saddoriel that she knew was somewhere here.

Roh was methodical in her approach, trying to cover her half of the vast wall before moving up again. From what she could see, Yrsa was doing the same. Both of their brows were shining with sweat, and Roh could feel beads of it trickle down her back and ribs.

'You need to go faster,' Odi called from below.

Roh gritted her teeth and didn't bother with a reply. They knew she was going as fast as she could. She was at least fifteen feet above them now, and if she or Yrsa fell, it would be the end of them, and Harlyn.

It was Harlyn's voice that carried up to Roh now. 'Whatever happens, do not break the glass,' she was saying over and over like a prayer.

With trembling fingers, Roh reached up and misjudged the sturdiness of the rock above. It crumbled beneath her weight and time slowed as she flailed, scrambling to find another ledge to grip. Her fingernails tore and fear exploded in her chest.

'Roh!' someone yelled.

But she held on. She *held on*. Long enough to hear a strangled noise from Yrsa. Roh's gaze snapped to hers, sweat stinging her eyes. She didn't want to say the words aloud, lest they not be true, lest they ignite hope in Harlyn, only to condemn her to death moments later.

Yrsa knew what she was asking and she angled her hand so Roh could see the glint of red between her fingers. 'But it can't be,' the Jaktaren murmured, even as she started her descent.

'You've found it?' Odi shouted. 'Hold on, Har – hold on!'

Yrsa had to have the Gauntlet Ruby; she was scaling down the wall fast.

Roh chanced a look in Harlyn's direction, only to see her friend craning her chin upwards, trying to avoid the grain covering her mouth.

'*Hurry!*' Odi's scream tore through the cavern.

Roh's legs weren't working fast enough. She was slipping, making stupid mistakes in her rush to get back down and run to Harlyn.

She heard Yrsa's boots hit the ground, heard her racing towards the tank. Roh jumped. Pain shot up her legs as she struck the floor, but she scrambled to her feet, staggering towards the tank, where Harlyn's face had disappeared below the grain. Roh could see her hands clawing at the glass.

'Yrsa,' Roh rasped as she closed the gap between them, reaching for the tank.

The Jaktaren fitted the red shard to the latch, pressing it down firmly.

Something clicked.

The glass doors swung open, grain spilling across the ground, Harlyn with it. Roh lunged for her, dragging her up. Harlyn was choking, gasping and then retching.

'You're alive,' Roh sobbed. 'You're alive.'

No one spoke as Harlyn recovered, her eyes red-rimmed and watering, her voice a rasp.

Roh barely dared to hope, barely dared to believe that Harlyn was whole and alive … She didn't move from her side. Roh didn't move at all except to hold her friend, to feel the shallow rise and fall of her body as she breathed.

But at last, although still unable to speak, Harlyn squeezed her hand.

A sob of relief escaped Roh then, and the others seemed to sag as they too allowed themselves to hope.

'You're alive,' Roh repeated into Harlyn's hair.

'And you have the Gauntlet Ruby,' Harlyn rasped.

Boots crunching atop the spilt grain sounded and there was Yrsa kneeling before them. 'Not exactly,' she said, holding out her hand.

Roh stared at the red gem that winked at her from Yrsa's palm. The Mercy's Topaz sent the pulse of warmth she had so desperately longed for through her crown, confirming that it was a true birthstone of Saddoriel, but something wasn't right.

For the Gauntlet Ruby wasn't whole ...

The piece Yrsa held was only one half.

CHAPTER THIRTEEN

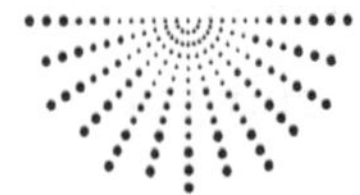

Roh stared at the glimmering half-gem, a cold fury washing over her as she took it from Yrsa. She held it to the light between her bloody forefinger and thumb, marvelling at the precise cut and wondering how they'd halved it so perfectly.

'Do you think the other half is in the wall as well?' Yrsa asked, patting Harlyn on the back and handing her a canteen of water.

Harlyn coughed and spluttered as she tried to drink, her eyes bloodshot.

'No,' Roh said, not taking her eyes off her friend, not certain they were out of the woods yet. 'That would be too simple.'

'They can't do this,' Odi said, hovering near Harlyn.

Roh gave him a pointed look. 'If there's one thing we've learned about the Council of Elders, it's that they can do *whatever* they want.'

Ignoring the knots of tension in her upper body, Roh removed her crown again and fit the half-stone to its inset. Yrsa handed her back the sapphire as well. When all but half a birthstone were in place, Roh shook her head, not in disbelief, but in resignation. She was far past the point of berating herself for not predicting such an outcome. Staring at the crown and the birthstones, she rallied what little strength she had left. She could not let despair win now. There was half a gem to go …

'Roh,' Finn called as he jogged towards them. 'The doorway has sealed. We can't go back the way we came.'

'I'm not surprised,' Roh replied.

Harlyn nudged Roh and pointed across the cavern to where another doorway was tucked almost out of sight.

'They left that way?' Roh asked her.

Harlyn nodded, still unable to speak.

Roh took her arm. 'Let's get out of here.'

She led Harlyn and her companions from the cavern, feeling their eyes on her the whole way. Were they expecting her to break down? To give up when they were so close to having it all? Roh walked with her chin held high. The council had not broken her when they had tormented her mind in Akoris' temple, they had not broken her when she thought Finn had fallen to his death … And they had not broken her when they had stripped her of her deathsong. She would not break now. But anger? Injustice? She would feel every ounce of those in her core, for they demanded to be felt.

'Should we be worried about traps?' Kezra asked as they entered a new passageway.

'No,' Roh replied, her eyes falling upon the markings on the wall, realisation dawning. 'They want me to see this …'

It was a crypt.

Roh heard Deodan's intake of breath as he too realised where they were.

'Elna *did* say the council wanted me to face my ancestry,' Roh murmured, moving further into the crypt, taking in its arched ceiling and antechambers. In each of these antechambers was an elevated casket.

Goosebumps rushed across Roh's skin; the air had turned chilly.

'Gods …' Yrsa peered into one of the antechambers. 'They've …'

Roh was at her side instantly. 'What?'

'They've defaced the graves,' Yrsa said, pointing.

Roh found herself staring at spatters of black and red across the pale stone. She didn't know if it was paint or blood, but there was no denying that the sacred site had been vandalised. There were cracks in the caskets, as though someone had attacked them with axes. Insults had been carved into the walls, and yellowed bones had been littered across the floors.

'Does their hatred know no bounds?' Odi said quietly as he helped Harlyn to a stone bench nearby. She was still wheezing, but the colour had returned to her cheeks.

Roh didn't answer. She didn't have one. Instead, she continued through the crypt, her heart heavy, recognising the same name over and over: *Cadelle*. The deeper into the tomb she went, the more graves there were. It was not only caskets, but headstones and carvings on the wall, all equally defaced by her people. Unease unfurled in her gut. Once, this had been a place where the Lochlorians had farewelled their dead in the human-like tradition Roh had once read about; a grave for each soul lost.

Roh moved forward, taking in the sight of the cracked, moss-covered headstones, weeds sprouting at their bases even down here, their words faded with age. No fear spiked in her chest, and she experienced no creeping sensation that she was being watched. She walked carefully between the markers, slowly noticing the pull of the gems in her crown – they were guiding her … But why? Surely, the council hadn't hidden the second half of the ruby here? With only the ghosts of warlocks long gone to defend it?

The others had stopped exploring the tomb and had gathered at Harlyn's side.

'What are you doing?' Kezra called. 'Isn't it time we left this gods-awful place?'

Seeing that Harlyn was well cared for by Odi, Roh waved Kezra away. She kept her eyes peeled for a gleam of red, deep as blood. The soft dirt sank beneath her boots as she walked the length of the crypt, scanning each and every grave. The gems continued to pull her along, warming her against the chilled air as she placed one foot in front of the other.

How many graves are there? She scanned the rows before her and the caskets in the antechambers. *A hundred? More?*

And then she stopped.

The guidance of the birthstones ended here, amidst a row of headstones all vandalised, covered in muck, spider silk and vines.

Roh dropped to her knees, her heart leaping. If the guidance ended here, it meant … It meant the rest of the ruby was somewhere here. In a frenzy, she swept her hands across the earth and stone, pushing aside all manner of filth, hoping that her hands would brush against the hard surface of the gem.

Damp soaked through the knees of her pants and she clawed at the dirt with her talons, desperation suddenly taking hold.

'Where is it?' she cursed, the note in her voice bordering on hysteria. She tore away the vines and dirt, sending chunks flying across the graves, and sat back on her heels, looking around wildly.

'What is it, Roh?' Finn called.

But he sounded far away. Then, she saw it. Carved into the headstone she sat before was a name …

Eadric.

Roh's breath caught in her throat. It couldn't be …

She reached out and traced the name with her dirt-lined talons, her gaze dipping to the rest of the inscription.

In memory of Eadric Cadelle.

A fearless leader. A fierce friend. A free man.

Someone had tried to scratch out the words, but there was no hiding what they said.

'But … that's not possible,' Roh whispered, her fingers still lingering on the inscription. The birthstones of Saddoriel told her otherwise, sending a beat of warmth through her again. Sincerity, truth, and a touch of clarity from the half-ruby … it was all here. The gems hadn't been leading her to the Gauntlet Ruby … They had brought her to her father and his family, the *Cadelles*. Her father had come from a long line of water warlocks, it seemed.

'His body is back in the lair,' Roh murmured weakly.

Another pulse of warmth. Another truth.

The dirt shifted as Finn knelt beside her, reaching for her hand. Roh leaned into him, resting her head on his shoulder, still staring at her father's memorial.

'For so long I have wanted to know my origins, I have wanted a history … And now that it may be within reach, I feel myself straining and folding, under the weight of all I cannot and will not be …'

'That's what they want,' Finn replied. 'Don't let them win.'

Gazing upon her father's would-be grave, the vision the Csillan mirror pool had shown her swam before her: a future self with wings. But beyond the newfound inkling of magic she felt within this territory, her father's homeland, she had known no true power: there had been no sign of these so-called wings of hers coming into being and she was no closer to mastering warlock magic.

'I would know, wouldn't I?' she asked Finn. 'If I was a descendant of the goddesses … I would know.'

Finn said nothing, but continued to hold her hand.

Deep down, Roh knew that without her deathsong, there was nothing special about her, nothing noteworthy. She pondered that thought for a moment, realising with a start that she had no idea of how much time had passed down in the tomb and that they still had the second half of the ruby to find. While she appreciated the gesture from the topaz and the sapphire to visit Eadric's memorial, it brought her no closer to the ruby, and unlike in her mother's old chambers, she felt no presence here, no echo of who her father might have been or the words he might have spoken once.

Roh felt another hand on her shoulder. Harlyn stood behind her.

'How's your voice?' Roh asked, getting to her feet.

Her friend winced as she touched her throat.

Fresh rage coursed through Roh and she hugged Harlyn to her. 'I'm so sorry.'

But Harlyn shook her head. She didn't want apologies.

Roh understood that; she knew that feeling better than most. But it made it no easier to quell the fury. What if Harlyn never got her voice back? What if she too became a songless cyren? Roh looked from her friend to the vandalised graves of her ancestors and felt her rage deepen and surge.

'Let's leave.' She was already moving towards the far end of the tomb.

The journey back up to the forest was a blur, and by the time Roh was climbing the steep, narrow steps to the surface, she was shaking with fury. The months of torment and danger and pain at the hands of the council flashed before her, the near losses of both Finn and Harlyn sharp in her chest. She had been told to surrender again and again – for a moment she saw Odi and Deodan in the flamed circle of sacrifice, their faces tight with horror. Each step fuelled Roh's wrath. It gathered momentum within her like a terror tempest through the Csillan gorges. She could think of nothing but the wrongs that had been done to her and her companions. With every leg of their quest, the council had spat in Roh's face, all the while feeding generations of Saddoriens lies about the bloody history cyrenkind had left in its wake.

Roh's anger burned and burned. It wasn't until the dappled light of the afternoon sun hit her face that she realised they had broken the surface of the tombs. Waiting for them was Elna, her arms folded over her armoured chest, her expression self-righteous. Roh could contain her fury no longer. She launched herself at the keeper of Lochloria, shoving her up against a nearby tree, her fingers closing around Elna's throat.

Roh had never strangled someone before, but the first thing that struck her was how *easy* it was, how effortless wrapping her hands around the column of Elna's neck was, how natural it felt to *squeeze* the life from an enemy.

Elna's eyes bulged and her hands flew to Roh's, her talons unsheathed, clawing at Roh's death grip. Blood trickled from the backs of Roh's hands, but she did not let go. She held firm, squeezing harder, feeling Elna's windpipe strain beneath her grasp.

'I told you I'd set my sea drake upon you,' she whispered in the cyren's ear as she choked her. 'But I decided *I* want to be the one to end you. I want to see the life fade from your eyes.'

Roh couldn't feel the slices to her own hands and arms, nor the warm trickle of blood on her face as Elna desperately tried to claw at her.

'Roh!' a foreign voice rasped, their hands pulling at her, trying to drag her away from Elna. 'Roh, stop this.'

It was *Harlyn,* her eyes watering at the pain of speaking. 'This isn't you,' she croaked. 'This is not the sort of queen you want to be.' She took a ragged breath. 'You don't want to be feared by your people. You don't want to be a murderer. That's not you. You're not Cerys.'

Roh's grip faltered.

Elna snatched the opportunity, batting Roh's hands away and

lunging out of her grasp, falling to all fours in the dirt and gasping for air.

Roh looked at her hands to find them shaking, red with her own blood. 'I …' But words failed her. What she'd done … A madness had taken hold of her.

A scaled snout nuzzled her shoulder, followed by a low growl.

Valli.

She turned to face her sea drake, pressing her face to his and closing her eyes against the guilt that now festered within. What would the others think of her? After everything they had been through together, they had witnessed her undoing in the most poisonous way.

'Well …' Elna's raw voice sounded.

Startled, Roh twisted to look at her, noting the ring of red around her throat and the bloodshot colour of her eyes.

Elna coughed. 'I can't say I wouldn't have done the same,' she managed, massaging where Roh's hands had nearly squeezed the life out of her. She looked at Roh as though she was seeing her for the first time.

Roh stared back at her. 'The ruby was not whole.'

'No. It wasn't. There is a second part to the test.'

Roh didn't have the energy to express her outrage. She had already guessed as much and she was still struggling to still her trembling hands, even as she rested them against Valli's warm scales.

'The other half of the ruby lies within the heart of a backahast foal,' Elna told her.

'What?' Odi's voice sounded behind Roh.

Leaves crunched beneath boots as her companions gathered around her, gaping at the keeper of Lochloria in disbelief.

'What do you mean?' Odi pressed.

'I mean there is a local herd here, human. And that the council saw fit to place the final part of the ruby within one of the foals.'

'Backahast are notoriously protective of their young,' Deodan explained, his expression grim.

'Precisely,' Elna allowed. 'Soldiers have riled up the herd, sending them stampeding down the valley. At their current pace, they should be upon us shortly.'

Finn swore.

'Had you not dawdled in the tomb, you would have had more time,' Elna said sharply.

Heart sinking, Roh waited.

'You will need to separate the foal from the herd, or risk certain death at their wrath. While a cyren can manipulate water and breathe in it, an angry herd of backahast can drown even the strongest of our kind.' She pulled out a weathered map and laid it upon the forest floor, pointing. 'Here is where we are now. The backahast are moving down this valley and then journey south ... There is a small window ...'

Roh's mind began to churn, and at last she summoned the courage to look at her friends. 'One last challenge?' she asked, fearing what she'd find in their eyes.

But she was greeted with nothing but understanding, and determination.

'Harlyn needs to sit this one out,' Odi declared.

'Agreed,' Roh said instantly. 'As do you.'

She expected her human friend to argue, but he simply nodded. 'I'll stay with her.'

'Good,' Roh said, crouching to study the map.

Finn, Yrsa, Deodan and Kezra did the same, gathering around her.

'Can we use Valli?' Deodan asked. 'Perhaps he could block off part of the pass? There?' He pointed to a section on the map. 'We could then force them towards the mirror pool.'

'You realise they're not cattle, don't you?' Kezra snapped. 'We can't just run at them and expect them to move.'

'We can if we have fire,' Roh interjected. 'We'll each carry torches from the tomb, and round them up that way. Backahast hate fire.'

'And how do you propose to isolate the foal?'

'As a pack of wolves would separate the weakling from the herd,' Finn replied. 'We split up, each of us manipulating the direction of the stampede.'

'Exactly,' replied Yrsa. 'But we're running out of time. We need to get in position if we have any chance of making this work.' She ran her hands over the map. 'Valli can block this path here.' She pointed. 'Then, we use the terrain to our advantage. I've seen these creatures move before – we can do this. See this narrow fissure here? Finn, you'll be stationed there. Use oil and from one of the torches draw a line, and as soon as you see the foal pass into the gorge, set the oil ablaze, cutting off the rest of the herd behind it.' Yrsa's brow creased in concentration and she turned to the Csillan Arch General. 'Kezra, you and I will be stationed at this fork in the valley. We separate the herd again there, forcing the portion surrounding the foal south, where Deodan and Roh will be waiting.'

'Got it,' Kezra replied.

Yrsa forged on, her jaw set with determination. 'Deodan, Roh. You'll be stationed by the mirror pool. The surrounding forest is dense there and it'll be your best chance of isolating the foal from what's left of the herd. Take this ridge here to get to your position. It'll be the fastest way to get ahead. From this vantage point, you should be able to see what's happening below.' Yrsa jabbed a finger at the map again. 'Taking the ruby is up to you.'

There was no more time for questions. Yrsa snatched up the parchment and got to her feet.

Roh followed suit and went to the entrance of the tomb, taking several torches from the walls and handing them to her companions. The events of the day faded into the back of her mind as she tried to prepare herself for the final task – the last piece of the unending puzzle to holding the cyren throne.

'If we manage to isolate the foal, how do you mean to get the ruby?' Deodan asked her as they started towards the valley.

'I plan to take it,' Roh told him simply, recalling how a lifetime ago, a backahast had wrapped itself around her in the first trial of the Queen's Tournament. And with that, she looked up at Valli. 'We're going to need your help this time, my friend.'

'Everyone to their positions. Now!' Yrsa called, breaking into a run.

Roh did the same. Her boots pounded the earth as she sprinted through the forest, following Yrsa's lead to where the valley opened up at the foot of the mountain. Branches and trees crashed alongside her as Valli tore through the undergrowth; the sea drake seemed to revel in his inclusion at last.

Roh turned to him. 'You stay here,' she said breathlessly. 'Block the pass into the forest. They'll be forced to go around you.'

Valli seemed to understand and stood rigid in position.

Without a moment's pause, Roh and Deodan split up from the others, everyone sprinting to where Yrsa had instructed.

'Hurry!' Deodan shouted as the pair approached the ridge. 'I can see them.'

Wind whipped Roh's face as she pushed herself even harder, silently praying that the torches they carried would not extinguish. Her legs burned as the incline began, but Yrsa was right – it was a decent vantage point. She could see clouds of dust billow up into the air above the tree line. The backahast were exactly where Elna said they would be and the noise was thunderous.

Roh got her first glimpse of the herd: beautiful water horses, their transparent bodies muscular and powerful, their numbers in the hundreds as they pelted down the valley.

Finn's words rang in her ears. *As a pack of wolves would separate the weakling from the herd.*

Roh and Deodan ran.

Valli's roar shook the mountains. Roh chanced a look over her shoulder to see the backahast scrambling to avoid the sea drake, shrieking in terror as they were driven to follow the base of the mountain range rather than careen towards the scholar's city.

'Hurry!' Roh shouted to Deodan over the thunder of hooves that echoed up the ridge. The plan was *working*. Which meant they had to get into position and *fast*.

Her lungs burning, Roh scanned the hundreds of backahast for the foal as the herd bottlenecked into the fissure Yrsa had described. They moved as fluidly as a river and were packed densely together. Roh knew her target would be right at the heart —

A flash of orange blazed across the fissure and suddenly thick smoke billowed up into the air.

'Yes!' Deodan shouted beside her as they sprinted along the ridge.

Finn had cut off hundreds of backahast in the narrow fissure. The herd was now two thirds of its original size.

A smile tugged at Roh's lips, but she pushed on; it was far from over. From above she could see where the narrow fissure forked, where Yrsa and Kezra would be waiting.

'We're not in position yet!' she called out to Deodan. 'We need to hurry, so when Yrsa —'

'I know!' Deodan grunted.

And so they ran, the ridge at last starting its descent towards the forest and mirror pool below.

Roh tried to recall the map and pinpoint their place, but everything was moving so fast.

'We're nearly there,' Deodan yelled.

As they descended, the sound of the stampede grew louder. From the corner of her eye, Roh saw orange flames and knew that at the forked path, Kezra and Yrsa were corralling segments of the herd elsewhere.

Suddenly, Roh and Deodan were at the foot of the ridge, the forest and mirror pool in sight, as was the opening of the gorge where the backahast would soon emerge. They were in position and Roh's heart was in her throat.

The ground vibrated beneath them as the last third of the herd burst forth from the fissure.

'Gods,' Deodan murmured, his eyes wide. Although the herd was much smaller now, it was still a force to be reckoned with.

Roh braced herself. 'Here they come …' She had lost one of her torches in the chaos, but held onto the other tightly as she tried to see through the bodies of water charging right for her, for the foal.

Suddenly, she spotted dozens of Deodan's water birds flitting between the horses. Deodan whistled and the sparrows dipped in and out of sight at his command. 'The foal's in there somewhere, the herd is —'

Icy air whipped Roh's face as the herd wrapped around them.

'Over there!' Roh shouted, pointing to where several of the water birds circled, snatching her attention to the far left.

Roh saw it then, the ruby hovering in the heart of the small water horse. It gleamed from within, beckoning to her, as the other gems before it had.

Without another thought, she ran towards it, with no care for her own safety or the chaos surrounding her. Backahast charged for her, but she cut through them as though she was made of water herself. She didn't question how.

She was so close she could taste it. The ruby gleamed at the foal's heart, and Roh was suddenly just an arm's width away.

A high-pitched shriek sounded, turning her blood to ice and Roh was knocked from her feet, hitting the ground hard. Winded, she scrambled, desperate to thrust her hands through the foal's watery body and wrap her hands around the Gauntlet Ruby —

She was violently knocked again, and this time she was sent sprawling in the opposite direction of the foal. She cried out as the ruby slipped away from her. How could she ever have thought she would emerge victorious? How could she ever have imagined a world where –

Suddenly, Roh was wrenched from the ground, someone grabbing a fistful of her cloak and shirt, hauling her up onto … A backahast.

Deodan sat behind her, grasping the watery lengths of the beast's mane with one hand, and trapping Roh between his body and the backahast's neck.

'How are you doing this?' Roh bellowed.

'They're made of water,' Deodan shouted back. 'Can't you feel their magic?'

Roh hadn't tried to, she'd been too caught up in the stampede, in the race for the gem. But as the words left Deodan's mouth, she felt a flicker of something within.

'Have you seen the foal yet?' Deodan yelled.

'Yes!' Keeping her shock at bay, Roh pointed at the smaller backahast, the one that had been surrounded by a dozen or more mares.

'Can you get us over there?' she called back to Deodan, pointing to where the violet haze of the mirror pool had come into view.

Deodan didn't bother replying, but directed their backahast with a tug of its watery mane and the squeeze of his heels. They forced their way through the galloping herd, towards where his birds fluttered once more.

'They're splitting again!' Deodan called, confused. 'Why?'

Roh didn't care, they were so close. They veered sharply and she brandished her torch, trying to corral the mares away from the foal.

'You'll need to ride solo!' Deodan barked.

Before Roh could answer, the warrior warlock had leaped from the backahast's back, into the fray of mares, waving his own torch and cutlass, feeding their panic.

It's working, she realised, as the foal at last broke away from the group, racing around the edge of the mirror pool. Roh clung to her own backahast for dear life, trying to direct it as she would a regular horse, towards the foal.

As a pack of wolves would separate the weakling from the herd.

The pandemonium of the final stampede faded around Roh as she closed in on the small water horse. Not taking her eyes off the ruby that glinted inside it, she leaned against her backahast's neck, forcing it forward, water spraying into her face as she did. She almost had it. The gems in her crown pulsed in anticipation, so close to being united as they had been once.

The violet haze of the frozen mirror pool called out to her and Roh's heart suddenly shot to her throat.

The backahast that had parted from their young at Deodan's urging were now on the opposite side of the frozen water, watching her with a white-hot fury as she closed in on their now isolated foal.

What are they doing? she wondered as she pushed on, her attention snatched from the ruby and its bearer just out of reach.

Voices. She could hear voices.

Carried along with the icy air and the gentle notes of the wind chimes, was the sound of two nestlings. Where, out on the frozen mirror pool, Nym and Maiella were crouched at the centre, playing on the ice.

As Roh's gaze fell upon them, the foal veered away from her, and in horror, she realised just how intelligent the backahast were. For the herd now stood at the edge, pawing the ice with their hooves, water magic rolling off them in waves to form a crack in the supposedly unbreakable ice.

'No!' Roh screamed. She looked from the innocent nestlings

playing on the now deadly mirror pool, to the ruby held in the heart of the backahast foal.

She could only choose one.

Her muscles went rigid as everything she'd done to reach this point flashed before her eyes. The deadly tournament trials in Saddoriel, the Rite of Strothos and its horrors, all that had occurred on the Bridge of Csilla and everything since then … She had always believed she would do whatever it took, no matter the cost, to succeed, to see herself upon the cyren throne.

But in that moment, Rohesia of the Bone Cleaners at last discovered the line she would not cross.

With a broken sob, she abandoned the foal and the ruby and flung herself from the backahast towards the ice. She clapped her hand across her mouth as she stumbled to the pool's edge – she couldn't alarm the nestlings. Any sudden movements might cause the ice to crack even more beneath the backahast's strength and spell, and Roh knew deep in her bones that the little ones would not survive the fall into the freezing depths.

Where is Deodan?

There was no knowing how much weight the ice could take, or how long it would hold … But she couldn't leave them at the mercy of the enraged backahast and the splintering surface. Crouching, she inched out onto the pool.

A low groan sounded from the ice and Roh stopped in her tracks.

Nym gave a delighted squeal and pointed to something on the other side of the mirror pool. Upon seeing whatever her sister was showing her, Maiella clapped her hands together, laughing. It was the escaped foal, whinnying softly to its kin.

Panic spiked hard and fast in Roh's chest. Movements of any sort on the ice were *bad*. She winced as Maiella clapped again, the sound echoing between the mountains that loomed above.

Additional pressure on the ice could send a giant fracture through the whole pool, sending the nestlings to their deaths.

'Rid yourself of your inner voice – the one that drags you from thought to thought ...' Deodan's voice filled Roh's head. *'Start by focusing on the small sensations ...'* Roh took a trembling breath. Could she call on her warlock heritage to help save the nestlings? Watching them was like watching the final grains fall in an hourglass. Inevitable. She had to do something.

'Listen for water. Send your senses outwards.'

Roh closed her eyes, welcoming the darkness over the heart-stopping sight of the children at risk. She repeated Deodan's words to herself, focusing on the frost creaking beneath her boots and the faint whisper of wind between the mountains. She had to hear the water, had to gather it as she'd seen Deodan do so many times before.

'Draw from its power ... Draw it together ... Try to shape it into what you need it to be.'

Roh felt her entire body strain with the effort of trying to harness a magic she did not understand. But she heard no quiet call, not a breath of magic in the breeze.

More exclamations from the nestlings carried across to her, but this time, they were full of terror. Roh's eyes flew open and she felt the ground beneath her feet rumble. Leaves from the weeping willows above fell to the ice as the earth quaked.

The herd of backahast started to charge across the ice towards their foal.

There was no way for Roh to quieten her mind now. There was no magic within her grasp. The ruby and the cyren throne were lost to her, and now she could only —

The near-deafening sound of the ice cracking echoed through the trees and the nestlings stood, dazed at the sight of the horde surging towards them.

Then, Maiella and Nym began to scream.

Roh didn't think; she was already on the ice, her boots slipping across its perilous surface. She was mad, she *had to be mad,* to be putting herself in the path of an enraged herd of backahast over a sheet of ice. But the nestlings' screams were in her ears and she couldn't get to them fast enough as they tried to run, but slipped over and over.

A shriek of horror tore from Roh as the ice split, shelves of it loosening and tipping.

The charging herd didn't matter as soon as the surface cracked and folded. Roh threw herself towards the nestlings, desperate to close the gap between them. She reached Maiella first, wrenching her into her arms and thrusting her up towards one of the weeping willow branches.

'Grab hold!' she yelled, her battered body straining as she reached up, praying that Maiella got a good grip. 'Hurry!' she cried, feeling the precarious shelf of ice groan beneath her. She felt the nestling find purchase and pull herself up towards the branch. That was all Roh needed. She lunged for Nym, sudden movements be damned.

'Hang on,' Roh shouted, hoisting and shoving the child towards her sister, who was holding out a hand. They grabbed hold of one another and Roh gave one final push to make sure Nym reached the safety of the willow branch.

The herd was charging. And the ice gave way with an almighty crack.

Roh let out a strangled cry, grasping for anything to hold onto, but there was nothing other than crisp air and the swirl of backahast around her.

For a moment, time slowed and all Roh could see was the violet hue of the ice, so beautiful and deadly. She took one last ragged breath, trying to fill her lungs as much as she could, but it was too late.

Roh went under.

CHAPTER FOURTEEN

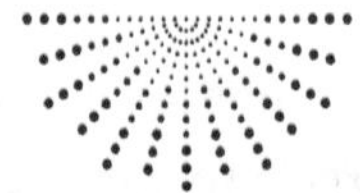

The cold was a thousand blades to her skin. It sliced through her flesh, a thousand cuts, a thousand sharp punctures, unlike any pain she had ever experienced before. It was everywhere, on every inch of her. She didn't know if she was screaming out loud; the rest of the world was so silent it hurt. Around her, the water was foreign, not of the river and not of the seas, something else entirely, tightening its agonising hold on her.

If this is death, let it be over soon, she thought distantly. She had always known her quest for the cyren crown could lead her here, but that knowledge was of little comfort. She just wished it wouldn't hurt so much.

Suddenly, violet ice gave way to a place that Roh was far more familiar with: the bone cells of Saddoriel's Prison. Only this time it was different. There were no dead water warlocks stationed outside her mother's cell and the passageways were lit with numerous torches. It was not the prison as she knew it, this was *before* ... Before she was born, she understood, though how long before she couldn't tell. The corridors and cells looked to be frequented regularly, and yet … Her mother was there, as she always was, behind those gleaming bars of bone.

The pain had stopped and Roh knew instantly that her mother could not see her. That she did not currently have a bodily form. She was simply here to witness what had been once. She peered inside the cell, drinking in the sight of her mother, whose hair was waist-length and whose talons were intact for once, despite the carvings of wings etched into the walls. There was something else about Cerys that unnerved Roh … a brightness and alertness to her green-flecked lilac gaze that she had never seen before.

'Eadric,' Cerys breathed his name as though it was an answer to a prayer.

Roh started, her heart immediately in her throat as she stepped back and surveyed the passageway. There he was: her father. In the flesh, he was a far cry from the half-snarling warrior she'd seen so many times before, frozen in the rage he'd felt upon his death. Here, he was warmer, softer – handsome, in a rugged sort of way.

'Cerys,' he said, rushing towards the bars, reaching through them, desperate to touch his wife.

Cerys threw herself at the bars, leaning into his touch, closing her eyes as she savoured the feel of his skin. 'You came.'

'I told you I would,' he replied.

Roh watched on in disbelief as his hand brushed over the curve of Cerys' swollen belly, a detail she hadn't noticed before beneath the loose shift.

'I would never leave you and our daughter.' His voice was quiet but strong, laced with determination.

'You can't know it's a girl,' Cerys told him, placing her hand over his, following his gaze to her stomach, a normal moment shared between husband and wife, not two outlaws.

'I can and I do.'

Cyren and warlock locked eyes then, studying each other, as though memorising each other's faces.

'I'm going to get you out of her, Cerys,' Eadric said, drawing her as close to him as the cell bars would allow. 'I will not rest until you are free of this place, free of Deelie.'

'I know you won't ...'

Eadric seemed to gather himself, glancing around, scanning for anyone who might be listening in.

Roh's heart skipped a beat as her father's warm brown eyes skimmed through her.

I'm here, she wanted to scream. *I'm right here.* But she knew it was no use. Her father was long dead and this was but an echo of the past, a memory that Lochloria was gifting her before she died.

'I found out something about the mirror pools, after all this time,' Eadric told Cerys, his voice low and his body tense. 'I don't have time to explain the whole history, but —'

'I trust you,' Cerys interjected.

Eadric forged on. 'There's an enchantment I can teach you, one that you can sing to our nestling, while she grows within you, when you first nurse her.'

'You will be there for that, Eadric.' Cerys' voice was full of warning.

Eadric smiled sadly. 'I hope that I am.'

'I will not hear you say otherwise. We do this together, as we have done everything that came before.'

Roh's father nodded solemnly, pausing as though there was something else he wished to say. He seemed to think better of it, inhaling deeply through his nose. 'The enchantment will stop her from crying,' he continued. 'It will stop her from shedding tears that can be sacrificed in the First Cry.'

'And what will that do?'

Eadric cupped Cerys' face in his and he stared intensely into her eyes. 'It will free our child from the grip Deelie has on the rest of cyrenkind. It will allow her to reach her full potential, without interference from the queen. And when the time is right … it will ensure that she is strong enough to face Delja, and be victorious.'

Cerys loosed a shaky breath. 'All that from one little enchantment?'

'More,' Eadric said, still cupping her face, pressing his forehead against hers through the bars of bone. 'It will give her wings, Cerys. *Wings.*'

The vision started to spiral before Roh and she thrust out her hands, as though she could physically anchor herself in the past, as though she could hold onto the memory of her parents with both hands. She wasn't done with them, she hadn't seen enough of her father, of her mother when she was … like that. From that brief glimpse, she knew that they had made a formidable pair, and seeing them together, it had –

Roh knew she wasn't meant to be here. The tension in the air was thick enough to cut with a knife and the small group of warlocks gathered before her all gripped their weapons too tightly. Roh didn't know exactly where *here* was … in some sort of secret alcove, by the looks of things, but her instincts were screaming that this was *wrong*, that something bad was about to happen.

Her father, Eadric, was at the head of the group, his jaw clenched and his body tense beneath his frayed travelling cloak. He assessed his companions critically, as though trying to weed out any final weak link in his armour.

'You're all ready?' he asked, his voice gravelly. 'The guards have been taken care of?'

'Yes, sir,' said the woman to his right, whose scythe was poised for violence.

Roh tried to swallow the lump in her throat. She recognised that weapon, that woman … She'd seen her many times, preserved in all her rage outside Cerys' cell … She had seen some of the others, too; their blue-tinged faces in the shadows of Saddoriel's Prison were hard to forget.

Roh stiffened as her father drew his quartz dagger from his belt, the very same dagger he had clutched in his dead hands for eighteen years, the very same that she'd worn at her thigh since Akoris.

'You all know the risks,' Eadric was saying, his hard gaze scanning the faces of his companions.

'But we also know what's at stake,' the woman said. 'We need to get Cerys out of there. We will not see your daughter born in a cyren prison cell, sir.'

Eadric nodded. 'She's not just my daughter … She's a chance for us to come back from what we lost in Lochloria, to be something *more*. She will be the one to root out the poison that has spread across cyrenkind. She will be our salvation.'

The woman raised her scythe in salute. 'We wait with all the hope in our hearts for that day to come.'

Murmurs of agreement sounded all around them.

'You're quiet, Midrah,' Eadric noted, his sharp eyes honing in on a warlock who'd lingered at the back of the group, keeping his head down.

The man lifted his chin, his gaze meeting his leader's. 'Are you sure?'

'Sure?' The word sliced through the air like a blade.

'Are you sure this nestling is all that you say? Your wife … She is the Elder Slayer, after all.'

One moment Eadric was three feet away, the next his hands were around the warlock's throat, shoving him up against the jagged wall of the alcove. The man choked and sputtered, his hands clawing at the giant fingers closed around his windpipe.

Alarmingly, Roh was reminded of how she'd done the same to

Elna not all that long ago, her hands still bearing the bloody marks from the Lochlorian keeper's talons.

'You dare doubt Cerys?' Eadric's voice was low, full of malice. 'You dare doubt *me*? On the precipice of her rescue mission no less?'

Roh's gut churned as she watched. *Rescue mission?* They were going to *rescue* Cerys?

Midrah rasped for air, his eyes wide. 'We ...' he wheezed. 'We place our lives in your —'

Eadric threw him to the ground. Midrah landed on all fours, dry-retching into the dirt and gasping for air.

'You had ample opportunity to voice your concerns when the stakes weren't this high. There is no room in this mission for doubters. You remain behind,' Eadric said coldly. 'The rest of you, with me.'

They were on the move. Roh followed closely behind, dread burning a hole in the pit of her stomach as her father led them through a network of hidden passageways in the depths of Saddoriel. Two of his companions held torches that illuminated the paths, but apart from those flickering flames, darkness engulfed them. With their weapons at the ready, they moved at a run in a single file, which was the only formation the narrow passages would allow.

Where are the guards? Roh thought, the emptiness of the rocky corridors nagging at her. Her father had mentioned them being taken care of, but she knew from experience how heavily guarded this place was ... But perhaps long ago the surveillance of Saddoriel hadn't been as strict?

It wasn't long before Eadric turned onto a path that Roh knew intimately. It was the one she had often taken to visit her mother in secret, the passageway where she'd learned to play the card game Thieves with the solo guard, Bryah. Where was Bryah now? If Cerys was currently pregnant with Roh, it meant that this slice of history was a little over eighteen years ago … Bryah had still been a guard then, Roh was sure of it.

Up ahead, Eadric signalled for the group to stop.

They halted immediately; their small unit was a well-oiled machine, with each of them utterly in tune with one another. Anticipation thrummed between them all, poised to attack, but nothing happened. Eadric waited a second longer before motioning for them to continue.

Roh recognised the unofficial entrance to Saddoriel's Prison instantly, her heart pounding in her throat. She had the sinking feeling that she knew what was about to happen here, but she had no choice other than to follow, an invisible ghost bearing witness to all that had unfolded in the past.

They entered the prison without incident. Eadric navigated the rows of cells as though he had done so a hundred times before. Roh realised with a start that he must have, for hadn't she been *conceived* in the prison? Eadric had been visiting Cerys *for centuries*. Why had it taken him this long to attempt a rescue? Roh stopped herself. She knew *nothing* of her parents and what they'd been through. Eadric very well could have been trying to help Cerys from the moment of her capture, for all she knew.

There was a strangled gasp as they rounded a corner and Roh's eyes fell upon her mother, standing at the bars of bone, fear dripping from her entire being.

'You're here.' Her gaze found Eadric instantly.

'I'm here,' he said, reaching through the bars and gripping her hand, as though physical touch would anchor them, would prove that their reality was true.

A flurry of movement burst around Roh as her father's companions sprang into action. The woman with the scythe produced several vials of water, similar to those Deodan carried, and set about pouring them into her hands. She and Eadric whispered enchantments to the liquid, which soon took the form of a dozen little insects. They set the creatures on the numerous locks of Cerys' cell.

Cerys was taking deep breaths, a hand resting on the swollen curve of her stomach, her eyes darting around the passageway before her. Roh could practically smell the fear pouring out of her.

Eadric reached for her again. 'It will be alright,' he told her, his grip strong.

'I ...' Cerys croaked, watching the insects eat away at the locks. 'I have a bad feeling about this, Eadric.'

'We're going to get you and Rohesia out of here.'

Roh's name on her father's lips was like a blade to the heart, especially as she saw his gaze dip to Cerys' belly, his hardened expression softening. He had loved her. He had loved her from the very beginning.

A loud crack sounded.

Roh stifled a cry as the locks fell away from the bars of Cerys' cell.

Cerys burst through the door, throwing her arms around Eadric and kissing him hard, the iron shackles around her ankles rattling.

'Sir?' the warlock with the scythe warned.

The pair broke apart reluctantly.

'Let's get you out of here,' Eadric whispered into Cerys' hair.

Cerys nodded, straightening. Despite the round stomach, she was thin and unsteady on her chained feet. 'I've been training,' she said quietly. 'But my strength isn't —'

Eadric waved her away. 'You can do this. We'll get you out of those irons as soon as we can.'

Cerys' eyes widened, a realisation hitting her like a blow. 'My song ...' she managed. 'My song is still silent. I thought once I was free of the cell ...'

'They put it in your food,' Eadric told her, motioning to his unit. 'Something to suppress your power. Once we're out of here, it will come back.'

'Sir, we have to go.' The warlock's words were urgent.

One of the warriors handed Cerys a cloak, which she fumbled with, drawing it closed over her filthy shift.

'Did you bring my sword?' she asked.

Eadric motioned to one of his companions, who came forward, holding out a scabbard.

Something in Cerys' face changed as her hand reached out, her fingers curling around the grip and drawing the weapon from its sheath. She stared at the blade for a moment as though she'd forgotten what a sword looked like, but suddenly, she looked stronger. The green flecks in her eyes seemed to brighten and her expression hardened to match her husband's.

'Now I feel like myself,' she said.

Pride shone in Eadric's gaze. 'Move out,' he barked, pulling Cerys to his side.

They exited the way they had come, through the hidden passageways of Saddoriel, still no guards in sight. Their torches only illuminated a few feet before them, but they ploughed into the relative darkness with complete confidence.

Roh followed them, in awe of the cyren and warlock who seemed to move as one, anticipating the other's move without half a thought, despite centuries apart. Cerys didn't let the shackles around her ankles slow her pace.

Deeper and deeper into Saddoriel they wove. Roh's inner compass was quiet as she hurried after her parents, but then … she wasn't truly here, was she?

'You came via the pool?' Cerys asked quietly.

Eadric nodded, eyeing the tunnel up ahead. 'Just as we planned. It won't be long now and you'll breathe the mountain air of Lochloria once more.'

Without warning, the terrain beneath Roh's boots changed and she knew where they were going. Grit and gravel no longer crunched beneath her. Instead, the ground was soft and spongy. Roh squinted in the poor light and saw that moss carpeted the path, a vibrant green, the colour of her eyes.

The unit came to an abrupt stop before a solid wall.

Odd, Roh thought. *I don't remember that being here ...*

Eadric was running a hand across the stone, feeling for something. He murmured foreign words before sliding his quartz dagger to some invisible lock.

Roh suppressed a gasp. She had seen Deodan do the same thing in Akoris.

A quiet hiss sounded and the wall opened up.

Dazed, Roh followed her father and mother through the temporary archway, where an immense cavern lay beyond ...

The Pool of Weeping.

'Come on,' Eadric urged the others.

The vast body of water greeted them, surrounded by weeping willows on the banks, their leaves like curtains, hiding a good portion of the pool from view. The trees and the surrounding jagged rocks were reflected on the water's surface, as flat as a pane of dark, polished glass.

Eadric and Cerys reached the edge of the pool —

'Did you not think it was too easy, Eadric?' a melodic voice sounded.

Roh knew that voice. She'd know it anywhere. Just as her parents did, Roh whirled around.

Queen Delja stood on the stony shore, her great wings outstretched, her beautiful face calm.

'Deelie,' Eadric breathed, drawing Cerys closer to him.

'*Don't* call me that,' Delja snapped, her mask of serenity slipping fast.

'Deelie, enough of this,' Cerys said. 'Let us go, you are still queen. We want nothing but —'

'I said, *don't call me that.*'

The unit of warlocks froze at the water's edge, looking to their leader for orders. But Eadric's gaze didn't leave the queen, didn't miss the three dozen cyren warriors creeping forth from the shadows behind her.

Run! Roh wanted to scream, but she was rooted to the spot.

Delja considered the couple, her expression taut with anger. 'You thought you could just waltz in here and take her? That I'd let you?'

'You've had me for centuries,' Cerys said, her voice hard. 'I have taken your punishment —'

'Your punishment is *five millennia,* Cerys. You're not even close to done. You're not going anywhere. And now, nor is Eadric.'

The Saddorien soldiers stood behind their queen now, poised for attack. Roh could hardly breathe. Her parents and the warlocks were outnumbered six to one …

Cerys took a step towards the queen, lifting her sword. However weak her spirit may have become in the prison, something stronger overcame it now: rage.

'You bitch,' Cerys spat. 'My family gave you *everything.* And this is what you become? This is how you repay centuries of friendship? Of sisterhood?'

'But that's just it, isn't it?' Delja said smoothly. 'You believe I *owe* you. That's not family. That's not friendship.'

'I *never* felt that way,' Cerys snapped. 'Not until you did what you —'

'*Seize them!*' Delja ordered sharply, pointing a trembling finger at Roh's parents.

The scraping of blades being unsheathed echoed across the water.

'You'll never take me.' Eadric twirled his dagger between his fingers.

Delja eyed him coolly, tucking her wings behind her back. 'As you wish,' she said. 'Take the Elder Slayer back to her cell. See that no harm comes to her. Kill the rest.'

A silent scream formed on Roh's lips as the Saddorien Army surged forwards, stones crunching like bone underfoot. The first ear-splitting strike of steel rang out over the glassy pool as Cerys swung her sword at her attacker. Their swords clashed in a blur of silver. Roh didn't know where to look. At her mother who blocked and parried, despite the thick irons around her ankles and the perils of the uneven ground; or at her father, who fought three soldiers at once, wielding a broadsword and his dagger, a dancer of death, slicing and kicking his opponents into one another.

Shouts punctuated the ring of clashing weapons. Two of the warlocks had already gone down, one peppered with crossbow bolts, the other with a dagger sticking out of their neck. Roh's attention snagged on movement by the entrance – Midrah, the warlock who'd questioned her father, lingered in the shadows, impassive.

Eadric and two of his companions were still upright, with Cerys fighting her way towards them, bleeding from a gash in her arm.

'Get to the water!' she yelled, cutting down another soldier. 'We can still —'

As the soldier fell, he grabbed the link between her irons, causing her to stumble and fall hard on her front, on her pregnant belly.

'Cerys!' Eadric screamed, the sound razor-sharp with panic. He severed a cyren's hand as he cut his way through the unit to get to his wife.

All the while, Delja watched on, her hands clasped together before her, her expression impassive.

'Get to the water,' Cerys ground out as Eadric pulled her to her feet.

A piercing scream of pain tore through the cavern, causing a ripple to pulse across the glassy surface of the pool.

The warlock's scythe clattered to the ground as her hands went to the sword protruding from her gut, blood pouring from between her fingers. Her eyes met Eadric's from across the shore.

'Sir …' she murmured, her voice faltering. 'I'm sorry —'

A crossbow bolt shot through the air and hit her in the chest.

The warlock gasped, looking down in shock at her wounds. 'I'm sorry,' she said again, before dropping to the ground, her eyes wide, even in death.

'No!' Eadric yelled, lurching towards his friend, Cerys at his side.

And still the Saddorien Army advanced.

It was a bloodbath, a senseless slaughter, and Delja surveyed it like a proud queen over her kingdom. Only Cerys and Eadric were left, the blood of warlocks staining the pale shores.

Roh scrambled towards her parents, only to see a soldier hand Delja a trident.

Eadric! Roh screamed silently.

The trident was a blur soaring through the air and time slowed as her father turned, too late, his mouth open in shock as it pierced his chest. His legs gave out from underneath him, hitting the ground hard, mere fingertips away from the water's edge.

The scream that ripped from Cerys was primal, a gut-wrenching sound that carved through the realms. She went down with him.

'Eadric, no …' she gasped, her hands pressing around the prongs of the trident, trying to staunch the bleeding.

Suddenly Roh was beside them, watching her father's blood leak into the Pool of Weeping, a sacrifice far greater than tears. He reached for Cerys, cupping her face with a bloodstained hand.

'You … You remember the enchantment?' he rasped. 'You remember the words?'

Cerys was sobbing. 'Don't go,' she begged. 'I can't ... I can't do this without you.'

Eadric's hand drifted from her face to her stomach. *'Hush, hush, little cyren, so strong yet so small ...* Tell me, Cerys, tell me the words.'

'Eadric, no. I won't. I won't let you go. You can't –'

'Tell me the words,' he whispered.

Tears tracked down Cerys' face, Eadric's blood blooming beneath her hands. As her husband took his last breath, she nodded and leaned in close.

'For down in deep Saddoriel, we let no tears fall.'

A blinding pain tore through Roh, as though her deathsong was being ripped from her soul all over again. But something snatched at her sleeves, dragging her up, up towards the surface. The thousand blades of ice melted away from her as she moved through the water.

She broke the surface with a ragged gasp and struggled to take the air in as she inched towards the shore. Scanning the pool wildly for whoever had helped her, Roh's feet hit the stony bottom, her sleeves now loose at her sides as she lurched through the water.

The cold ebbed away from her as she staggered from the Lochlorian mirror pool, her blurred vision slowly sharpening.

She couldn't believe what she saw.

Two miniature water sea drakes flapped their wings nearby, spraying her with violet droplets from the now thawed pool.

Their presence told Roh all she needed to know.

Rohesia the Songless had emerged from the icy depths of the mirror pool with water warlock magic at her fingertips.

And it had saved her life.

CHAPTER FIFTEEN

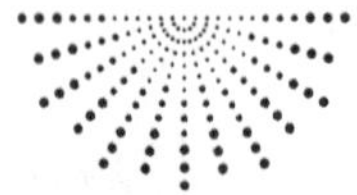

Above the surface, the lavender-and-blush hues of dusk had settled around Lochloria and the air was cold against Roh's wet skin. She barely felt it. What she *did* feel was the powerful current of the warlock magic within her, and the invisible cord between her and the strange miniature water drakes flitting about her shoulders. She watched them, with a surreal sense of wonder. *How?* How had she managed to manifest water warlock magic beneath the agonising ice? Her mind had been anything but quiet and the pain that had lanced through her had been unimaginable.

She had just watched her father die, she had watched Delja kill him ... She wished she could unsee it. She wished she'd never known the sound of her father's voice and the defeat in his final words, knowing he would never meet the daughter he'd fought so hard to free. And now ... Now Roh had failed him. The ruby was lost to her, as was the cyren crown. Despite her father's enchantments, she had no great wings at her back. All she had left in her wake was a trail of destruction and disappointment.

A loud crack sounded behind Roh and she turned to see the

remaining sheets of ice in the mirror pool dislodge from one another, the shelves tipping on their sides and sinking into the pool. The way back to Saddoriel was clear, but Roh no longer needed it.

Her warlock magic drakes vanished with a splash as she stumbled to shore. At the water's edge stood Elna, her daughters clutched to her chest. Roh felt a breath of relief leave her at the sight of them. They were safe. It had not been for nothing.

Beside them, Yrsa, Finn, Deodan, Harlyn, Kezra and Odi stood rigid, their mouths agape as they took in the sight of her. Soaked to the bone, Roh knew she had a haunted look about her, just as she had after the Rite of Strothos. Finn came to her side, wrapping an arm around her waist and supporting her as she limped up the shore.

'Roh …' Harlyn's broken voice sounded. 'What happened down there?'

Roh shook her head. She could not speak of it, not yet. 'Where are the backahast?' she managed, craning her neck to look for the herd.

'Gone,' Finn told her gently. 'They bolted as soon as the mirror pool gave way.'

Gone. The word echoed in Roh's skull. As was the ruby. This had been her final test, the final obstacle between her and the cyren throne. And it was *gone*.

From the corner of her eye, she noticed Finn had a bloody lip, as did Odi, while a bruise bloomed high on Deodan's cheek and Harlyn's knuckles were grazed.

'There were some disagreements as to whether or not we should retrieve you from the ice,' Harlyn explained with a cold look at Deodan and Kezra as she wrapped a cloak around Roh's shoulders.

Roh waited, glancing at Elna and wondering why she hadn't left. Roh's failure meant Elna's wishes would be met – no warlocks in Lochloria, and she would remain the territory's leader. Why was she lingering?

'Some of us tried to get you out,' Odi was saying. 'But Kezra and Deodan ... Well, they had other ideas.'

'Oh?' Roh asked, the weight of exhaustion hitting her with full force. She wasn't sure she cared about their disagreements. It hardly mattered now.

Deodan rushed to her, gripping her hands in his, his eyes desperate. 'Roh, it wasn't like that,' he blurted. 'It was about the prophecy. Kezra and I ... Well, we were sure you would emerge from the pool with wings ... You have to understand,' he pleaded. '*Stone will crumble and land will fester, until the winged one flies forth* ...'

'It's fine, Deodan. I don't care.'

'But, Roh, we would never have left you, we were so sure —'

'It's fine,' Roh repeated, numb. 'Though I'm sorry to disappoint you. I don't have any wings, do I?'

'We really thought —'

'Perhaps the prophecy does not refer to wings of Rohesia's own,' Elna offered quietly. Still clinging to her nestlings, she closed the gap between them and came to stand before Roh on the banks of the mirror pool. There, she pointed up, where Valli circled above. 'Perhaps he is the *winged one* the prophecy cites.'

Roh looked from the ring of bruises at Elna's throat to the territory around them. Lochloria looked no different to her, no more prosperous, no less dilapidated. 'I don't think it matters now,' she said, reaching for her crown. She held it out to Elna. 'Take it.'

'Roh – don't!' Deodan lunged towards the crown, but Kezra blocked him easily with a firm arm thrust out.

Elna stared at the crown of bones as Roh forced it into her hands.

'Take it,' Roh repeated, her voice hollow.

The keeper of Lochloria looked shocked, turning the crown of bones over in her hands, eyes wide, as though she never expected to touch such a revered object. Roh wondered abstractly if the council had even allowed Elna a glimpse of the Gauntlet Ruby before they'd cleaved it in two and hidden its halves within the perils of her territory.

'There is something I have to do,' Elna said suddenly, sounding far away as she met Roh's gaze. 'Given you saved my daughters from certain death, I assume I can leave them safely with you for a brief interval?'

Roh's skin prickled, suspicion stirring within. With the mirror pool now thawed, perhaps Elna was to alert the council of her failure? Roh felt her friends exchange baffled looks, but Roh merely shrugged. She didn't care, not anymore.

Elna seemed to nod to herself. 'Good. You should take the next few hours to regroup, clean up ... Rest if you can.' She cleared her throat, a flush creeping up her neck and she fidgeted, apparently uncomfortable. 'I will host a dinner tonight,' she told Roh. 'As a thank you for saving my daughters. Be at the Residence Halls at the twentieth hour.'

Roh was too exhausted to be surprised. Someone else must have voiced their agreement, because soon, she was walking away.

'You should have seen her, when they were in danger,' Yrsa murmured.

Curiosity piqued briefly. Roh didn't know what had happened to the others after they'd split up. 'You saw her?'

Yrsa nodded. 'We had separated part of the herd and were trying to move them east away from the foal, which was where Elna went after the tomb trial. Apparently, the nestlings had run away from their guards. Elna was *distraught*, Roh. I had never imagined she'd fall apart like she did. With a stampede of backahast on the loose —'

'We lost control of the herd,' Finn interjected. 'That's when we spotted Maiella and Nym on the ice and the backahast, well … They're clever, aren't they? They knew they had leverage.'

'We were too far away to help,' Yrsa continued. 'As was Elna. You were their only hope. And you saved them. I think Elna's in shock. I think she needs a moment to process that she now owes a bone cleaner a debt.'

Numb, Roh nodded. She peeled herself away from Finn's support and stared dead ahead as the sun dipped further below the horizon. Her breath formed clouds of mist before her face and she realised for the first time since breaking the surface of the pool just how cold she was. Her teeth were chattering and her toes felt like frozen bricks in her boots. And yet she didn't want to lean into Finn's warmth, or rest her weary head on Harlyn's shoulder. Like Elna, she wanted to be separate, away from them all. She knew her friends were watching her, she could feel their concerned gazes lingering on her, but she said nothing.

All the while she'd been under the ice, she thought she was dying, that the visions of her parents were some final gift from the gods, knowing that she would never get the answers from the *Tome of Kyeos*. But she had survived … And now she lived on with no ruby, no wings, no song, no crown … That was her legacy.

Maiella and Nym ran ahead, laughing as they pointed up at Valli, who flew low to the ground, seeming to enjoy their amusement. Roh stared after the nestlings, at their unabandoned joy, at their innocence. It was because of them that Roh would never be queen, it was because of them that she would never *be the one to bring them all together*, as Marlow had predicted. Roh would never know what had happened between her parents and Delja to have it all end in such a way. She had failed so completely and utterly that she had no words left. But watching the young cyren sisters, Roh couldn't bring herself to regret it. Harlyn had been right. She hadn't wanted to be that sort of queen – cold and ruthless.

Maiella and Nym's laughter echoed through the trees.

Roh knew that faced with the decision again, she would do the same, but that knowledge gave her little comfort.

Her friends seemed to understand that she wasn't ready to speak yet. They made small conversation between themselves as they crossed the Lochlorian grounds and passed the old greenhouse. The door was still on its hinges, though the glass panels in its windows were smashed in. Everything within was grey and dusty, rows of empty garden beds lined the ground and broken workbenches lay discarded by the decaying walls. Roh couldn't help but linger, imagining what it once was to those who had come before ... For a moment, she pictured greenery, flowers and the scent of fresh herbs in her nose and on her tongue. She could see the neat rows of plants and the fruit vines climbing the trellises at the back, the warlocks and healers gathering supplies in woven baskets. Roh imagined the warlock Killian sitting in the corner somewhere, scrawling in one of his journals, documenting the remedies he'd attempted that day and the effects they'd had on his patients. She wondered if her father had walked its length ... Or if he was too much of a warrior to tend to bushes and take cuttings from shrubs ... It hit her anew that whatever his plans had been, he had died for nothing. She had not been the salvation that the warlocks had sought. They had all perished.

As the greenhouse disappeared behind them, Roh drew a shaky breath. How could it all feel so real, and yet she'd never been here before? She glanced across at Deodan. His expression was faraway, as though he too was picturing what once was, and what could have been. That was all she felt. The rest of her was as empty and hollow as the greenhouse.

. . .

The hair on Roh's arms stood up and she realised that the subtle notes of the windchimes had returned, the unruly melody sweeping up around them.

'Come on,' she heard herself say, her voice hoarse.

When they reached their accommodations, Roh sat on one of the benches and stared into the hearth as Odi rekindled the fire from the hot embers.

'What now?' she asked, not speaking to anyone in particular. 'The quest for the throne is lost. We cannot return home.'

It was Yrsa who spoke. 'We give ourselves tonight,' she said firmly. 'We make no plans, no decisions.'

Harlyn was nodding vigorously. 'Agreed.'

Yrsa locked eyes with Roh from across the room. 'Tomorrow,' she vowed. 'Tomorrow we'll know what to do.'

It wasn't long after that that Roh found herself in the bathing chamber with Harlyn, who peeled away Roh's filthy clothes and heated water for the baths. As Harlyn worked, Roh could hear her wheezing, as though whatever grain she had inhaled during her ordeal was still rattling around in her lungs.

But she waved Roh off when she asked about it, instead insisting on cleaning Roh's bloody fingertips from where she'd clawed at the wall of rubies in the tomb. Had that only happened this morning? It felt like a lifetime ago.

She ignored the stinging as Harlyn cleaned her cuts and bruises, watching Harlyn's expression tighten with worry.

'I'm alright,' she tried to reassure her.

'You don't *have to* be alright,' Harlyn replied, her voice still a rasp. 'I don't know what you went through beneath the ice. But I do know what you've lost ... It's not just the crown. It's the dream of a better Saddoriel, not just for you, but for all of us. So you can scream. Cry. Break down. Fall apart ... Whatever you need to do. You should know by now that we'll all still be standing here at the end. We've proven that much I think?' There was a note of reproach in Harlyn's tone.

Roh shook her head. 'I'm not ready, Har.'

'I know,' Harlyn said. 'But when you are, we're not going anywhere.'

Just before the twentieth hour, battered and uneasy, Roh found herself at the entrance to the Residence Halls as Elna had requested. Inside, the keeper of Lochloria was nowhere in sight, but the whole battalion of Saddorien warriors was waiting.

Harlyn gripped Roh's arm, panic flashing on her face. 'It's a set-up,' she hissed. 'She means to hand us over to the council.'

Scanning the hall, Roh noted that it was in much better condition than the rest of the scholar's city. Fires blazed in two hearths at either end of the space, while long tables stretched the length of the room beneath several chandeliers.

The battalion eyed Roh and her companions warily, but made no move to detain them.

'I don't like this,' Harlyn said.

'Me either,' Odi agreed, pushing his hair back from his furrowed brow.

'What do you want to do, Roh?' Deodan asked, his hands resting on the grips of his cutlasses.

'Elna wouldn't have left her nestlings with us if she meant us harm,' Yrsa argued, turning to Roh.

'Well, she knows now we'd never harm them,' Harlyn countered. 'That doesn't mean she won't harm *us*.'

An icy shiver ran the length of Roh's spine, creating a rush of goosebumps along her arms. She tugged her cloak tighter around herself and waited for the familiar pulse from the gems, only to realise she didn't have her crown. She'd given it to Elna. Deodan had tried to stop her, but she'd forced it into the hands of the

Lochlorian keeper, the one thing she had to discern truth from lies.

'We're defenceless,' Roh said, fear spiking in her chest. Wrapped up in her own grief, she'd thrown away the one thing they could have used as leverage. She'd gifted their only advantage to the enemy. 'We need to leave.'

The doors to the Residence Halls burst open.

Roh and the others jumped, unsheathing their weapons and bracing themselves for violence.

Elna stood in the doorway, dripping wet, determination blazing in her stare as she sought Roh amongst the crowd.

'Get out of here,' Roh hissed to Harlyn. 'You and the others flee. It's me the council wants.'

'Rohesia of the Bone Cleaners,' Elna's voice seemed to magnify and echo between the chandeliers. 'I would speak with you *now*.'

There was no way Roh believed that all Elna wanted with her was to exchange a few words. Whatever this trick was, it had the council's dirty hands all over it and she wasn't about to leave her friends at their mercy.

Blood roaring in her ears, Roh gave Harlyn a shove. 'Go!'

'We're *not* leaving.'

Elna peeled off her soaking cloak. 'You will want your companions here for this, Rohesia Irons,' she said, her voice strange. From one of her pockets, she removed the crown of bones and placed it on the table to her left, the two-and-a-half gems shining bright.

Roh's hands were shaking. So, Elna hadn't given it to the council. Did she want it for herself? Is that why she had stationed the battalion here?

But Elna closed the gap between them, that same determination gleaming in her gaze as her hand shot out and snatched Roh's.

Instinct had Roh reeling back, but the keeper of Lochloria held firm, forcing something into Roh's palm, something cold and hard.

With her heart in her throat, Roh gazed down, opening her hand, shock settling around her. She opened and closed her mouth several times, blinking down at what gleamed against her skin.

She held the other half of the ruby.

CHAPTER SIXTEEN

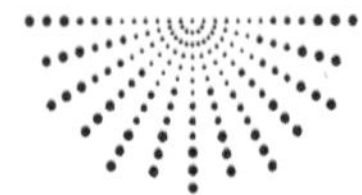

The only sound was the crackle of the fires and the drip of Elna's wet hair onto the floor. The rest of the world seemed to slow as Roh stared at the Gauntlet Ruby, so vibrant against the pale skin of her palm.

'It's yours,' Elna told her.

'Is this some sort of trick?' Roh managed, the warmth of the gem spreading to her fingertips. She marvelled at the depth of its colour, its modest size in contrast to the significance of all that it meant.

'No.'

Roh didn't move, her heart hammering against her sternum as she tried to convince herself that what was happening was *real*. She turned her head and gazed at the others, waiting for one of them to say something, to warn her that it was a trap, or a deceit of her own mind. Perhaps she so desperately wanted it to be true that she'd projected her imagination –

But Finn was at her side in two long strides and he laced his fingers through hers, closing Roh's hand around the ruby, the final birthstone of Saddoriel.

The jagged edge of the gem pressed against Roh's palm and sent a powerful jolt of energy through her, causing her grip to tighten around the stone in shock. Finn's hand fell away from hers, but Roh remained rooted to the spot.

'Why?' she croaked.

The entire hall was still. Anticipation pulsed in the air around them as everyone waited for what came next.

Elna met Roh's baffled gaze. 'The council told me of you before you arrived on these shores,' she began. 'They spoke of an *isruhe* with a poisoned mind, determined to carry out Cerys the Elder Slayer's work of forcing cyrens to their knees before water warlocks ...'

No one else made a sound.

'They spoke of your mixed heritage, your traitorous nature, your unworthiness ... That you want to win at all costs ...' Elna drew breath and glanced at her daughters, who had stowed away in a corner and were playing quietly with a pair of dolls. 'That is not the cyren I saw today. Today, I saw a Saddorien who would sacrifice her crown for an enemy's nestlings. You chose to save my daughters, knowing what it would cost you and your court. Even after my treatment of you. Even after you had wished me dead. I know no other who would deem two short lives more important than centuries of unparalleled power.'

Roh's mouth was dry. 'I ...' But the words wouldn't come.

Elna eyed her knowingly. 'My husband once told me that there would come a cyren to shake my rigid beliefs to my core. He was rarely wrong. You are that cyren, Rohesia. I know that now. Your sacrifices, not just today, but upon the Bridge of Csilla make you worthy of the birthstones. I felt it when you were beneath the ice, felt the realm shift.' She glanced at Roh's companions then. 'We all felt it.'

Roh's friends were nodding, expressions of awe on their faces. It was Odi who broke away from the group and retrieved her crown from the table. He smiled when he stood before her, his amber eyes bright, no longer the scared human trapped in the lair of bones, but her friend, her family. He held the crown out to her.

Roh's hands trembled as she set the piece of ruby in its rightful place. A glimmer of light touched her fingertips as the two halves merged with a quiet hiss.

'Today I saw a cyren become a queen,' Elna said. 'You are that cyren, Rohesia of the Bone Cleaners. You are *my* queen.'

A shiver rushed across Roh's skin as Odi lifted the crown to her head.

Energy surged, a wave of glimmering silver cresting and breaking upon the hall in a vibrant flash before fading away. Magic hummed across Roh's brow as it never had before, now that the Gauntlet Ruby sat whole alongside the Mercy's Topaz and the Willow's Sapphire. The individual power of each stone was strong, but stronger still was the combined fortitude of all three. They complemented one another, filled in the gaps of magic … coaxing her own power, whatever it was, to thrive in her veins.

Movement caught Roh's eye as she straightened the crown of bones. People were bowing. Deodan knelt before her, as he had done once before back in Csilla, but he was joined by Odi and Elna, and Harlyn and Kezra. The Jaktaren knelt too, as did the battalion filling the hall, in one powerful, unified motion. Even little Maiella and Nym came to stand at their mother's side and bent at the waist as she did.

Roh's heart was in her throat. She had *won*.

'The pool is completely thawed. You have your way home, Majesty,' Elna said, looking up at her in awe from where she bowed. 'But I beg you to stay the night, feast and celebrate.'

Choking back emotion, Roh gestured for her friends to stand. 'Please,' she managed.

As the word left her lips, a gift from each gem pulsed down through her … From the Mercy's Topaz: a clear direction, for she was no longer lost; from the Willow's Sapphire: a push of endurance, for there was more she had to do; and from the Gauntlet Ruby: a beacon of clarity, for now she knew her path.

Roh turned to Elna. 'We would love to celebrate with you.'

The keeper of Lochloria beamed and ordered soldiers to bring food and drink from the cellars. It wasn't long before the hall was a hive of activity, a simple but generous feast spread across the tables, toasts to the new queen echoing all around.

Roh was suddenly surrounded by cyren soldiers bowing and clasping her hands in theirs. The panic she had felt in crowds since Akoris did not come. Instead, she accepted their handshakes and pulled them up from their bows with the strange sensation that she was not quite in her own body. Goblets were raised in her honour and she thanked her wellwishers, smiling broadly. This was what it meant to be accepted ... She didn't allow herself to wonder about how the reception might differ in Saddoriel. For now, she would enjoy this.

Roh was led to a bench where she sat with Elna and her friends, the crown resting proudly atop her head, its gems subtly humming with power. She couldn't remember the last time she'd felt so at ease, so complete, so uncontainably joyous, if she ever had ... She could feel the pull of the crown towards Saddoriel, knowing that the pool awaited her. But she looked around at Odi, Harlyn, Yrsa, Finn, Deodan and Kezra, feeling her chest swell with pride, with gratitude. They were laughing and stuffing their faces with food, their eyes bright. Without them, she would never have made it this far, and so she would give them this night.

'It's truly something,' Elna said beside her, following her gaze. 'What you have achieved, who you have unified ...'

Roh smiled. 'Thank you.' She took a sip of wine and thought of the other cyrens she had meant to unify, to protect.

'You mean to ask after the Akorians?' Elna guessed, reading her furrowed brow.

'I do. They're not safe by Lamaka's Basin, not with —'

'I've already sent for them,' Elna replied. 'After I retrieved the gem from the backahast foal, I sent a small unit of soldiers to bring the Akorians here. They shouldn't be long.'

Roh stared at her, still not quite able to comprehend that the cyren beside her was the same one who had greeted her with so much hostility at the gates of Lochloria.

'You must have truly thought me awful,' Elna allowed quietly.

Roh shifted in her seat; there would be no advantage to dishonesty. 'You still bear the marks of what I thought.'

Elna's hand went to her throat, where a ring of bruises still marred her skin.

'I'm sorry for that,' Roh told her.

'It is forgotten, My Queen.'

Roh's stomach flipped at the formal title, but she decided not to press the matter. Instead, she eyed the thick fur around Elna's damp shoulders. 'How *did* you get the ruby?' she asked.

'Ah.' Elna grinned. 'That is some tale.'

Kezra leaned across the table, splashing a generous pour of wine into both of their goblets before refilling her own. 'Now there's a story I want to hear,' she said enthusiastically.

'Us too, us too!' cried Maiella and Nym, who appeared from beneath the table.

To Roh's surprise, Elna laughed and clinked her goblet against Kezra's. 'Then I had best do it justice,' she said, raising her drink higher. 'To the new queen!'

'To the new queen!' came the echo.

The celebrations went on well into the early hours of the morning, but Roh did not tire. She ate and drank with the rest of them, her elation knowing no bounds. Her cheeks ached from laughing and her heart was full of hope. Slightly addled by the wine, she embraced each of her friends every chance she got, thanking them profusely for all they had done, for never giving up.

It wasn't until the first rays of dawn kissed the skies that Roh and her companions stumbled out of the Residence Halls.

Valli was waiting for her.

Roh smiled at her companions. 'Take the morning to rest,' she told them. 'Then meet me back here at noon.'

No one objected. They seemed to understand that she needed this moment, needed to be alone with the patient sea drake who'd hardly left her side these past few months.

When her friends had left, Roh turned to Valli, stroking his neck. 'I think it's time we saw the territory from above, my friend,' she said. She had been thinking of this for weeks now and she hadn't been the only one, it seemed.

Joy sparked in Valli's molten-gold eyes as for the first time Roh clambered up onto his back, his scales cool and smooth beneath her grasp. Valli didn't wait. The giant creature pushed off from the ground, shooting up into the sky.

Roh braced herself, not daring to blink as the drake's glorious form soared through the cloud, the dawn light breaking through. She leaned into him, veering when he did, letting her body follow her instinct, as though they had been flying together since the beginning of time. The sensation of being groundless was utterly exhilarating. In just seconds, the wind whipped her face and the buildings became specks below as she touched the clouds hanging between the great towering mountains. For a second, she imagined she had her own wings. There was nothing like this feeling – *nothing*. It was pure freedom.

Valli gave a contented shriek, taking a playful dive. Together they spiralled through the sky, a laugh bubbling at Roh's lips. Never in her wildest dreams had she ever imagined *this*. She had no song, but instead she had the cyren crown, warlock magic and a drake who carved through the realms. From up here, Lochloria was beautiful. Roh hadn't realised just how large the territory was until she and Valli followed the mountain range north. The jagged, snow-capped peaks and dark ridges spanned more land than she could fathom, while low-lying clouds hung between the sheer drops. Even further north, a strange fog carpeted the lands so she couldn't see the forest beneath.

Valli flicked his tail and elegantly turned them back around, leading them towards Lochloria, the ice blue of Lamaka's Basin yawning wide below. Roh shook her head in disbelief at its size. It had to be one of the largest inland bodies of water in existence, and beyond it, she could see the sea stretching to the horizon.

Even in the low light of dawn, the vastness of the sea called to her, the dark expanse glittering below the half-orb of the orange sun. Valli strained beneath her, pulling towards it, as though its song beckoned him as well, the current summoning its prince.

Roh leaned into the drake. 'Let's land,' she whispered.

With another small shriek to the waves beyond, Valli took another dive, this time towards the great lake of Lamaka's Basin.

As the stony shore grew closer, Roh felt the creature slow his descent, sliding into a glide. The peacefulness was lost on her as the rocks around Lamaka's Basin grew larger and larger.

Valli landed clumsily, skidding across the shore, pebbles flying everywhere, sending Roh tumbling from his back. She hit the wet banks of the lake on all fours, sand flying into her mouth and eyes.

'Urgh.' She spat out a lump of dirt and got to her feet, face flaming. 'Not as graceful as I would have liked,' she muttered to Valli, who eyed her as if to say, *it's not as easy as it seems*, before looking to the horizon.

Roh couldn't help but stare at the sea drake, who'd changed so much over the last few months. From that moody little thing snapping at her fingers, to the majestic creature before her. It was quite the transformation. And now, all three gems in her crown told her it was time …

Roh pressed her forehead to Valli's and closed her eyes. Their flight together had confirmed what she knew in her heart. Valli didn't belong trapped grounded at her side. He was meant for the skies and the seas.

'You belong with your own kind,' she told him, her eyes burning behind her lids. 'I do not regret taking you, not for a second. But I want you to have what's yours: freedom.'

Valli nuzzled against her and she knew he understood every word she spoke.

The warmth of the birthstones pulsing down from her crown told her it was the right thing to do, she had just needed one more memory with him, just him and her amongst the clouds.

'Go and find your kin,' she said, her voice cracking.

Valli gave a soft growl, his scales vibrating beneath Roh's touch.

She pulled away from him, turning to the great lake and taking in its glistening waters that led to the sea. 'You'll be much missed, my friend.'

The sea drake blinked at her, his molten-gold eyes seeming older now. He nuzzled her one last time in the crook of her neck before stalking towards the lake's edge and spreading his wings.

Roh pressed a hand to her already aching heart as Valli pushed off from the ground and soared into the sky, heading straight for the sea, the beat of his wings causing waves to break across the lake's shore.

'Roh,' came Deodan's voice, alarmed. 'Why did you …?'

Roh turned to find her companions standing behind her, watching Valli grow smaller in the distant skies.

'He was never my captive,' Roh told him. 'He is his own master, as we are our own.'

'But —'

'He belongs amidst the currents, Deodan. He always has.' She touched her crown. 'This helped me realise it.'

That silenced the warlock, for the gems had not led them astray yet.

Odi, Harlyn, Yrsa, Finn, Deodan and Kezra approached her tentatively, each of them surveying her, that strange tension of awe still raw between them.

'You flew with him,' Harlyn said unnecessarily when she reached Roh's side, looking like she wanted to reach out and touch Roh.

Roh smiled. 'I did.'

'And?' Harlyn pressed eagerly.

None of the words were right. Nothing she said could do justice to what it had felt like gliding overhead, close enough to touch clouds and mountain peaks. 'It was incredible,' Roh settled for.

Yrsa grinned, folding her arms over her chest and turning expectantly to Roh. 'We decided not to sleep the morning away,' she said.

'So I gathered.' Roh smiled back.

'We packed up the gallery, saw Valli descending towards here ... We thought there might be some more pressing matters to attend to rather than indulging our hangovers ...?'

Roh cast her gaze across each of her companions, noting the packs at their feet and weapons sheathed once more at their sides. In the quiet of the blue-hued morning, she nodded, turning towards the scholar's city and beyond it, the path to the mirror pool, no longer frozen over.

'It's time to go home,' Roh said. 'It's time to go back to Saddoriel.'

CHAPTER SEVENTEEN

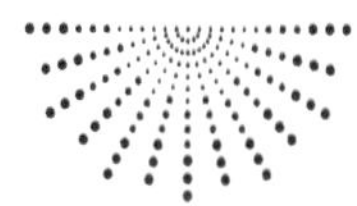

Standing at the water's edge by one of the war beacons, Roh assessed the Lochlorian pool with surreal calmness. She had learned much in such a short space of time here, but now, the birthstones in her crown, the violet ripples and the *Tome of Kyeos* beckoned her back to the lair of bones. With warlock magic tingling at her fingertips, Roh turned to Odi, the companion who'd been with her since the very first moment of this quest.

'It's your choice,' she told him. 'I will support you whatever you decide, the rules be damned. You can come with us, back to Saddoriel, or I'll have Deodan escort you home to the Isle of Dusan ...' She let her words sink in before she continued. 'There is no shame in either path. And either way, I will free your stepbrothers and I will tear that ledger in two, perhaps even burn it for good measure.'

Odi opened his mouth. 'I ...'

Roh wasn't finished. 'There is no pressure from me. I want you to know that. I will respect the decision you make.'

'I want to see this through, Roh,' he said, his amber eyes full of conviction.

'It will be dangerous for you.'

'Naturally.'

Roh gripped his shoulder, squeezing gently. 'I need you to understand … I don't know what's ahead.'

'Nor do any of us,' Finn interjected, coming to stand beside Odi. 'He said he wants to see this through, so he'll see it through.'

Odi shot Finn a grateful look and nodded. 'Until the end.'

Roh glanced between Jaktaren and human, their alliance, their friendship so unlikely and yet now so defined before her. She squeezed Odi's shoulder again and smiled. 'Until the end, then,' she said.

Elna approached them, bowing her head when she reached Roh. 'I have not travelled via the pool,' she offered. 'So, I cannot tell you what to expect, or how to direct your travel.'

Roh adjusted her crown, which was radiating warmth. 'I am not worried,' she told her. 'The pool knows where we need to go.' She was sure of it.

Elna placed a hand over her heart, and when she spoke her voice was quiet, full of a humility that seemed strange coming from her. 'Whenever you need us, we will be there.'

Feeling the reassuring thrum of the gems, Roh shook Elna's hand, knowing how much a vow like that meant from the cyren warrior. 'Thank you.'

At last, Roh turned to her friends, who were waiting patiently. 'Are we ready?' She offered Finn her hand.

His palm was warm and firm against hers. 'Ready,' he said.

When the Elder Council had entered the mirror pool in Akoris, they hadn't held onto one another, but in this moment, it felt right to Roh. She nodded to the others to link hands, and as they did, she walked into the shallows.

Instantly, the water surged, swelling around her boots and then parting before her, just as she'd seen in the monastery. She pulled the others in after her, the violet water no longer touching her, but shifting to create a pathway to the heart of the pool.

'Gods ...' she murmured, quietly savouring the magic of this place as the sun dipped behind the mountains beyond.

Roh led her companions deep into the pool, where a portal shimmered before them. She knew where it would take them, she knew deep in her chest that the birthstones would not lead her astray. She crossed the threshold and stepped into the portal.

The sensation of a thousand butterflies tickled her skin as darkness swallowed her. She heard the intake of breath from Harlyn somewhere behind her, but she could see nothing. A cool wind whipped through her hair and suddenly she was falling, a cry of surprise catching in her throat. She gripped Finn's hand tightly, sensing him falling nearby, but he made no sound. For a second, Roh wondered what would happen if Valli had been with them and his wings had caught the wind beneath them, where would they end up? But Valli was free now and she allowed the mirror pool to take her, surrendering to the portal completely. She only hoped that the others were doing the same.

On and on they fell, through space and time; a tunnel cut the realms, flashes of colour occasionally puncturing the inky black around them. Roh tried to imagine Delja and the council travelling like this, Marlow, too, and somehow she couldn't picture it, all of them falling with utter abandon.

That sensation of butterflies on her skin started up again, a delicate tickling across her arms and face, and she knew it was almost over. The flashes of colour increased, and suddenly, they were surrounded by ice blue. Roh's boots hit solid ground.

Still holding Finn's hand, she began to walk. All she could see was the blue shimmering all around her, a body of water that parted for her. With her crown of bones at last complete with all three birthstones of Saddoriel, Roh emerged from the mother source of the cyren territories' mirror pools, The Pool of Weeping.

But as her boots crunched upon the shore, a loud rumbling sounded in the distance. Above, the ceiling of stalactites rattled. She braced herself as the others left the pool behind her and looked around at the enormous grotto, half expecting the council to be there, waiting for her, but there was no one.

The ground trembled.

'Roh?' came Harlyn's uncertain voice.

Roh made to step forward and the rumbling sounded again. This time, Roh swore as the shore shook violently beneath her, causing her to stumble and ripples to pulse across the pool. Dread churned in her gut as she looked around wildly, spotting pieces of rock break away from the ceiling.

Kezra yelled as a stalactite shot down at her like a dagger. 'Roh,' she panted. 'You know what this is ...'

Roh didn't want to say it aloud. 'We have to get to the entrance,' she shouted over the noise, instead. 'We have to find the council. And Isomene Sigra!'

Roh led the race through the grotto, leaving the pristine banks upon which her father had died behind, following the path of emerald-green moss that she remembered well. Her inner compass guided her through the lair, horror gripping her as she recognised a sound drifting through the trembling passageways.

The mournful notes of two fiddles, playing somewhere amidst the quaking lair.

She didn't stop, didn't glance in Odi's direction.

The song of the Eery Brothers was immaculate, clear, cutting through the chaos as though the musicians stood right beside her. An invisible fist clamped around Roh's heart with the knowledge that the poor humans were being forced to play, even now.

When they reached it, the archway of bones towered taller than she remembered. Its ivory tones were stark against the otherwise dark cavernous walls of Talon's Reach; the thousands of pieces had been expertly placed within the imposing structure. As

Roh and her companions passed beneath it, the music that filled the air became clearer and more sorrowful, even as the lair around them seemed to break apart at the seams.

A cage of bones, similar to the one the Eery Brothers had been trapped within back in Csilla, stood in the near centre of the great cylindrical space, the stone galleries overlooking it, stretching over a hundred feet above. Rocky bridges joined the upper levels, while at the heart of it all, a thick, jagged column, the cyren throne, loomed high. Roh had admired that structure once, but it looked different to her now.

Odi broke away from the group, running towards his stepbrothers. Roh surged after him, skidding to a stop at the base of the horrific contraption. She couldn't help but gasp upon seeing the humans inside. They were shadows of their former selves … Roh vaguely recalled thinking them handsome for human men at one time, but now … Now they were shells of men, skeletal, with dark hollows beneath their eyes, their cheeks sunken and their bodies hunched over.

'Mason, Brooks …' Odi rasped upon seeing them. 'Gods …'

The men behind the bars of bone didn't so much as glance down at their brother. They kept playing, their fiddles tucked beneath their bearded chins, the melody that poured from their instruments more poignant and bereft than Roh had ever heard.

'I'm so sorry,' Odi croaked, his half-gloved hands gripping the bars, tears lining his amber eyes.

Another tremor rocked beneath Roh, strong enough that she had to catch herself before she lost her footing. 'We have to get them out, *now*,' she yelled.

'I'm afraid you can't do that,' a cold, familiar voice sounded.

Taro Haertel stepped forward, seeming determined to assert his power over Roh even now. But he blanched at the sight of her completed crown.

She rounded on him, gesturing to the falling debris around

them. 'Didn't you get my messages? Have you done *nothing* to protect the lair from what's coming?'

Suddenly, the rest of the mighty Council of Seven Elders was there, panicked, bowing their heads together and whispering in low, hurried tones. Where they came from, Roh didn't know, nor did she care as the world she knew fell apart. There was no sign of the former queen.

'What's happening?' Elder Rasaat cried, flinching as more stone and debris fell.

There was no mistaking it now. The entire lair shook with force.

Roh pushed back her shoulders and fixed him with a hard gaze. 'The terror tempests are here.'

Above, glass shattered in one of the domes, showering them with falling shards. A long, piercing scream echoed through the hall as one of the gallery railings gave way and a cyren fell, his flailing body shooting towards them and hitting the ground with a sickening thud.

Roh grabbed Harlyn from the path of another falling piece of stone, while Odi and Finn hacked at the bars of bone with their blades, trying to free the Eery Brothers.

Yrsa gripped Roh's arm. 'We have to get out of here,' she urged. '*Now.*'

As all of Saddoriel trembled and pieces of the hall fell away in great, deadly chunks, it was every cyren for themselves. The Elder Council was darting across to the other side of the entrance towards the Great Hall and Roh motioned for her friends to follow, Odi and Finn half-carrying Mason and Brooks, who were at last free of their cage.

Roh didn't think of the fatal drop on either side of the bridge within the Great Hall, she just ran, trailing the billowing robes of the council elders. They burst into the foyer of the Upper Sector residences. Everyone's eyes were wide, chests heaving with panicked breaths as the whole lair rumbled and shook around them, more screams echoing through the lair in the near distance.

Roh faced the council and demanded again: 'Didn't you get my messages?' Her whole body tensed as her home continued to shake.

Isomene Sigra opened her mouth. 'We —'

'Ignored them? Dismissed them? Didn't prepare? Thought them the schemes of a traitorous bone cleaner?' Roh cut her off angrily.

The council stared at her and her crown. She didn't know what had become of the warnings she and Floralin had sent through, detailing the increased rate of terror tempests and the rise of the warrior warlocks under Sybil's rule. But it didn't matter, not right now.

It was Isomene Sigra who stepped forward, bowing at the waist. 'What are your orders, My Queen?'

Roh would have liked to savour the moment, the very second that an elder acknowledged her as their ruler, but there was no time. She quelled that fiery panic inside her, a cold, calculated calmness washing over her.

'Evacuate the nestlings and the fledglings from Talon's Reach. Use the mirror pool and take them to Csilla. It's the safest of our territories.'

Rasaat's eyes widened. 'What of —'

Roh threw up a hand, silencing the cyren. 'There was a unit of warrior warlocks stationed at Lamaka's Basin, readying to attack. Akoris is in ruin and is the base for the warlocks. Csilla is safest.'

Kezra stepped forward. 'I can escort them.'

Roh gave her a nod, her mind already three steps ahead of the plans unfolding before them. 'Taro, you're in charge of our population. You will oversee the evacuation of the nestlings and fledglings.'

To Roh's deep surprise, there was no objection from the

council elder. He merely nodded and motioned for Kezra to follow him.

Roh turned back to the remaining elders. 'Where is Delja?'

'She … uh …' Erdites Colter spluttered, looking around as though she had been right behind them.

'She's not here?' Roh pressed.

'We … we don't know.'

Roh clenched and unclenched her hands at her sides. 'Fine. We'll deal with that later.' Ignoring the pounding in her ears, she continued. 'Any human musicians being held here must be freed immediately.'

Erdites Colter gasped audibly. 'You can't free them. You're not officially queen and it's the Law of the Lair.'

'*There will be no lair* if we don't move quickly. They go free.' Roh faced Odi. 'I want you to take your stepbrothers and any others and use the passageway that leads to the Isle of Dusan. You know the one.'

'Roh, that passageway was affected too.'

'From what Deodan has learned, the terror tempests will be drawn to the heart of Talon's Reach, where the most magic gathers. The passage may shake, but it will hold. Should the tempests cleave into Saddoriel and break the weaker enchantments, you have no chance. I want you to go, escape here. And don't look back.'

Odi hesitated, reaching for her and glancing at Harlyn. 'But, Roh …'

Roh shook her head, her mind made up. 'We'll find a loophole in the rules about you not being with me if and when the time comes. Go! You heard me, *don't look back*.'

This was it, this was exactly what she had feared – inheriting a kingdom on the precipice of destruction. But she would not break now. 'Colter,' she barked.

The elder stared at her, bewildered.

'Take Odi and the fiddlers to any other humans you have in the musician holdings. Free them. Give them talismans against the lure of the lair and take them to the passageway that leads to the southern human lands.'

'You … you can't make me.'

Roh looked pointedly to both Yrsa and Finn. 'See to it that he does as I've said.'

The Jaktaren exchanged savage grins as they unsheathed their weapons and surged for Elder Colter, who visibly paled.

'I will not –'

'You heard the queen,' Yrsa snapped, menacingly brandishing her loaded sling and broadsword.

Roh froze as Odi launched himself at her, throwing his arms around her neck. 'There's no time for goodbyes,' she said hoarsely, returning his embrace.

'Then it's not goodbye,' Odi told her gruffly as he released her and turned to the Jaktaren.

Roh paused, just for a second, as she watched them leave, the lair still trembling violently around them.

'Roh?' Harlyn prompted. 'What now?'

Roh took a deep breath, feeling the remaining elders' eyes on her. 'Someone send for the mentor of the bone cleaners,' she ordered before turning to Deodan. 'Do you think between us we could identify the weakened parts of the lair? Where the strength of the warlock enchantments are wavering?'

Deodan nodded. 'I could feel thinner parts of magic since we got here.'

A particularly violent shudder ripped through the lair and everyone threw themselves towards the nearest wall, pressing their backs up against it as more debris fell from above. Roh could hear shouts nearby and she prayed to the goddesses that Kezra and the youth of Saddoriel would make it to the Pool of Weeping.

Isomene Sigra stepped forward. 'I also know several passages that compromise the lair's defence.'

'Good. That's a start.' Roh turned back to the warrior warlock, finding his gaze intense. 'Can they be repaired?' Roh pressed urgently.

'Reinforced at least,' Deodan told her.

'Good, I'm untrained, so I will need guidance.' She pushed her shoulders back. 'We'll take as many vials from the pool as we can, and Deodan and I will tend to the compromised parts of the lair.' She faced Harlyn next. 'Find Jesmond, she'll help. Take her with you to the Pool of Weeping. Fill as many vials as possible with its water.'

'I'll escort them,' Elder Winslow Ward offered, her lilac eyes cool and determined.

'Very well.' Roh faced the remaining elders: Arcus Mercer, Koras Rasaat and Bloodwyn Haertel. 'Where is the safest, most secure place in Saddoriel?'

'The Vault,' Bloodwyn replied instantly, her eyes narrowing.

'The three of you are to take shelter there.'

'What —'

Shock rippling across their faces, the three council elders jumped at her final word and darted across the foyer to a corridor on the other side.

'You're just going to let them hide?' Deodan objected, incredulous.

'They're in my way,' Roh said through gritted teeth before addressing Isomene Sigra. 'Let's get to these compromised tunnels.'

'Right away, Majesty,' the elder bowed and set off towards the Great Hall once more.

Roh and Deodan sprinted after Isomene Sigra across the stone bridge once more, artwork and railings and pieces of ceiling raining down on them, the tremors rattling the entire hall. But there was nothing for it – they had to reinforce Saddoriel and it had to hold against the onslaught of terror tempests.

Talon's Reach was eerily empty – with the nestlings and fledglings hopefully long gone and the rest of the Saddoriens taking shelter where they could, the passageways were wide open for Roh and her companions as they darted through them towards the most dangerous parts of the lair.

As Roh's boots pounded the floor, Floralin's words came back to her: *'In order to reinforce the enchantments, there would need to be a call for magic across the lands, a gathering of power that no longer exists in the realms as we know them today.'*

Before his suspicions about Valli's connection with Roh being the key, Deodan had implied that her deathsong had been that power, a power to rival them all. And for a time, Roh too had wondered as much. But her deathsong was gone, thanks to the cruelty and schemes of the very council she now sought to protect. Were it not for them, the answer to saving Saddoriel might just be on the tip of her tongue.

Even with her warlock magic, Roh had no idea how she might help the lair, and the resentment bubbled into bitterness as Isomene brought them to a stop in a passage Roh didn't recognise.

'This,' Isomene said, reaching for Roh's hand and placing it flat against the damp stone wall. 'This is compromised. It's been hit several times in the past.'

Roh ignored the anger rising hot in her chest at the knowledge that the threats had been ignored and instead focused on the rocky grain against her palm, sensing a hollowness, as though the wall was an all-too-thin barrier, the sea pressing against it and weakening it from the outside.

Deodan did the same beside her, his face grim. He fumbled with his vials, shoving several into Roh's hands before pouring the sacred water into his own palms and whispering his enchantments. Glowing blue vines formed in his cupped hands and drifted towards the wall, as though securing it in place. He moved further down the tunnel, working quickly and with intense focus.

'What can I do?' Roh called after him desperately.

A warm hand gripped her shoulder and suddenly her uncle, Marlow, was there. There was no time for relief, to revel in the joy of seeing his familiar face in what was becoming one of her darkest hours.

He offered no greeting, but uncorked a vial. 'Empty this into your hands, imagine containing it …'

Much of the water spilled through Roh's fingers. She swore.

'Not so fast,' Marlow told her. 'Try.'

But there was no time to try. This was not the moment for trial and error. For the life of her, Roh couldn't recall how she had manifested those water sea drakes in the Lochlorian mirror pool. They had come from a place deep within, perhaps so deep she couldn't access it in the here and now.

'Draw from its power ... Draw it together ... Try to shape it into what you need it to be.' Deodan's words echoed in her mind again. *'Anything that takes on the shape and mannerisms of a living being is very complex magic ...'*

So, water sea drakes were out of the equation …

'Something simple. A shape. A shield. A symbol.'

A shield. She'd seen Deodan do such a thing only seconds before.

Roh took another vial from her uncle and poured the water into her cupped hand again. This time, her focus was unbreakable as she listened to the call of the cool liquid and concentrated.

'That's it,' Marlow said quietly. 'Picture it knitting together and covering the cracks … Very good, Rohesia …'

Roh felt a bead of sweat trickle from her brow, but she didn't break contact with the sacred water, watching in awe as her magic created a shield from the inside of Saddoriel. It was not as strong as Deodan's, she could tell just by looking at it. But it was all she could do and it was better than nothing.

Shouts from nearby echoed down the passageway and Roh wrenched Isomene out of harm's way just as a stalactite dislodged from the ceiling and came spearing towards her.

'Thanks,' the elder rasped, her chest heaving in shock.

'Deodan!' Roh called. 'Send a water bird to Harlyn. She'll need to bring those vials soon. As many as they can carry!'

Gritting his teeth, the warrior warlock nodded and did as Roh bid. Seconds later, a water sparrow flitted away down a dark passage.

Together they worked tirelessly, seeking out the thinning parts of the enchantment, with Deodan whispering to his water magic and reinforcing the weakened areas with all his strength and power.

Roh did the best she could, listening to Marlow when he pointed out a fault in her work or a better angle for the shield, but she was all too aware that she was weak and untrained in the face of all that threatened them. The lair shook and its foundations groaned under every ounce of pressure.

Just as the warrior warlock used the last of his vials, Harlyn and Jesmond found them, their pockets bulging with more bottles and flasks of water from the Pool of Weeping.

'We brought as much as we could,' Harlyn panted, thrusting a whole canteen at Roh.

'Thank you. What's it like back there?' she asked.

Harlyn exchanged a grim glance with Jesmond. 'They're panicking.'

'How badly?' Roh pressed.

'Those who aren't taking shelter in their residences are fleeing to the passages of Outer Talon's Reach. They're practically trampling one another.'

Roh swore. Wiping the sweat from her brow with her sleeve, she braced herself. 'We need to canvas the whole lair,' she said.

'Not possible,' Marlow replied. 'The lair is *enormous,* Rohesia. And there is only one of us with magic strong enough to make a difference.'

'I'm doing everything I can,' Deodan snapped.

Marlow clicked his tongue. 'Who said I was speaking of you?'

Roh ignored their griping, knowing it was borne of fear. She watched Deodan work, the back of his shirt dark with perspiration as he coaxed another shield of water vines in place across a weakened wall.

Roh struggled to hold her own magic in place. 'We've barely covered a third of the Upper Sector. And I will not leave the Mid and Lower Sectors vulnerable. Marlow's right. We can do this for days and still the tempests might —'

'But it's not enough,' Deodan finished for her, pausing to rest his forehead against the wall and taking deep breaths, his eyes closed in defeat.

'No ...' Roh agreed. 'It's not enough. And ... don't think I don't know what this means, for a warlock to protect this place.'

'It won't mean anything if it falls.'

As if in answer, the lair quaked again, hard enough to make Roh's teeth chatter.

Deodan's magic sputtered upon the creation of his next shield, as though he was reaching his last reserves. The exhaustion and sweat on his face confirmed as much to Roh.

'What else can we do?' Roh threw up her hands. 'Can we evacuate the whole lair? Can we use the pool?' Her gaze went to her uncle, who gave a subtle shake of his head that confirmed her suspicions. That would take too long and it would also leave Saddoriel to its fate at the mercy of the terror tempests.

Deodan sagged against the wall, panting. 'I just need a minute,' he said between ragged breaths. 'I just need to gather myself.'

But Roh could see his hands trembling under all the strain he'd put on himself and she knew that the best of his magic had been drained.

Straightening her shoulders, Roh sweated as she worked, attempting to knit the water vines together and attach them to the holes in Saddoriel's defence. But she worked much slower than Deodan and she knew her efforts wouldn't hold as strongly as his – she was undisciplined, with only a drop of his trained warlock magic.

She was all too aware of the eyes boring into her back as she tried to strengthen the lair one tiny patch at a time, but she ignored them, focusing on the task at hand –

A sharp jolt hit Saddoriel.

The ground beneath Roh shook, as though the whole lair was rocking from side to side.

'It's getting worse!' Isomene called out, throwing herself against the wall with a pointed glance at the deadly stalactites hanging above them.

'Take cover!' Roh yelled, shoving Marlow back against the wall.

More stalactites dislodged, shooting down towards them like daggers.

Roh swore again. 'It's not enough, my magic isn't enough. Not since I sacrificed my deathsong,' she murmured to her uncle.

Marlow whirled to face her, gripping her shoulder, his gaze wild. 'Hasn't anyone ever told you that there's no such thing as a songless cyren?'

Flinching as more stalactites shattered around them, she churned the words over in her mind and her gaze shot to the weakened warrior warlock. 'Deodan. Deodan said that. But that was before.'

'Before what?'

'Before my sacrifice!' Roh yelled. She didn't mean to, but all the anguish, the emptiness came flooding back to her, as did the despair she felt now. Had she not given up her deathsong, she might be powerful enough to save Saddoriel. 'You were there, Marlow,' she rasped. 'You saw the sacrifice I made.' She eyed Isomene bitterly. 'Because of them.'

'It was *one song*, Rohesia,' Marlow said, his voice low.

'What?'

'You only sacrificed *one song*,' Marlow insisted, his lilac eyes frantic. 'There is more magic within you. More than one song. Look deep, Roh ...'

Roh stared at him. *There's no such thing as a songless cyren ...* Was it possible it didn't mean what she thought it did? Not that a cyren didn't survive without a song, but that ...

Go where the fear is darkest ... Roh could hardly remember where she'd first heard that phrase, that strangely familiar voice, but it echoed in her mind as the gems thrummed in her crown of bones ...

Finn's voice filled her head. *'Something brought me out of unconsciousness. A song ... There was no mistaking who that song belonged to, there's nothing like it.'*

Then Roh was taken further back in time ... *Song erupted from her. An unleashing of all that restlessness and magic that had simmered for so long beneath her surface. She didn't think about what she was singing, only that the sound was coming from her very core, every single note a reflection of her, of everything she had ever gained and everything she had ever lost, a fluid dance between love and sorrow and magic ... She looked down in utter disbelief, the final note of her melody caught in her throat. A ragged gasp escaped her.*

Tiny dark wings flared, breaking through shards of shell.

And a pair of molten-gold eyes stared up at her.

Roh's body jerked as each memory rushed to her. *All at once, magic rushed into Roh, coursing within her like a river breaking through a dam, restlessness dancing with it, escaping through song, through her. Several notes. She knew in her very core that they belonged to her and her alone ... Something tickled the side of her foot and she jumped, scrambling back, her eyes flying open. A flower. A small lilac bloom was sprouting from the sand, swaying in the gentle breeze ...*

Harlyn reached across and pushed Roh's hair from her brow, tucking the flower behind her ear. 'Funny where life can flourish, isn't it?' she said with a smile.

Roh staggered forward, the realisation hitting her with full force to the chest. Marlow caught her.

'Life,' she croaked. 'My song was at its most powerful when it created *life*, not death ...'

Marlow was smiling knowingly then.

'I have a *lifesong* ...' Roh murmured. 'They took my deathsong, but ... That wasn't the most powerful part of me.'

The others were staring at her, but Roh ignored them. She knew what to do.

As the lair threatened to crumble around her, she tipped her head back and sang.

CHAPTER EIGHTEEN

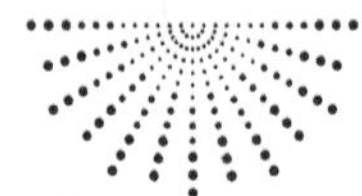

The music poured from Roh's very soul. A gold essence flowed from her mouth, her talons and her heart, dancing before her in a chaotic melody. It was magic at its purest and most powerful, expanding outwards as though it were life itself, taking a long-awaited breath. The song drifted to the weakened patches of the lair, reinforcing the defences she and Deodan had already placed there, welding together, healing, creating a stronger, impenetrable barrier.

The presence of Marlow, Deodan, Harlyn, Jesmond and Isomene fell away from Roh as she sang. She was untethered from Saddoriel, becoming one with the music she felt manifesting deep within her chest, building and building before it flowed through the passageways of Talon's Reach, bracing the thinning old enchantments. She followed it through the Upper and Mid Sectors, down into the darkened tunnels of the Lower Sector. She reinforced it all, gold glittering in the blackened stone around her. She was without her body, drifting through the narrow passageways, illuminating the dark paths and the structures made of ancient bone.

This song was home to Roh. She knew it intimately. It had saved Valli and Finn before this moment and now it would save Saddoriel, and the friends who had become her family. She found herself and her magic at the official entrance to Saddoriel's Prison, greeted by a portcullis of bones, fortified with iron, casting long shadows across the wet ground. In her ethereal form, Roh gazed upon the thick, rusted chains and heavy locks wrapped through the latticed grille and a solid wall of algae-covered stone standing on either side.

Strangely, this part of Saddoriel had no weakened spots. The protective warlock enchantments were as strong as they had ever been down here. Deep in her heart, Roh knew that it was no coincidence. Here, her father's magic thrived in the crawling plant of white oleander, its vines firmly wrapped around timber beams, its delicate flowers peppered across bone and iron alike.

In ribbons of gold, Roh's song reached out, sensing the magic in the blooms that had held fast for centuries. An enchantment deeper than protection against terror tempests, an enchantment forged with blood and sacrifice, with love. Roh could almost envision her father standing here in the past, casting the enchantment, just in case he didn't survive the rescue attempt. An enchantment with a single purpose: to protect his wife and unborn child.

Whatever guards were stationed here had fled, and Roh paused a moment, resting a palm about the portcullis, her magic still flowing freely from her. Driven by instinct, there, she wove her protection in as well.

She projected her awareness and power outwards, still seeking the weakened patches across all of Saddoriel and Talon's Reach. Her magic connected with every trace of live enchantment, drawing them all together in a massive golden net of protection, a reinforcement of the magic that once was.

As every piece connected, Roh slowly felt herself slip back into her body, her boots firmly planted on the ground, ground that was no longer shaking. She blinked and looked around.

Harlyn was kneeling before her. 'You did it,' she managed, her eyes wide with awe. 'You did it, My Queen. Yours is the *gathering of power that no longer exists in the realms as we know them today …*'

Roh examined her hands, the ribbons of gold at last ceasing to pour from her fingertips. 'Do you think …?' she murmured.

Harlyn got to her feet and cupped Roh's hands in hers. 'Yes,' she said firmly, peering into Roh's face, her gaze full of reassurance. 'You are our queen. And you have saved Saddoriel.'

Roh loosed a tight breath and looked to Marlow. 'All this time, I've had a lifesong?'

'We had hoped … Cerys and I …'

'Do many cyrens have lifesongs?'

'Not that we know of, but it's possible. It's our understanding that the chances increase with mixed heritage such as yours,' Marlow told her. 'Your father, he was adamant that you would have one, that the choices and sacrifices you would make would draw it out.'

For a brief moment, Roh allowed that possibility to settle inside her, but she was not left with her thoughts for long. To her surprise, it was Isomene Sigra who came forward and bowed deeply at the waist. 'With your permission, Your Majesty, I would have the queen's residences readied for you at once.'

'She needs a coronation immediately,' Marlow interjected. 'Her crown needs to be made official.'

Isomene nodded. 'I will have your coronation underway as soon as the lair is in order.'

In a daze, Roh gave her a stiff nod before turning to Harlyn, Deodan and Jesmond. 'Tell the elders in the Vault that the worst of the tempest is over. That Saddoriel will hold. Then find Finn, Yrsa and Kezra.'

'Consider it done, Majesty,' Jesmond bowed with a wicked wink.

'I …' Roh faltered, realising for the first time just how much time had passed and how much had changed since she'd been home. 'I don't know where I'll be …'

'We'll find you.' Harlyn squeezed Roh's hand in reassurance before helping Deodan down the path to find the others.

Now, it was just Roh and Marlow.

'You're tired?' Marlow asked, his brows knitting together in concern.

'You could say that.' Roh sighed. 'You know … the prison …'

'What about it?'

Roh pushed a loose strand of hair from her eyes. 'It was the most protected part of Saddoriel.'

Something flickered behind her uncle's eyes, but he simply shrugged his shoulders. 'Imagine that,' he said.

Roh huffed a laugh, picturing the white oleander flowers laced with her father's magic. 'Imagine that …' she murmured.

At her request, Roh and her uncle descended the levels of Talon's Reach together. They employed the same pulley system they had used at the very beginning of the tournament. The one that made her stomach squirm with the falling sensation, as the box jolted and began to descend. Roh couldn't help but think of Orson, who'd squeezed her arm in sympathy the first time they'd journeyed into the Upper Sector. Roh had to believe that their friendship had been real at that point, that it hadn't all been part of some long-winded plan to best her when the time came.

The numerous levels of Talon's Reach passed as they tunnelled down into the leagues under the seabed. Darkness greeted them, punctuated by glimmers of torches and valo-beetle jars, the screech of the chains snatching Roh from her thoughts as they lurched to a stop. They stepped out from the crate into the Lower Sector of Saddoriel, Roh's home.

It was quiet. A dark, cramped, hopeless place. Roh could even smell the bone shavings drifting down from the workshop.

'Why are we here, Rohesia?' Marlow asked at last.

'I … I felt the protection around the prison,' she said. 'But … I have to see the Lower Sector … I have to see for myself that my fellow lowborns are safe.'

'But your coronation –'

'Can wait,' she countered. 'Saddoriel has suffered a trauma. It is my duty to make sure that its less privileged inhabitants are safe.'

Marlow seemed to struggle to find the words, and in the end he simply bowed his head and followed her down the passageway she'd know in her sleep.

The quiet, square workshop smelled of bone shavings and sawdust, as it always had. Pieces of ivory gleamed on the floor in the flickering candlelight and barrels of bones stood by each workbench, ready to be cleaned and sorted the following day. Windows had shattered in the chaos and glass crunched beneath Roh's boots as she stepped inside, checking that no one lay injured within.

She turned around to find Marlow standing over his desk staring down at something, his spectacles perched on the bridge of his nose.

'What were you working on?' Roh asked, peering over his shoulder at the canvas lying there.

'From time to time, I restore the art that hangs in the Passage of Kings. This one has been gathering dust for years. Arcelia Bellfast noticed and asked me to tend to it. I was in the middle of it when I received word that you were here.'

Roh stared at the artwork on her uncle's desk. 'I've seen that before,' she said, her eyes roving over the painting she'd seen on the Bridge of Csilla when Floralin had told them of the terror tempests. Valli had been particularly enamoured with the scene: King Asros' consort, Freya, slaying a sea drake, defending Saddoriel.

'There were many replicas made,' Marlow was telling her. 'A fine moment in cyren history.'

Roh realised that Marlow had no idea about Valli, that up until a few hours before, she had had a great sea drake at her side. 'You think they're all bad?' she asked.

Marlow studied the painting thoughtfully. 'Actually, I've always been of the school of thought that Freya was trying to save the beast.'

'*Save* it?'

'Yes. There are a handful of scholars who believe she was trying to pull the dagger from the beast, not pierce its heart.'

'Oh.'

For the first time since Roh could remember, Marlow was looking at her, *really* looking at her, and the crown that now sat atop her head. 'You did it,' he croaked, as though only just realising it.

Roh stared back at him. He was here, like he'd always been, in the workshop, the mentor of bone cleaners ... But he wasn't only a *mentor* to her. She chewed the inside of her cheek. 'Do you mind that I've been calling you Marlow?' she asked suddenly, gripping the doorframe as the words came tumbling out.

He froze by his desk. 'What would you like to call me?'

Roh took in the sight of his lined face. 'Ames doesn't seem right anymore.'

'Alright.'

'But nor does "uncle".'

Was that a flash of hurt in his eyes?

He cleared his throat. 'Then it seems my true name suits best.'

'Marlow ...' Roh tested the name again, realising that she had already started to think of him as such. Marlow, her uncle, her family … She supposed he had been the closest thing she'd had to a father all these years. 'Marlow works,' she said.

Marlow nodded. 'It's settled, then.'

The timing was perfect because Harlyn burst through the doorway and nearly crashed into Roh. 'Ames!' she shouted, shoving past Roh and throwing herself at their mentor.

Roh nearly laughed at how uncomfortable Marlow looked with Harlyn's arms wrapped around him. He patted her awkwardly on the back before pulling away.

'Glad to see your arm is on the mend, Harlyn.'

Harlyn grinned. 'Nothing much has changed around here, then?'

'We're calling him Marlow now, Har,' Roh told her friend.

'Really? I thought "Uncle Ames" had a nice ring to it.'

Roh scoffed. 'Of course you did.'

But Harlyn's face was all seriousness as she looked sternly at Marlow. 'I do hope you realise that you've gained *two* nieces, not just one.'

'Never doubted it for a second,' Marlow said, a soft smile gracing his face.

Harlyn gave him a grin before turning to Roh. 'Jesmond said for us to meet in the dining hall.'

'How does Jesmond know …?'

Marlow gave a sigh. 'I've come to accept that that girl knows most things before the rest of us.' He returned to his desk, gathering a number of delicate brushes scattered there and placing them in their tins. 'An exhausting habit of hers.'

Harlyn nudged Roh. 'The others are waiting outside.'

Roh hesitated, wanting to ask Marlow more, wanting to stay with him, but he gave her a knowing smile. 'Go. You wanted to see the Lower Sector for yourself. I think you will find it much changed, Rohesia.'

Out in the passageway, all her companions waited, even Odi.

Without thinking, she smacked him on the shoulder with the back of her hand. 'What in the realms are you still doing here?'

Odi grinned. 'I said I'd be here till the end, didn't I?'

'But —'

'I saw your magic,' Odi interjected. 'It rushed down the tunnel we were in and reinforced the walls. It was incredible, Roh. I knew it was you, knew I could come back.'

'But your brothers —'

'Are safe. I told them the way, told them to keep their talismans close. They're leading the other musicians to the Isle of Dusan.' Odi squeezed her shoulder gently. 'It's alright, Roh. This is where I'm meant to be. If you truly are the one to bring us all together, then you need a human at your side.'

'I …' Roh wanted to protest, but the words didn't come. She knew he was right.

Odi turned to Harlyn, surveying the dank passage. 'I thought you were going to eat me the first time I was down here,' he said.

A laugh burst from the former bone cleaner, as it had the first time Odi had voiced his concern.

Roh felt a grin split across her own face. 'At least there's more meat on him now,' she quipped with a pointed look at Odi's shoulders, which had broadened over the course of their journey.

Harlyn snorted.

'I'm right here,' Odi objected.

Harlyn barked another laugh and threw her good arm around him. 'That you are, Prince of Melodies, and have been since the beginning.'

Roh could have sworn Odi leaned into Harlyn's embrace.

'While I very much enjoy jokes at the human's expense,' Finn drawled, 'don't we have a coronation to prepare for? Why are we down here?' He was leaning back against the rock wall, arms folded over his chest as he waited expectantly, amusement in his eyes.

It took Roh a moment to realise he was talking to her. 'I … I wanted to check on the lowborn cyrens.'

This seemed like a good enough reason for everyone, and as she led them down the narrow passageway, salt glimmering in the dark stone walls, Finn caught up with her.

'So …' he said, a smile tugging at the corner of his mouth, his dimple showing.

Roh glanced at him. 'So …?'

'This is where you grew up.' He looked around.

Roh refused to blush. 'It is. And?'

But he wasn't teasing her, she realised, his lilac eyes lingered on her, brimming with a meaning she couldn't pinpoint, flicking up to her crown and then meeting her gaze again.

'And look at you now,' he said, still smiling, a note of pride in his voice. 'Saviour of Saddoriel …'

It took all of Roh's willpower not to stop in the middle of the path, not to reach out and bring his face to hers. Instead, she loosed a breath and kept walking. 'Yes,' she murmured. 'Look at me now.'

To her surprise, despite where they were and who could see them, Finn laced his fingers through hers. Roh looked down at their linked hands, calloused palm to calloused palm, Jaktaren and bone cleaner … And Finn didn't let go.

'Roh!' Harlyn near shouted, surging ahead. 'Look!'

Roh followed Har's pointed finger to the walls of the passageway ahead. There, banners and streamers adorned every possible surface, flowers, too. Roh's chest tightened as she drew closer. The last time she'd seen such festivities, they'd been in honour of the water runner, Neith. A power play from the highborn whose hand she now held. A tactic that had undone her at the time.

But this … Roh stopped and stared at the squares of material hanging from the walls, messages scrawled across them …

Queen of Bones.

Rohesia for Queen.

Rohesia, Saviour of the Lower Sector.

Long Rule the Crown of Bones.

CHAPTER NINETEEN

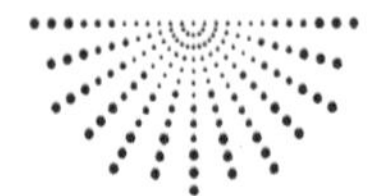

Roh stood there gaping at the words, words she'd longed to see since the second she'd entered the tournament. She had often dreamed of this support, of this moment …

'Who did this?' she breathed.

Deodan came to stand beside her and gaze upon the wall. 'Your people,' he told her.

Her people … Despite the three birthstones in her crown, despite the coronation currently being planned in her honour and despite everything she had done to reach this point, part of her still hadn't believed it. That a bone cleaner could be the Queen of Cyrens, that a bone cleaner would have the support of *her people*.

'Roh?' Harlyn pressed. 'Jesmond said to meet in the dining hall?'

Harlyn led the way to the Lower Sector dining hall, Roh close behind her. Finn and Yrsa were particularly quiet as they navigated the lowborn levels. Roh knew that Finn had been down here at least once before when he had commissioned his bone transporter for the second trial of the tournament, but perhaps he hadn't seen all that much of the Lower Sector, for his and Yrsa's expressions were tense. After all, they had never belonged down here.

Deodan and Kezra remained at the back of the group, looking equally shocked to see where Roh had spent the majority of her life. Roh didn't say anything to them. What had they expected when they'd heard she was a bone cleaner?

Roh could hear the bustle of the dining hall well before they reached it. A pang of guilt lanced through her as she remembered the last time she'd walked through those doors. It had been then she'd convinced Jesmond to present the card game as her own idea, the morning that Orson's mother had yelled at them, calling Harlyn and her *blood-hungry orphans* for getting her daughter mixed up in their deadly games.

The doors swung inwards. The dining hall seemed untouched by the terror tempest, and inside the lowborns fell silent, all eyes falling to Roh.

Uncertainty swelled. Had she completely misjudged her place here? Had those banners been a cruel joke? Had —

Applause erupted, thunderous and near deafening.

Dazed, Roh stepped into the dining hall. Her fellow lowborns swarmed around her, clapping her on the back, heartily congratulating her and marvelling at the birthstones in her crown. Roh had always known Harlyn was the most popular of their trio, but that didn't seem to matter now. There would be a lowborn queen, someone to change the ways of the Lower Sector for the better, that's what mattered to her people.

Unlike the panic she'd felt in Akoris when the fanatics had surrounded her, Roh felt at ease here. The faces and voices were familiar and encouraging; she wondered what they'd be like if she revealed her warlock magic. Roh kept it hidden; now was not the time or place. Her friends waited by the doors, watching as the entire sector welcomed her with open arms. It was how she'd imagined it once, long ago.

And they were all whole and healthy – the terror tempest had not broken them or their spirit.

But then she spotted a figure hunched over in the corner of the hall, paying no heed to the festivities unfolding around her … Roh froze, expecting the cyren's gaze to lift to hers and for a whirlwind of rage to spiral towards her. But there was no eye contact, not even a flicker of recognition in Roh's direction. Orson's mother was a shell of her former self, all her rage and fire gone, as though grief had scooped out her insides and left her empty. Her face, which was once so like her daughter's, had aged drastically in the months that had passed.

Harlyn was at Roh's side then, the chatter of the crowd falling away from the pair of them as they looked towards their friend's mother. 'Do you think we should say something?' she asked.

'What is there to say? That we're sorry we entered the tournament? That we're sorry she chose to challenge me? That we're sorry she ever met us at all?' Roh shook her head. 'Not now. We don't say anything now. Not with everyone here.'

Slowly, Harlyn nodded in agreement. 'Her *meesha* is gone,' she whispered.

'She is,' Roh murmured. 'But we can only cling to the fact that it was Orson's choice, can't we?'

Suddenly, the doors banged open again and a stern, older cyren's face came into view, as did a trolley of hefty tomes being pushed towards Roh, the wheels squeaking noisily.

'That book you borrowed is *long* overdue,' Andwana barked when he reached her, his voice gruff.

Roh tried not to smile. 'My apologies. I returned it to the Akorian library.'

'It was overdue even then.'

'That it was,' Roh allowed, waiting for the moment of realisation to hit him.

A second later, it did. Andwana's eyes widened as his gaze

caught the crown atop her head and the three gems gleaming there.

'You're –'

'Not here in a bone cleaner capacity, no,' Roh finished for him.

Andwana's cheeks reddened. 'Well …' He cleared his throat and straightened. 'Well, you still owe me a book, Majesty.'

Roh smiled freely then. 'I suppose I do.'

Shock rippled across his face and through the rest of the crowd. Roh guessed that wasn't how a queen might speak to a lowborn making demands of her … But she had decided long ago that she didn't want to be a ruler like the rest, that she wanted to be different.

Roh turned to the crowds. 'There is to be a coronation in the Great Hall of the Upper Sector,' she said, projecting her voice to the far corners of the hall. 'Elder Sigra will send word with the details, but I hope to see each and every one of you there.'

Some time later, Deodan noticed Roh swaying on her feet and insisted that they retire for a meal and rest. It wasn't long after that Roh found herself at the silver doors to the queen's private residences, her companions at her side. She placed a hand on one of the doors. It opened beneath the slightest of touches and Roh entered the grand hallway, greeted by pristine white walls and a floor of shining blue marble that reflected the chandeliers of bone above. But Roh's attention went immediately to the feature she remembered best from her brief visit to these residences … At the end of the hallway, from floor to ceiling was a veil of shimmering water. An enchanted portal to the turquoise sea surrounding Talon's Reach. A private door to the currents and tides.

But she was ushered into a room, where a servant greeted them at the creamy white doors.

'Roh, this is Ellis,' Yrsa explained. 'He usually oversees my aunt's residence, but I thought he could help us here temporarily. I wanted someone we could trust.'

'Good idea,' Roh said gratefully.

Upon seeing Roh and her crown, Ellis threw himself at the floor. 'Your Majesty, it is the greatest honour —'

Roh pulled the cyren to his feet, flushing furiously. 'It's fine,' she assured him. 'It's not official yet anyway.'

'You wear the birthstones of Saddoriel, Majesty. It is simple in my eyes. You are queen.'

'Well, I thank you for that,' Roh said awkwardly.

Ellis was suddenly all business, turning to Yrsa with a renewed purpose in his gaze. 'You must be famished. I have prepared some food in the drawing room.' He gestured inside.

At the mention of food, Roh's stomach gurgled loudly and she realised with a start that she had not eaten since the night before in Lochloria, nor had she slept ... She entered the room to find every feature elegant and well designed, ensuring a flow throughout the entire space. Four turquoise lounges created a square at the centre, a low silver table placed in the middle, upon which trays of food had been carefully placed. Finn threw himself down on one of the seats unceremoniously, smacking a cushion into a more comfortable position.

Roh sat down next to him slowly. It felt strange to be amidst finery once again, their dirty travel clothes and muddied boots in stark contrast to the luxurious furnishings and polished floors.

Harlyn sank into the thick pillows with a satisfied sigh and propped her legs up on Odi's lap.

Odi raised a brow at her. 'Make yourself comfortable, why don't you?'

Harlyn gave a lazy grin. 'Oh, I intend to.'

There was another loud sigh from the opposite lounge, where Deodan had kicked off his boots and lain down lengthways, resting his feet on the rounded arm, his holey socks visible to all.

'Your feet are worse than mine,' Kezra scoffed as she inched away from Deodan on the sofa beside him, her nose screwed up in disgust, though it clearly didn't affect her appetite. Kezra reached forward, taking a plate from the pile and starting to load it up with pies, cheeses and sauces. 'Well,' she said, taking a massive bite of a honey-soaked roll. 'Everyone should eat.'

'And sleep,' Harlyn moaned.

Roh's gaze paused on her friend, realising that it had been some time since she had asked about the voice that had plagued Harlyn. She didn't doubt that Harlyn would tell her about it when she was ready, but it didn't stop Roh wondering about the source of the voice and what it meant. Was it a result of Harlyn's guilt about Orson's terrible fate? A figment of her imagination? She quietly surveyed Harlyn's relaxed posture and her lingering looks at Odi … Perhaps Harlyn hadn't mentioned it because the antidote she'd been given had done its work …?

Harlyn will talk to me when she needs to, she thought, deciding to leave the subject alone for the time being.

And so at last, she turned to the generous spread of food before them and ate well. As she did, her mind wandered to what it would be like to look upon her mother after all this time, with the crown upon her head. There would be time for that soon enough, she told herself, time after she had gazed upon the *Tome of Kyeos* and had determined the truth of things for herself. Then and only then would she visit Cerys the Elder Slayer. She pushed the thought away, exhaustion at last gripping her in its talons.

Despite the weariness, Roh finally shoved her plate aside and rested her elbows on the table, her mind ticking through everything she had learned upon her return to Saddoriel. She had saved Saddoriel from a terror tempest, she had a *lifesong*, a *following*, her coronation ceremony was supposedly underway … and yet something nagged at the back of her mind.

'What do you suppose they're up to?' she asked, assessing her companions.

'The council?' Finn asked.

Roh nodded. 'I have not been challenged a third time, which seems unlikely. But once I'm officially crowned, there will be no opportunity for that, so there must be something else they're plotting ...'

'Perhaps they've finally accepted you,' Harlyn offered. 'You've done everything they've asked, you've achieved everything the extension clause dictated. You *saved Saddoriel*. You're the rightful queen, they must know that now.'

'Knowing and accepting are two different things,' Yrsa said.

'Agreed,' Roh murmured.

Yrsa motioned for Ellis to enter the room. 'Ellis, can you please send word to Elder Sigra and Elder Ward and enquire about the delay with Her Majesty's coronation? Stress that this must take place as soon as possible.'

Ellis bowed his head. 'At once, Mistress Ward.'

'Thank you.'

Roh shot Yrsa a grateful look. The Jaktaren's decisiveness helped ground her, but there was another matter plaguing her mind. She needed a moment to herself. Roh left the drawing room, and in the hallway outside exhaled shakily and leaned against the wall, pressing her forehead to the cool plaster there, which was where Yrsa found her.

'There are still things we need to discuss, Yrs,' Roh managed wearily.

'After.' The Jaktaren put an arm around her and started to lead her down the hallway. 'We all should rest. Ellis will find me when there is more to know and we can go from there.'

Relief washed over Roh. What she craved more than anything else was a long, hot soak, but she soon realised that she had no idea where she might find a bathing chamber in the queen's residences.

Yrsa seemed to pre-empt her needs. 'Ellis told me where everything is,' she said quietly.

Making her excuses to the others, Roh followed Yrsa from the drawing room down a wide hallway, passing several doors leading off into various chambers. The floor shone beneath her mud-caked boots and she chastised herself for not taking them off at the door. Yrsa took her to a carved door at the end of the corridor and pushed it open.

'This is the master bathing chamber. There are fresh towels and clothes within. I had Ellis gather some choices in your size.'

Inside was a lavish, tiled marvel and an in-ground tub full to the brim with steaming water.

'Thank you, Yrs,' Roh managed.

With that, her friend left her to it, seeming to sense that after everything, Roh needed some time alone.

Roh felt oddly numb as she stripped off her own travel-worn clothing. Her arms, face and neck were flecked with dirt and her hair was a tangled mass. A quick glance in the spotless mirror revealed that she'd lost weight and a haunted, hollow gaze stared back at her.

Where was the cyren from the Csillan mirror pool? The wings, the lilac eyes, the long hair ... and the fierce determination ... Where were all those things in her reflection? Had she not just saved Saddoriel from the deadly wrath of the tempests?

With steady hands Roh reached for her crown, placing it carefully on the vanity. Leaving her clothes in a heap, she eased herself into the tub, hissing at the heat of the water on her skin. She submerged herself fully, knowing that when she resurfaced, it would be a rebirth, as the Queen of Cyrens.

With little concept of time, Roh had finished bathing and dressed, only to emerge to a quiet residence. Exhaustion had latched onto her; she didn't have the energy to go searching for the bedrooms, so she curled up on one of the lounges in the drawing room, pulling a heavy blanket over her and sinking into a deep sleep.

Roh woke with a start, her heart racing, her skin tingling. It was not from the dream she was having; the birthstones of Saddoriel were humming quietly in her crown. It had slipped from her head, but the warmth of the stones kissed her face. She found herself standing, placing the crown upon her head once more and moving towards the door.

Is this a new dream? she wondered, following the pull of the gems' magic.

Soon, she stood before the mesmerising veil to the sea and she knew this was no dream. *She* was the queen and this veil belonged to her now. Slowly, Roh walked towards it, the song of the sea calling out to her, as vibrant and powerful as any melody. Her own magic uncoiled within, answering to the power that beckoned beyond. Roh lifted a hand to the veil. The barrier of it glimmered and moved with the rhythm of the water on the other side.

I could dive straight through this and feel the kiss of the sea on my skin, Roh marvelled. She needed no one's permission. She belonged to herself and herself alone. Her magic thrummed within at the thought and the gems pulsed within the crown. She was her own master.

Her fingertips brushed against the silvery surface of the veil —

'Roh.'

She would know that voice anywhere, low and melodic. But she didn't turn around. She was enchanted by the call of the current beyond the veil, as she had been the first time she had entered these quarters as a lowly bone cleaner, mesmerised by the depths of the sea … How long had it been since she'd swum freely through its waves and bent its tide to her will? How long since she'd tasted salt on her tongue and the soft graze of sand against her skin?

'Roh.' Finn's breath tickled the side of her neck.

Roh knew if she leaned back, the wall of his body would catch her. His scent wrapped around her, warm and masculine.

'You're alright?' she murmured.

'We're all alright,' he told her, a reminder of what they had been through and that they had emerged victorious. 'Are you? You look like you're about to jump through the veil and not look back.'

He stood so close behind her and yet he hadn't touched her, hadn't closed that final gap between them.

'I'm not going to do that.' Her voice was suddenly hoarse. 'That's not what I want right now.'

'No?' There was more than one question laced in that word.

Roh turned to face him. 'No,' she said, rising up on her toes.

Finn's words caught. 'Well … that's …'

Roh kissed him. Everything else fell away. The violence of the terror tempest, the call of the seas, the power of her lifesong and her impending reign all faded into the depths beyond the veil. Finn deepened the kiss, drawing her to him and crushing his body to hers. Roh arched into him, a thrill rushing down her spine as his tongue brushed against hers and the heat of his hands soaked through the thin fabric of her shirt.

'This is happening?' he murmured against her lips.

'Yes,' she told him.

Together they stumbled towards the closest door, bursting through it, still tangled in one another.

'This is the kitchen,' Roh realised, pausing to survey the pots and pans lining the walls. She'd only ever been in one room of the queen's quarters before.

'I don't care,' Finn said roughly, pushing her up against a bench and grazing his teeth against the column of her neck.

Roh gasped, her hands finding the buttons of his shirt. Her

fingers weren't working. They trembled as she tried to undo the top one. Finn's hand came up and tore clean through the material.

Roh pulled back for a moment, drinking in the sight of his ridged abdomen and the vicious scar that marred it – courtesy of the sea serpent she'd saved him from. Inhaling sharply, she pushed the scraps of shirt from his shoulders, exposing his muscular torso, tracing every old wound. She trailed soft kisses across his skin, his whole body tense with anticipation as she worked her way down his chest.

He pulled her back up to his mouth, lifting her so she was seated on the bench, her legs on either side of him. He kissed her deeply, bunching her shirt in his fists.

'Take it off,' she said.

'This?' He waved the material back and forth.

'Yes. But maybe don't rip it – it's not mine.'

'You are queen. Everything is yours.' There seemed to be a double meaning there and he ripped it anyway. With contrasting gentleness, he brushed the straps of her camisole from her shoulders and the fabric that clung to her breasts fell away to her waist.

Finn stepped back and gazed upon her. 'Gods, you're beautiful,' he said breathlessly. He drew them together again, his hands tracing the curves of her body. 'You said you haven't done this before.' It wasn't a question.

Roh shook her head anyway, her heart hammering in her chest, her skin utterly alive. 'You have?'

Finn paused. 'No.'

'No? I thought …'

Finn broke away from her and Roh felt suddenly self-conscious. She pulled her camisole up to cover herself, but Finn kicked off his boots and his hands went to his belt. He didn't take his eyes off her as he unbuckled it and then undid the buttons of his pants, pushing them over his hips. He pulled them away from his ankles, and there, in the kitchen of the queen's private residences, Finn Haertel of the Jaktaren guild stood naked before her.

'Have you forgotten that no one knew about my leg?' He gestured to where flesh met prosthetic.

Roh's breathing hitched. But she wasn't looking at his leg. Nearly every inch of him was corded with muscle and the other parts … Her mouth went dry. He was glorious. She wondered if she should say it aloud, but the words got tangled on her tongue.

'Apart from my family, no one ever knew about me. Until you.' He watched her watch him, tension rippling off him. 'So no,' he said finally. 'I haven't done this before …' Still naked, he went to the shelves against the wall and pulled an armful of linens onto the floor. He met her gaze again. 'But gods, do I want to.'

Roh slipped down from the bench and removed her camisole entirely. She pushed aside any remaining self-consciousness and slid her pants free, too.

'So do I,' she said as she went to him.

They drank in the sight of one another, like cyrens starved of the sea. Finn tugged her down to the table linens. The floor was hard beneath them, but it didn't matter. Finn pulled her on top of him.

Roh gasped at the heat of Finn's bare skin against hers; her breasts against his chest and the hard length of him pressing between her legs.

'Roh …' he moaned against her mouth.

It was intoxicating, the feel of him, the taste of him, the sound of him. He kissed her fiercely and she kissed him back just as hard, her talons dragging down his back. He reached between her legs and —

Pleasure rushed through Roh. She moaned, her cheeks flushing and heat spreading down her neck across her chest. 'I thought you hadn't —'

'I didn't say I was a saint,' he murmured, circling that intimate part of her with his fingers.

Roh moaned into his mouth and pushed against his hand. She wanted more, more of him, more of *this*. Feeling bold, she reached between them, touching him.

Finn swore, his head tipping back.

Roh jumped, snatching her hand away. 'Did I hurt you?'

The Jaktaren laugh huskily. 'Only when you stop.'

Roh suppressed a smile. 'Then I won't stop.'

Finn's hand gripped the back of her neck and drew her mouth back to his. 'Good.'

Roh couldn't believe this was happening. She was naked on the floor of the queen's residences with *Finn Haertel*. *Finn Haertel* was kissing her. *Finn Haertel* was touching her, creating a build-up of pleasure. *Finn Haertel* was on top of her.

He lowered his mouth to her neck, trailing kisses along the curves of her breasts and the plane of her stomach. Roh's back arched as his hands slid to her thighs, opening her to him. She was utterly bare. The vulnerability sent a delicious shiver to the base of her spine and she held her breath, unsure of what came next.

Her whole body bucked as Finn put his mouth on her. Coils of pleasure tightened within as his tongue explored. She moaned again, loudly. 'What are you doing?' she gasped, writhing on the floor beneath his touch.

'Worshipping you,' he murmured against her skin, creating wet, heady circles with his tongue.

It was Roh's turn to swear as his finger brushed –

She couldn't stand it any longer, she wrenched him back up to her, desperate to feel the full weight of him on her body. A gasp escaped her as the hard length of him brushed against the place he'd left wet and wanting.

'What about …?' Roh didn't want to ruin the moment with talk of protecting against pregnancy, but …

'I take a certain tonic,' Finn told her softly.

Roh stared. 'Really?'

'Since Akoris. I didn't know … Well, I didn't know *this* would happen. But I knew I wanted it to. I thought I should … you know.'

'You've wanted this for that long?' Roh asked.

Still poised above her, Finn raised a brow, mischief shining in his lilac eyes. 'Haven't you?'

Roh drew him to her, excitement and nerves churning within. 'Yes.' She wrapped her legs around him.

'You're sure?'

'I'm sure.'

Finn moved then, lacing his fingers through hers and holding them above her head. Slowly, he pushed into her.

A sharp breath caught in Roh's throat. She could feel herself stretching as he entered her. She froze beneath him, inhaling through the pain.

Finn halted. 'Should I stop?'

Roh shook her head. Harlyn had told her it might be like this the first time and that it would get better, that she would adjust. 'Just take it slow,' Roh whispered, her lips finding Finn's once more.

'Promise me you'll tell me if it —'

Roh locked eyes with him, pulling him deeper into her with her legs around his back. 'I promise,' she said, opening herself to the pain, breathing through it and focusing on the addictive feel of him.

Finn moaned, his hot breath tickling her face. 'Gods.'

The next time Finn moved inside her, Roh moved with him.

Eventually, clutching their discarded clothes and tablecloths around their naked bodies, Roh and Finn found the master bedroom. The opulence of it rivalled all the fine things Roh had seen since leaving the Lower Sector put together: an enormous canopy bed, layers of silk sheets and cushions, a walk-in robe brimming with highborn fashions and a bathing chamber the size of the bone workshop, with an in-ground tub large enough for several cyrens. But none of it mattered to Roh. Content and tired, the pair collapsed in a heap on the luxurious mattress, the candles burning low around them.

Roh gazed at Finn, noting his heavy lids and sleepy smile.

'Does me being queen matter to you?' she asked him, stroking his arm lightly with her talons.

'I kissed you long before you were queen,' he murmured, his voice thick with exhaustion as he lay back. 'I kissed you when we were just two cyrens standing at the edge of a ravine.'

Roh huffed a laugh. 'I was the one who kissed *you*,' she told him. But he didn't hear those words, sleep had already claimed him.

For a time, Roh watched Finn sleep, the steady rise and fall of his chest, the way the harsh lines of his face softened. She lay on her side, still feeling as though it had all been some sort of beautiful dream, only the pleasant soreness of her body telling her otherwise.

Happy. This is what it feels like to be happy, she realised. No sooner than the realisation hit her, another feeling crept into the hollows of her chest. She swallowed the lump forming in her throat, trying to cling to the breathtaking sight of Finn Haertel in her bed … Roh had thought that by now, she was intimately acquainted with fear. Gods knew she had experienced it on so many levels since entering this godsdamned tournament, but the cold panic in her heart was a different terror, its older, darker cousin perhaps. The terror that came with being so wildly happy that each step was shadowed by the panic that everything might be wrenched away. Terror that settled in the back of one's mind, watching every move, waiting for some fatal coin to drop.

Knowing that happiness was so paramount that any movement could only be one towards its inevitable demise.

Roh eased herself off the bed, careful not to disturb Finn. She couldn't let happiness and fear for that happiness derail her. But she also couldn't let the beautiful cyren in her bed distract her from why she was here.

Word would soon arrive of her coronation, but before then, there was something she needed to do. Urgency gripped Roh, rushing through her as she dressed in the flickering candlelight and placed her crown atop her head. Every fibre of her being told her that *now* was the time, and that she had waited long enough.

Roh slipped from the bed chambers and went to find the *Tome of Kyeos*.

The Vault was exactly as she remembered it. She stood alone where she had once stood with Delja, in the dimly lit cavern. A thick, circular iron door stood before her, a large wheel at its centre, embellished with an array of intricate locks, gears and mechanisms, like the inside of a clock. Roh grasped the wheel at the door's centre, turning it once, twice, thrice, before stepping back as she'd seen the former queen do.

A tiny part of her expected nothing to happen, for there to be yet another unknown obstacle standing in her way, but the gemstones in her crown thrummed and three lines of coloured light hit the giant door, unlocking whatever enchantments were woven into this place. Then, the door groaned loudly beneath its own enormous weight and slowly began to spin, round and round, gaining speed as it went. Its detailing blurred as it spiralled, making a whirring sound that continued to amplify. Roh remembered thinking last time that it might shoot off its invisible hinges, but as soon as the thought crossed her mind, the door snapped to a stop and swung outwards.

Nothing stood between her and the Vault, or her and the *Tome of Kyeos* now.

Hands trembling at her sides, wondering for the first time if she truly wished to know the truth of it all, Roh stepped inside. There was no mistaking it. The beam of light in the heart of the chamber illuminated the very thing she had nearly destroyed herself and those she loved for.

The thick tome hovered in the light, as though weightless, which struck Roh as odd given everything the book held. During the Rite of Strothos, she had hallucinated this moment, her fingers slipping through the tome; forever unattainable, a mirage, a trick of her damaged mind. And so when she reached out now, she held her breath, expecting the worst, expecting to have the *Tome of Kyeos* stolen out from under her.

Her fingertips brushed against the leather-bound spine. A ragged sob escaped Roh as her hand closed around it and pulled it from the beam of light. The book was so heavy in her hands, smelling of must and ink and history. Hinges creaked and another shaft of light hit the cylindrical inside of the Vault. Part of a bookshelf had swung inwards, revealing a small chamber beyond.

Still not quite able to believe she was, in fact, holding the *Tome of Kyeos*, Roh stepped inside, her mouth hanging open in shock. The room held nothing but a sturdy oak desk and a high-backed velvet chair, the walls bare except for the half-dozen sconces and torches. There were no windows, no belongings, nothing that suggested another being had ever stepped foot in this place.

A study, a place to uncover the true histories of cyrenkind.

Roh's throat was tight as she carefully slid the tome across the desk and sat down in the chair, staring at the book in awe.

'Am I ready?' she whispered to herself, daring to run her talons across the front of the book. The birthstones in her crown pulsed. She was ready. She had always been ready. Roh braced herself and opened the *Tome of Kyeos*.

CHAPTER TWENTY

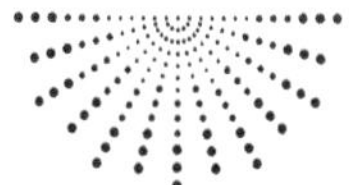

MANY CENTURIES AGO ...

In the brilliant light of a crisp winter's morning, Deelie stood before the great gates of Lochloria, dishevelled after months of travel. Her shoulders were sore from the pack she'd lugged around from one territory to the next, from continent to continent, scouring far and wide. She had left her friends in the scholar's city in search of two things: a magic wielder who dealt in time and immortality, and to learn of the cyrens in the distant lands, who according to lore, had wings like their ancestors. Now, she stared at the gates, willing herself to step inside but finding she was unable to. Throughout her travels, she had wondered if she would be missed, if her plight for uniting those she loved across the ages would be worthwhile, or if she would be forgotten, as she had always been, by her mother, her sisters ... All long gone now.

A memory came to her then, as clear and bright as the day around her: three nestlings arriving at the scholar's city with awestruck faces and wide eyes. Deelie remembered that first afternoon well. How she, Cerys and Marlow had run the perimeter of the vibrant quadrangle, exclamations of glee on their lips, with a tentative wonder for the warlock magic thick in the air while Sedna Irons watched on, smiling openly.

Those first few months in Lochloria were some of the happiest of Deelie's life. When Marlow was whisked away to healers, it was just her and Cerys. They explored the forest and the mountains unsupervised; adventurers who answered to no one. They played warriors and warlocks by the mirror pool, duelling with sticks and collapsing to the ground in fits of giggles when neither could best the other.

The recollection, as well as the smile it had brought to Deelie's lips, faded. Now that she had returned home, she didn't know how to feel about what she'd brought back with her: *knowledge*. More knowledge than her friends could possibly imagine. She rocked on the balls of her feet, mentally sifting through all that she had learned. She wondered how she would share it, how her friends would react to what she had done … Perhaps now wasn't the time to explain herself, perhaps she should turn right around and stay away a little longer. What if Cerys and Marlow and Eadric hadn't missed her at all? What if they liked their group better without her?

Deelie felt the familiar burn of panic rising in her chest.

Yes, she told herself, allowing her fears to take root in her heart. *Perhaps I'll head north again, and give them some more time without —*

'Deelie!' called a voice from behind her.

Killian, her handsome warlock friend, approached. No more was he the long-limbed apprentice who had run her childhood lessons in Lochloria, but rather a fully fledged scholar under the tutelage of the Warlock Supreme himself.

Deelie too had changed since they'd first met all those years ago. She was no longer a curious fledgling who gasped wide-eyed at the sight of warlock magic, nor did she fear her mother's outrage at her entanglement with their kind. Deelie had matured into a strong Saddorien cyren, with a powerful deathsong at the tip of her tongue, and now the knowledge to change the course of cyren history. Plus, her and Cerys' plans were well underway, plans that would see them enter The Dawning, the epic tournament for the next ruler of their kind.

Grinning, Killian navigated the path towards her with two buckets of fresh fish in his hands, eagerness gleaming in his eyes. 'You're back!'

Deelie hesitated.

Killian didn't notice, all but throwing the buckets to the ground and swinging an arm around her shoulder. 'You've been gone an age. You must have some tale to tell. Shall we get the others? Make an afternoon of it?'

Deelie felt a smile tug at the corner of her mouth. 'That sounds nice.'

The warlock was practically bouncing. 'Gods, I can't wait to hear all about it. Outside of Lamaka's Basin, I've only ever been to Saddoriel, but you … You've seen it all!'

Killian's enthusiasm was catching. Deelie found herself nodding, an ember of hope flaring to life in her chest.

'I have seen quite a bit, recently,' she allowed, giving him a shy smile. Although they had both lived for more than decades now, Deelie was always aware that Killian was *older*. He had walked the realms for longer than she had and their relationship had started with him as her teacher … It didn't seem to bother Killian; he treated her as he treated all his friends, with a cheerful keenness and kind interest in everything that she did.

'That settles it, then. Why don't you get cleaned up and I'll grab some food? Cerys and the others won't be far. I'll meet you at the stream in the quadrangle?' Killian's words tumbled from him in hurried excitement.

He was already through the gates with his fish before Deelie had finished agreeing. But it didn't matter. She adjusted her pack and shook the fears from her head. She had let her insecurities get the better of her yet again. Her friends were *always* glad to see her. She *had* been missed. Eagerness sprang to life in her once more. She couldn't wait to see Cerys, she couldn't wait to continue their planning together. Many times on her journey, Deelie had pictured them winning The Dawning together, being crowned Queens of Cyrenkind. Together they would make history.

Deelie gave a contented sigh. She was *home*. And soon, she would see her family.

The Irons' residence was empty when she arrived and Deelie's body sagged with relief as she looked around. Everything was as it should be, and the faint scent of sandalwood soap was comforting and familiar. Dropping her pack by the door, Deelie crossed the room and threw herself down on her bed. She'd missed her soft mattress, she'd missed seeing Sedna's armour hanging proudly on the wall and she'd missed the neat row of shoes by the door. She didn't know why she'd come here first. She had her own rooms in the Resident Halls, but ... it wasn't the same. It never had been. It had been a long while since they'd all shared these chambers, but Sedna had always insisted that they come and go as they pleased, that they always call this place *home*.

Deelie set about bathing and changing into a fresh set of clothes, savouring the familiarity and the nostalgia of the rooms that had been her childhood sanctuary. Deciding it would be rude to keep the others waiting, she tugged on one of Sedna's fur-lined winter cloaks and left, heading for the stream as Killian had told her.

Outside, the day was bright, the winter chill of the mountains settling around her, with just a touch of the sun's distant warmth kissing her skin. Deelie breathed in the crisp air, laced with the scent of freshly cut grass and yellow wattle, the flowers of which fell into the babbling stream in the gentle breeze. The quiet notes of the timber wind chimes danced around her as she walked across the quadrangle, the chance music coaxing her own magic to the surface and playing with her song.

'Deelie!' someone shouted.

She turned just in time for someone to barrel into her, nearly knocking her off her feet.

'Marlow!' she cried, returning his embrace heartily before pulling back to examine him. He was a far cry from the tremor-racked nestling she'd met long ago. 'You look good!' she said. 'Much better than when I left.'

'I *feel* good!' Marlow told her. 'Treatments have been going well. But who cares about that, I want to know where you've been all this time. Come and sit!'

Smiling from ear to ear, Deelie followed Marlow to where Killian waited beneath one of the enormous purple-flowered trees. He'd set up a rug and a basket of food.

'Thought you'd be hungry,' he said by way of greeting.

'I'm famished,' Deelie admitted. She'd travelled through the night to get here, urged on like a horse close to home. She dropped to the rug, curling her feet up underneath her, and reached for an apple. 'Where are Cerys and Eadric?' she asked, taking a bite.

'They said they'd be here soon,' Killian replied happily, looking expectantly at Deelie.

'Soon?' she pressed, frowning. 'What are they doing?'

Killian shrugged. 'They're in the Archives, on the verge of some grand discovery, as usual.'

Deelie stopped eating. She hadn't seen Cerys in *months* and now she wouldn't stop messing around with the old books to come and see her dearest friend, *her sister*?

Marlow seemed to sense her unhappiness. '*We're* here, Deelie,' he said, offering her a canteen. 'Why don't you tell us about your adventure?'

Disappointment soured the remaining piece of apple in

Deelie's mouth and she swallowed it with a grimace. 'But I'll just have to repeat everything when they get here,' she replied, trying to keep the edge of frustration from her voice. She couldn't help the anger that bubbled within, boiling to the surface. She had travelled far and wide, had faced countless dangers, had risked her life *for them*. And now they didn't have the decency to welcome her home?

'Deelie?' Marlow was saying, tugging on her sleeve.

'What?' she snapped.

Marlow flinched at her anger. 'I was just …'

Deelie softened at once. 'I'm sorry,' she said quickly. 'I'm just tired from the journey. What were you saying?'

'Only that by the time we eat something and Killian and I tell you our news, the others will be here and you can tell us all together. How does that sound?'

Deelie's heart swelled and she gave Marlow a grateful smile. Age hadn't hardened any of his beautiful qualities. He was just as sweet and innocent as he'd always been, never failing to look out for everyone, always tending to the cracks in their friendship, smoothing over any ridges and bumps.

'That sounds lovely,' she said, giving his hand a squeeze and noticing how steady it was. Even the patch of discoloured skin on his neck had faded somewhat. 'You really are looking well,' she told him.

Marlow grinned. 'Well, it's all thanks to Killian. He's been finding all manner of new potions and enchantments to help me.'

'That's wonderful,' Deelie said, turning to their warlock friend. 'The Warlock Supreme must be impressed with your work.'

Colour flushed Killian's cheeks. 'He seems happy enough.'

'Well, why don't you tell me about these enchantments? While we wait for Cerys and Eadric?'

Killian beamed.

For the next half-hour, Deelie sat quietly as her friends filled her in on all the developments they'd uncovered in the Greenhouse and the Alchemy Halls. Killian truly seemed to be making strides in his never-ending magical studies under the supervision of the grand warlock leader. Deelie tried to be as present as possible while she listened to their tales, the tales of the two friends who'd *actually* showed up for her, who were always by her side. But as time wore on, she grew more and more impatient, anger leaking into her system like a poison.

Where are Cerys and Eadric? Do they truly not care that I'm back?

Deelie knew it was unfair of her, to sit in the company of two wonderful friends and stew over the absence of others. But Cerys was something more to her, a sister. Did she no longer feel the same about Deelie?

Deelie had lost track of what Marlow and Killian were saying, so she sat quietly, nodding where appropriate and sipping on a flask of Vallian wine. She had all but given up on an appearance from Cerys when a magical water bird came flying into view. It burst before her, showering her with cold droplets.

A familiar laugh followed.

Deelie was on her feet in an instant, scanning the quadrangle for her friend. Sure enough, there she was, walking alongside the warlock, Eadric.

Cerys waved to her. And that ugly thing inside Deelie blackened. They hadn't seen each other in months and Cerys was *waving*? Deelie rooted herself to the ground, stopping herself from bolting towards her friend like an infatuated nestling. The images of her and Cerys with matching crowns upon their heads seemed to go up in flame before her.

When Cerys reached her, she threw her arms around Deelie, squeezing hard. 'I'm so glad you're back!' she cried. 'We have so much to tell you.'

Stiffly, Deelie patted Cerys on the back and pulled away. 'We?'

Cerys nodded. 'Me and Eadric. We've been in the Archives and —'

Deelie's gaze shifted from her friend to the warlock who stood just behind her, smiling.

'Hello, Deelie,' he said, dropping to the rug and digging into the food.

Deelie had to stop herself from staring at Eadric in disbelief. *The sheer nerve of him!*

Cerys pulled her down to the ground. 'We'll tell you about it all later, you're the one with the news. Where in the realms have you been? I thought you were only going away for a week or two.'

'So … you did miss me?' The words had left Deelie's mouth before her self-control could snap in place.

Cerys' brows furrowed and her hand hovered above a pastry. 'Of course I missed you, what are you talking about?'

Deelie reined herself in. 'Nothing,' she said quickly. 'I've been everywhere.'

'Everywhere?' Cerys scoffed.

Deelie met her gaze. 'Yes,' she told her. '*Everywhere.* I went north, to the Upper Realms. I navigated the Valia Forest and bent the currents of the East Sea, I crossed the scorching plains of the Janhallow Desert and explored the dark market of Battalon …' She let her words sink in, at last finding her audience enraptured by her presence and her tale. 'I —'

'What were you looking for?' Eadric interrupted. 'Will you finally tell us that?'

Deelie shot him a glare. It was just like him not to let her finish speaking, just like him to —

'Don't interrupt,' Cerys snapped at him.

Satisfaction welled in Deelie's gut, but Cerys turned to her. 'Though now that he has … Will you tell us, Deelie? It's been driving me mad.'

Deelie sighed. 'That's all you care about?'

'You've been gone forever!' Cerys said, gripping Deelie's hands in hers. 'I'm dying to know what it's been all about.'

Deelie considered her friend. Things had certainly changed over the decades. They were no longer the two nestlings huddled together in lessons, the two of them against the rest of the world. In fact, Deelie could pinpoint the exact moment things had started to change between them … It had been in their first campaign in the Age of Chaos, when they'd been separated from their unit, with Sedna at the heart of the fighting. They'd become stranded on an island, only to be rescued by *a human* of all creatures. Something had changed in Cerys during those weeks, something that no matter how hard Deelie tried, she couldn't bring back and couldn't understand.

Deelie had loved that time on the island with Cerys and the human, working on the cottage. *'It's a simple life, but that's the best kind of life, eh?'* the girl had always said. But Cerys had grown restless there. *Because of Eadric.* They had left the peace and beauty of the island to be thrown back into the fray of sea battles and dirty politics *because of the warlock boy*. Deelie had stayed by Cerys' side – they were sisters, after all, and she could never leave her sister. But it had bothered her, more than she could ever admit aloud. Which was precisely why she'd travelled so far, to ensure that they could never leave one another … that not even death could part them.

'Deelie?' Cerys pressed.

Deelie chewed her lower lip.

'What is it?' Marlow asked, his voice laced with concern as he studied her face. 'You've done something …'

'I …' Deelie stammered, cursing herself. She should have been more prepared for this.

'What did you do, Delja?' Eadric said, the use of her true name blanketing the group in seriousness.

'Nothing … I …'

Cerys squeezed her hand again. 'Deelie, please, you can tell us.'

But Deelie felt the exact opposite, especially with how Eadric was looking at her, suspicion clouding his eyes.

Half-truths, Deelie told herself. *A half-truth is always more believable than an outright lie.*

'I found that magic wielder you mentioned,' Deelie said with a nod to Killian.

Killian leaned in, mouth agape. 'The one who could take and distribute years of life?'

'Yes, that one.'

Killian sucked in a breath. 'What do you mean you "found him"?'

Deelie lifted her chin. 'I scoured the realms. And when I found him in a place called Oremere, I went and spoke to him.'

'What are you talking about, Deelie?' Cerys asked.

Is that a hint of fear in her voice? Deelie wondered, studying her friend for a moment. The selfish part of her hoped that it was. Perhaps Cerys would stop treating her like a simpering fool, perhaps she'd realise that she was just as mighty a Saddorien as she, and that she'd make a formidable ally in The Dawning.

'There is not enough time for us,' Deelie said, her tone hard. 'Not for what we want to achieve.'

Cerys leaned in eagerly then. 'You found something to help us? To help us win the tournament?'

'Better,' Deelie replied. 'I found something to help us rule for centuries, long after we've won.'

Cerys' face went slack, and her eyes drifted to where Eadric sat. They exchanged a look Deelie didn't understand, a look that caused suspicion to roil in her gut. Not for the first time, she got the distinct feeling that the pair had discussed her in private, that slowly but surely Eadric was turning Cerys against her.

'Deelie ...' Cerys said carefully. 'What *exactly* do you mean?'

Deelie felt her nostrils flare and she glared at her friend. How could they sit there and pretend to not understand that what she had sought and what she had done was all *for them*? That she had combed the realms for a power that would ensure they would all stay together, forever.

'What did you do?' Eadric demanded again, turning to face her fully. 'What did you do, Deelie?'

Deelie rounded on him. 'Nothing,' she spat furiously. 'Nothing you won't benefit from later. Which is something you're incredibly good at, swooping in and taking advantage.' She leaped to her feet, emotion suddenly surging inside her, threatening to break free in a powerful wave. 'Just leave me alone. I should never have come back.'

With that, she turned on her heel and left.

A part of her hoped Cerys would follow. In the past, she would have. And Deelie knew if it was just the two of them, they could make sense of everything together, but Eadric … He was a blight on her friend, on their sisterhood. Deelie didn't think about where she was going, she just stormed off, the wind whipping through her hair and goosebumps racing along her arms as the anger dissipated and the lonely sadness of it all set in.

She had been walking for some time when she finally realised where she was going. The other piece of the puzzle, the other half of the knowledge she had obtained in her travels across the seas and the unknown lands.

Before her lay the mirror pool of Lochloria.

A twig snapped behind her and Deelie whirled around, her heart suddenly racing, hope flaring. *Thank the gods, Cerys has come to her senses.*

But it was Killian, dragging the tip of his boot through the dirt, watching her with concern. 'Are you alright?' he asked quietly.

Sighing, Deelie turned back to the pool, folding her arms over her chest. 'I … I overreacted,' she said, her cheeks flushing.

Killian came to stand beside her. 'They're not the most

sensitive pair,' he offered with a shrug. 'They don't realise they leave the rest of us out.'

Deelie's eyes snapped to his. 'You think so, too?'

'Yes,' he said firmly.

Deelie felt a rush of affection for the warlock. So, he knew what it was like to live life in the shadows of the much-loved Cerys Irons and Eadric Cadelle. 'Thank you for checking on me.'

Killian smiled. 'Of course. Always.'

Was Deelie imagining it, or was there an additional meaning between his words? She peered curiously at him, her skin prickling. Cerys had suggested on more than one occasion that the warlock felt more for her than friendship. Perhaps it was time to test the theory.

'Killian?' she asked, keeping her voice soft.

'Hmm?'

'If I asked you a question, would you promise not to tell the others?'

He seemed to brighten at that. 'Of course. I can keep a secret for you.'

Deelie smiled openly at him. 'Alright, then.' She nodded to the mirror pool. 'You know that all cyrens partake in the First Cry?'

'Yes, everyone knows that. They sacrifice their first tears – their essence – to the Pool of Weeping in Saddoriel.'

'Exactly.'

'What is it you want to know, Deelie?' Killian asked gently.

'I want to know if there is a way to extract my essence? To remove it entirely?'

It was clear by his furrowed expression that whatever Killian had been expecting her to ask, this was not it. But he seemed to think on the matter, his hand rising absent-mindedly to scratch his chin.

'Remove your essence, you say?'

'Yes.' Deelie nodded keenly, moving closer. 'From the First Cry ritual.'

'I've never heard of such a thing being done,' he murmured thoughtfully. 'But ... that doesn't mean it can't be done ... Why?'

'I learned of something when I was away ... About the suppression of cyren power,' Deelie told him, trying to decide then and there how much information to divulge and how much she could trust him. 'I ... I just want to know.'

Killian seemed to sense not to push her, not after her emotional outburst with the others. 'I'll find out for you,' he said. 'Then you'll tell me why?'

'Of course,' Deelie replied, reaching for his hand. Gently, she took it in hers and gave it a squeeze. 'Thank you, my friend.'

A few days later, Deelie travelled with Killian in secret to Saddoriel. She hadn't spoken with Cerys since their picnic in the quadrangle. Cerys had visited Deelie's apartments once and knocked on the door, but Deelie had hidden in her room. Cerys didn't come back after that and it made Deelie all the surer of her plans.

Killian was easy to talk to, as he had always been, and they chatted all the way to Talon's Reach, taking one of the less-travelled tunnels. If Deelie had been a highborn or a queen, they could have used the mirror pool, a much quicker alternative.

One day, Deelie vowed. One day she would use the mirror pools to travel wherever she wished.

Nevertheless, in Killian's company, the journey went quickly, and as they both knew, time shifted differently down in the passageways of the lair. When they reached the heart of the territory, they moved in the shadows, careful not to draw attention to themselves as they made their way towards the sacred site.

At last, Deelie looked upon the Pool of Weeping, its still waters glistening in the torchlight, reflecting the canopies of the willows at its banks.

'Are you sure you want to do this?' Killian asked her, his brows knitting together in concern. 'I'm worried it might hurt you.'

'I can handle pain,' Deelie told him. She had lived with it most of her life.

'I know you're strong, but —'

Deelie placed a reassuring hand on the warlock's arm. 'I'm sure, Killian. Please, remove my essence from the pool.'

Killian retrieved a vial from his belt. 'You have to tell me what it will do first.'

'You won't tell the others?'

'I already gave you my word.'

Deelie set her shoulders straight and gazed out onto the source of all cyren power and deceit. 'It will give me wings,' she told him.

CHAPTER TWENTY-ONE

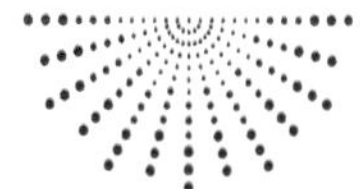

MANY CENTURIES AGO ...

Deelie had told Killian it hadn't worked. That there must have been something missing from his enchantment, or an unforeseen magical barrier around the pool. But now, as she felt the itch of dried blood on her skin and sprinted through the outer passageways of Talon's Reach with Cerys at her side, it took all her willpower to stop her secret wings from materialising at her back. It wasn't time, not yet.

She and Cerys had made it to the final trial of The Dawning – a race through the lair, with any manner of obstacles, including fellow competitors, thrust in their path. The blood that stained Deelie's skin was Sangor's, whom she'd cut down only moments earlier, saving Cerys from a fatal blow to the head.

'Come on,' Deelie panted, glancing back at her friend, who was unsteady on her feet.

'Did you kill him?' Cerys asked, her voice ragged.

'I don't know. But it was you or him,' Deelie snapped, gripping her dripping sword as she skidded to a stop and checked around the corner. 'It's clear,' she said, darting ahead. She felt no guilt for what she had done; everyone knew that The Dawning was life and death. There was no way she would allow a cyren other than her and Cerys to take the crown at the end.

'We're in the lead?' Cerys called.

'Yes by my count, we're not far now. Can you feel it? Feel Saddoriel calling to you?'

'I can,' Cerys murmured, close behind.

Notes of music from the heart of the lair drifted down to wherever they had found themselves, scrapping in the mud, fighting beast, cyren and element to claw their way to the crown. They had trained for this for years. They had known what they were getting into, what they'd have to do, what they'd have to sacrifice to survive ... And Deelie had sacrificed much to safeguard their future.

'Are you alright?' Cerys asked her, pulling her to a stop.

'Fine,' Deelie said hurriedly. 'We can't linger here, we need to make it to the archway.'

Cerys smiled. 'Deelie ...'

'Yes?'

'We're going to do this ... It's happening.'

'I know.'

'We're going to be —'

'Don't say it,' Deelie hushed her. 'Don't say it until it's true.'

Cerys grinned widely and Deelie was suddenly with the eager fledgling she'd learned to spar with in the forests of Lochloria, her heart near bursting with joy. She couldn't help but grin back. 'Alright then, let's go.'

The two cyrens set out at a jog, each on high alert for any incoming attack, any danger lurking in the dark. They had already faced gruesome traps and backstabbing peers, a tunnel of flame and an enchanted veil to the sea that Cerys had suspected led to a sea drake's nest. She had all but dragged Deelie away from it, until the lure wore off and Deelie could see straight again.

Deelie's pulse raced in excitement. There was something so

inherently thrilling about being down here, facing off with death, her friend by her side. This was something no one could take away from them, something that no one else would ever share with them. *No one.*

Up ahead, torchlight flickered at the base of a pulley system to the Upper Sector.

'We've made it,' Deelie breathed as they approached.

Cerys hesitated at the crate. 'It can't be this easy.'

'Easy?' Deelie's brows shot up. 'Look at us.' She gestured to their blood-soaked and singed clothing, the cuts to their skin, the mud that caked their legs up to their thighs.

'Well, perhaps "easy" was the wrong word.'

'You don't say,' Deelie scoffed, crossing her arms over her chest. But she knew what her friend meant; the pulley system just stood there, waiting for them. Presumably to take them to the Upper Sector, to the entrance of Saddoriel, where they would take the crown as their own ...

'It's not like we have a choice, I suppose,' Cerys said, studying the inside of the crate that was to transport them between levels.

'We could take the passageways, but that would take hours. Then whoever's behind could jump in here and beat us to the archway,' Deelie countered.

'So, we're in agreement?'

Deelie nodded. 'We take the risk.'

'We take the risk,' Cerys echoed, offering Deelie her hand. 'Together?'

Deelie grasped it in her own. 'Always.'

The pair stepped inside the crate and closed the doors, Deelie pressing the large button to start their ascent. The heavy metal box groaned as it began to lift upwards. Still holding Cerys' hand, Deelie scanned the interior of the pulley system, suspicion uncoiling, raising the hairs on the back of her neck.

Cerys opened her mouth to speak, but Deelie's finger shot to her lips, a silent plea for no noise. Buzzing, Deelie could hear a quiet buzzing nearby.

Cerys' eyes widened as she too heard it.

Seconds later, Deelie spotted the source. A nucrite, fluttering by a valo-beetle jar in the top-right corner of the crate – a tiny winged insect that in a swarm would eat the flesh off their bones.

Deelie froze, using her eyes to show Cerys what accompanied them. For where there was one, there was usually more.

The two cyrens were as still as death. Deelie could hardly breathe as she spotted another nucrite creep from a crack in the wall, and another, and another. Soon, there were dozens buzzing around them, the flutter of their wings sending goosebumps around Deelie's arms. All it would take was one sound to send them into a flesh-eating frenzy; she only hoped her heart didn't hammer in her chest too loudly.

With her blood roaring in her ears, Deelie remained perfectly still, inhaling and exhaling ever so delicately through her nose, careful not to disturb so much as the air around her. The levels of Saddoriel flew past outside in a blur, but still Deelie and Cerys did not move. Deelie could feel the sweat lining her palms, her shirt growing damp with perspiration.

Of course the council elders had saved the worst for last: an agonising, messy death that would have both of them screaming for Sedna before the end. And so they made not a sound, not a flicker of movement.

Deelie clenched her entire body to stop it from trembling as a bead of sweat formed at her brow and rolled to her temple, sliding down her cheek and neck. The nucrites continued buzzing around them, as though poised to attack at any moment.

The pulley system lurched to an abrupt stop, causing Deelie and Cerys to stumble. The doors burst open and the nucrites swarmed from the crate, only to be obliterated by some invisible net.

A ragged gasp escaped Deelie as she dragged Cerys from the crate, her mouth open in disbelief.

'Gods.' Cerys bent over to gather herself.

But Deelie looked ahead, as she always had. 'Cerys ...'

'Give me a second, Dee—'

'Cerys.' Deelie's voice was all command as she pointed to the archway of bones that awaited them. To Deelie, the bones gleamed brighter than they ever had before. The artistry of the structure was more immense, more magnificent than she'd ever noticed.

'We made it,' she breathed. Utterly elated, she threw her arms around Cerys, the pair jumping up and down and grinning like fools.

'We made it,' they chanted together. 'We made it.'

Deelie's chest was full to bursting. Everything they wanted, everything they had planned was coming to pass. She hugged Cerys to her tightly, willing every ounce of her joy into her friend. 'Long may we reign,' she whispered.

Hand in hand, the two cyrens passed through the entrance of Saddoriel, where beyond, the cyren throne loomed in a column of jagged rock and King Uniir the Blessed stood at its base.

Deelie hardly registered the crowds peering down upon them from the galleries, the whispers and the coin exchanged, the faint applause trickling down from the highest levels. She only saw the king and the Council of Seven Elders at his sides.

When she reached them, she did not bend at the waist as every instinct within her bid her, and her hand shot out to prevent Cerys from doing the same. 'We do not bow,' Deelie murmured. 'Not anymore.'

King Uniir gazed upon them critically, as though he couldn't believe that two female cyrens had clawed their way through the violence to usurp him. But his eyes shifted from Deelie and Cerys to the council and then to the crowds above. They had followed the Law of the Lair, and now, he had to do so as well.

'Welcome to a moment in cyren history,' he called up to the spectators, projecting his voice to the far reaches of the galleries. 'It has been five decades since our last tournament, and this one, like the ones before it, was a demonstration of our kind's courage, tenacity and cunning. The challenges faced by our competitors were designed to push their limits, to test their endurance and the very fibre of their being. They did just that. The efforts of all were nothing short of valiant ...' He cleared his throat. 'For the first time ever, we have two victors at the finish line. Delja Silvah of the Second Infantry and Cerys Irons of the Trident Warriors, you have won The Dawning. Come forward.'

Deelie stopped herself from looking at Cerys. Instead, she kept her eyes ahead, refusing to tear them from the former king as she approached.

King Uniir cleared his throat again. 'Our victors will be taken to be fitted for their crowns in the council's chambers and taken to be blessed in the goddesses' temple before their coronation here at sundown.'

There was no applause as Deelie had imagined. Perhaps it was too much of a sacred moment. Still, she did not look at Cerys, not wanting to appear unsure of herself or weak. They would talk later, once they were Queens of Cyrenkind.

King Uniir turned to them. 'Follow me,' he said, sweeping his robes from the floor and starting towards the Great Hall and one of the many passageways beyond.

Anticipation flooded Deelie's senses as she walked in the former ruler's footsteps. She had never seen the inside of the council's chambers, and now ... now she would know it intimately, with her friend, her sister, by her side, always.

When they entered the room the first thing Deelie noticed was a round stone table at the centre. The next was all the portraits hanging from the walls – the kings past, Uniir the Blessed and Asros the Conqueror, and those who came before, all the way back to the first cyren king, Taaldin the Great. All kings, all men who had failed their kind, leading them from one war to the next, leaving a bloody trail in their wake.

At last, she looked to Cerys. Together, they would be the first Queens of Cyrenkind. The thought made her heart swell. But for some reason, Cerys' face didn't mirror her own. There was no joy there as she had expected. Only resignation, and anger.

That was when Deelie noticed the coral crown at the heart of the table, the birthstones of Saddoriel glimmering at each apex.

A *single* crown.

'You never intended for us to lead together,' she realised, the words tasting like ash in her mouth.

'Of course not,' said one of the elders. 'What an absurd notion.'

'Then why allow it in the first place?' Cerys asked, stunned.

'Saddoriel and its territories are free kingdoms. We could not introduce a rule against it,' the elder Deelie recognised as Indra Haertel spoke, her voice sounding distant, tinged with regret.

Deelie's skin crawled with dread. 'Well, what now?'

The elders gathered around the table, their eyes flicking to the coral crown at the centre and back to the two Dawning victors.

'You will partake in an additional challenge,' one elder told them, her face smug. 'You will duel for the crown. To the death.'

The shuck of a blade being drawn rang through the chamber and time slowed as Deelie turned to Cerys, her friend, her sister, the cyren who now brandished her sword against her.

'Deelie, please,' Cerys pleaded. 'We don't have to do this.' Her lilac eyes flecked with green were distraught.

Magic tingled at Deelie's talons, a deadly calm washing over her. 'I'm not the one who has drawn a weapon, Cerys ...' She spoke slowly and deliberately, allowing her words to sink in. Deelie could feel the eyes of the council upon them, but they meant nothing to her, they never had. Only three cyrens had ever meant anything to her and now ...

'Cerys,' she murmured. 'I thought by now you'd know I'd never … I would never hurt you.'

Cerys faltered. 'You've just … Since that trip all those years ago, you've —'

'I've what? Spent years planning to win the throne with you? Shared knowledge and power with you? Saved your life in this very tournament?'

'You've just been different.'

And then the cloud of shock lifted from Deelie like a strange fog. 'Those are Eadric's words,' she said, her voice full of venom.

'No.'

'You're the one who's different, Cerys. You're weak, because of him.'

'I'm the same, Deelie.'

Deelie closed the gap between them so she could see the stains of blood on the blade pointed at her. 'You still haven't sheathed your sword.'

Cold. Deelie felt nothing but cold, brutal power pushing against her heart. 'I've not drawn a weapon for this supposed duel and yet still you hold your sword to me.'

'Deelie … please. We're meant to rule together.'

'That was always the plan, wasn't it? But I see you for your true ambitions now. To seize power, to reinstate the warlocks in Lochloria.'

'They're our friends, our family.'

'They are *your* friends, *your* family. I have none to call my own.' As the words rushed from Deelie, hot and furious, the magic that had flickered at her talons unleashed itself, flooding her whole body and taking hold.

'Delja —'

But it was too late. Deelie tipped her head back to the ceiling and a relentless, violent chaos broke free, surging through the room.

Then, the screaming began.

Deelie's song was a poison-tipped arrow through the council elders she sensed opposed her. They begged for their lives, begged for their mothers, but she did not yield. They bled from their eyes and noses, from their ears and from their talons, ripping them on the door that seemed locked from the outside, a prison of their own making.

Deelie sang and sang, relishing their pain, their regret and their desperation to live. They deserved it all and more. It was their secrets, their broken systems, their hierarchy that had seen her family abandon her one by one, that had ripped her mother and her sisters from her, and Sedna, too, in the end. Yes, they deserved it. Suffering rained down upon them at her behest, the power surging through her making her feel giddy and drunk, godlike and triumphant. Blood ran in rivers across the floor, soaking into the soles of Deelie's boots.

Let them bleed, she chanted to herself, caught up in the magic of her deathsong –

Someone was screaming her name, a different sort of pain threaded through their voice as they begged.

'You're killing him!' Cerys shrieked, crouched over a limp body on the floor. 'Deelie! Stop!'

A sharp pain sliced through Deelie's arm and she came back to herself, seeing her own blood join that which flooded the chamber. She looked from the cut on her arm to Cerys, who had thrown a dagger, her face etched in horror as she cradled Marlow in her lap on the ground.

'What have you done, Deelie?' she whispered, rocking her brother in her arms, a trickle of blood leaking from his nose.

Deelie faltered. 'Where did he come from?' she demanded. 'He wasn't with us.'

'He snuck in, just before –'

'I-I didn't know,' Deelie stammered. 'I –'

Marlow's chest rose as he took a ragged gasp. He was still alive. Cerys sobbed in relief. Deelie felt it in her own chest. Marlow had never done anything to her. She was sorry she'd caused him pain, but ... She felt herself harden again as she watched Cerys on the floor. Here was the daughter of the legendary Sedna Irons, cowering before her, a mess, incapable of delivering more than a mere scratch.

Deelie was more Sedna's daughter than Cerys had ever been, and she was done hiding. She took a deep breath and looked from her former friends to the surviving two council elders.

At last, she allowed her magic to show its true form, *her* true form.

Great wings materialised at her back.

The elders and Cerys gasped. Deelie let them drink in the sight of her, a goddess incarnate.

She reached for the coral crown, almost daring someone to stop her, before she placed it atop her head and stretched her wings outwards.

'You have all witnessed the atrocity that unfolded here today,' she said, her voice strong and clear. 'The day that Cerys Irons became The Elder Slayer of Saddoriel.'

'What?' Cerys croaked.

Deelie turned to the two snivelling council elders. 'I trust you saw what I saw? That you can see past the illusion that this warlock-lover cast? That you wouldn't doubt the word of a goddess?'

The elders exchanged terrified glances, already shaking their heads. 'No, Your Majesty. We do not doubt your word. The slayer used mind trickery and murdered our own kin.'

Deelie expected Cerys to plead, to gaze upon her wide-eyed and in shock. But Cerys did no such thing. Still holding an unconscious Marlow, she lifted her chin, meeting Deelie's eyes with a look of defiance.

'You are no goddess,' she said, her voice steely.

Rage rattled in Deelie's bones. 'You question my ancestry? My power? In spite of the wings you see before you now?'

'Those wings are a lie. We will find out what you have done, Deelie. If not today, if not tomorrow, some day. Eadric won't rest until he's uncovered your deceit.'

Deelie sneered, her wings flaring at her back. 'It's always about Eadric, isn't it? Well, I will not allow him to undo all I have worked for, all I was born into.'

A chair on the other side of the table crashed to the floor and King Uniir, whom Deelie had all but forgotten about, rose to his feet, blood smeared across his face. He gaped at her, his mouth opening and closing several times before he staggered across the chamber to her.

'A goddess among us,' he murmured, staring at her wings and her unsheathed talons.

'Do you not bow before the likes of me?' Deelie asked coldly.

Uniir fell to his knees, enraptured. 'I bow, Majesty.' His eyes brimming with awe, he clutched at the hem of Deelie's trousers, as though to prove to himself she was more than a vision before him. 'I have touched a goddess.'

'You have,' Deelie allowed, eyeing him with disgust, suppressing the urge to shake him from her like an insect. 'But you have also betrayed a goddess, with your lies about the two crowns and the additional challenge.'

Uniir threw himself to the ground. 'Forgive me, Goddess, forgive me. I did not know who you were.'

'Perhaps you should have. A cyren who spends as much time in worship as yourself should know a god when he meets one.'

The former king was weeping. He drew a long dagger from his belt and sliced into his palm. 'I give you my blood as penance. Forgive me, Goddess.'

Detached, Deelie watched the cut ooze red, watched as Uniir bled at her feet.

'Do you think that's enough?' she asked, her head tilting.

'No,' Uniir gasped, desperate for her approval. 'No, it's not enough. Not for you.' He turned the dagger on himself and thrust it into his abdomen with a scream.

Time slowed.

All Deelie could hear for a moment was a strange gurgling noise escaping through the former king's lips as blood stained his teeth and dribbled down his chin. On his knees, he lost balance and fell to his side, twitching.

Feeling nothing, Deelie took a deliberate step over him and the pool of blood towards the door. 'Guards!' she shouted.

A Saddorien Army unit burst into the chamber a second later, their eyes scanning the carnage of the room before staring in shock at Deelie, her crown and her wings amidst the bloodbath.

'Seize her,' Deelie commanded, pointing to Cerys. 'You are hereby stripped of the name Irons. I will not tarnish your family's name further. You will be called Cerys the Elder Slayer for centuries to come, reviled by all of cyrenkind. Take her to the prison.'

Cerys didn't fight them, she didn't scream or beg. She simply gazed upon Deelie one last time.

'You are no goddess,' she said. 'You are no queen.'

CHAPTER TWENTY-TWO

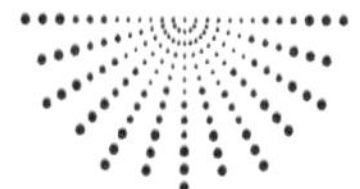

Roh's heart pulsed in her throat as she stared in shock at the pages before her. She hadn't simply read about what had happened between Delja and her mother, the words had lifted from the tome and wrapped around her, pulling her into the past.

She had been there and witnessed it all.

She had felt Deelie's fear of abandonment and her rage. She had felt Cerys' confusion and despair. Roh had felt the blood pool at her own feet in that chamber, just as she had during her fevered nightmare on the way to Csilla all that time ago.

Cerys was innocent.

Delja was the Elder Slayer.

Their whole history was a falsehood.

And there was so much more.

Somewhere in this lair, Delja walks free. The realisation came to Roh, a horror forming low in her gut. She tasted bile at the back of her throat, recalling how she'd *embraced* Delja at the end of the Akorian challenge, something she'd never been able to do with her own mother. She remembered how she'd felt *grateful* for Delja's presence, her support. All the while, the cyren's true nature had hidden in the shadows, the real Elder Slayer of Saddoriel, a king killer.

Roh's hands went to her crown. How could she not have known? With the gems sitting in her crown? Were they not supposed to guide her towards sincerity and truth? To show her the way when she was lost? She sifted through her memories, trying to determine when she'd obtained the stones and when she'd come into contact with Delja and how, but … She felt sick as the realisation hit her. Delja had taken the crown from her in Akoris when she had asked for the truth …

'You will come to find that sacrifices must always be made.' Delja gazed upon the crown and held out her hands. 'May I?' she asked.

It seemed a strange request given that she'd just placed it on Roh, but Roh could find no reason to object, and so she passed her the crown and the topaz it housed.

'Is that what you told my mother? That sacrifices must be made?' Roh asked sharply.

Delja sighed. 'It's actually what Cerys said to me. Before she tried to kill me. And her brother, Marlow.'

'What?' Roh's hand went to her scar …

Delja inhaled, her eyes lined with tears. 'We defeated our fellow opponents and emerged victors of one of the most brutal Dawnings in our whole history. We were about to be crowned joint rulers of

Saddoriel and cyrenkind, but Cerys ... It wasn't something she wanted to share in the end. A sickness took hold of her. Winning The Dawning wasn't enough for your mother. She wanted full autonomy, complete power.'

In that moment, Delja had taken the power of the gem away from Roh, and lied. And Roh had believed her.

Roh's body trembled as she stood, closing the *Tome of Kyeos* and taking it in her arms back to the Vault. There would be time enough to unravel more of Saddoriel and Delja's lies later. She placed the book back in its beam of light, the thick volume drifting from her grasp and hovering where it always had in the heart of the chamber. She gave it one last look, vowing to return time and time again until she had the knowledge that the former rulers of cyrenkind had dismissed or not bothered to learn. But first, there was someone she had to see.

Cerys Irons stood waiting for Roh behind the bars of bone. There was no manic glint to her lilac-and-green gaze, only understanding as she beheld her daughter before her, taking in the crown full of gems she wore.

'All this time,' Roh said softly, suddenly overcome by emotion. 'All this time and you said nothing, not one word about what really happened.'

Cerys continued to study her, her expression unreadable. 'So, you know.'

'I know.' Roh swallowed the lump in her throat. 'I know what she did to you, to ...' she trailed off, and for the first time knowing exactly who he was, looked upon the preserved warlock opposite her mother's cell. 'To my father ... To all of us.'

'Deelie did many things,' Cerys murmured, following Roh's

stare to the man who had been Eadric Cadelle. The longing in her gaze was poignant. 'As did Eadric and I.'

Roh frowned. 'But it was Delja who went looking to extend and link all your lives. It was Delja who sought out distant cyren legends to learn about the origins of our wings. It was Delja who used that information against you – against us all, to take the crown.'

'She did what many cyrens would have done. She used her cunning to get what she wanted,' Cerys countered, her voice devoid of emotion. 'To keep hold of her power.'

Cold dread uncoiled in Roh's stomach. 'Is that what I have done?' she whispered.

'Perhaps,' Cerys replied, toying with the ends of her uneven hair. 'But it was a path your father and I put you on from the moment you were born.'

Roh gripped the bars of bone. 'I made my own choices.'

'I would expect nothing else from an Irons.'

Roh sucked in a breath. 'I'm going to get you out of here.'

'I have no doubt of that, Rohesia.'

Roh imagined her mother standing by her side at her coronation, the truth at last revealed about Delja and the council and king she had slaughtered. She envisioned telling Finn that it was *Delja* not Cerys to whom the Haertels owed a death debt. But there was a part of what she'd learned that niggled at her.

'I … I don't know where to start,' she admitted aloud, the doubt churning in her gut.

'You tell the truth.' Cerys said it as though there was no other option.

But Roh hesitated. 'I could … I could share everything, everything except one detail …'

That last kernel of knowledge the *Tome of Kyeos* had shown her lingered at the forefront of her mind like a fog.

'Could you really do that, after everything you have learned?' Cerys asked, a shadow crossing her gaze.

Roh's thoughts were racing. 'Would it not cause even more trouble, to give cyrens more power than they already have? What would it mean for the warrior warlocks? Perhaps it's best if I keep —'

'That depends,' Cerys said sharply.

'On what?'

'If you think you are mightier, worthier than the rest of us.'

Shocked at the steel in her tone, Roh met her mother's gaze, brimming with challenge and fire despite the centuries of confinement.

'Well?' Cerys prompted.

It didn't matter that she stood there in nothing but her dirty shift, her hair tangled and uneven, her talons jagged and torn. It didn't matter that there were bars of bone and a lifetime of separation between them.

Roh wrung her hands, her cheeks heating. 'No. No, I'm not —'

She froze as Cerys' hand reached out, wrapping around her own that still gripped the gate of the cell. Roh watched in wonder, abstractly trying to recall if her mother had ever touched her before.

Cerys seemed just as mesmerised by the contact, her fingers smoothing over Roh's skin, as though trying to convince herself that her daughter was real.

Movement sounded further down the path and Roh whirled around. Who would be down here at this time? What did they want with Cerys? But as the sound grew louder, Roh determined that it was more than one pair of boots sending stones scattering along the gravelled path.

'I told you she'd be here,' Odi announced loudly.

Torchlight suddenly illuminated the whole passageway and Roh's friends came into view.

'We've been looking everywhere for you,' Finn interrupted from behind Harlyn and Yrsa, their faces tight with worry.

Roh felt a twinge of guilt in her chest for leaving after they had ... Finn looked like he'd rolled right out of the sheets to find her; his hair dishevelled, his shirt untucked. But his expression darkened as he looked past Roh to the cyren standing in the cell.

'Cerys the Elder Slayer.' He moved as quick as a shadow and was instantly standing before the bars, gazing in, his eyes full of loathing.

But Cerys didn't flinch, didn't so much as blink. 'You must be a Haertel ...' she said slowly. 'Your great-grandmother had the same jaw.'

'Before you killed her,' Finn spat, smacking a hand against the cell door.

Roh was at his side in a second. 'Finn.' She tugged at his shirt. 'Finn, it wasn't her.'

Finn gave a dark laugh. 'It wasn't her? What mind games has she played with you now, Roh? What twisted story has she told —'

'She told me nothing,' Roh said, her voice hard. 'The *Tome of Kyeos* showed me.'

Finn's hands dropped from the bars and he whirled around to face her. 'You went to the Vault?'

'I did.'

Finn stared. 'Without me?'

'I —'

'We had a deal, Roh.'

'I had to go alone.'

'So, the first thing you did when you left my bed was betray me?'

A harsh silence fell, pulsating through the group as what he'd said settled like dust on the ground.

Roh's cheeks burned. 'I'm going to tell you.'

'That's not what we agreed.'

'Finn,' Yrsa barked. 'We have more pressing matters at hand.'

Roh turned to her. 'What is it?'

'There's something happening at the Pool of Weeping. We've received no formal word, but cyrens are gathering there. We don't know why.'

'Are more evacuated Saddoriens returning?'

'We don't know,' Harlyn replied.

Roh looked to Finn. 'Cerys didn't kill the council elders,' she said. 'Delja did. They won The Dawning together and then Delja turned on her, taking the crown for herself.'

A muscle twitched in Finn's jaw, but he said nothing.

'And that's not all,' Roh told them, pulling her father's dagger from its sheath and fitting it to one of the multiple locks on Cerys' cell. While she worked, using her limited warlock magic and the quartz blade, Roh told them what she'd seen in the *Tome of Kyeos*, she told them *everything*.

When Roh was done, she pocketed a stone marked with the blood of her cyren friends; a final weapon, enchanted by Deodan; the key to proving the deeper truths she had learned from the ancient time; the key to extracting a cyren's essence from the pool. And as though they had been waiting for the opportune moment, Roh felt the urgent tug of the birthstones, pulling her to the Upper Sector, to the ancient Pool of Weeping. Anticipation thrummed in her veins alongside her magic, telling her: *something is coming, something is about to happen.* The birthstones pulsed too, a rhythm of reassurance from her crown. She was on the right path, she was heading the right way, her instincts rang true. With the others close behind, Roh made her way up through the passageways of Saddoriel towards the sacred site, her mind racing through the array of options. She didn't bother to try to quieten it. Now was not the time for warlock magic, now, she would be more cyren than ever before.

Something is coming, something is about to happen. The sensation beat against her like a war drum, as did the knowledge she now held close to her heart.

'Were there any warnings of more tempests?' she asked over her shoulder.

'Not that we know of,' Kezra called.

'No word from Elder Sigra about my coronation?'

'None.'

'Your coronation wouldn't take place at the pool,' Yrsa told her.

Roh's gut churned. She had guessed as much. Something, whether it was instinct or the gems in her crown, told her that whatever was coming was a different sort of battle. She increased her pace, the lair passing by in a blur as she followed her inner compass through its winding tunnels and levels. She had never taken this route before, but it didn't matter, the birthstones sang their truth to her. This was where she was meant to be.

Roh's eagerness to reach the pool increased the more ground she covered, and when she was near, when she recognised the spongy moss beneath her boots, she nearly cried out in relief.

At last, Roh came upon the Pool of Weeping. It was like the terror tempest had never happened. Its water was still again, reflecting its surroundings like a pane of polished glass, mirroring the ceiling of stalactites that hung down like daggers. Dozens of weeping willows were rooted at the banks, their hanging leaves veiling much of the pool, with jagged rocks framing the water's edge. The shore was pristine now, but Roh could still see the violent red where Eadric had lain dying, where her father's blood had stained the pale stones and run in narrow rivers into the ice-blue water.

Her eyes did not linger there, her gaze snagged on a figure standing on a plinth at the base of one of the war beacons.

Delja's wings were out and majestic, and she was wearing a coral breastplate. Holding a blazing torch, the former queen looked across at her, taking in all three birthstones in the crown of bones and the once-unlikely companions at Roh's back.

Saddoriens had gathered around the edge of the pool, watching on in a mix of fear and awe. But Roh ignored them. She kept her sights on Delja, who fidgeted where she stood.

'Welcome home, Rohesia,' she called, her voice echoing off the water. 'You have done our kind proud.'

Once, Roh might have flushed with pleasure at those words of praise, but now … Her skin prickled, knowing all too well the duplicity and agenda behind them.

'What are you doing here, Deelie?' Roh asked coolly, not acknowledging the burning torch in the former queen's grasp.

Colour drained from Delja's face, a vein pulsing in her neck. 'What I have always done.'

Roh noted the anger in her voice for the name once used by her family. 'Lie?' she prompted. 'Deceive your people?'

Around them, the Saddoriens gasped. No one had ever dared speak to Delja the Triumphant in such a way, not in six centuries, crown or no crown.

Delja cast a hateful gaze across the crowd, as though she resented their presence, before training her stare back on Roh. 'You're just like me,' she retorted. 'You should have been *my* daughter. You're just as ruthless, just as cunning as I am.'

Roh said nothing.

'Imagine what you'll be like in six hundred years. Eight hundred. A millennia. *I* can share that power with you – the power of long life. We can make you an immortal queen, just like me.'

For a moment, Roh saw a vision of herself. In it, she ruled over Saddoriel and its territories with all the power she had ever dreamed of. Her eyes shone bright lilac and her dark hair flowed to her waist, she stood before the masses, who listened to every word of hers, enraptured. The image was a mesmerising one, where she was revered amongst her own kind, respected and loved. Across the many realms, all knew her name, all knew of what she had achieved, of what she had sacrificed to become their queen.

But it wasn't real. It was a picture Delja was painting with her own cruelty and selfishness.

Roh's voice was quiet, but not weak when she spoke. 'No.'

Delja brandished the fiery torch in her grasp. 'You will see one day, Rohesia … Power corrupts all hearts eventually … You've given me no choice.' She took a deep, satisfied breath. 'You have not been formally crowned. Therefore …' Delja touched the burning torch to the war beacon. 'I challenge you, Rohesia of the Bone Cleaners.'

CHAPTER TWENTY-THREE

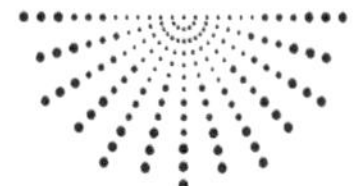

Blue flames burst to life at the tip of the beacon, and around the Pool of Weeping, four other beacons caught alight, the reflections shimmering across the glassy surface of the water. But it was not just the reflections moving – ripples pulsated across the pool and the water surged.

Roh met Delja's eyes across the shore; triumph glinted there.

Someone nearby gasped and Roh's attention snapped back to the pool, where the water had parted. From the depths, cyrens from Csilla emerged, Floralin and Piri at the forefront. Roh also recognised the tattered robes of a handful of Akorians, those who must have been hiding in the warlock-held monastery. Elna, Maiella, Nym and the battalion from Lochloria also appeared, filling the space.

Delja had lit the war beacon, she had called every living cyren to witness Roh's final undoing.

They gathered around the pool's edge, their faces grave. Even those who Roh knew to be her allies watched on with hardened expressions of resignation. A goddess of the realm had challenged her, with only one criteria left – *magic*. And Roh had no deathsong, no means of attack. Everyone knew that.

She stared as Taro Haertel stood at Delja's side. 'You have all been summoned here to bear witness to the end of one of the darkest periods in cyren history. It was an error on our part to allow an *isruhe* to enter the Queen's Tournament in the first place.' He gestured to Roh, his face distorted with disgust. 'But we have given her every opportunity to prove herself better than her reputation. But throughout her quest and the challenges she's faced, all she's done is show us how corrupt and ill-suited she is to rule.'

Roh felt one of her friend's hands on her arm, but she didn't look away from the elder. She felt *nothing* as he spoke.

He continued. 'Retrieving the gems matters not. We will never accept the daughter of Cerys the Elder Slayer as our queen, a bone cleaner, an *isruhe*. Not when we have the descendant of a goddess in our midst. Delja is the one true queen.'

An eerie quiet fell across the water. There were no cheers of support, nor outbursts of rage. Not a single cyren made a sound.

Delja stepped forward then. 'I understand that some of you may have started to question our ways, that Rohesia has obtained the birthstones of Saddoriel, and that means something. Which is why I do not simply take the crown for myself, but challenge her fairly, as the rules of this tournament dictate —'

'Deelie,' Marlow's voice suddenly rang out across the pool. 'Deelie, please. Don't do this.'

Is he begging for my life? Roh wondered, finding her uncle amidst the crowd, his weathered face distraught.

The former queen silenced him with a hand and gave Roh a hard look. 'Enough. I wish to banish this imposter from our lair, from our territories and the realm for good. I am the only descendant of Dresmis and Thera in centuries.'

'That's where you're wrong.' Roh's voice cut through the cavern, strong and unyielding.

She had learned many things from the Lochlorian mirror pool and the *Tome of Kyeos*. Pieces of a centuries-long game had fallen into place and her mother had confirmed it all in hurried whispers in the prison's passageways.

Roh had come of age in the scholar's city. A seemingly quiet rite of passage that had set her on a different path to all of those who had sacrificed their infant tears to the Pool of Weeping ...

She closed her eyes and searched deep within herself. She passed the shimmering presence of her lifesong, so intricately entwined with who she was now. She moved past the flickers of warlock magic in her veins, seeking something more ancient, more primal; a fundamental part of what it meant to be a cyren.

Heat flared at the centre of her back ...

She heard the unified intake of breath from the throngs at the water's edge as she found the thread of power coiled within herself and pulled.

At her shoulderblades, a pair of great wings manifested, casting shadows across the shore. Roh could feel power in every inch of them, in that pull at the middle of her back, in the bone-like structures that now bowed to her every thought. She unfolded them, stretching her wings outwards, revelling in their generous span and immense physical strength.

The vision she had seen in Csilla had been true.

Roh beat her wings powerfully for all of cyrenkind to see, causing a gust of wind to surge across the cavern, rippling the water and catching in the leaves of the willow trees.

Cries and exclamations of shock echoed at the pool's edge.

'*— the bone cleaner is a goddess —*'

'*— a direct descendant of Dresmis and Thera —*'

'*— there are two goddesses in our midst —*'

Roh ignored the declarations around her. She focused on Delja, whose face had slackened.

Deathsong, lifesong, it mattered not. Roh was a descendant of the gods and there was no denying her place amongst cyrenkind now. She let the former queen see the truth radiate from her.

'You are not the only child of the gods,' Roh said, lifting her chin in defiance and stretching her wings.

'What is this heresy?' Taro Haertel shouted, unable to tear his eyes away from Roh's wings. 'What have you done?'

'I know exactly what she's done,' Delja growled, stepping down from the plinth and moving towards Roh, her eyes full of loathing. 'She has done only what an *isruhe* knows to do. She has created an illusion with that warlock blood of hers. She betrayed Saddoriel, all of cyrenkind, just like her elder-killing mother.'

'Rohesia is not the deceiver here.' A new voice cut through the cavern, raw but strong. 'Just like it was not me. It was you,' Cerys Irons said, coming to stand at Roh's side. 'It's still you. It's always been you.'

Delja froze mid-step. '*Cerys* ...' she rasped, raising a trembling talon and pointing. Panic was wild in her eyes and she scanned the cavernous space desperately. 'See?' she cried, her voice increasing in pitch. '*They're working together.* The bone cleaner has freed the Elder Slayer. She'll kill us all.'

Roh met her mother's gaze, which was deadly calm. Cerys gave her a single nod.

'You are the deceiver here, Deelie,' Roh said, taking a step towards the former queen. 'You have spent *centuries* suppressing the truth and true nature of cyrenkind. You have spun lie after lie, all for your own gain, your own power —'

Delja's wings flared outwards, and with several powerful beats, she was airbound, glaring down at them all. 'We are here for a challenge of magic,' she spat, a vein bulging in her neck. 'Let's see what you can do against me, bone cleaner.'

Suddenly, Delja's chest expanded as she filled her lungs with air, tilting her head to the ceiling and opening her mouth. The world around her seemed to pause; an intake of breath before chaos descended.

A piercing note sounded from Delja's lips and two black ribbons of magic uncoiled from her as she began her deathsong, aiming it straight at Roh.

Dark whips of oblivion lashed out towards her. Roh shot into the air without thinking, her wings beating effortlessly. She didn't hesitate. She reached deep within, finding those familiar threads of power and drawing them steadily to the surface. She called upon her gift, a vibrant river of gold pooling at her chest.

And then she sang.

The notes poured from her, rich and vibrant, a collection of every ounce of magic she had inside herself. She felt it in the air she exhaled, in the tips of her talons, in every beat of her heart.

The cruel chords of Delja's deathsong flayed against Roh's own gilded melody, unable to break it, unable to find its mark and annihilate her into a pile of bones.

Blood streamed from Delja's hands where she clenched her talons into her fists. Veins and tendons strained against the skin of her neck as she sang and sang, those onyx bonds of death lashing relentlessly at Roh.

But Roh's lifesong held.

A high-pitched scream of fury tore from Delja's throat and her fiery eyes met Roh's, triumph flashing across her face.

'You may be an Irons,' Delja yelled over the beat of her wings. 'But you're forgetting whose song was so powerful they discovered it *at eight years old*.' The former queen laughed darkly, manically. 'Your pretty tricks might be enough to save your own hide, *isruhe*, but ... can it save *them*?'

A guttural roar exploded from Delja and the whips of her power multiplied and coiled back, ready to strike all of those who watched on from below. Screams pierced the air as Delja's darkness descended. But with every fibre of strength she had left, Roh summoned her own song, casting it not at Delja and her vengeful melody, but outwards, coaxing it into a barrier between the former queen and her subjects.

A golden shield fell into place. And Delja's deathsong did not pierce it. The deadly black ribbons of magic touched no one.

'It's over,' Roh said quietly, her voice cutting through Delja's vicious notes. She beat her wings to stay in place above the Pool of Weeping, watching the former queen carefully.

Delja's eyes flew open, widening in shock as she surveyed the unharmed cyrens gaping up at her. 'What …?'

'It's over,' Roh said again. This time, she glanced down at Finn, Yrsa, Kezra, Odi and Deodan, who had arrows aimed at Delja.

It was then that Roh reached into her pocket and withdrew the stone marked with the blood of her cyren friends and family. The stone Deodan had enchanted to remove their essence from the waters below. She dropped it, leaving it to hit the Pool of Weeping with a splash.

'You are not the only child of the gods,' Roh repeated. 'And nor am I.'

A forceful wind hit her as a wave of power rolled through the cavern. All at once, behind Roh flew Cerys, Yrsa, Finn, Harlyn and Kezra, great wings beating at their backs.

Delja screamed her rage, the sound flung outwards, rattling the walls of the cavern and dislodging several stalactites from the ceiling, which shot down like arrows, crumbling to dust as they hit Roh's golden shield.

But Roh and her companions hovered before the former queen, steadfast and unrelenting. Roh sang a final note, her magic flaring once again, more gold ribbons leaving her, at last reaching out, to Delja. Powerful, glimmering binds closed around Delja's flailing limbs, fastening her hands together and wrapping around her mouth, muffling her deadly song and screams of rage.

Slowly, Delja was dragged back to the ground.

Roh's own feet touched the shore. The Saddorien Army looked to her now. 'Put her in treated shackles,' Roh ordered with a nod to Delja. 'Take her to the prison.'

Delja staggered in the guards' grip, gazing at Roh in astonishment. She looked as though she wanted to say something, but as the irons snapped into place around her wrists and ankles, her face paled. Roh remembered that feeling from when she'd been trapped by Tess back in the redwood forest, the nauseating sensation of having her magic snuffed out.

Cerys came forward and wrenched the coral breastplate from Delja before the guards dragged her away. She continued to stare at Roh until she'd been taken from the cavern entirely.

Roh heaved a weary sigh, the golden song shield having taken much of her energy. But she was not done here. The stares still boring holes in her wings told her there was more that needed to be said. She stood amongst her people now, and at last, they deserved to know the truth.

Her friends looked expectantly to her, Yrsa pointing to the plinth upon which Delja had stood. There was no sign of Taro Haertel, who only moments ago had denounced her in front of all of cyrenkind. Roh kept her head high as she made her way towards the platform, taking comfort in the soft thrum of the three gems in her crown, guiding her every step. Ignoring the heaviness in her chest and the exhaustion dragging her down, she took to the plinth and gazed upon the crowds gathered before her.

She took a trembling breath. 'This is not how I imagined I would first address you.'

Quiet settled. Roh could hear the thundering of her own heart. She took another breath. 'This is not how I imagined I would first address you, but too long have you been kept in the dark. For too long have you been oppressed by the talons of a power-hungry and desperate ruler. You heard what I said. Delja is not the only descendant of the gods. Nor am I. And,' she paused. 'Nor are my friends.'

Roh took a pause, letting her words wash over the cyrens of Saddoriel and the smaller numbers of Lochloria, Csilla and Akoris.

'Centuries ago, long before Delja entered The Dawning, she embarked on a quest to distant lands, to seek information on the degeneration of cyrens' wings from faraway clans. There, she discovered that millennia ago, our ancestors sought to control us, to create further divide between our kind, further divide between those with power and those without. And thus, the First Cry ritual was born. A supposedly sacred, mandatory rite of passage where all cyrens must sacrifice their first tears to the Pool of Weeping. Enchantments were placed on the pool, ensuring that any cyren who had sacrificed their tears would be unable to grow wings, would have no knowledge of their existence. All evidence of such was wiped from our records. History was rewritten.'

Roh scanned the crowds. Why would they believe her? And when they didn't, then what? She would stand before them, a liar in their eyes? But Roh's gaze fell upon the green-speckled lilac eyes of Cerys once again. Her mother had changed from her filthy shift into a worn shirt and pants, but she looked every bit the Irons warrior that Roh had heard tales about as she gripped the coral breastplate she'd ripped from Delja. That gave Roh strength, and so she forged on.

'Delja obtained that knowledge, and keeping it for herself, convinced a warlock to extract her essence from the Pool of Weeping. After Delja and Cerys won The Dawning together, Delja turned on her and the council. It was *Delja* who slayed several council elders. It was *Delja* who was responsible for the death of King Uniir. It was *Delja* who created the tale about Cerys the Elder

Slayer, when it was Delja herself who murdered those council members. And it was *Delja* who kept the knowledge of cyrenkind's wings all to herself.' Roh's voice had grown louder and louder as she burned through the list of Delja's crimes. She knew it was personal to her because of Cerys, but surely, it was personal to every cyren, for they had been robbed of their birthright?

'We are *all* descendants. We *all* have the ability to grow wings at our backs, as true cyrens always have.' Roh steadied herself. 'I will not force this choice on you, it is yours to make. But should you wish to be returned to the form we once were, to the form you are owed, it can be done,' she told them, walking down the steps of the plinth and coming to stand at Deodan's side. 'We have an ally in our midst. The choice is yours.'

All Roh could hear were her own shallow breaths, her own heartbeat in her ears. Perhaps they didn't believe her. Perhaps even after everything she had been through, after everything she had achieved, she was still just a bone cleaner to them. Perhaps cyrenkind was not ready to align itself with water warlocks ... Perhaps Roh's ambitions had been too grand from the start.

Sorrow churned in her chest and she found herself looking at Deodan, tears lining her eyes. 'I'm sorry,' she managed, her voice breaking, along with the shattered remains of her hope.

Deodan's expression was one of shock. Clearly, he too couldn't believe where they'd ended up. Roh made to leave, tugging on his sleeve. But Deodan was rooted to the spot, his gaze transfixed on something nearby.

Roh turned back, looking towards the crowds that had simply stared and stared without a word, unable to process what she was seeing. For, one by one, at the water's edge, cyrens began to come forward.

CHAPTER TWENTY-FOUR

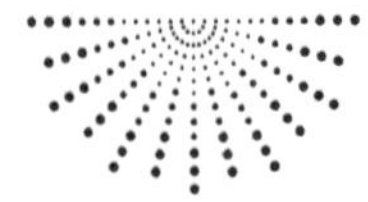

Roh left Deodan at the Pool of Weeping to find Cerys and Marlow in a darkened antechamber off the main cavern. The reunited siblings sat side by side on a stone bench, not touching, but talking softly in the lone candlelight.

Cerys looked up upon Roh's approach, taking in the wings at her back. 'You did it,' she said, her voice gravelly.

The words hung weighted between them. Roh didn't know what to say, she was still in shock herself, and she had no idea what came next. She had faced one obstacle after the other, with no moment for reprieve, for planning or strategising. And not a second to adjust to the new part of her; it took every fibre of her willpower to stay on the ground, when every part of her was screaming *fly, fly, fly*.

It was then that Marlow took his sister's hand in his. 'We did it,' he told her, with a glance at Roh. 'Our plan worked. After everything you have endured, Rohesia is queen.'

'Not quite yet,' Roh murmured, watching them in a quiet awe. Brother and sister shared the same weary but hopeful expression, the set of their eyes so similar that Roh was surprised she'd never noticed it before. But then, she hadn't spent much time with Cerys over the years. It didn't matter now. They were her family, and at last they were all together.

'How do you feel, Rohesia?' Cerys asked.

Unable to remember the last time someone had asked her that question, Roh hesitated for a moment. She savoured the sound of her name on her mother's lips. She could count on one hand how many times she'd heard it there.

Cerys waited.

'I don't know,' Roh admitted, wringing her hands in front of her as she sifted through the questions in her mind. 'I just ...'

'Just what?'

'I just don't understand why Delja did it all. And why she helped me along the way, only to oppose me at the end.'

'Perhaps that's something you need to ask her,' Marlow said cautiously.

But Cerys gave a dark laugh, the laugh of someone who had not seen the light in a long time. 'Deelie has always warred with her two sides. The side that yearns to belong, the side that loves fiercely and is desperate for family. That against the side that craves to be unique, special, better than the rest ... I was a fool not to see it, all that time ago. There were signs of her unhappiness, signs that she was turning down a dark path, but —'

'It's not your fault,' Marlow interjected firmly.

Cerys sighed. 'I should have seen it,' she repeated. 'As for you, Roh ... I believe part of Deelie truly wanted to take you under her wing. For you to be the family she lost when she betrayed me and Marlow. But knowing her, she never truly intended to give up that power.'

Roh paced the small chamber as she mulled over the words. It seemed to fit with her experience of Delja, of her contrary actions, but ... Marlow was right. What drove the former queen to do what she had done was not something Cerys, nor even the *Tome of Kyeos* could tell Roh. It was something Delja and Delja alone could answer. But that was not the only question eating away at her. She faced her uncle.

'Why didn't you tell me about the wings and my lifesong?' she asked. 'You had eighteen years of opportunities —'

'No,' Marlow said, his voice suddenly sharp. 'What I had was eighteen years of *terror*, Rohesia. Terror that someone would discover what Eadric had done with that enchantment, that you hadn't partaken in the First Cry, that you were *different* from all the rest ... Do you know what would have happened if Delja had found out?'

'Marlow,' Cerys said softly, placing a hand on his arm to soothe him. 'She is only asking.'

Marlow's shoulders slumped. 'A cyren's wings do not manifest until they come of age,' he explained, expelling a long exhale. 'It was safer not to tell you.'

Roh started to argue. 'I wouldn't have told —'

'A secret like that is a heavy burden for a fledgling to bear,' Cerys cut in. 'We kept it from you to *protect you*. To protect all of cyrenkind. You have seen what Deelie's envy and wrath can do ... You saw it in the *Tome of Kyeos*.'

Roh opened her mouth to speak, but closed it again, looking down as the images of that horrifying event filled her mind.

'As for the lifesong,' Marlow continued. 'That was less straightforward. We didn't know for certain that you would have one. It was a gamble on your father's part. All the literature and histories with that particular detail had been wiped from existence, except for one small inscription in an ancient language in the warlock tombs of Lochloria.'

A shiver passed over Roh at the mention of that place. She had walked those very crypts not all that long ago ...

'It always seemed like a far stretch to me, but Eadric was convinced that a nestling born of mixed heritage had a far bigger chance of having a lifesong within them. It was another part of cyrenkind that had been suppressed for millennia. Somewhere along the way, we were taught our power lay in death and destruction, and so lifesongs were all but forgotten, with a deathsong becoming the crown jewel of a cyren's power. But it was Eadric's guess that the former might come to the surface in ... well, dire situations. When something a cyren loved was threatened.'

'It was all speculation,' Cerys added, shaking her head. 'And we gambled everything on it.'

Cerys herself had paid the highest price, Roh realised. 'How ... How did you bear it? How did you survive in that cell?'

Cerys rubbed her temples, the day taking a visible toll on her. 'There was a time when I thought I wouldn't ... A time when I reached breaking point. That's when Eadric came. He cloaked the cell in warlock magic and created an illusion from the outside. He managed to break in and stayed with me through my darkest times. Those times became the happiest I had had in decades. In that cell, Eadric crafted a life for us. Those beyond the bars of bone could see only me in my state of despair, but within that cell was magic, was love and life ... That was when we conceived you, Rohesia.'

Roh stared at her mother.

Cerys sighed heavily. 'For a time, I stopped caring about the realm and the cause beyond my prison, but Eadric's magic couldn't sustain us in there forever. We received word that Delja had started to suspect that Eadric was moving against her ... She had some of Eadric's warlock colleagues captured and interrogated, and while they knew nothing of his plans, their ignorance only fed her paranoia. So, I feigned madness ... For someone who had lived a false life in a cell of Saddoriel's Prison, I only needed to reach out a hand to find it ...'

Cerys' voice strained. 'Deelie believed my performance,

believed what she so desperately wanted to believe, that I was weak and she was strong. She loosened her grip, became complacent, and Eadric was able to leave, to go about his work ... To find the keys to undoing all that had been done to cyrenkind.'

All that Cerys and Marlow had said fell upon Roh with an intense solemnity. She was keenly aware of the weight of her wings at her back and the press of the crown on her head. They had given everything. They had –

'Breathe, Rohesia,' Cerys told her gently. 'We have had a long time to come to terms with all of this. We do not expect you to do so in the space of a few hours. Go and prepare for your coronation.'

Roh heaved a heavy sigh, tucking her wings in tightly behind her. 'Will you come with me?' she asked Cerys.

Cerys gave a sad smile. 'I think the opulence of the Upper Sector residences would be too much for me at this time. I was just telling Marlow before you found us, it's already an assault on my senses, even in this chamber here.'

'You will adapt,' Marlow told her.

'I always do,' Cerys replied before turning back to Roh. 'Get ready with your friends. Celebrate. There will be enough time for us later.'

Roh tried not to let her disappointment show. She didn't know why she suddenly wanted Cerys by her side. She had managed for the last eighteen years, what was one more day? With a final nod to her mother and uncle, Roh left. There was something she had to do.

The preparations for her coronation were well underway, but Roh paid the bustling lair no heed as she went about her business. She somehow knew that no one had *ever* taken the *Tome of Kyeos* from the Vault throughout cyren history; she would be the first. There were to be many firsts carved into history from here on.

Roh sent word to the others to meet her in the queen's private residences once more and she was relieved to find them there, waiting for her amidst the rich mahogany furniture and lavish lounges. Any trace of Delja had been keenly swept away and the residences were now a blank canvas for her to make her own.

Her friends stood as she entered the sitting room of what was now her home. Harlyn and Yrsa were grinning, flexing their wings at their backs, and Deodan, Odi and Kezra bowed. Roh's gaze lifted to Finn's, anger still plain in his lilac eyes. It was to him that she went, moving to stand before him. She held out the *Tome of Kyeos*.

'I made a vow,' she said, her voice cracking. 'I'm sorry to have made you doubt me.'

Finn blinked, clearly not expecting her to place the actual book in his hands as she was doing now. 'You took it from the Vault?' he gaped.

She nodded. 'I expect the tome will find itself moving more freely about the lair during my reign.'

Finn took the hefty volume with a look of disbelief, running his hands across the leather just as she had done.

'I thought about it, you know,' Roh admitted, her voice soft. 'Keeping the knowledge to myself.' Finn and the others deserved to know that about her, that the selfish, power-hungry part of her existed and for a moment had threatened to swallow her whole. She could feel their eyes on her and she knew they didn't know what to say.

Finn was still close enough that she could feel the energy of his body. He watched her thoughtfully. 'But you didn't.'

'I thought about it,' she repeated.

Finn shrugged. 'And that makes you a Saddorien through and through. The fact that you shared the knowledge in spite of that?

Well, that makes you, *you*. Makes you a leader unlike any we have had before.'

'Does that mean you forgive me?'

Still holding the tome, Finn drew her to him. And in front of everyone, he kissed her deeply, pressing his body flush against hers.

'Is that a yes?' Roh said against his lips.

He kissed her again. 'What do you think?'

Someone – Deodan – cleared his throat pointedly. 'As much as this union thrills me, can you take it elsewhere?'

Roh laughed. She realised with a start that it was the first time she'd genuinely laughed since her return. With Finn's arm around her shoulder, she turned to the others.

'We need to ready ourselves,' she told them. 'I expect all of you by my side at the coronation.'

With that, Harlyn rushed forward, extricating Roh from Finn with a gleeful grin and tugging her in the direction of the master bedroom. 'We'll meet back here within the hour,' she called to their friends. 'That should be enough time to make this bone cleaner queenly.'

Laughing again, Roh followed Harlyn to the master bedroom and watched her throw open the doors to the walk-in robe dramatically. As her friend disappeared inside and palmed through the various gowns and glamorous attire, a tinge of sadness lingered between them. Though they didn't mention it, Roh knew they were both thinking of the last time they had prepared for her coronation: Orson had been joyfully tearful and now her absence was palpable.

'I've been hearing her again,' Harlyn admitted, running her hands over the fine fabrics. 'Since we returned.'

Roh started, her gaze shooting worriedly to Harlyn's. 'Shall we get you some more of the antidote?'

'Well, that's the thing isn't it ... It was only a temporary solution, it seems. There's something about Saddoriel that's drawing her to me, or me to her. I can't tell which. I just know that her calls are stronger here. Almost pulling me in a particular direction …' Harlyn shook her head, as though remembering where they were and why they were here. 'It can wait. We have more pressing matters to deal with.'

'But —'

'Honestly, Roh, it can wait.' Harlyn did her best to emulate happiness for Roh, despite the strain, and emerged with her arms laden with outfits.

'These are for me,' she said, lifting one arm of shimmering fabric. 'And these are for you.' The selection she had chosen for Roh was more understated than her own, showing that she knew Roh well, for Roh wasn't one for sparkling dresses.

Harlyn, however, paused, her gaze stuck on the dishevelled sheets of the bed and the discarded cushions on the floor. 'You know … I almost completely forgot with all the dramatics about the wings and the pool, but …'

Roh's cheeks were already heating.

Harlyn all but threw the clothes aside. 'What's this about you *bedding* Finn Haertel?! And *why* was I not informed of every detail *immediately*?'

Roh burst out laughing. 'Would I have done that before or after reading the *Tome of Kyeos* and going up against our former queen?'

'Well,' Harlyn allowed. 'I suppose *after* suits.' She picked up her pile of dresses and started to smooth them out over the end of the bed, deliberating what to try on first. 'I can multitask.'

'There's not much to tell,' Roh said.

Harlyn froze over a particularly bright silver dress and gave her a long, hard look. 'Don't for one second think you're getting away with that.'

Roh huffed another laugh. She certainly hadn't thought Harlyn would be satisfied with next to no detail, but she wasn't sure she was ready to share what had happened between her and Finn. She wanted it to be just theirs, if only for a little longer. It was no secret now; he'd made sure of that with his outburst in the prison, and he'd kissed her in front of everyone. But what had occurred between them in the kitchen, and in the bedroom after … She wanted to hold it close to her chest and not let go.

Harlyn was watching her. 'I see …'

'See what?'

'The thing between you and Haertel … It's not just for fun, is it?'

Roh stared at her. Fun? She could describe Finn Haertel in many ways, but *fun* wasn't the first thing that came to mind. What they shared was darker, deeper, intangible even.

Roh found herself shaking her head. 'No,' she said. 'It's not just for fun.'

Harlyn smiled. 'Then say no more, my friend. You'll tell me when you're ready.'

Roh nodded. 'I expect I will.'

'Good, now let's get your outfit sorted.' Harlyn was suddenly business-like, holding up various dresses for Roh to consider, each one more beautiful and luxurious than the last.

'None of those feel right … They don't suit me, Har.'

Harlyn was frowning at the most recently rejected dress. 'Hmm … They're all like this, though. And imagine what the rest of the lair will be wearing. This is a big moment in history.'

'I know.' Roh felt uneasy in her own skin. 'I don't want to pretend to be something I'm not, today of all days. I don't want to start my reign like that.'

'Then what do you want to do?'

'Do you know what you're wearing?' Roh gestured to Harlyn's ever-growing pile.

'Oh yes,' Harlyn replied enthusiastically, pointing to the silver dress she'd initially looked at. 'I knew from the moment I saw it. I just wanted to raid the rest of your wardrobe for any future occasions.'

'Well in that case, perhaps you could ask Yrsa if I could borrow something simpler from her?'

'Simpler?' Harlyn looked taken aback as she slipped into her chosen gown.

'You're acting like I'm planning on going in my undergarments,' Roh quipped. 'I just want to be comfortable, Har. I want to be myself.'

'Alright, then.' Harlyn shrugged. 'I'll go find Yrsa.'

'Thank you.'

Roh watched her friend leave with a quiet sense of relief. She had expected Harlyn to push back, to insist that she needed to look the part of the Queen of Cyrens. Alone now, Roh ran her fingers through her hair and looked around the room, unsure of what to do with herself. It was rare indeed for her to have time to herself these days. A soft knock on the door interrupted her thoughts of solitude. She supposed this was what it would be like from now on; the notion felt surreal to her.

'Come in,' she called, her gaze lingering on the dishevelled sheets and discarded piles of clothes.

Finn entered the room, wearing a simple black shirt and pants, no Jaktaren leathers in sight, holding something under his arm. 'You're not ready?' he asked by way of greeting.

'Harlyn's getting me something from Yrsa,' Roh replied. She nodded to the parcel he was carrying. 'What have you got there?'

Finn's cheeks were tinged with pink. 'A gift.'

'Because of the coronation?'

Finn shrugged. 'Just because.' He offered it to her.

The package was heavier than Roh expected. She sat on the edge of the bed and tore through the brown paper. It was the sketchbook he'd bought her back in Thornhill, the one that she'd discovered upon what she thought had been his death.

'I've been waiting for the right time … I finished the inscription,' he said, his voice low. The mattress sank as he sat down beside her and leaned across to open the leather-bound book.

Roh's gaze fell to the neat scrawl of handwriting on the very first page, looping across the thick, high-quality parchment.

Roh, I thought of you when I saw this. I wanted your ideas, your drawings to grace its pages. Just as you have graced my life with your fire. Never forget this part of yourself, the part that wants to create, to build things, to contribute to a better world.

Yours,

Finn

Roh loosed a breath, her eyes prickling. *Yours.*

'This is the most beautiful gift I've ever received,' she told him. She left out the fact that it was one of the *only* gifts she'd ever received.

Finn nodded. 'I'm glad you like it.'

Roh twisted to face him, her hand slipping around the back of his neck. 'I *love* it.'

Finn flushed deeply, but seemed pleased with himself. 'Good,' he said and kissed her.

Roh kissed him back, her tongue brushing against his. This thing between them was so new, so *alive* that she could hardly contain herself. His hands were at her waist, finding her curves and drawing her closer to him.

'There's no time,' she murmured against his lips.

'I know.' But he didn't stop kissing her.

Roh slid the sketchbook onto the bed beside her so her hands were free to explore the sculpted torso beneath his shirt. The absurdity of their union struck Roh anew as she traced the muscles of his chest. It was *Finn Haertel's* broad shoulders beneath her touch, *Finn Haertel's* nipples hardening against her palms, *Finn Haertel's* fingers at the buttons of her shirt. She wondered abstractly if the shock of it all would ever wear off.

Roh leaned into Finn's heated touch, each brush of his skin against hers sending a thrill down her spine –

The room trembled, violently enough to rattle the chandelier above the bed.

Roh broke away from Finn. 'What was that?'

They were on their feet in an instant, surging for the door, Roh cursing herself. Had she truly been so naive as to think she'd stopped the terror tempests? That her magic and her magic alone could protect all of Talon's Reach from the most powerful force of nature?

She went straight to the veil at the end of the hall, gazing at the seas beyond. Around her, the lair shook again, causing her knees to buckle and black spots to swim in her vision.

'Gods,' Finn murmured beside her.

Beyond the veil, the currents churned violently, but not just at the mercy of a tempest.

Roh followed Finn's gaze further and her legs weakened at the sight. Through the turquoise waters she saw them: the bottom of several war ships.

Terror burrowing itself tight in her heart, Roh turned to Finn. 'Sound the alarm,' she ordered. 'We're under attack.'

At last, the Warlock Supreme had come for blood.

CHAPTER TWENTY-FIVE

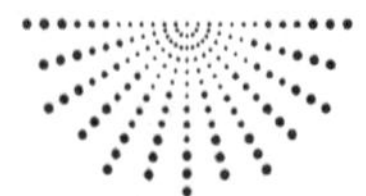

A terror tempest raged anew, rattling all of Saddoriel and Talon's Reach, more savage than any Roh had seen before, spurred on by warlock magic and war weapons of the mighty ships. The whole lair shook, pieces of lifesong enchantment flaked away from the walls and Roh knew that her magic would not be enough to save them this time, not with the warlocks lying in wait above. Their ships seemed to be magically protected from the worst of the battering winds and violent currents, patiently bobbing above the waves for the opportune moment to attack.

Roh called for Deodan and Odi. First, she turned to the warrior warlock. 'Sybil knew of the recent tempest, knew when to strike, as you predicted months ago.'

Deodan nodded stiffly, his knuckles white as he gripped his cutlasses. 'Exactly. The lair is weakened and in disarray …'

Roh took his hands in hers. 'I do not want to ask this next thing of you.'

'Ask it anyway.'

Roh swallowed the lump in her throat and tried to keep the

tremor from her voice. 'Bring us allies, Deodan. You feel it in your bones as I do … We will need them before long.'

Deodan gripped Roh's fingers and traced the symbol of their alliance on the back of her hand – *wings*. 'I cannot promise anything, but I'll go at once.'

'Use the mirror pools.'

With that, Deodan bowed low before turning on his heel and leaving, his tattered cloak billowing in his wake.

Next, Roh faced Odi. 'You should have left with your brothers. There may still be time yet, time to flee.'

'I'm not going anywhere,' Odi said firmly.

Roh ran her shaking fingers through her hair, her mind lingering on the word that had been with her since she'd first witnessed the rage and hate of the Warlock Supreme in Akoris; the word that had slowly grown louder in her head as she'd crossed new lands and faced one trial after another.

'*War*,' she rasped. 'War is coming.' They had all known it was, but it was one thing to know, and another thing entirely to say it out loud in the face of it. 'Odi, if the lair falls …'

'Then you and everyone we know falls with it. I am not without my uses, Roh. I can help. And I will not abandon you, abandon —'

Harlyn rushed to them. 'What are you doing standing there?' she yelled, eyes wild as she spotted the warships for herself beyond the veil.

'Roh's trying to get me to leave.'

Harlyn whirled around to face him. '*She's right*, you need to get out of here. You need to *run*. Get to the mirror pool. You can at least make it to Lochloria, or Csilla. If the warlocks breach —'

But Harlyn was silenced as Odi crushed his lips to hers.

Roh took a step back, not quite able to look away from their private moment as Harlyn threw her arms around the human's shoulders and pulled his body to hers.

Reluctantly, Odi drew back. 'I'm not going anywhere,' he said breathlessly.

Roh shook her head in disbelief, and with a final glance at the warships closing in, she made for the door. 'So be it.'

Warning bells rang out, echoing down the passageways and herding non-fighting cyrens once more to the Pool of Weeping. Roh and her companions did not head that way. Roh carved through the crowds, leading Finn, Yrsa, Odi, Kezra and Harlyn to a place she'd never been before: the War Room.

There, Isomene Sigra, Winslow Ward and former tournament competitor, Toril Ainsley waited for them. A huge map of Talon's Reach had been unfurled and laid across a long table at the centre of the chamber, held in place by various weapons in its corners.

'Where is the rest of the council?' Roh asked, standing at the head of the table.

'On their way, Majesty,' Elder Sigra told her with a bow of her head.

'I'll believe that when I see it,' Harlyn muttered at Roh's side.

Roh was inclined to agree with her. The council would undergo some serious changes under her rule, if they survived this.

Toril Ainsley came forward, the white burn from a reef dweller at her right temple stark against her skin, and her voice silvery and thick when she spoke. 'It's an honour to fight for you, Majesty,' she said, bowing low.

For a moment, Roh merely blinked at her. Then she came back to herself and cleared her throat, asking the first question that sprang to mind as the wheels of her cunning and strategy began to spin. 'Have we sent scouts out to get an idea of the warlocks' numbers?' she asked.

'We have, Majesty,' Toril replied. 'As soon as I saw the ships. They should be back within the hour.'

Roh bit back her retort that they might not have an hour, not with the way the lair was shaking and falling apart at the seams.

The chamber door flew open and in strode Cerys and Marlow, their resigned expressions matching one another. Cerys came straight to Roh, holding something out for her.

A coral breastplate.

'This was your grandmother's,' Cerys explained as she fitted it to Roh's chest. 'The armour of the great Sedna Irons.'

Roh heard gasps from those around the table.

Sure enough, it was the very armour that had been hanging in the Irons' quarters back in Lochloria, the very same breastplate that had graced the walls of the battalion leader's residence. How had Delja got her hands on it?

And then it hit Roh. The war that she'd told Odi was coming, was here. She was in the *War Room* of Saddoriel, surrounded by those who wished to defend her, defend the lair.

Her body jolted as her mother started to fit the armour to her body. The gesture felt incredibly intimate, as though they should have shared this moment in private. Roh's face flushed as she felt her mother struggle to buckle the straps.

'It won't fit,' Roh said quietly.

'Lift your wings, Rohesia,' her mother replied.

Roh did as Cerys bid. The powerful weight of her wings shifted up and spread outwards, dark and membranous, across the width of the War Room. Time seemed to slow as she did this, and Roh heard several intakes of breath.

'If there was any doubt about your right to rule,' Kezra said slowly, taking in the sight of Roh's great wings, her crown and her armour. 'It is long gone now.'

Roh felt the last clasp of the breastplate snap into place and she nodded her thanks to Cerys before tucking her wings away and bracing herself against the table. She looked to Elder Sigra and Toril. 'I hope to the gods that you have a plan,' she said.

'You'll need to reinforce the lair as best you can, Majesty,' Elder Sigra said.

'I'll do what I can with my lifesong, but I'm not sure it will hold this time.'

As if in answer, the entire lair shook again, an empty sconce dislodging from the wall and clattering to the ground nearby.

Roh turned to Cerys. 'You fought in the Age of Chaos. What was the defence strategy then?' She expected Elder Sigra and Toril to object to Cerys' inclusion, but they merely turned their attention to the former prisoner and waited. Perhaps they recognised her value; neither of them had ever defended the lair to such an extent before.

Cerys' expression hardened. 'Back then, the warlocks were on our side. Not fighting against us. I see we do not have even one left with us?'

'Deodan is elsewhere for now.'

Cerys seemed to accept this. 'We need to rally our army units in the outer passageways and by the veils closest to the surface of the sea. We need to move as one force against them and stay close to their ships – they're protected from the terror tempests, so we need to utilise that cover, lest we get caught in the storms ourselves. Our cyren magic will be useless against those whirlpools.'

Roh was nodding and she turned to Elder Sigra. 'Do you have a rough guess how many the Warlock Supreme has at her disposal?'

'There are at least ten ships by my count,' Elder Sigra offered. 'We won't know the figures until the scouts return, but I would suggest we strategise under the assumption that we are greatly outnumbered.'

'That's putting it lightly.' Cerys folded her arms over her chest.

Roh addressed her friends next, those who had become her family. 'We've always beaten the odds,' she said, her voice sounding steadier than she felt. She turned back to the elder. 'Have your units armed and ready while we wait for the scouts. I'm assuming you have formations and tactics within each force?'

Elder Sigra nodded. 'Are you ready?'

'Yes. Where would you like me and my court?' she asked.

'You're going to fight?' Toril Ainsley gaped at her.

Roh gave her a hard look. 'I'm no trained soldier,' she said. 'But the blood of warrior cyrens and warlocks runs through my veins and I will not hide in the shadows while others die for my kingdom.'

'Very well, Majesty,' Elder Sigra said, bowing her head again. 'I would have you and your court by my side. We'll attend to the veil closest to the sea. We should be able to see everything from there, and we'll have almost direct access to their ships.'

Roh nodded. 'Good. I wish to address the army.'

'Of course, Majesty.'

Together, Roh, Isomene Sigra, Toril Ainsley and Cerys Irons hunched over the map of Talon's Reach, plotting out where their forces would be stationed and from which vantage points they could best defend Saddoriel. Every now and then, Finn and Yrsa would interject their opinions, too, for they had travelled the passageways extensively in their time as Jaktaren, while Odi pointed out several popular methods of sea attacks and Kezra speculated as to what sort of magic the Warlock Supreme might rally against them.

'Do we have any larger weapons?' Finn asked. 'The ships will have cannons and likely bolt throwers, too.'

'Bolt throwers?' Roh questioned.

'They're like giant crossbows,' Finn explained.

'The enemy will use those to weaken the protective barrier around the lair and break through the already vulnerable spots,' Toril suggested through clenched teeth. 'We have bolt throwers of our own, though.'

'Gods ...' Harlyn murmured.

'Not sure they're going to help us now,' Roh muttered.

Harlyn snorted. 'That's comforting.'

Roh stared at the map, her eyes scanning over the markers they'd put in place, the last line of defence between the attacking warlocks and her home.

'Are we ready?' she asked no one in particular.

It was Toril Ainsley who answered. 'As we'll ever be, Majesty.'

Roh nodded as she fought against the panic constricting in her chest. 'Good. We'll go to the armoury and then —'

A loud crashing sound echoed through the lair and the ground beneath Roh trembled violently.

Grabbing the side of the table, she steadied herself. 'Armoury first,' she confirmed. 'Then take us to the veil.'

Elder Sigra nodded and made for the door.

Roh found Harlyn at her side. 'This is really happening?' her friend asked, wide-eyed.

'I'm afraid so,' Roh told her, resting her hand on the grip of her father's dagger, the coral breastplate pressing against her chest. 'You don't have to fight,' she said.

'I'll make myself useful, like I did in Serratega.'

'Alright,' Roh agreed.

Together, they left the War Room and hurried through Talon's Reach, the lair rattling violently all around them. Roh stayed at Elder Sigra and Toril Ainsley's heels, her friends and family close behind them as more stalactites fell from the ceiling and high-pitched screams echoed down the cavernous tunnels.

Roh did her best to reinforce the lair with her magic as they went, but found that her lifesong power was depleted after the first bout of tempests and protecting her people from Delja's attack. She knew her shield would not hold.

There was no segregation between the sectors now. Highborns and lowborns alike crammed into pulley systems and passageways, their faces panic-stricken, their loved ones clutched close. Long gone was the notion that all cyrens were vicious warriors. Now, the lair smelled of ripe fear. Cyrens gaped at Roh and the others as they charged past. Roh knew that she was doing all she could for them now and couldn't stop to reassure them. She wasn't sure what she'd say anyway.

Saddoriens were fleeing and cracks began to form in the walls, creating deafening rumbling noises and vibrations through the whole of Talon's Reach. Several times Roh stumbled forward, losing her balance as the ground shook, but she caught herself each time. They only stopped for Roh to try to reinforce the shield enchantments, but for each layer of magic she added, another wave of the terror tempest struck, causing fissures in her barriers.

'You've done all you can,' Marlow said, grabbing her arm. 'You need to get to the armoury and get to the veil.'

Pushing the hair from her damp brow, Roh gritted her teeth and nodded. Her uncle was right, there was nothing more she could do for Saddoriel with her water magic and lifesong.

A huge line of Saddorien soldiers snaked from the armoury all the way down the passageway Roh and the others had turned onto.

'This way,' Elder Sigra said, pushing past the soldiers. Those who weren't frozen in shock bowed low as Roh passed, awe momentarily cutting through their fear.

'It's good for them to see their queen amongst them,' Elder Sigra murmured to her as they reached the doors to the armoury. 'Boosts morale. Word of your magic, your backbone has spread far and wide since you returned home, My Queen.'

Roh simply nodded. The elder's words only added to the mounting pressure she felt on her shoulders. What if she couldn't save them? What if the lair fell to the warlocks? They were greatly outnumbered, with a vast supply of ammunition, both tangible and magic, stacked against them. Roh couldn't help but glance back at the lines of cyrens anxiously awaiting their armour and weapons, her imagination painting several pictures of what might become of them. Her gaze fell upon several particularly young faces and she twisted questioningly towards Elder Sigra.

The hardened cyren led her into the armoury. 'Those who want to fight, will fight,' she said.

The armoury was lined with shelves and shelves of shields and tridents, swords and axes, helmets and spears, and weapons Roh had never even seen before. At Toril Ainsley's instruction, a space was cleared for Roh and her companions towards the back of the chamber.

Finn and Yrsa took over the task of handing out the armour to the rest of their party. Roh ran her talons over the abdomen of her coral breastplate. It was spotless, but she couldn't help wondering how much blood had once stained its surface. She looked up to find Cerys watching her, a curious expression on her face.

Marlow elbowed her. 'Flashbacks?' he asked, with a pointed look at Roh.

Cerys all but grunted. 'You could say that.'

Roh couldn't imagine what this must be like for her mother, thrust from the dank, dark cell of the prison into the heart of an upcoming battle. Especially when only hours ago, she had mentioned feeling a sensory overwhelm. But by the looks of things, these surroundings were familiar to Cerys and she strapped coral gauntlets around her forearms as though she'd done it a million times before.

'Fighting has never been your strong suit, brother,' Cerys said to Marlow. 'You shouldn't be here.'

'No, I shouldn't.'

'Then leave. Your talents can be useful elsewhere.'

Marlow nodded. 'I will go and seal off the passageways where I can, lest these outer tunnels be breached.'

Cerys gripped her brother's shoulder. 'Until we meet again.'

Marlow grasped her hand and peered into her green-speckled, lilac eyes. 'We will meet again, sister.'

Roh tore her gaze away from their private exchange, scanning her friends instead. Their faces were weary but lined with determination as they readied themselves. Cyren armour wasn't the heavy, clunky steel of mortals. It was streamlined and lightweight, designed not to interfere with their mastery of the water.

'Whatever happened to cyrens fighting in nought but their shifts?' someone nearby asked.

'We evolved,' another called.

'The enemies see what they want when they hear our songs,' a third voice offered.

Roh met Finn's gaze across a sea of weapons, his words from before the Rite of Strothos coming back to her in a powerful wave: *'They needed no armour, no weapons to shield themselves against the realms ... They were magic, cunning and power incarnate. And they answered to no one.'*

The pair didn't speak, only exchanged a final glance before Roh turned to Toril and Elder Sigra. 'We're ready,' she said.

The foreboding atmosphere was thick in Saddoriel as they yet again took to the passageways and navigated the levels and twists and turns of the lair. Elder Sigra led them further and further up Talon's Reach, which Roh expected. They were to be as close to the battle as possible; the thought made her stomach churn. By now, Roh had seen her fair share of conflict, of violence and death, but this ... This was different. This was about her home, her friends, her family ... Everything and everyone she knew and loved was at stake.

Oddly, the words Deodan had spat at Finn in Csilla echoed in her mind as she took in the crumbling of the walls, the flakes of magic protection peeling away and the panicked shouts of her kind.

'Why not let nature succeed in its purpose? Wipe out the Saddoriens and start afresh.'

Roh's mind went to a dark place then. Would the realms be better off without cyrenkind? Despite all her efforts, would she have made the world a better place when she left it? If that day was today, could she make her peace with that? With what she'd done?

But she didn't voice her fears, didn't let them show in her eyes as she gripped the sword and the dagger at her hip, ignoring the increasing trembling of the lair around her.

Elder Sigra held up a closed fist, signalling for the unit to halt. She snatched a discarded crate from nearby and placed it on the ground before Roh. 'You said you wanted to address the army. This might be your only chance.'

Roh's mouth went dry, and for a brief moment she thought she might be sick all over her boots. But a kernel of something within forced her up on that crate and she found herself standing upon it straight-backed, looking across the battalion that would soon fight for Saddoriel's survival. She breathed deeply.

'The odds against us are no secret,' she told them, her voice raised over the chaos descending around them. 'You know what it is we face out there. But before we charge through the sea know this ...'

The Saddoriens were silent.

'For centuries, we have been fed lies and hatred about the realms and people beyond our own. This day will not be the day that we succumb to those notions again. For today, we do not fight the warlock race in its entirety.' Roh steeled herself. 'We fight *one warlock* and her misguided followers. The actions of the warlocks beyond the veil are the actions of a select few. They do not represent the beliefs of all —'

'I can attest to that,' came a familiar voice.

Roh's heart stuttered as Deodan moved through the parting crowd. A flurry of movement at Odi's back caught Roh's eye and she spotted a dozen or more hooded figures, heavily armed, all bearing the same symbol painted on their jerkins.

A pair of wings.

Hope flared in Roh's chest. Though their numbers did not change the odds, their presence meant everything. She lifted her chin, placing her hand over her heart as she spoke again, her voice projecting to the far reaches of the passageway.

'It is my hope that this is the last time we fight warlocks in such a way. It is my hope that the price we pay today will secure a different future for both our kinds. What we fight for today is more than victory. We fight, not only for a better Saddoriel, but for a better *world*. And I am honoured to do so at your side.'

A chorus of near-deafening cheers burst from the battalion as Roh stepped down from her makeshift podium, echoing throughout Talon's Reach.

Flushing furiously and wanting nothing more than to fade into the crowd, she looked upon the allies Deodan had brought to her aid. The man at the front lowered his hood and Roh recognised him instantly.

'Barrow,' she blurted. 'You were in Lochloria. You opposed Deodan and me, you —'

'I have since seen the error of my ways, Cyren Queen,' he said, his eyes full of earnestness. 'We have come to make amends, to assist you where we can. Our *true* Warlock Supreme found us in Lochloria and brought us to you. He has told us of your vow again ...'

'That vow holds true,' Roh told him. 'When this is done, Lochloria will be returned to your people. Deodan will be the keeper of the scholar's city.'

Barrow bowed low at this. 'Then we offer you our fealty, our swords and our lives, if the task demands them.'

The rest of Roh's companions had gathered around, shocked to find themselves among those who had once fought against them.

Roh looked from the newcomer to Deodan, who gave her a nod of confirmation. That was all she needed. She offered Barrow her hand.

'Good,' he said, shaking it. 'Because we've got a plan to commandeer one of their ships.'

'Fine.' Roh motioned for Elder Sigra to keep the battalion moving while they talked.

Deodan cleared his throat. 'I want to be clear, Roh … I do not wish to kill my own people if I can help it. I realise they have left us with little choice, but our preference is to weaken what ships we can and force them to retreat. We want to unite our people, not obliterate them.'

'Do what you can, Deodan,' Roh said, noting the respect of his companions clear as day on their faces. 'But we defend our own first, and the lair, at all costs.'

Deodan bowed his head gravely. 'Odi, Barrow and I will lead our new allies on the surface. We're sitting ducks down here.'

Roh nodded at this. 'Good. I'd prefer Odi to be on a protected ship than exposed to the weakening enchantments of the lair. If Saddoriel is breached, he's particularly done for.'

'Thanks.' Odi laughed darkly, adjusting his crossbow over his back. 'That's the support I've always dreamed of.'

'Live through this and I'll throw you a damn support party,' Harlyn told him.

Odi grinned at her before Barrow continued. 'If we can get a hold of one of their ships, we can turn their own cannons and bolt throwers against them and hopefully damage some of their hulls so they take on water. Just one ship can buy us time to get your cyren forces up there and onto the decks. Is that how you intend to fight?'

Roh didn't want to, but she gave a stiff nod. They had already assumed most of the enemy warlocks would be wearing protective talismans against deathsongs, so their intentions were to meet in hand-to-hand combat where they could use the current against the warriors, to sweep them from the safety of the decks and into the roaring whirlpools of the terror tempests.

Roh's talons cut into her palms when they reached the veil. She had never seen this one before, had never been to this part of Saddoriel. The veil was enormous, like the entrance to a giant cave that looked out onto the shimmering waters. Roh could see the bottom of several warships and the waves that thrashed against them in the thunderous storm above.

She looked to the warlocks and Odi, with Deodan now taking the lead.

'Deodan's already given me something for the seasickness,' Odi told her. 'I'm as ready as I'll ever be.'

'Funnily enough, that wasn't at the top of my concerns,' Roh said. 'How do you intend to get to the ships?'

'If you give us an escort, two or three cyrens to help propel us quickly through the water, we can swim. It's not far to the top.'

'Swim? Are you mad?' Roh asked. 'There's a godsdamned terror tempest out there!'

'As soon as we reach the ship we'll be under the warlocks' protective enchantment,' Deodan insisted. 'Get us there, Roh, and we can take the ship for you. We can buy you some time.'

The thought of sending Odi and Deodan out into the savage seas made her feel nauseous. But the set of the warlock's shoulders and the grim determination on Odi's face told her there would be no arguing with them, and that if they achieved what they set out to, it could turn the tide of this battle for them.

'Alright.' Roh nodded to Toril.

Toril stepped forward, her hand on the hilt of her sword, and called to a pair of soldiers. 'You two! You're with me,' she shouted. 'We'll see the warlock allies to the ship. Lose no one, leave no one behind.' They gathered at the veil. 'On my mark,' she said.

Roh didn't have so much as a second to say goodbye to the

warlock and human. Both Odi and Deodan sucked in a deep breath, as did the warlock allies. At Toril's command, the small unit wrapped their arms around them and leaped through the veil.

With her farewell and wishes of luck caught in her throat, Roh watched them swim. The Saddoriens bent the current around them to their will, propelling the warlocks and human towards the surface as fast as they could.

Roh could make out Odi kicking with all his might.

'Gods,' someone nearby gasped.

For the warships seemed to be closing in.

A flash of brilliant, white light temporarily blinded Roh and she staggered back, shielding her eyes.

'Was that ...?' Yrsa said behind her.

'Lightning,' Finn replied as another bolt struck the seas in a jagged line.

The lair shook so hard that everyone scrambled to find purchase, staggering about wildly. Another great fork of lightning lit up the dark depths of the sea and the near-deafening thunder rattled Roh's bones.

A strangled, desperate scream caught in her throat as Talon's Reach was cleaved open to the seas.

CHAPTER TWENTY-SIX

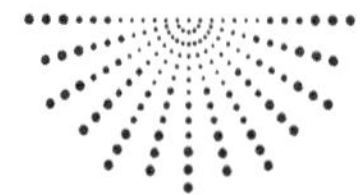

The veil before Roh vanished and she was thrown violently into the thrashing sea. The water hit her hard, stealing the breath from her lungs as she kicked out in shock. Chaos ruled the seas now. Powerful tides did not discriminate as they dragged all manner of creature and debris into their clutches, drilling down in the dark depths and stirring up the seabed hundreds of leagues below, turning the waters murky.

As though time had slowed, Roh's friends and the battalion drifted limply in the choppy currents, their cyren natures momentarily stunned by the force of the tempests and the battering of their home. Roh could see the yellow glow of the moonlight above the surface, and the enclosing hulls of several great warships. The warlock and human forces were taking keen advantage of the break in Saddoriel's defences and the shock of its army.

Numb, Roh blinked. Cannon balls and bolts plunged through the depths, narrowly missing several cyrens as they hurled towards the non-existent defence between the sea and Saddoriel.

Gods, this may be over before it has even begun ...

With her heart in her throat, Roh threw a prayer for Marlow towards where the veil had separated the lair from the water, hoping that he'd managed to seal off the passageway and that Talon's Reach had not already been lost. But she could not stay suspended in the current forever. She had to *move*. She reached down within herself, finding that kernel of power that was inherently Saddorien, and drew the air from the water around her, filling her lungs as the magic from the sea tingled at her talons. She spread her wings, too, understanding that they were just as powerful in the water as they were in the air.

The current foamed around her, making it near impossible to see where Finn and the others were now. She had to get to the surface, had to take in the surroundings before she could form any sort of strategy. The sea surged at her command, propelling her through the water towards the churning waves above. She tried not to linger on the red blooming around her and what that meant for her kind. They needed to gain the upper hand, and fast. They were sitting ducks in the depths below.

Roh jolted as a metal bolt tore past her, grazing the skin of her upper arm and narrowly missing her wing, adding her blood to the seas. She felt nothing, nothing but urgency to break the surface and rally the cyren warriors around her.

At last, she burst into the chilled night's air, the rain of the terror tempests stinging her face and lashing the black seas. The warships loomed enormous and imposing above and Roh whipped her head around in search of anyone she recognised. Using her magic, she gathered the current around her, pushing her up into the air, her stomach muscles straining as she beat her wings and took in a clearer view of the warfare.

A few yards away, amidst the churning foam, Toril Ainsley and a unit of cyren warriors were suspended in the currents, archers at the ready.

'Loose!' Toril bellowed over the raging storm.

Arrows flew towards the decks of the ships. The tempest drowned out any cries of pain from the warlocks.

Roh whirled around in the water, trying to discern the ship Odi and Deodan had aimed for. Had they succeeded in commandeering it? Her heart hammered wildly against her sternum as she beat her wings harder, meaning to fly above the rest. But the gale-force winds were too strong, threatening to tear her wings from her back.

The old-fashioned way it is, then, Roh thought, feeling the power of the sea surge at her fingertips as she spotted the figurehead of Odi's ship. She manipulated the water around her, pushing towards the ship and propelling herself towards the deck, ignoring the whipping blast of air carving through the seas.

The moment her feet hit the timber deck, Roh palmed her father's dagger.

'Roh!' Odi shouted over the downpour from behind a cannon. His hair was plastered to his face, Finn's crossbow still strapped to his back.

Roh darted towards him. 'Have you seen the others?'

'Deodan is on the upper deck,' he yelled. 'Roh, I can't believe it worked! The enemy warlocks were washed off. The next ship won't be as easy, but Finn and Yrsa have it in hand.' He pointed to one of the vessels a league or so away. 'If we can get close enough to the enemy, we've got grappling hooks.'

'Where's the Warlock Supreme?' Roh helped him steady the cannon which was threatening to slide across the drenched deck on its wheels.

'Haven't seen her,' Odi grunted, fitting the weapon to its gunport.

Roh squinted through the rain towards the enemy's fleet. Canvas sails tore in the wind, strips of material flapping uselessly in the wind. Roh could hardly see the units on board the ships, but

—

She spotted the eagle, surmising that it must be under Sybil's magical protection against the storms.

'There!' she cried. 'The Warlock Supreme must be on that ship. I need to get to her.'

'To do *what*?' Odi readied the cannon, aiming it for an enemy vessel.

'I –'

Odi shoved his wet hair out of his eyes. 'Help me fire this thing!'

Roh held the weapon fast.

'Ready!' Odi yelled. 'Aim …'

Roh sucked in a breath as flint was struck and a flame miraculously burst to life.

'Fire!'

The barrel of metal sent her flying across the deck as it recoiled. Roh's head hit the ground and she saw stars. Pain blooming at the base of her skull, she staggered to her feet, gripping the rail so she didn't tumble overboard. Her head was spinning and she stared hard at the water below, trying to focus her vision, but colours flashed before her eyes: black, turquoise, green and gold.

Gold …?

Wincing, she closed her eyes and pinched the bridge of her nose as a means of applying pressure elsewhere to distract her from the pain of her throbbing head. She needed her wits now more than ever.

'Roh?' Odi shouted. 'Are you alright?' He was already loading another ball to the cannon.

Roh gave him a reassuring wave and trained her gaze on the aim of the weapon at his hands, where it had blown a considerable hole in the side of one of the enemy's ships.

'Why isn't Deodan helping?' she yelled as she stumbled across the slippery planks towards the human.

'He and the warlocks are using their magic to protect our ship, to line it up with the others.'

But Roh had stopped listening. She watched in horror as an enormous, roaring funnel of storm raged straight for Toril Ainsley and the ship her battalion was attacking. Warrior warlocks fell from the bow as cyren arrows shot through their hearts and throats in a dark splash of blood, only to be swept away by the savage whirlpool. Screams pierced the night as cyrens too got sucked into the ravenous vortex, the terror tempest devouring anyone unprotected in its path.

'Get in line!' Toril's voice carried across the sea as she struggled to unify her force of archers amidst the storm. Roh thrust her weakened lifesong outwards, creating a wavering shield to protect the cyren commander.

Roh's own ship lurched into the waves, making straight for one of the enemy crafts. She could just make out Deodan's shape at the wheel, barking orders at his warlock allies. They came scurrying down on deck, carrying hefty grappling hooks and chains between them.

Shock settling deep in Roh's bones, she helped Odi move the cannon to the starboard side, as Deodan's intentions became clear: he meant to bring their ship parallel with the enemy's and join them together.

'He said sea warfare is always more brutal than land battles,' Odi shouted in her ear. 'Retreat is next to impossible. All that awaits them is a watery grave.'

'That's our upper hand,' Roh yelled back, a fire reigniting within her. She ran to the rail and clambered over it. She heard Odi scream her name before she dived overboard.

The sea rose up to greet her and she welcomed it, sculpting a body of support around her as she ducked incoming arrows and spears and soared towards the Warlock Supreme. Roh knew she must be concussed because those colours from before still flickered in the churning waters before her. But she shook the spotty vision from her head again and launched herself up towards yet another ship, where the giant eagle circled above, and Sybil herself stood shouting orders from the bow. Deodan's mother looked fierce and unflinching, a sword clutched at her side. She was clearly trying to keep a tight control over her fleet, but the savage rain and whirlpools were making it near impossible, despite whatever enchantments they'd used on the warships.

Out of the corner of her eye, Roh saw Deodan's ship collide with another, the grappling hooks swinging overboard and finding purchase. The small force of ally warlocks heaved on the chains, wrapping them around the base of the mast and forcing the two ships together. Roh tore her gaze away from the skirmish towards Sybil, whose eagle had landed upon her shoulder. The Warlock Supreme now took measured steps towards Roh.

'So, you came for me,' she said, her voice managing to cut through the roar of the storm.

Out of the shadows, more water warlocks emerged, brandishing their weapons, their faces streaked with rain and blood.

'I did,' Roh told her, unsheathing her father's dagger once more and eyeing the encroaching force. She saw Sybil's eyes widen at the weapon, recognising it for what it was – the blade of a warlock legend.

Roh took advantage of her pause. 'We don't have to do this. Together we can stop the tempests, we can —'

'We will do nothing together but battle against one another,' Sybil snapped, her blue eyes filled with an ancient fury.

The enemy unit of warrior warlocks surged forward. But Finn, Yrsa and Kezra shot out of the darkness and landed before Roh, swords raised and at the ready. They were all soaked to the bone, their expressions as wild as the storm around them. Roh didn't know how many of the enemy her friends had felled, but judging from their torn clothes, split lips and bloody gashes, it had been a great many.

Someone gave a shout. Sybil's guard charged. A dozen men against two Jaktaren and the Arch General of Csilla. The first spray of red hit the deck and a warlock soon after.

The clang of steel and iron rang out across the ship, close enough to Roh that the storm didn't mute the ear-piercing sound. Enraged screams sounded from the rest of the group, but Roh fixed her gaze on the older woman, who continued to stalk towards her in the downpour, ignoring the cries of agony of her own people.

'Nothing will sate your bloodlust, then.' Roh gripped her dagger hard, wishing she had borrowed a second so she could dual-wield as Finn had taught her.

Sybil smiled. 'I can think of something.' She reached for a vial on her belt and poured it into her palm. Her eyes were bright with triumph and didn't leave Roh as she whispered her enchantment to the sacred water.

Three small water eagles burst from Sybil's hand and circled her in a mania before diving straight into the seas.

In that moment, Roh knew *exactly* what the warlock leader had planned, that the ships and terror tempests were just a distraction, bait to get the Queen of Cyrens and her army out in open water.

She felt the blood drain from her face as she looked to Finn, Yrsa and Kezra, who were down to the last five warlocks. The Jaktaren fought as a unit, slicing and thrusting their blades with pinpoint precision, while Kezra covered their backs. They were a whirlwind of their own, a blur of wicked movement, delivering powerful blows and swift deaths.

But suddenly, everyone was backing away from the side of the ship, the skirmish forgotten. Even the cyrens had stopped fighting …

The vessel lurched and several screams followed. Over the side of the ship, a giant black sink hole had opened up, waters circling, sucking at floating debris and threatening to swallow the whole fleet.

Satisfaction was smug on Sybil's face as not one, but *five* enormous reef dwellers emerged from the darkness. Poisonous tentacles shot out of the black water, snatching up cyrens, humans and warlocks alike as though they were mere playthings. Blood-curdling screams sounded, cutting through even the loudest roar of thunder. Bodies went flying. Limbs were torn from torsos. It rained red.

All at once, it was clear to Roh. This invasion wasn't about taking Saddoriel, nor was it about putting the warlocks in power. The Warlock Supreme didn't so much as flinch as her own people suffered the blows alongside their cyren enemies.

A thunderous groan sounded from nearby as another ship's mast cracked in two, crashing into the ship alongside it.

Roh stared at Sybil in horrified disbelief. 'You'll kill us all,' she shouted. 'Your own kind as well.'

'This is just the beginning,' Sybil said, smiling menacingly as she murmured to the water eagles that had sprung up from the sea. The little creatures beat their wings and darted away, straight for the slimy mass of reef dwellers, riling them up, seeming to direct their attack straight for Roh.

Sybil brandished her sword, but she didn't strike; she was waiting.

Finn, Yrsa and Kezra rallied at Roh's sides, but she held up a hand, ordering them to stand down. Whatever was coming could not be bested by blade alone.

Roh stood with her feet apart, trying to keep her balance on the swaying ship. Her gaze flicked to the waters, those same colours burning into her eyes: black, turquoise, green and ...

Gold.

Something clicked into place in Roh's mind and she felt a gentle acknowledgement on the other end of the connection. She took a trembling breath of the icy night air and met the Warlock Supreme's stare as the reef dwellers rallied threateningly behind her.

'You need not throw me to the monsters, Sybil,' Roh said, her voice steeled. 'They come when I call.' A single note left Roh's lips, a ribbon of gold dancing through the night air.

In answer, a near-deafening roar split the sea in two, and a great sea drake burst from its depths.

Valli.

Roh's jaw dropped as her enormous sea drake took to the storm-drenched skies, the whirlpools and bolts of lightning doing nothing to deter him from beating his powerful wings, hovering protectively above her, snarling at the Warlock Supreme and her tentacled allies.

'He came back …' Roh murmured, gazing up at the gold scales and vicious talons. He had grown so much more during their time apart. Now, he was as big as – Roh had no creature to compare him to. His wings could span the width of the Bridge of Csilla; his long, muscular body could not be contained by any structure she knew of.

He gave another roar, sending flecks of spittle flying towards the Warlock Supreme.

Around them, the fighting had ceased in the presence of the legendary creature – there was no plan, no protocol for this.

But Sybil sneered. 'We fought that creature once before and nearly bested him. We will do so again. There are five of the reef dweller's friends now.'

Valli tilted his head to the star-littered sky and shrieked, the sound sending its own powerful wave across the sea.

Several giant gold masses shot up from the water.

Roh's knees buckled beneath her.

Valli had found his family.

Four sea drakes nearly the same size as Valli beat their golden wings amidst the terror tempest, the storm seeming to lull slightly in their presence. The battle ceased as enemies and allies stood side by side and took in the unbelievable sight before them. Even Sybil gaped now, realising that perhaps the tides of the war had turned against her.

'What ... what is this sorcery?' she stammered, a mix of fury and fear shining in her eyes. She reached for her vials with a shaking hand, but Valli roared again, the sound echoing across the choppy waters and keeping the tunnelling hurricanes at bay.

An icy wind slammed into the ship, nearly capsizing the whole vessel. Sybil dropped her vials, and they smashed into a million pieces on the deck and she fell to her knees amidst the shards, her face showing no pain – only wonder. Her neck was craned to the sky.

A gasp escaped Roh as she too saw what had captured the Warlock Supreme's attention.

Another sea drake.

Far mightier, far larger than the rest, even Valli, its gold scales glimmering in the rain and moonlight, its smooth underbelly reflected in the waves. Something protruded from its chest, glinting in the night.

Though Roh had never truly faced her, had only fled from her and only just managed to avoid the gnash of her fangs, she knew now who had answered Valli's call.

The mother drake.

It was the creature who had hunted Roh across the shores of the realms. The beast who'd had Roh's scent from the moment she'd snatched that egg from an unguarded nest nearly seven moons ago now.

The bellow that escaped between the mother drake's fangs was louder and deeper than any other sound; the sound of an ancient promise, of ultimate power, of the true queen of the sea.

While she beat her gold wings, Valli and his siblings circled the black hole, corralling the cowering reef dwellers towards it, jabbing at them with their poisoned barbed tails. Roh saw that amidst the waves, there were sea serpents carving through the currents as well, ensuring no reef dweller remained amidst the battle.

But the mother drake … she made straight for Roh.

Roh didn't need the guidance of the birthstones – she knew what to do.

Shrugging off the protests of her friends, amidst the torrential downpour and lashing storms, Roh went to the mast of the ship and began to climb. Wild wind stung her face and whipped through her hair, causing the rope ladder beneath her to swing dangerously above the deck. But Roh kept climbing. She knew this was something she had to do, had to face alone.

When she reached the crow's nest, the mother drake was waiting for her, beating her enormous wings, creating vicious waves in the sea below.

Ancient gold eyes met the moss-green of Roh's. And they were indeed ancient, for in her heart, Roh knew the drake to be the very same one Freya had faced in the Age of Chaos, hundreds of years ago, the hilt of her bone dagger still protruding from the creature's scaled breast.

Those same ancient eyes seemed to say to Roh: *I know you.*

Roh eyed the bone hilt of the dagger, the twin to the one sheathed at her thigh. *It will find you,* Marlow had said. And it had.

Roh reached for it, her fingers closing around the grip. She knew she would have to be fast, she knew her actions in the seconds that followed would shape the course of her entire life and the future of cyrenkind. With all the strength she had, Roh pulled.

Blood spurted and the mother drake shrieked in agony. But Roh tilted her head to the stars and sang.

What was left of her lifesong poured from her in ribbons of gold, curling around the sea drake, filling its wound with magic, with power. Beautiful notes escaped Roh, and still singing, she watched as her magic knitted the mother drake's wound together, smoothing over the scales that had broken and bent around the quartz dagger millennia ago.

The lifesong went on, drifting outwards, exploring the raging storm around them and touching each of the sea drakes' foreheads. Valli glowed, magic thrumming from his body and pulsing outwards towards the remaining storms.

Roh sang, the three birthstones of Saddoriel pulsing in her crown, guiding her through each note. A net of golden magic was cast over the entire fleet, washing over the blood and anguish, causing any remaining pain and anger to ebb away. Roh felt the power thrum from her entire being; felt every cyren, warlock and human it touched.

When the final note left her lips, her magic drained at last, the raging sea below was still.

CHAPTER TWENTY-SEVEN

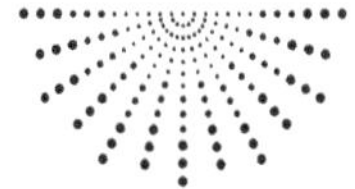

In the yellow light of the moon and several small fires burning in the warships, Roh looked from the twin quartz daggers in her hands to the bloodied waters below. The mother drake beat her wings and soared upwards, before taking a great dive towards the sea, Valli and his kin following. Roh hoped she would see them again, to give thanks.

There was no sign of the reef dwellers, only the carnage they had caused. Roh could see the smears of entrails on the decks and the bodies floating in the now gentle lap of the tides. She sheathed her daggers and slowly started the descent from the crow's nest, her knees weak and her hands shaking. When she reached the deck, she saw that their warlock and human opponents had set down their weapons and white flags of surrender flew at their masts. The shock of battle was stark on their faces, dazed eyes and trembling limbs, and Roh knew her own expression mirrored theirs. She sought her friends amidst the gathering groups. Finn and Yrsa stood side by side, alert, their weapons still at the ready. She couldn't see Harlyn, and could only hope that she'd retreated to safety. Deodan and Odi were on the next ship over, she knew that much. They had both been in one piece the last she'd seen them.

She staggered across the deck, staring out at the aftermath of battle. Debris littered the sea; burnt sails, various chunks of warships torn apart by cannon fire, severed tentacles of the reef dwellers, pieces of weaponry … The bodies of cyrens, warlocks and humans alike floated like ragdolls amidst the wreckage. Roh's chest tightened at the sight. She had known there would be heavy losses on all fronts, but to see it was something else entirely. The dead that drifted in the gentle lull of the waves hadn't known upon waking that morning that it had been their last. Roh's gaze sought Finn and Yrsa once more; it could have been any of theirs. But they had survived while others had perished; there was no sense or reason to it.

Roh became suddenly aware that everyone was waiting. Faces lined with pain and exhaustion peered at her from every angle.

'Where's Toril and Elder Sigra?' she heard herself ask no one in particular, her voice hoarse.

Murmurs broke out across the deck and Roh gathered that they were passing the message along, trying to find her battle leaders amidst the devastation. Roh avoided leaning against the mast. She knew if she did, she might very well slide to the ground and not get back up. She waited, straight-backed and patient, despite the heaviness of her mind and heart; her people were depending on her.

Eventually, she received word that both Toril and Elder Sigra were on the next ship over, the same vessel that held Odi and Deodan. Thanking the messenger, Roh stretched out her wings, silently praying that she had the strength to fly across the way to meet with her council.

Somehow, she did. Her wings beat powerfully on either side of her and her boots left the deck, the crisp night air once more kissing her face, this time soothing some of the residual panic caged in her chest. She felt rather than saw Finn and Yrsa following her. The three of them landed deftly on yet another blood-soaked deck, the atmosphere immediately prickling Roh's skin. Something was wrong. A deeper wrong than the aftermath of battle.

She scanned the ship, her eyes instantly snagging on Deodan's allies, who were gathered around something she couldn't see. Toril and Elder Sigra were there, too, their heads bowed together as they discussed something urgently.

Roh crossed to the starboard side in several quick strides and the warrior warlocks dispersed, allowing her access instantly.

Roh fell to her knees with a ragged gasp. Deodan lay on the timber planks, blood soaking through his shirt at his abdomen, an enormous arrow protruding from his middle. His wet hair was plastered to his head, which he tried to hold up but kept dropping to his chest as he came in and out of consciousness. His breathing was shallow and he was cold to the touch.

'Gods,' Roh muttered, trying to get a better look at the wound. She reached within herself, for that healing lifesong that had done so much good already, but her magic was spent. She had nothing left to give.

Odi was at Deodan's side, his face ashen, his hand resting on the warrior warlock's shoulder, murmuring words of comfort Roh couldn't hear.

'When did this happen?' she asked.

Odi looked up, his eyes wide, as though surprised to find her there. 'I ... I can't be sure ... Before Valli showed up?'

'He's been like this for that long?' Roh gaped. 'My song did nothing?'

Odi shook his head. 'I could see you in the crow's nest from here. I know your song touched us all, but it ... Perhaps if we removed the arrow —'

'Don't!' Roh nearly shouted. 'If you remove it he might bleed out in moments. We need to get him to a healer.' She stood up too fast, her head spinning and the base of her skull still throbbing as she tried to find the familiar faces of Toril and Elder Sigra, black spots making her vision swim. She steadied herself on the tailing and found them waiting for her.

'Elder Sigra,' she said, commanding the tremor in her voice. 'I want you to assess the damage to Talon's Reach. I want to know if sealing off that tunnel worked and if we have a lair to return to.'

'Yes, Majesty.' Elder Sigra bowed and instantly took to the waters, towards where the veil had stood between the seas and the cyren territory.

Roh turned to Toril and one of her soldiers. 'I want a scout sent to find Cerys, Harlyn and Kezra. I need to know they're alright. And, Toril, I want you to organise envoys to each of the ships. I accept their surrender. They have permission to gather their dead and burn them on the warship of their choosing. May their warriors find peace atop the waves.'

Toril nodded. 'And our own?'

'Record their names and return their bodies to the seas, as is custom.'

'Yes, Majesty.' With that, Toril too was gone.

Odi looked up at Roh. 'What about Deodan?' he asked.

Roh could see the perspiration beading at his brow and she wondered for how long exactly he'd been trying to staunch the bleeding.

'As soon as we know the state of the lair, we'll move him.'

'You can't heal him yourself?' Odi pressed.

'I … I have nothing left, and even if I did … I don't know how, not a wound like this,' Roh said, trying to keep her voice from breaking. She wanted to say more, to offer some sort of reassurance to Odi and the rest of her friends, but she had none. The battle had scooped out her insides, had drained her of any words of comfort she might give, and so she sat beside Deodan and waited for news of Saddoriel.

Roh listened to the sounds of the survivors gathering their dead amongst the waves – the shouts of humans and warlocks as they lifted the bodies from the sea with a pulley, water splashing over the decks anew. The overwhelming smell of burning pyres and charred flesh filled her nostrils as a blood-red dawn began to glow on the horizon, dark plumes of smoke drifting into the early-morning air.

Cerys, Harlyn and Kezra had been located on one of the enemy ships, bruised and battered but otherwise unharmed. Apparently, they were tending to the wounded cyrens there, and all Roh could do was take the messenger's word for it.

Deodan looked worse by the minute, and no medical supplies on board would do for the wound in his gut. They needed a skilled healer and fast. Roh stayed at his side with Odi, fear seeping into the quiet between them. She remembered acutely how it felt to lose a friend, and she prayed she would not experience it again so soon.

At last, Elder Sigra appeared on deck once more and signalled for Roh to join her in the captain's cabin. Leaving Odi to guard Deodan, Roh got to her feet, feeling unsteady, motioning for Finn and Yrsa to follow.

'Well?' Roh said, folding her arms over her chest when the door clicked closed behind them. The movement was as much to warm herself as it was to demand an answer.

'The veil is destroyed,' Elder Sigra told them gravely. 'As is the sealed tunnel to Talon's Reach. However, Ames – I mean, Marlow – managed to seal off the tunnel after that, which protected many of the outer passageways.'

'What's the damage to Saddoriel?' Roh pressed.

'Minimal,' the council elder said swiftly. 'There is some general damage from the terror tempests' blows – some caved-in tunnels, flooded passages and cannon wreckage in the outer regions, but Saddoriel itself remains in one piece, all the sectors. There is rubble and superficial damage, but it holds. Once we met the warlocks in battle, much of the attack was diverted to us. We can return home.'

Roh let out a tight breath. 'It's safe to return? Do we have terror tempest readings from Csilla? Is the lair structurally sound?'

Elder Sigra bowed low. 'It's safe, Majesty. Your magic saw to that.'

Yrsa nudged Roh. 'It was you,' she murmured. 'You made the call for *a gathering of power that no longer exists in the realms as we know them today*.' She smiled. 'You saved Saddoriel, Roh. You saved it again.'

Roh's throat went dry, all her thoughts with her bleeding friend back on deck. The exact cost of saving the lair was yet to be clear. 'All precautions have been taken in securing Talon's Reach?' she asked Elder Sigra.

She nodded. 'Marlow has seen to the necessary tests and reinforcements. He assures me that the lair may be inhabited once again.'

'Good,' Roh said, her voice rough. 'See to it that our best healers are on standby to receive Deodan. Inform them of his injuries. Have one of your envoys invite the warlock and human survivors to regroup in Saddoriel. They will be treated as guests, not hostages; fed and treated for their wounds.'

Roh half expected the council elder to argue, for there had never been humans and warlocks in such numbers in the lair, least of all people who until moments before had been their enemies. But Elder Sigra nodded and gave another bow before sweeping from the captain's cabin to carry out her orders.

At last, Roh allowed herself the support of leaning against the captain's desk, her body nearly collapsing with relief. She prised the coral breastplate from her chest, stifling a moan, and wiped a hand across her grubby face, trying to keep the exhaustion at bay. She looked to Finn and Yrsa, who finally appeared as tired as she felt.

'Are you both alright?' she asked, scanning them critically.

'A few cuts and scrapes,' Yrsa reassured her. 'And you?'

Roh waved her away. 'I'm fine.'

Finn made to approach her, but she held up a hand. 'Please,' she said, 'not here. I need to stay strong, I need to attend to Deodan. If you hold me, I'll fall apart.'

Finn nodded. 'I understand.'

Roh tried to smile at him in thanks, but she knew it was more of a grimace. She wanted nothing more than to collapse into his arms, to be taken away from the carnage and destruction of all that had occurred amidst the lashing terror tempests, but a queen could not walk away so easily. To wield a crown was more than the thing that sat atop one's head. It was to think deeply beyond one's self, to consider the experiences of all, and to strive to make them better.

She straightened and made for the door. Outside, Odi and Deodan had not moved, but Roh was surprised to see a new figure at her wounded friend's side.

'What are you doing here, Sybil?' Roh practically growled.

The enemy leader was crouched by her son, her face lined with grief and regret. 'I heard he was injured,' she murmured, her wrinkled hand clasping Deodan's. 'I had to come. I had to …' she trailed off.

Deodan was unconscious, completely unaware that it had taken his blood spilling across the deck to bring his mother back to him, a trace of long-lost maternal concern at last finding her.

But Roh's sympathies didn't extend to Sybil and a glance at

Yrsa told her that the Jaktaren felt much the same. Roh drew herself up to her full height, her hands resting on the grips of her quartz daggers, and turned to the cyren soldiers standing warily nearby.

'Take her into custody,' she ordered. 'Seize any remaining vials from her belt. Ensure she has no other weapons or warlock contraptions. Put her in treated irons and take her to Saddoriel's Prison. She will remain there until we can set a trial.'

'A trial?' one of the guards blurted.

'Yes,' Roh confirmed icily. 'Get her out of my sight.'

The edge in her voice spurred the cyrens into action and Sybil was dragged away from Deodan, limp in the arms of her captors, as though grief weighed her down. Roh turned her back on the former Warlock Supreme, shaking her head in disbelief. Deodan needed her.

She crouched by her friend. 'We're going to move you soon,' she told him quietly, placing her hand gently on his arm, unsure if he could hear her. 'You'll get the help you need. I won't let you die,' she promised.

Next to him, Odi seemed to sigh heavily, resting his head back against the rail and closing his eyes momentarily.

'He's going to be alright,' Roh told him.

With his eyes still closed, Odi smiled. 'With the Queen of Bones by his side, I have no doubt.'

The golden orb of the sun had risen by the time a team of healers with an enchanted stretcher came for Deodan. Roh had to bite her tongue to stop herself from hissing at them every time they jolted him around. But Deodan was still unconscious, so still that she had checked his breathing against the back of her hand on multiple occasions.

The healers' faces looked grim, but Roh told herself it wasn't only Deodan they feared for, there were many more injured parties needing transport and treatment. Roh anchored herself in the logistical tasks of getting warlocks and humans into the lair without drowning them.

With Cerys and Marlow guiding them, some of Deodan's warlock allies created a portal from the deck of the ships to the entrance of Saddoriel. Roh had never seen such a thing created before and even in her bewildered, shocked state, she marvelled at the beauty of warlock magic. She watched on as the healers took Deodan to her home, praying that they could find a way to save him.

Roh stayed behind on deck for as long as she could stand, telling cyrens, warlocks and humans alike to go to the Queen's Conservatory, where she had ordered food and drink to be served to anyone who needed it. It had been a long night and an even longer morning watching on as people from all walks of life struggled to process the battle that had savaged the seas and carved into the stronghold. In part, Roh stayed to feed magic into the portals, in part she stayed out of her duty as queen, but deep down, she knew that she stayed because she wasn't ready to face what awaited her in Saddoriel: an entire kingdom waiting for her command, a dear friend on the brink of death and a mountain of decisions in the wake of all the destruction she'd witnessed, or perhaps even brought upon cyrenkind by herself.

But when Roh finally swayed beneath the weight of exhaustion, someone caught her under the arms and held her upright.

'It's enough now, Roh,' the familiar voice said. 'You've done all you can.'

Finn's hands gripped her, gentle but strong, and led her away. Roh didn't remember entering the portal. She didn't remember getting from the ship to the archway of bones. Nor did she recall the journey from the entrance of Saddoriel to the residences currently being used as an infirmary. All she knew was that she was now at Deodan's side. He was lying on a narrow bed, as pale as death beneath the grime and dried blood. He was shirtless. Someone had removed the arrow from his abdomen, a thick white bandage now wrapped around his middle, marred with red.

Roh inhaled shakily, pressing her trembling hand to Deodan's heart, to reassure herself that it was indeed beating. His pulse was slow, scarily so, and she looked around the chamber for the first time, in search of some explanation, or an answer to a prayer.

'He's lost a lot of blood,' Finn said quietly.

'Will he die?' The words flew out of Roh's mouth, but there was no other way to put it; Deodan was standing at the gates of the underworld.

Finn squeezed her shoulder gently. 'I don't know ... But you need to get some food and something to drink, or you'll be in the bed next to him soon enough.'

'Finn's right,' Yrsa added. 'Go to the conservatory, there's plenty to eat there. You need your strength.'

Though she had no appetite, Roh found herself nodding. She felt depleted; using the amount of magic she had, had hollowed her out in a way she'd never experienced before.

She squeezed Deodan's hand and leaned in close. 'Please don't die,' she begged him, before getting to her feet once more and allowing the Jaktaren to lead her from the infirmary.

Roh hadn't stepped foot inside the Queen's Conservatory since the tournament gala. Now, it was a far cry from the decadent and formal space it had been then. On her orders, long tables had been set up along the walls and stacked with food and drink. Piles of clean plates and mugs were at the ready, welcoming anyone to serve themselves whatever they needed. All around the room beneath the bone chandeliers, dazed-looking humans, cyrens and warlocks sat on the floor with plates in their laps and cups by their sides, purple smudges beneath their eyes, many of them still covered in the gore of battle.

When Roh entered the grand doors, many made to stand and bow, but she raised a hand.

'Please,' she said, hoping that was enough.

It was. Her guests lowered their heads and continued to eat, the quiet scrape of cutlery and the soft murmurs starting up again.

Roh gratefully took the plate Yrsa passed to her, and she was relieved to see Odi on the far side of the conservatory. She crossed the grand room and sat down beside him, suppressing a groan as her muscles seemed to give out beneath her.

'I don't know if I'll be able to get back up,' she admitted.

Odi huffed a laugh. 'You always do,' he said.

Roh glanced at him then, hearing the utter exhaustion in his voice. To her surprise, he was drenched with sweat, despite the neutral temperature of the conservatory. She watched him reach for his mug with a trembling hand and drain its contents as though he was a parched beast in the desert.

'Are you alright?' she asked, putting her plate down and turning to face him.

He seemed to have trouble swallowing before he answered her. 'I'll be fine,' he told her, before he swayed at the waist.

Roh caught him, preventing his face from colliding with the marble floor.

'Odi?' Panic spiked in her chest. 'Odi? Can you hear me?'

He was limp in her arms, his eyelids fluttered as he tried to focus on her face. 'I can hear you ...' he breathed. 'But I can't see you much.'

Roh looked around wildly – this couldn't be happening. 'Help!' she cried, but it came out a faint croak; her voice was trapped inside her like a nightmare.

She spotted Finn and Yrsa sprinting across the room. Odi's

skin was clammy against hers. 'What's happened?' she asked him, desperation rising within. 'Odi?'

Odi huffed a pained laugh, still unable to hold himself up in her arms. 'Deodan said something about a cannon.'

Roh's blood went cold. 'A cannon?'

Yrsa, who had been listening, crouched beside Roh, her hands going to the hem of Odi's shirt and lifting it.

Roh choked back a sob.

Yrsa and Finn both swore.

For Odi's abdomen was purple and swollen, visibly pulsating beneath Yrsa's touch.

'Gods, Odi!' Roh cried.

Yrsa's voice broke. 'You've been bleeding internally this whole time …'

'You fool,' Finn whispered, his face leaching of colour as he took in the sight of the injury.

'Someone get help!' Roh screamed across the conservatory.

She heard glass shattering, and hoped it meant someone was scrambling for a healer.

'We can't wait,' she realised. 'We have to take him to the infirmary, *now*.'

But Odi's half-gloved hand reached out, for her. She took it.

'Gods, Odi … Why didn't you say something?' she cried.

Odi licked his cracked lips. 'Didn't know it myself,' he managed. 'Not till I got here.'

'You …' Roh trailed off, remembering the exact moment on the warship. She'd gone flying in the opposite direction – Odi's hands had shoved her violently. 'You saved me. You saved me and this was the price. Gods, why did you come back to Saddoriel? You were nearly safe. Why —'

She was crying openly now, for deep in her bones, the realisation settled, cold and hard.

Odi's hand blindly found her face and he cupped her cheek.

She blinked at him through the tears, seeing the line of blood leaking from his mouth.

'Why did you come back?' she croaked. 'This wasn't meant to happen. You —'

'Because,' he rasped. 'You're the one to bring us all together, Roh. You're the one to make the realms a better place.'

'I was meant to do it with you.'

'I told you I'd be with you till the end.' He coughed then, blood spraying across the pristine marble.

'Odi ...' Roh sobbed.

'Bring us together, Roh,' he said again. His elegant fingers twitched before falling away from her and he wheezed, gasping for air.

He did not exhale. He did not move again.

For the Prince of Melodies had taken his final breath.

CHAPTER TWENTY-EIGHT

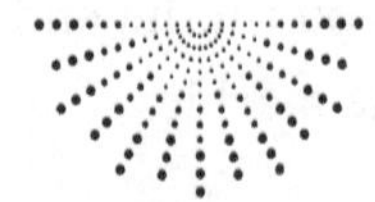

Roh didn't know how long she knelt beside Odi's lifeless body, clutching his hand to her aching chest. She felt rather than saw the others gathered around them; a squeeze of her shoulder, words whispered in her ear, but they fell away to nothing. It was just her and Odi, as it had been from the start.

'I know this song,' he had said, his first-ever words to her.

Roh inhaled deeply, the air burning her lungs but ceasing to fill them entirely. Her heart felt swollen and exposed. Her face was wet with tears, though she couldn't remember crying. She kept waiting for someone to tell her that this wasn't real, that she'd imagined the whole thing, that it had been some cruel trick of her overly active, exhausted mind. But no one did, and Odi's hand remained cold and limp in hers.

This wasn't how it was meant to be.

Someone had shut his eyes, she didn't know who.

'Roh …' someone was saying from far away. 'Roh, we have to move him.'

'Can't —' The word grated out of her like a rusted blade and she panicked, unable to gulp down enough air, as though Odi had taken it with him. But he couldn't be gone, could he?

'Breathe, Roh …' Yrsa, it was Yrsa beside her.

At last, Roh tore her gaze away from Odi and met Yrsa's red-rimmed stare. Fresh tears tracked down her face, but she held onto Roh, strong and steady.

'We have to move him,' she said again.

The cold logistics of death sank its talons into Roh, and slowly she nodded. But she did not release Odi's hand, even as Finn and Kezra lifted him from the ground. She didn't release his hand as the crowd of humans, cyrens and warlocks parted for them with their hands resting on their hearts. They carried their dead friend to the infirmary.

'What's wrong with him?' a deep voice cut through their shock as they entered the makeshift medical quarters.

Deodan was sitting up in his narrow bed, the colour returned to his cheeks, a bowl of broth clutched in his hands.

'He's …' But Roh couldn't say the words. She didn't –

A primal, gut-wrenching scream carved through her panic, curdling her insides. Suddenly, Harlyn was there, her bad arm in a fresh sling, her eyes wide in horror as she took in the waxy pallor of Odi's skin.

The others set him down carefully on an empty bed. The pain and tension had ebbed from his expression in death and now he looked at peace, as though he was only sleeping.

Harlyn reached for him, but her hand instantly recoiled as it touched his already cold face and her eyes shot to Roh's in disbelief, frantically seeking reassurance, an explanation.

Roh had none to give, so she held her friend's gaze and shook her head.

Harlyn's mouth fell open, a hand clutching her chest. 'No.'

It was that single word, that desperate refusal to believe the stark truth before them, that finally forced Roh to drop Odi's hand. She went to Harlyn, her chest cracking open anew at the sight of her oldest friend's heart breaking right in front of them. Harlyn collapsed into her arms, rasping for breath as Roh had only moments before.

Roh clutched Harlyn to her chest, trying to lend her any ounce of strength she had left. Harlyn's body heaved against hers, half fighting Roh's embrace, but not being able to stand without it.

'How?' Deodan asked, his voice stripped of all emotion.

But when Roh looked to him, tears streaked the warlock's blood-caked face, his eyes fixed on Odi's body.

'How?' he asked again, placing his bowl on the side with a wince.

Roh struggled to find her voice, and when she did, it sounded like it belonged to someone else. 'Cannon fire ... He ... He didn't tell us. We didn't know.'

Deodan covered his mouth with his hand, shaking his head. Roh felt his sorrow in her own chest, knowing that both she and Deodan would forever feel responsible for not realising their friend was hurt.

'I thought I saw it happen,' Deodan managed. 'But he insisted he was fine, that it had barely grazed him.'

Finn dragged the bed Odi was on closer to Deodan's, so the warlock could see for himself. The Jaktaren then sat on the end of Deodan's bed, the mattress sinking beneath his weight. Yrsa came to stand beside him, and Kezra beside her. Roh brought Harlyn closer, so they were all gathered around Odi.

The shock and raw grief settled over them in a blanket of heavy silence, the rest of the infirmary fading into nothing.

'He's truly gone ...' Roh wasn't sure if she'd said it or one of the others had, but it was the truth all the same. She still held Harlyn in her arms, the embrace just as much for her sake as her friend's. If she let go she knew she would slip away and melt into the dark abyss of grief that awaited her. She stared at Odi, who looked less and less like himself in death. Roh prayed he had gone somewhere with music, somewhere with light.

'Majesty,' a voice sounded from the door.

Roh's head snapped up, her heart jolting as though snatched from a dream.

Elder Sigra and Toril Ainsley waited, clearly uncomfortable at the sight of the scene before them.

'Your Majesty, there are matters …' Elder Sigra began.

Roh raised a hand and the cyren fell silent at once. Roh's chest ached as she motioned for Yrsa to take over holding Harlyn, which she did, Roh easing Harlyn's weight into the Jaktaren's arms. She would not sully Odi's deathbed with talk of cyren politics. Taking a deep breath, she straightened and motioned for her council to take the conversation outside. It hurt to leave Odi. It hurt to leave her friends in their sea of grief, but the cold hard actuality of being a ruler dragged Roh from the throes of her sorrow.

She closed the door to the infirmary behind her and out in the passageway turned to Elder Sigra and Toril Ainsley.

'What is it?' she asked, her voice hollow.

Elder Sigra's face was lined with regret as she spoke. 'Majesty, I am sorry for the loss of your friend, but … there is much to be done.'

Roh nodded. While Odi's death halted her world, the rest of the kingdom did not stop moving, she knew that. 'Have the Saddoriens started returning from evacuation?' she asked.

'They have, Majesty.'

'See to it that no deathsong or death chorus is used. No human or warlock guest is to be harmed or intimidated. They are to be treated with the same respect we would our Akorian, Csillan and Lochlorian kin.'

'Already done, Your Majesty,' Toril replied with a bow.

'Good.' Roh mulled over her thoughts for a moment. 'Find the rest of the council elders and have them gathered in the War

Room within the hour. I want Cerys and Marlow Irons there as well.'

'Of course.'

'Round up any willing and able water warlocks to reinforce the old enchantments of the lair. I don't want a single fissure in our protection.'

Both cyrens were nodding.

'And what of your coronation, Majesty?' Elder Sigra asked. 'The Council of Seven Elders will expect —'

'I don't care what they expect,' Roh snapped. 'Where were they when Saddoriel nearly fell?'

'I —'

'You stood by me, Elder Sigra, as did Elder Ward,' Roh allowed. 'I do not hold you responsible for their actions. But *they* will be held responsible.'

Roh let her threat settle in the space between them before continuing. 'As for a coronation … It's not appropriate to hold an event like that in the wake of so much loss. And I will not be crowned until my friend is given the farewell that he deserves.'

Elder Sigra bowed her head. 'Of course, Your Majesty. Shall we prepare him for the cyrens' last rite?'

'The Prince of Melodies will not be given to the seas. He gave the seas enough already,' Roh said quietly, choking down the lump in her throat. 'My companions and I will escort him back to his homeland, to the Isle of Dusan.'

'But, Majesty, the lair —'

'The lair will wait.'

'Are you —'

Roh eyed both leaders coldly. '*The lair will wait.*'

Her words seemed to echo down the passageways and both leaders bowed low.

'We'll have the council waiting for you within the hour, Your Majesty,' Elder Sigra said.

To Roh's relief, that was the end of the discussion and the cyrens left. With a deep sigh, she leaned back against the wall, allowing it to take some of her weight. She felt so heavy, so tired and hollowed out. Closing her eyes, she ran through the list of risks she was taking by insisting she escort Odi back to the Isle of Dusan ... Saddoriel was still bleeding from battle, the vulnerable still camped out in the Queen's Conservatory, and her first instinct was to *leave*? Before she had even been formally crowned? While she trusted Cerys and Marlow to oversee things in her stead, she knew that the news of Cerys' innocence was still fresh and to leave a kingdom in the hands of a newly freed prisoner was a precarious move. However, Roh knew deep in her bones that she could not give Odi to the seas.

On their first journey together, Odi's amber eyes had met hers. *'If you're crowned queen, will you let me go?'*

'Let you go?'

Odi had nodded. 'Will you set me free from Talon's Reach?'

Roh had sighed and touched a finger to the fresh scar on her cheek. 'When I'm crowned queen,' she said, 'I will grant you your freedom.'

Odi exhaled shakily. 'I have your word?'

'You have my word.'

Fresh tears burned her eyes and spilled down her grimy face. 'I'll take you home, Odi,' she whispered between quiet sobs. She had promised, after all.

Roh told Finn, Yrsa, Harlyn, Deodan and Kezra of her plans and left them to wrap Odi's body in a shroud, which they would take on a stretcher through the outer passageways of Talon's Reach to the Isle of Dusan. It was the same path she and Odi had taken during the official tournament to retrieve supplies for their piano, the same path Odi had guided his stepbrothers and fellow humans to as the first terror tempest struck. It seemed only right he would travel it one last time with her.

Roh met the Council of Seven Elders, along with Cerys and Marlow Irons in the War Room an hour later. She had done her best to clean herself up, to wash the dirt and grief from her face, but a fresh shirt and a polished crown didn't hide that she was a wreck. Her sorrow was on display for all to see, and she didn't care.

Roh listened to the excuses of Taro and Bloodwyn Haertel, of Erdites Colter, Arcus Mercer and Koras Rasaat with a blank expression, her fury simmering just below the surface. But she made no hasty decisions, not before she had been officially crowned. She eyed each and every one of them coldly.

'I'll take it under consideration,' was all she said to them.

Roh then listened to the progress reports on the reinforcement of Saddoriel and the state of the lair. There were only a handful of tunnels that had fully caved in during the savage terror tempests, none of which would affect the daily running of Talon's Reach for the time being.

According to Winslow Ward, the evacuation of the children had been a success, and slowly, they were now returning to Saddoriel, families uniting all around the lair and praising the power of their new queen.

There had been one or two issues with older cyrens refusing to accept the presence of warlocks and humans. The culprits had been reprimanded and taken to Saddoriel's Prison to await the queen's justice.

'Let them rot a little while longer down there,' Roh said without hesitation. 'I'll address the matter upon my return.'

'Return?' Taro Haertel blurted. 'Where are you going?'

'Your Majesty,' Cerys growled from across the table. 'Where are you going, *Your Majesty*.'

Taro Haertel flushed furiously, his eyes narrowing at the sight of Cerys Irons before him. But he bowed his head. 'My apologies, Your Majesty.'

Roh felt her nostrils flare. 'To the Isle of Dusan to return the Prince of Melodies to his home and family.'

'Surely, you don't mean to leave Saddoriel without a leader.'

'She's not,' a firm voice sounded from the door. 'She's leaving me in charge to oversee her orders. An Arch General of a cyren territory is surely temporary leader enough for such a task.'

Roh's chest swelled with gratitude as Kezra Wisehand strode into the War Room and took up a place at her side. She glanced up at the towering Csillan. 'You're sure you don't want to come with us?'

Kezra gave her a sad smile. 'I have said my goodbyes to the master musician,' she said. 'I think it's only right that you and your companions take him home alone.'

Roh's eyes burned again – would they ever not? But she blinked back her tears and gave a stiff nod, scanning the faces before her, which were a combination of shock and fury.

'I leave Saddoriel in the capable hands of the Csillan Arch General until my return. It will only be a matter of days. Cerys and Marlow Irons will assist her in all important matters.'

'As you command, Your Majesty,' Bloodwyn Haertel said, bowing her head.

Roh had to stop herself from sneering. The Haertel elders clearly knew they were on thin ice … For a moment, she wondered if they even remembered that it was they who had captured and thrust Odi into the Queen's Tournament. Were it not for them, he might never have set foot in Saddoriel.

Roh shook the thought from her mind. It would do her no good to dwell on such matters now. She cleared her throat and dished out the rest of her orders. Aid was to be sent to Akoris and Lochloria immediately, with any displaced refugees of the Akorian conflict to be given shelter and food, whether they were cyren, warlock or otherwise. Although they had received word that the Csillans hadn't detected a single flicker of a terror tempest since the battle, Roh ordered that additional resources be sent to the gorges to help monitor any incoming storms at a granular level; she was taking no chances.

They covered refugees, displaced Saddoriens, supply shortages and increased protection of the outer passageways. Erdites Colter tried to bring up the sentencing of the Warlock Supreme, but Roh silenced him with a flick of her hand. The fate of the Warlock Supreme would not be decided until the warlocks had been reinstated in Lochloria, until Deodan was officially named their leader. The resentment was thick in the air at that decree, but Roh did not yield.

The meeting went on for hours, to the point where Roh's eyelids became heavy and she could no longer follow the discourse. They seemed to be going around in circles and it became clear to her why Saddoriel hadn't changed its ways in centuries. Without warning, she got to her feet and braced herself against the table.

'All the urgent matters have been addressed,' she announced. 'You all have your orders. See to it that they are carried out in my absence. I expect full reports upon my return. This meeting is now at an end.'

Roh remained upright as she watched the council leave one by one, until only Taro Haertel lingered in the doorway.

'What is it?' she asked him, her patience on its last legs.

Elder Haertel lifted his chin. 'It's my understanding that there is to be a union between our houses, Your Majesty.'

Roh blinked at him.

The elder shifted from foot to foot. 'You and my son —'

'Your son?' she retorted. '*Now* he's your son?'

'Finn has always —'

'Don't say another word,' Roh snapped, her talons unsheathing and digging into the tabletop. 'Get out, before I throw you out.'

'Your Majesty –'

She straightened, feeling her power surge, an almost tangible mix of grief and fury. 'I won't tell you again.'

Wisely, Taro Haertel left, his robes swishing behind him.

'I can't say I didn't enjoy that,' Kezra said dryly.

There was a murmur of agreement from Toril Ainsley and Elder Sigra.

But Roh's vision blurred, her knees buckling under the weight of her exhaustion, which had at last found the cracks in her armour. Suddenly, the world was tilting and she was falling into oblivion.

Roh awoke in the queen's – in *her* – private quarters, the bed luxuriously soft beneath her. For a moment, she allowed herself to come back to the world, believing it had all been a dream … But the ache in her heart was as poignant as ever and she spotted Finn asleep in an armchair by the bed; even in sleep, his face was etched with grief.

Roh slipped from the bed, taking a blanket and draping it across Finn before closing the door behind her. The residence was quiet. She hoped her friends had all sought out some rest before their journey.

Roh found herself in front of the veil to the sea, staring out at the turquoise currents, no longer stained with blood. She paused to give thought to the dozens of cyrens who'd given their lives in that battle, whose bodies had been returned to the sea, to become one with the waves. How many souls drifted alone out there? Part of her very much wanted to join them, to float through the veil and out into the tides, to be carried away from all that anchored her in sorrow. Her fingertips reached for the filmy barrier between Saddoriel and the sea –

A flicker of movement in the depths stopped her.

A flash of gold.

Valli was somewhere out there, and that more than anything gave her comfort.

Gnarled roots crept through the surface of the path before Roh. She wore a pack high on her shoulders and held the front end of the stretcher that carried Odi, with Finn at the rear. Despite his injuries, Deodan had insisted on joining them.

'I will not miss the opportunity to say goodbye to a friend,' he had told them firmly as he'd wrapped his bandages tightly and taken a tonic for the pain.

Roh couldn't begrudge him that.

And so, Roh, Finn, Deodan, Harlyn and Yrsa took Odi through the outer passageways of Talon's Reach. Silent tears tracked down Roh's face as the wet ground beneath her boots became wider, and deeper puddles and the immense water forest greeted her. It was the same as it had been when she and Odi had walked the path alone: all manner of enchanted plants and shrubs flourishing in one of the lungs of Saddoriel. She remembered how entranced she had been, how she had felt the quiet yearning of the trees as strong as she did now. Odi had marvelled at it, too. It had been in the safety of Odi's company that she had spoken her fears aloud for the first time.

'Are you scared?' he asked.

Roh hesitated before she said her next words. 'I think part of me is always scared.'

'Of what?'

She had never admitted that to anyone, not even Harlyn and Orson. 'That ... I'll never be more than what I am. And I want ... so badly to be so much more.'

The memory was like a lance to the chest and Roh pushed it

away, palming the fresh tears from her face. For someone who had spent so much of her life unable to cry, it seemed now she could not stop.

The others moved through the water forest in silence, following her as she guided them in the direction of Odi's homeland. How far had he come before turning back to fight with them? Had his stepbrothers made it to safety? Roh swallowed the lump in her throat and pressed on. She supposed she would have those answers soon enough.

Roh and her companions made slow progress through the tunnels, due to sharing the weight of the stretcher between them and ensuring that Deodan didn't tear his stitches. They took frequent but short breaks. No one complained, no one sought to hurry them. Roh knew it was because once they reached their destination, they would have to say a final goodbye. None of them were ready for that.

Time ebbed and flowed strangely down in the dark passageways, but at last Roh felt the incline of the terrain increase and her calves begin to burn. Around them, the air changed, becoming fresh and crisp, a welcome relief to the stuffy, dank tunnels. And then, she saw the glow of sunlight ahead.

The others said nothing as they climbed the arduous ascent, pulling the stretcher up between them as well. Finally, the tunnel opened up to a vibrant woodland and Roh paused on the threshold, her boot hovering between her world and Odi's, as it had before.

But this time there was no tether, there was nothing confining her to the darkness of the lair. She was free to step out into the light. Her heart caught in her throat, for she had always meant to see the Isle of Dusan with Odi at her side. But that wish would never come to pass. So, she stepped out into the sunlight, a wave of goosebumps racing up her arms, a tight breath expelling from her mouth as the golden rays soaked into her skin.

No one had spoken in hours, but now she turned to Finn and Yrsa. 'Odi once told me it would take the better part of a day to reach his home from here. Can you find the Eery Brothers' tracks?'

Finn and Yrsa swapped places, so the latter took the weight of the stretcher. Finn strode ahead and crouched in the dirt, scanning the ground before him. 'Found them,' he said, pointing to a clear disturbance in the leaf litter. 'Let's take our friend home.'

Even with the stretcher, Deodan's injury and Harlyn's bad arm, they made it to Odi's hometown in half a day. Roh knew from what Odi had told her that it was one of three islands, best known for their chalk-white cliffs and verdant grasslands. Settled amongst the hills and cliffs were several neat buildings. Roh's stomach churned as they drew nearer, suddenly aware that upon the Eery Brothers' return, they would have told their story and that the townsfolk certainly wouldn't welcome the cyrens with open arms.

But there was no one around to bother them. They made for the tiny main street of the village, and without Finn's help knew immediately which was the Arrowood shop residence. A single music note, like those Odi had written to his brothers, hung on a wooden sign outside the window, rocking gently in the salty breeze.

Without a word, Roh led them to the door and pushed it open.

A small bell rang above her and she moved slowly into the shop, taking in the array of musical instruments and paraphernalia. It was only once she was inside that she wondered in a panic if bringing Odi's body into the shop was appropriate, but there was nothing to be done now. Harlyn, Yrsa and Finn stood behind her, holding up the stretcher, while Deodan blocked the entire doorway.

A crash sounded from the back of the shop, followed by colourful cursing that Roh had heard Odi mutter on numerous occasions; the thought made her chest hurt. Not long after, an elderly man appeared at the counter. He had Odi's amber eyes and the same lean frame and flop to his hair, though his was grey and wiry.

He paused, resting his hands on the countertop, surveying the cyrens and what they carried between them. He showed no sign of surprise.

'You've brought my son back to me,' he said, his voice laced with sorrow.

Roh stared at him for a moment. How was it that he knew? Word could not have travelled so fast, and from whom? Harlyn nudged her.

'We have, Mr Arrowood,' Roh told him, her voice sounding once more like that of a stranger.

The elderly man's gaze lingered on the shroud before his tear-lined eyes fell to Roh. 'And you must be the cyren queen my son died for.'

Roh felt as though she'd been punched in the gut. All the air was sucked from her lungs and she fought to stay upright. Somehow she managed to keep her head up, just. 'I am, sir,' she replied, her lip quaking.

Mr Arrowood seemed to consider her before he nodded. 'Then you'd best come in.'

Odi's father motioned for them to follow him through the storage of the shop, which led to modest apartments beyond. Roh could feel the shock rippling from the others behind her, but she kept her eyes forward. How had he known Odi was dead? How was he so calm? Did a unit of soldiers lie in wait, ready to kill them?

But it was only Mason and Brooks Eery who sat on a settee, drinking something amber. Odi's stepbrothers looked much better than the last time Roh had seen them. They'd been washed and fed, though their faces still bore the pain and weariness of months of imprisonment. Like their stepfather, they did not seem surprised to see a handful of cyrens and a warlock in their midst.

'You can put him on the table there,' Mr Arrowood pointed.

Roh and the others wordlessly slid the stretcher onto the table, all of them massaging their blistered hands.

'I'm so sorry,' Roh said, both to Mr Arrowood and the Eery Brothers. 'I promised to free him from Talon's Reach, and I failed him.'

The Eery Brothers were on their feet, suddenly pressing cups into the cyrens' hands. Brooks, the elder of the two, shook his head. 'We tried to stop him, but he wouldn't let you face it without him.'

'And now we face the realms without him,' Odi's father murmured.

Roh bit the inside of her cheek to keep from sobbing. She didn't want to imagine a world without Odi, but now his body had been returned to his family, the reality was sinking in, fast.

Brooks approached Roh. He seemed to suppress a glimmer of fear before placing a large hand on her shoulder. 'It wasn't your fault,' he said, his voice raw and brimming with emotion.

Roh rested her hand on his. 'It was, I should have found a way —'

Mason cleared his throat. 'It was his choice to go back. He insisted that for you to bring everyone together, to unite warring races, a human needed to be seen fighting at your side.'

Brooks' hand was still on her shoulder, as though he knew she needed its reassuring weight to remain grounded. Roh could hardly breathe.

'Thank you for telling us,' she said eventually, bowing her head. 'We're deeply sorry for your loss. Odi was …' Words failed her then, the grief she was holding back at last spilling over.

It was Finn who stepped forward and knelt before Odi's father. 'I was honoured to fight alongside your son, sir,' he said, his voice hoarse. 'And even more honoured to call him my friend.'

For the first time since their arrival, Mr Arrowood's tears fell.

Brooks Eery came forward. 'It was your crossbow he bore?'

Finn nodded. 'It was.'

'Then my brother felt the same for you.' Brooks pulled Finn to his feet and embraced him, hard.

When the emotion had settled once more, Odi's father looked to them. 'You will stay to say farewell? We'll do a ceremony at dusk.'

'We'll stay,' Deodan said roughly.

The Eery Brothers left the shop to spread the word of the ceremony throughout the islands. Mr Arrowood said that if they had more time, they knew people would have travelled from far and wide to pay their respects, but the harsh truth was that Odi had been dead for some time now and his body needed to be put to rest as soon as possible.

'He would have preferred it this way,' his father said. 'Nothing too fancy.'

Roh agreed.

While it was just their small group gathered in the shop, Roh forgot about Saddoriel and her impending reign. All of that fell away as she listened to her friends tell their favourite tales of Odi from their travels. Mr Arrowood laughed along with them, at Odi's sea sickness, at his immediate disdain for the newly hatched sea drakeling, at his hayfever in the moors between Csilla and the redwood forest, and his blushing when adoring fans asked him to sign scraps of fabric ... But then came the stories of his courage, his bravery. How he'd bartered their way into The Thorn with his musical talent, how he'd saved Finn's life in Serratega, how he'd fought off the reef dweller in Lamaka's Basin, and lastly ... How he'd saved Roh in the battle for Saddoriel and in the end, sacrificed his life for hers …

The tightness in Roh's chest refused to loosen. It only grew tighter still when she snuck glances at Harlyn. Her friend's eyes were red raw and it seemed she had developed a sensitivity to noise, constantly flinching at ordinary sounds around her. Roh knew Harlyn would be reliving those last moments she'd had with Odi for a long time to come; that heated kiss on the edge of battle, a promise of what could have been between them. Roh knew there was nothing she could say to comfort her, nothing that would ease the pain, and so she did not try. Instead, she stayed close and hoped that Harlyn knew she was there when she decided she was ready to talk.

The dusk light filtered through the grimy windows, and soon enough the townsfolk were gathered outside around the small hill at the back of the yard which overlooked the sea, their faces lined with the same disbelief that Roh still felt now.

'Are you ready?' Mr Arrowood asked them.

'No,' Roh said, but went with him anyway.

The Eery Brothers, along with some townsmen, had moved Odi to a pyre on the top of the hill, while some of the women handed out paper lanterns. Roh had never seen a human funeral rite before, so she didn't know what the lanterns were for, but she took one nonetheless.

No one spoke.

No one objected to the presence of cyrens.

Instead, the Eery Brothers lit the pyre, while the small crowd lit their lanterns. Suddenly, dozens of glowing paper lanterns drifted into the air, floating across the seas as Odi's body burned.

The Eery Brothers put their fiddles to their chins and began to play of their own free will. And there, upon the cliffs of the Isle of Dusan, Roh and her remaining companions said their last goodbye to the Prince of Melodies, their friend.

CHAPTER TWENTY-NINE

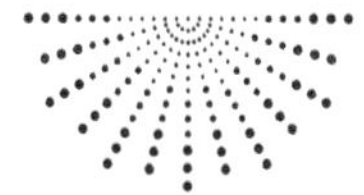

Saddoriel was a different place upon Roh's return. A deep change had occurred not only in the lair, but in its people, mirroring the change within her and her companions at Odi's passing.

With Cerys and Marlow at her side, Kezra had seen to it that all Roh's orders had been carried out. The remaining damage to the tunnels and protective enchantments had been attended to, many warlocks having stayed behind to ensure it. All the evacuated Saddoriens had returned to the lair and the refugees had been cared for.

Roh couldn't remember the last time she'd been alone, but on the afternoon of her return, she found herself in her own company in her private *queen's* residences. Her first instinct was to send for Finn, to seek the comfort of his body, but he had told her once that he was not a balm to be used on a wound. Deep down, she also suspected that she needed this time alone, a moment or two of solitude to process what she could, to feel what she needed to feel.

The walls of grief closed in around her, reminding her of the shrinking room in Akoris, only this she could not stop. The pain within was unbearable, creating a new voice in her mind that insisted Odi would be the first of many she'd lose, that death crept closer and closer to them all …

Her hand went to her pocket, where she had carefully stored the folded pieces of parchment given to her by the Eery Brothers. Mason had pressed them into her hands in the doorway of the shop before she left Odi's home.

'It's a script of music,' Brooks had explained. 'He gave it to us in the tunnels, asked us to make sure it got to you. He wrote it for you.'

Roh had stared at the yellowed folds of paper in a daze. 'But I can't read that language,' she had said.

The brothers had smiled sadly, and Mason had closed his hand over hers. 'It's not meant to be read. It's meant to be played.'

Roh's throat had tightened. 'Then … Can you play it for me?'

'We are not master musicians,' Brooks had answered, shaking his head. 'Not the standard that this piece demands.'

Roh had turned the square of parchment over in her hands. 'Then what –'

'You wait,' Mason had said. 'Wait until the next master musician comes along. Then ask them to play it for you. You'll know they're the one.'

Now, in the privacy of her chambers, Roh sat on the edge of her bed and unfolded the sheets. Her lip trembled as she scanned the beautiful markings she'd seen Odi make so many times before, sending melodies of his own creation back to Saddoriel for his fiddler stepbrothers. She could understand none of it, save for the title of the piece. For at the top of the first page, an Old Saddorien word was scrawled in Odi's hand.

Her heart constricted, a wave of dizziness washing over her. Roh placed the sheets of music down carefully, so her tears didn't mar the ink.

. . .

Later, when she could cry no more, Roh fixed herself a plate of bread and cheese in the kitchen and started to plan. Her coronation was to take place the following day, not giving her much time to get her affairs in order, of which there were many. Amidst the throes of grief and the lingering shock of battle, and since long before then, Roh had been mulling over the conversations she'd had with her friends throughout their quest for the birthstones. These conversations about change and ambition, about desire and selflessness swirled constantly at the forefront of her mind as she tried to prepare for the biggest moment of her life, all without Odi at her side. She wanted to summon Yrsa, to talk things over, knowing that the Jaktaren's wisdom always managed to soothe her. But she couldn't do that just yet. Her thoughts were too scattered, darting from one problem to the next that she needed to address. To be queen was no simple thing. There were many moving parts, countless responsibilities, and she wanted to do it well, to do it better than those who had come before. And for that reason, the night before she was officially crowned, Roh called her mother to her chambers.

Cerys Irons arrived wearing a simple black tunic and trousers, looking very much bewildered by the opulence of the queen's private residences. In the doorway, she eyed the veil to the sea at the end of the hall, a flash of longing in her eyes, but made no mention of it as Roh showed her into the drawing room.

Cerys sat down tentatively, as though concerned she might mark the furniture. Roh watched her mother take in the decadent space before her gaze fell to Roh's crown and the gems gleaming within it.

'Is this what you wanted for me?' Roh asked her quietly.

Cerys seemed to choose her words carefully. 'I wanted many things for you, Rohesia.'

'And for yourself.'

'I'd be lying if I said otherwise.'

'And now?' Roh pressed.

Cerys placed her hands in her lap. Her talons were sheathed, but the dark tips of her fingernails were still jagged. 'Now I am tired.'

Roh ran her hands through her hair with a heavy sigh. 'So am I.'

Cerys nodded. 'I expect you are. But you did not call me here to speak of rest and retirement, I gather?'

'No, I didn't.'

'Well, then?'

Roh rested her elbows on her knees and leaned forward. 'I have had an idea … Of how to restore balance to cyrenkind, to protect it from ourselves, to make things better … But I need your help.'

Something flickered behind Cerys' eyes. 'I'm listening,' she said.

The morning of Roh's coronation arrived all too soon, and alone again, she dressed simply for the occasion: intending to bear no jewels but for the birthstones in her crown, which had been taken to be cleaned and readied for formal presentation. She felt naked without it.

A sharp rap at her bedroom door sounded and Yrsa appeared.

'Are you ready?' she asked.

Roh huffed a laugh, the sensation feeling foreign. 'Are you?'

A hint of a grin tugged at the Jaktaren's mouth. 'Guess we'll find out.'

Finn, Harlyn, Deodan and Kezra were waiting for them in the hall. As Roh and Yrsa joined them, Roh mourned Odi's absence anew, wishing with all her heart that he could be here for this. His final words to her echoed in her mind.

'Bring us together, Roh ...'

I'll do my best, Odi, she vowed silently to her dead friend.

Roh and her fellow cyrens tucked their wings in at their shoulderblades, and along with their warlock companion made their way down to the entrance of Saddoriel, where the coronation was to take place. Roh heard the crowds before she saw them, the thrum of excitement from hundreds, if not thousands of cyrens from all across the realms. And sure enough, when they came upon the archway of bones and the stone galleries beyond, every space was crammed with Saddoriens, Akorians and Csillans. Roh spotted Elna and her daughters, beaming at Roh from their seats. Floralin stood nearby, trying to keep hold of the unruly nestlings, Sol and Mora, who were pointing and waving wildly to Kezra as she passed them with a grin. And by their side, was Piri, who gazed upon Yrsa with her hand on her heart and tears of joy in her eyes. Yrsa broke away from Roh and the group, throwing herself at her partner, drawing her into a fierce kiss and a hard embrace.

Many cyrens stood tall with their wings proudly on display. She hadn't realised that such a great number had chosen to have their essence extracted from the Pool of Weeping, and how many warlocks must have assisted in that process.

A large platform draped in luxurious fabrics had been raised beside the rock column throne at the centre. There, the Council of Seven Elders stood waiting.

Roh glanced at her companions, each of whom gave her a smile of encouragement. This was it. The moment was finally here, after everything she had endured. Roh did not hesitate. She made straight for the platform.

Bloodwyn Haertel eyed Roh warily as she ascended the steps,

her head held high. Roh gave her a single nod of permission. It was time to begin.

The elder cleared her throat and turned to the crowds above. 'Welcome one and all, to Saddoriel,' she started, her voice projecting to the far reaches of the galleries above. 'We have united here from across the realms to bear witness to a new age in cyren history: the reign of a new queen.'

Thunderous applause echoed through the lair and Roh had to hold her hands behind her back to keep from wringing them in anticipation.

'History has indeed been made, by Rohesia of the Bone Cleaners.'

'Rohesia Irons,' Roh cut in, not an ounce of compromise in her tone.

Bloodwyn blanched for a moment, a muscle twitching in her jaw, before she gave a bow of apology. 'By Rohesia Irons,' she corrected herself. 'Rohesia Irons not only emerged victor of the original Queen's Tournament seven moons ago, but has succeeded in her quest to obtain all three birthstones of Saddoriel from across the cyren territories,' Bloodwyn faltered.

'Not only did she retrieve all three gems,' Elder Ward stepped forward, tilting her head to the galleries. 'But she has also liberated cyrenkind from the web of lies our former rulers had spun.'

Another near-deafening applause rang out.

Elder Sigra stepped forward next. 'In spite of our treatment of Rohesia and her family, she has fought for us. She has saved our home and cyrenkind, proving herself a worthy queen time and time again.' Elder Sigra reached behind her, where a cyren held out a velvet cushion, upon which sat a crown. But it was not the crown of bones of Roh's travels and trials.

'When you become queen, will you have a different crown made?' Odi had once asked her. Roh had never given him a straight answer, but when Elder Ward had approached her with details of

her coronation, Roh had insisted. The original crown of bones was to be kept, for formal and historic occasions, but she would not wear it in her daily life. The crown she looked at now was made of white coral.

Elder Sigra cleared her throat. 'It is without further ado that the Council of Seven Elders officially offers the crown and throne of cyrens to Rohesia Irons. Please step forward and kneel, Rohesia.'

With her heart hammering in her chest, Roh did as Elder Sigra bid, kneeling before her crown with her head bowed.

'Rohesia Irons,' Elder Sigra called. 'Do you vow to serve cyrenkind, to protect its history, its legacy and its future, so long as you live?'

'I do.'

'Do you vow to adhere to the Law of the Lair, to rule over cyrenkind with justice and integrity, so long as you live?'

The galleries were silent, as though every being was holding their breath.

'I do.'

'Do you vow to protect the *Tome of Kyeos* and the birthstones of Saddoriel with your life?'

'I do.'

Roh could feel the anticipation pulsating in the air around her.

'Then it is with great honour that I officially crown you *Rohesia the Resilient*, Queen of Cyrens.'

Resilient. The word echoed through her, the answer to a question she had long asked. What would they call her? It was not Songless, it was not Bone Cleaner.

Resilient.

She supposed of all things, she was that.

Awe rippled across the crowds as the crown touched Roh's head. Slowly she stood, no longer a bone cleaner, no longer an *isruhe*, but a queen of her kind.

She touched a hand to Elder Sigra's shoulder. 'Thank you,' she said softly, before turning to face the crowds herself, the Council of Seven Elders dispersing from the platform.

'I am not one for pretty speeches and grand formalities,' Roh heard herself say, her voice clear and loud. 'But I am here to uphold my promises, both new and old.' She strode to the archway of bones, reaching deep within herself for that power that had rejuvenated since the sea battle. She called it to the surface with a single note.

Flowers bloomed at her fingertips, verdant leaves and vines sprouting, exploring the intricacies of the bone structure, wrapping around the ivory arch and covering it nearly completely.

'From here on,' she said. 'There will be no more bone cleaners, no more bone architecture.'

An audible gasp sounded from the crowd.

But Roh pushed on. 'I will not remove our bloody, shameful history from the lair, but I will make new history here today. Henceforth, to use a deathsong or death chorus against an innocent, human or otherwise, is outlawed. This is the dawn of a new era of peace between cyrens, warlocks and humankind.'

Roh's magic continued to encase the archway of bones with new life and colour.

The lair was silent, all eyes on her, a unified sense of wonder resonating through the crowds as Roh returned to the platform.

'There is a vow I need to uphold before you all today,' Roh announced, turning to Elder Erdites Colter, who stood below her. 'Bring me the ledger.'

She saw the hesitation in his face, but he dared not defy her, not now. There was a flurry of movement somewhere behind him and a thick book was brought forward to her. She took it in her hands, opening it to its final page, where a single name called out to her, written in a messy hand.

Odalis Arrowood, Prince of Melodies.

Roh braced herself, and as she had promised her friend, with all her strength, she tore the ledger in two. Shredded pages fluttered to the ground.

Erdites Colter could not suppress the gasp that escaped him, but Roh eyed him evenly.

'From this day forth, the purpose of the Jaktaren guild has changed,' she declared. 'From now on, it is the duty of the Jaktaren to find traitors to the cyren crown and bring them to justice.'

Murmurs of intrigue punctuated Roh's words, but she pressed on. 'Anyone who disagrees with such a mission is invited to leave the guild, and to speak with the new head Jaktaren, Finn Haertel, immediately.'

Finn Haertel stood with his arms crossed over his chest, wearing a fresh set of black leathers, his prosthetic limb showing beneath the gathered hem of his trousers. He stared right back at those surveying him, a sharp glint of defiance in his lilac eyes.

Let them challenge me, he had said to Roh when she had first mentioned the position to him. Now, she met his gaze across the chamber and smiled with pride.

'The first assignment for the new guild is to locate the former Arch General of Akoris and disclose this information to me. The queen's justice awaits him.'

The excitement of the crowd was palpable and Roh knew it was only a matter of time before they could no longer contain themselves. There was much to digest and debrief about, but she wasn't done yet.

'One last matter of business,' she called out.

All fell quiet once more.

'It has come to my attention over the course of my quest and the former Queen's Tournament that our ruling system is flawed, broken even.' Roh steadied herself, knowing with every fibre of her being that what she was about to say was the right decision, not just for her, but for the realms.

She cleared her throat and lifted her chin. 'Therefore, it is my command that from this day forward, there be not one, but two Queens of Cyrenkind.'

Disbelief coursed through the throng.

'It is my intention that there will always be a queen present in Saddoriel, who will maintain justice and order. But there will also be a queen to travel between the other cyren territories to ensure fair rule is always adhered to there as well. A dual rule offers balance. May we always keep each other accountable, may we always keep each other honest.' Roh waited for a moment, before reaching out to her friend. 'Yrsa Ward, please join me.'

Yrsa's cheeks were tipped with pink as she ascended the platform and stood beside Roh, who motioned to Cerys at the foot of the steps. Cerys came forward, offering another velvet cushion to Roh, atop which sat another crown of coral.

Roh took it in her hands and smiled at Yrsa. 'Please kneel,' she said.

Tears glistened in her friend's eyes as she did as Roh bid.

'Yrsa Ward,' Roh stated clearly, recalling the words Elder Sigra had spoken only minutes before. 'Do you vow to serve cyrenkind, to protect its history, its legacy and its future, so long as you live?'

Yrsa returned Roh's smile, tears spilling down her cheeks. 'I do.'

'And do you vow to adhere to the Law of the Lair, to rule over cyrenkind with justice and integrity, so long as you live?'

Once more the galleries were silent, the significance of the moment lost on no one. History was being made before their very eyes.

'I do,' Yrsa said.

'Do you vow to protect the *Tome of Kyeos* and the birthstones of Saddoriel with your life?'

'I do.'

'Then it is my greatest honour to officially crown you, Yrsa the Wise, the second Queen of Cyrens.'

Roh felt the burst of thunderous applause from the crowds deep in her chest as she pulled Yrsa to her feet, and together the two cyren queens faced their people for the first time.

CHAPTER THIRTY

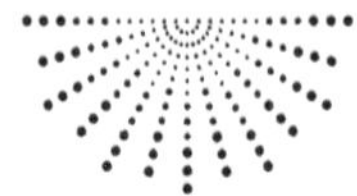

Rohesia the Resilient, Queen of Cyrens, stood before the entrance to Saddoriel's Prison. Her body was tense as she watched a guard use a flat chisel to scratch her mother's sentence off the stone above the portcullis of bones.

Cerys. Five millennia, it had stated. Now it was nothing but a blank mark upon which a new sentence would be carved, in time.

Roh thanked the guard and waited as the portcullis opened for her with a loud creak. Taking the torch offered, she stepped inside the prison, waving away her escort. There were some things a cyren needed to do alone.

Roh wandered the passageways, her inner compass and the birthstones in her crown guiding her through the network with ease. She had never entered the prison from the official gates, she had only seen past them in the visions of her father, shown to her in the Lochlorian mirror pool. It looked much the same as it had then: dark and dank, a place leeched of hope and comfort. Somewhere in here, the Warlock Supreme was being held and Roh wondered if she had asked after her son and if the guards had shared the news of Deodan's survival.

Goosebumps rushed across Roh's arms, but the thrum of the gems in her crown soothed the uneasiness within her as she turned another corner, reaching the cell she was most familiar with.

Cerys' cell. With all its wing carvings and madness within.

Only it was not her mother who stared back at her this time.

The former Queen of Cyrens did. Delja was anything but triumphant now, still wearing the same gown from her challenge at the Pool of Weeping, filthy and in tatters now. Her usually immaculate hair was lank and oily, her skin covered in grime and her expression one of self-pity.

'Rohesia,' she breathed, gripping the bars of bone desperately in her hands. 'You have to understand –'

Roh gazed upon her, knowing full well she now stood where Delja herself once had, looking down at Cerys in glee. 'That's exactly why I came,' Roh said evenly. 'To understand.'

'I thought you would just turn to the *Tome of Kyeos*,' Delja said, her voice raw.

'The tome has shown me many things. But I wanted to hear it from you.'

'Hear what, exactly?'

'Why,' Roh told her. 'Why you did any of it, to my mother and Marlow, to my father, to cyrenkind ... And then to me ... Why did you pretend to care for me? Why did you pretend to help?'

Delja's hands fell away from the bars and she paced her cell, before she sat on the filthy cot. 'There were many reasons, once.'

'You have to do better than that,' Roh said.

Delja put her head in her hands, but nodded. 'At first it was fear, I suppose. Fear that I would lose them, Cerys and Marlow. They were the only family I ever had.'

'Until you betrayed them.'

'Yes.'

'And then?'

'And then it was the power … I loved it. It was the one constant in life, the one thing that wouldn't let me down. Once you have a taste, you become unwilling to live without it. And that single taste is not enough.'

'You could have shared it, it could have been the two of you ruling together, like you always planned.'

Delja huffed a dark laugh. 'Crowns and magic aren't the only power, Rohesia. There is power in friendships, in history, in popularity … All of which Cerys had in abundance … and I did not. We might have hoped to share a throne, but her other powers far outweighed mine. We would never have ruled equally.'

'And so you had her husband killed and sentenced her to five millennia in prison?'

'I'm not proud of what I did.'

'Aren't you?' Roh pressed. 'You never undid that which you could. You never made things right.'

Delja looked up at her. 'I tried to, with you.'

'What?' Roh nearly snorted.

'I took you under my wing, I helped you. You could have been *my* daughter.'

'You betrayed me before the end, just like you did my mother.'

Delja inhaled sharply. 'Because you were *just like her*,' she hissed, shooting to her feet, fury flashing in her eyes. 'The same unapologetic ambition, the same perplexing moral high ground … I knew you would ruin all I had worked for, all that I had built.'

'You built *nothing*, Delja,' Roh said softly. 'You will leave nothing behind when your time is done. Your only legacy is the lies you fed our people. Your reign was six hundred years of deception and nothing more. That is how you will be remembered.'

Delja cursed, upturning her cot in a rage, the threadbare blankets hitting the puddles of filth. 'And what will your legacy be, *isruhe*?' she screamed, spit flying.

Roh looked at the former queen for what she knew would be the last time. She would not come back to the prison, she would not oversee Delja's trial. She would move on.

'I was never an *isruhe*,' Roh told her. 'And my legacy will be all that I can make it.'

With that, Roh left Saddoriel's Prison.

Cerys and Marlow were waiting outside the portcullis for her. It was still a strange sight to behold; the two siblings standing side by side, as though they hadn't been separated for centuries. Roh thought Marlow seemed younger next to his sister; he didn't look as frail and old as he had before.

'Did you get the answers you wanted?' Cerys asked, starting the walk back to the Upper Sector of Saddoriel.

Roh shook her head. 'I'm not sure even Delja has those.'

'I think you're right,' her uncle offered, a note of sadness in his voice. 'She is not the same nestling we grew up playing in the stream with.'

'None of us are,' Cerys answered roughly.

Roh could feel her mother's fury vibrating from her. She certainly didn't blame her for such feelings. Roh imagined they had all come rushing to the surface upon seeing the entrance to the prison. Her mother had vowed she would never step foot inside the place again, not even to see Delja suffer.

Several minutes passed as they walked the passages of Talon's Reach, putting more and more distance between them and the prison. With each step, Roh could feel Cerys' rage ebb away, little by little.

When she thought enough time had passed, Roh brought her mother and Marlow to a stop.

'Before we go any further, there was something I wanted to ask you both ...' she began, suddenly nervous. 'As you know, the

Council of Elders is changing. Several members are no longer fit to serve Saddoriel and cyrenkind.'

Cerys snorted. 'Indeed.'

Roh ignored this. 'Yrsa and I were wondering if you – both of you – would be willing to serve? As new elders?'

A second passed. Then two.

The Irons siblings exchanged a look, before Marlow took Roh's hands in his. 'We have been trapped over six hundred years too long in this godsforsaken lair, Rohesia,' he told her. 'We need the mountains, we need the crystal blue of Lamaka's Basin. We need to go home.'

Tears prickled in Roh's eyes, but she blinked them back. 'I understand ...' she managed to say.

Cerys put an arm around her shoulder then. 'We will return to Lochloria with Deodan, to reside there for the rest of our days. And while we do not wish to be part of the Elder Council, the very organisation that helped destroy us and our family ... Whenever you need us, we will be *your* council, Rohesia. Always.'

Roh leaned in to her mother's arms and squeezed Marlow's hand. 'Then that's more than enough,' she said.

Both cyren queens agreed that Yrsa was to remain behind in Saddoriel to oversee the beginning of the changes to the lair, while Finn, Harlyn and Kezra, along with Cerys and Marlow would return to the scholar's city for Deodan's ceremony.

However, on the banks of the Pool of Weeping, Harlyn pulled Roh aside. 'I want to stay here,' she said weakly, toying with Odi's shell token that she had worn every day since his passing. Its leather strap had tangled with that of the key from Csilla that she also wore around her neck. Roh's own grief compounded as she looked upon her oldest friend; the change in her was heartbreaking. Not only was her face thinner, with dark smudges of purple beneath her eyes, but there was no sign of the confident cyren she had once been. Her hair was unwashed and her clothes were wrinkled, but she seemed oblivious to those details, and most things around her. Once, she had stood straight-backed, head high, but now, her shoulders curved inwards, her movements that of a frail human.

'Harlyn …' Roh started to say. 'We agreed it might be good for you —'

'Please,' Harlyn interrupted. 'There's something I have to do.'

A wave of alarm washed through Roh and it must have shown on her face because Harlyn took her hand.

'It's not about … Odi,' she managed. 'Well … I don't know, it might be.' Harlyn rubbed her chest, as though the action might ease the pain there. 'After Odi … Well, I know I haven't really been able to … function, I suppose. Conversations have gone over my head, very few things had actual meaning to me, they still don't …'

Roh listened, still holding Harlyn's hand.

Fresh tears tracked down Harlyn's face as she spoke. 'But somewhere amidst all the buzzing in my head, *her* voice cut through.'

Roh's heart stuttered. 'Orson's voice?'

Harlyn nodded. 'Remember I told you that it had grown louder since returning to Saddoriel?'

Roh didn't trust herself to speak.

'And how it seemed to be pulling me in a particular direction?'

'Yes,' Roh breathed.

'I think I need to follow it …'

Fear spiked in Roh's chest. 'Harlyn, I don't know … It sounds —'

'Mad, I know.'

'I was going to say, *dangerous*.'

'Roh.' There was a pleading note in Harlyn's voice this time. 'It's something I have to do. I have to find out …'

Roh exhaled a long, low sigh. 'I understand. But I don't want you doing this alone. You will take two guards.'

'I thought I would take Orson's mother,' Harlyn countered. 'She knows her *meesha* best, doesn't she? She might understand …?'

Roh sensed the others watching them from the water's edge and found that her hand had grown clammy in Harlyn's grip. She squeezed her friend's fingers before releasing her. 'If it's something you must do, Har, then do it. But … be safe.'

Harlyn's gaze lingered on Roh's own, the words she hadn't spoken heavy between them: *I can't lose another friend.*

Harlyn nodded gratefully. 'Good luck in Lochloria,' she said, before swiftly walking away.

When Roh and her entourage emerged from the mirror pool in Lochloria, the day that greeted them was clear and crisp. Roh breathed in the fresh mountain air and the scent of pine with a grateful sigh. The birthstones of Saddoriel hummed contently in her crown and she felt at ease, knowing that she had left the lair in capable hands.

Roh heard her mother's intake of breath as they stepped foot on Lochlorian land, but Roh left her to be with Marlow, so they could take in the sight of their family's home together in privacy.

Finn slid his fingers through hers as they made their way through the forest with their friends, following the river towards the quadrangle where the warlock ceremony was to be held. The earth beneath Roh's boots was still scorched and dry, as was the grass of the quadrangle when they reached it, but it mattered not. The joy in the air was infectious, with warlocks from all over the realms having gathered together to see their homeland returned to them.

They had hung colourful banners and flags across the sandstone buildings and archways, and flagons of Vallian wine were being passed around generously. From amidst the crowds, Maiella and Nym darted forward, along with Kezra's nestlings, Sol and Mora, who both wore gold circlets across their brows. The group of terrors threw themselves around Roh's knees.

'Roh! Roh! Did you bring your dragon? Where is he?' Maiella blurted, looking up at Roh full of eagerness.

Roh found herself laughing, a sound that sometimes still shocked her. 'He's coming a little later,' she assured the nestlings.

The youngsters burst into excited chatter and Elna appeared, pulling them away apologetically as she shooed them off.

'So, that's why you're so popular,' Finn murmured in Roh's ear.

'One of many reasons,' she quipped, pulling him towards the stream that ran through the centre of the quadrangle, where Deodan was in deep discussion with some of his fellow warlocks, his mother's eagle sitting proudly on his shoulder.

'You're here!' he beamed when they reached him.

'Of course we're here,' Roh said, curiously eyeing the bird of prey. 'The creature is loyal to you now?'

'Its fealty is linked to the true warlock leader,' he explained. 'As soon as my people recognised me for what I am, the bird came to me. It is its nature.'

'I see ... And what of the former Warlock Supreme? Have you and your clan leaders determined a date for her trial?'

Deodan nodded. 'Two weeks from today.'

'Good. It will be a relief to put the matter to rest,' Roh replied before turning back to the quadrangle. 'So ... The ceremony ... What happens now? Is it all vows and serious sentiments?'

Deodan laughed. 'We leave most of that to you cyrens.'

'Well, what, then?' Finn asked.

Deodan gave a nod to Barrow, who stood close. 'It's time,' he told him.

'What do you need me to do, Deodan?' Roh hissed, suddenly panicked. 'I'm not familiar with this formality.'

Deodan smiled. 'Because it's never been done before. You'll know what to do, Queen of Bones.'

Nearby, someone struck a bell. The single note carried across the entire quadrangle and the crowds fell silent. For a moment, all that could be heard was the rustle of the wind in the trees and the rush of the small stream.

'Friends from far and wide,' Deodan spoke, his voice echoing between the buildings. 'Witness the return of the warlocks to our homeland, Lochloria. Where the blood of our ancestors was once spilled, so too our blood is spilled again.'

There was the flash of a blade across his palm and red dripped from Deodan's open hand onto the cracked earth.

The whisper of a breeze channelled through the crowd and Roh heard the faint notes of a wind chime. She closed her eyes, relishing the delicate song, feeling her magic rise up within as if in answer to a quiet question.

And Deodan was right, she knew what to do.

Feeling everyone's eyes on her, Roh went to Deodan and knelt in the dirt beside him. There, she placed her palm where his blood stained the earth, and tilted her head to the clear sky.

Rohesia the Resilient, Queen of Cyrens, sang her lifesong.

The notes poured from her soul and channelled her power into the heart of the scholar's city, seeking out the poison that had cursed its grounds for so long.

No more.

Life sprang up from the earth, the yellowed grass at their feet became vibrant greenery, the water flowed more powerfully in the stream, and verdant vines coiled around the buildings that were in disrepair, pulling them together like a healed wound, the sandstone no longer crumbling at a touch.

Roh's magic banished that dark mark upon Lochloria. And when the final note left her lips and she turned to her warlock friend, there were tears of happiness in his eyes. Around them, the wind chimes shifted in the gentle breeze, singing their own song of wild joy, and overhead, a sea drake and an eagle flew together.

EPILOGUE

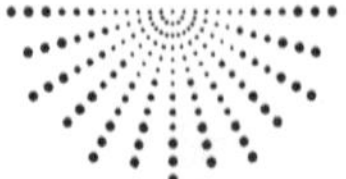

SIX MONTHS LATER

It took time to dismantle and rebuild an entire system, Roh learned as much at a frustratingly slow pace. She had never been the most patient cyren, which was why having Yrsa ruling at her side was one of the best decisions she had ever made.

The two queens had at last addressed the issues within the Council of Seven Elders by removing some of the longest-serving families from power. After Lochloria had been returned to the water warlocks, the Haertels, Mercer, Colter and Rasaat were all dismissed from their seats and had slunk away to lick their wounds in the shadows. Roh knew she had not seen the last of them, but for now, they held no power over her or cyrenkind.

Elder Sigra and Elder Ward remained, though the latter insisted she was due to retire as soon as the dust had settled. Roh wondered how long that would take. Both she and Yrsa faced a daily onslaught of complaints regarding their ongoing changes to the lair, but together they handled them.

The council now boasted two new members: Arcelia Bellfast, Roh's former lessons master who had helped her during the initial Queen's Tournament, and Floralin Wisehand, who agreed to the position so long as she could carry out her duties from Csilla and travel between the territories when required.

Roh had insisted that the seats on the council should not be filled for the sake of it, and so the queens had left space for three more elders to be sworn in, when a cyren came forth who was worthy of such responsibility. Much to the disdain of some of the older, male highborns, females now exclusively ruled Saddoriel.

Over the months that had passed, Roh and Yrsa had elected a pair of treasurers to assess the Saddorien coffers. To Roh's relief, Delja had not spent lavishly during her reign, and by selling off a number of unnecessary assets, the new queens were able to offer a weekly stipend to former bone cleaners to assist them in undertaking re-education or finding new occupations. Many of Roh's former colleagues wished to learn how to play music, for under the new regime, it was perfectly legal for a cyren to master an instrument. Roh and Yrsa encouraged this widely in the hope that someday, the cyrens of Saddoriel would fill the lair of bones with music once more.

With so many new accounts and schemes to manage, Roh had half joked that Jesmond would be perfect as a treasurer, but Yrsa the Wise had swiftly dismissed the notion, declaring that placing a known gambler in charge of an entire kingdom's funds wouldn't be the best way to start a new reign.

'Besides,' Yrsa had said. 'She belongs at Harlyn's side in Lochloria. That is where she is most needed.'

Roh couldn't have agreed more. She enjoyed working closely with Yrsa. They worked together as though they had never known another reality. Yrsa had shared the 'ledger' that she and Finn had kept over the years, rich with ideas on how to improve Saddoriel and the distant cyren territories. Sometimes Roh felt as though the competitors who had opposed each other in the Queen's Tournament were different cyrens entirely, as though those trials had been endured by others. The thought of the trials always made her chest twinge, as the memory of Odi by her side was still a raw wound.

True to her word, Roh not only gave Finn access to the *Tome of Kyeos*, but had the entire Vault modified so that any cyren who wished to read their histories could be admitted. Deodan had helped her enchant the volumes so that they couldn't be damaged by touch, nor could they be altered by those who wished to deny their bloody past. Arcelia Bellfast had also seen to it that the mandatory nestling and fledgling lessons be amended to reflect the true history, and even the Passage of Kings underwent renovations.

Cerys visited Roh regularly, and together they began training both Roh's warlock magic and cyren lifesong. Sometimes Marlow came too, offering his own insights on warlock techniques, as well as titbits of information about Roh's father. Cerys didn't speak of him, but Roh surmised that she would hear of Eadric when her mother was ready.

Under her family's guidance, Roh's power flourished, as did her mastery of the chaos within. She could feel herself growing stronger, despite the weight of the kingdom upon her shoulders and the ever-present grief in her heart.

She pushed on with Yrsa at her side, achieving changes one by one, day by day. They had seen to it that the stolen statues and artworks in the Akorian gallery were returned to their rightful owners across the realms, a peace offering and a step towards rebuilding their relationships and allies beyond the cyren territories. There was so much to learn, so much to navigate, but Roh found that the practicality of such tasks kept her mind occupied and the darkness of that grief at bay. Having Finn by her side helped with that, too. The handsome Jaktaren spent most nights with her and travelled with her when he wasn't busy with the running of the guild.

It was the guild that occupied Roh's mind as she woke with a start one morning, Finn's warm arm draped across her. The previous night, as she'd been sketching designs in the sketchbook he'd gifted her, Finn had brought her the news she'd been waiting for and she'd hardly slept. Every fibre of her being had been restless in the wait to take action. It was still early, but Roh could wait no longer. She slipped from her bed, careful not to wake Finn, and dressed in the dark. In the hallway of the queen's private residences – Yrsa had insisted she take them and that she was happy with her own – Roh wrote Finn a note explaining where she was going and why it was something she needed to do alone. She knew he wouldn't like it, but he'd understand. And with that comforting knowledge, she left her apartments and headed for the Pool of Weeping; Akoris awaited.

Roh had visited Akoris a handful of times on official business over the last few months. This, however, was *not* official. Her skin tingling, she emerged on the other end from the mirror pool in the cyren territory, not quite yet used to the strange form of transportation.

A quartet of guards greeted her in a flurry of bows.

'Your Majesty, we weren't expecting you,' one said hurriedly.

Roh gave a dismissive wave. 'I'm not here,' she told them.

The guards exchanged unsure looks, but didn't question her.

Roh nodded her thanks as she passed them and left the cavernous space with its willows and stalactites. She moved through the monastery with a reluctant familiarity. While many of the statues of Dresmis and Thera had been removed and the air was free of the scent of incense and hallucinogens, Akoris still made Roh's skin crawl.

The Rite of Strothos felt like a lifetime ago, but as she turned a corner and approached the temple, Roh could still taste the bitter tang of fear on her tongue. Gods, she hated this place. She wondered if there would ever come a time when she didn't.

Roh forced herself to peer inside. For a second, she saw the space as it had been for the rite – transformed into what the Akorians had called The Hollow, a giant poison-laced pool at its centre. But it didn't look like that now. Now, it was a simple temple. A few cyrens wandered freely about, though none were forced to their knees to pass hours in silent, drugged prayer. Those days had long gone.

Roh gave the worship hall a final glance before leaving the monastery behind.

An hour later, with five hooded figures at her back and the briny breeze tangling her hair, Roh crossed the dunes of Akoris to a place she had once treasured – the sea caves. She rested her hands on the grips of the quartz daggers sheathed at her sides, revelling in the comfort they gave her; one belonging to her father, the other pulled from the heart of a mother drake.

The hooded cyrens in her wake were silent. Roh could feel the anticipation thrumming between them, making the hair on the back of her neck stand up as they made their way into the sea caves.

Roh hated that Finn's news had brought her here. She didn't want this place tainted with something so bitter. She wanted to keep her memories of Odi and their friends leaping from the rocks with too much wine in their bellies and laughter on their lips. She decided then and there that she would protect those moments with all her power, that no one could take them from her.

Roh saw a flicker of torchlight up ahead and slowed her steps, careful not to make a sound. Ignoring the squirming discomfort in her gut, she took a steadying breath and pushed forward, closing the gap between her and the cyren she'd sought for months.

She stopped before him, her expression cold, her hands still resting on her daggers. He was exactly as she'd expected him to be.

Cowering beneath an overhanging rock was Adriel, the former Arch General of Akoris. His robes were in tatters, his once handsome face, gaunt. There was a desperation in his gaze and a terror to his mannerisms that sent a selfish thrill of satisfaction through Roh.

'I told you that your time here would end,' she said. 'Remember?'

Adriel gaped at her, at her crown and wings, at the steely determination in her now lilac eyes; one of many changes the vision in Csilla had promised. 'Majesty, I —'

'I told you that I wouldn't forget.' Roh's words cut through his pleas. 'You knew I would come for you.'

Adriel threw himself at her feet, going so far as to clutch the hem of her pants. 'Your Majesty, I beg for forgiveness,' he cried. 'I was not myself that night, I —'

'Take your hands off me,' Roh ordered.

He did.

Roh studied him carefully. Any trace of the imposing presence he had once possessed had withered away in the months he'd been in hiding. He was thinner and wide-eyed, downcast. Roh felt nothing.

'Please —' he started again.

But Roh held up a hand. 'Unfortunately, I am not who you have wronged most in this world.'

Confusion rippled through him. 'Majesty?'

Roh stepped aside, allowing the hooded figures behind her to show themselves.

Adriel choked, backing away. 'No.'

Slender hands lifted to the dark fabric, letting it fall, revealing

Seraphine, Adriel's former *oracle* and her sisters, long blades glinting at their belts.

Ignoring Adriel's pleas, Roh bowed her head to Seraphine. 'Tell me when it is done.'

With that, she left the former Arch General to his bloody fate, and the women to their revenge.

The high sun disappeared behind the canopies as Roh strode from the Lochlorian mirror pool into the dense woods. Beneath the shade, the air was cool against her skin and she breathed it in with a sigh of relief. She had long since realised that there was something reassuring about the mountain breeze, as though it greeted her with the presence of her ancestors. Following the pull of the birthstones, Roh found herself at her father's grave, which had been removed from the eerie tombs below. Cerys had requested that Eadric and his preserved companions be returned home to where they belonged, and at last he had been properly laid to rest in the fresh air of the forest. Now, Roh touched her hand to the stone, tracing the inscription. She hoped her father had found some peace in the next life, finally freed from the darkness of Saddoriel's Prison.

'I wish I could have known you,' Roh told him. Magic pulsed at her fingertips and she let small tendrils of power trace his name in farewell, but she couldn't linger.

She continued through the forest, following the stream towards the scholar's city, passing the spot where Deodan had attempted to train her warlock magic. Soon she entered the main part of Lochloria, the warlock students waving as she passed. She waved back, the warmth of the revived scholar's city slowly thawing the coldness in her heart. The warlocks weren't the only ones learning; after her initial refusal to visit Lochloria, Harlyn had eventually installed herself permanently in the restored

Resident Halls and was studying to become a lessons master. It was there that Roh found her, hunched over the beloved lute that Odi had fixed for her.

'You're finished your classes for the semester?' Roh asked by way of greeting as she entered her rooms.

'Yes, thank the gods. My mind has turned to liquid,' Harlyn replied, setting the instrument down on her bed. Grief had aged her, but she put on a brave face.

Roh smiled and looked to the disarray of clothes hanging from the half-open chest of drawers. 'And you're obviously packed?'

Harlyn scanned the mess and gave her a sheepish look. 'Obviously.'

Roh laughed and moved aside a pile of parchment to sit in the armchair opposite her friend. 'You're sure you want to go ahead with this?' she asked.

'More than anything,' Harlyn said. 'Are you sure Your Majesty has time for another adventure?'

'I *made* time. That's why I asked you to wait until now.'

Harlyn nodded. 'Right ... Good, good. Well ... considering I might need a few more, er ... minutes to finish packing ... Deodan suggested that you take a look at the new building beyond the arts sector.'

'Oh?'

Harlyn shrugged. 'I think you'll like it.'

Frowning in suspicion, Roh stood. 'Alright, then ... I've got something for Deodan anyway.'

'If you see Jesmond, can you send her this way?'

'Will do.' Leaving Harlyn to her packing, Roh left the Resident Halls and headed past the arts sector. Much of the architecture had been restored to its former glory and the sandstone glistened in the morning sun. Revelling in the bright day and the rare moment of solitude, Roh crested the grassy ridge and paused at the top of the hill, looking down into the verdant valley. Only it was no longer a valley alone. In the clearing, the foundations had been laid for a grand new structure, timber framework erected all around.

Roh racked her brain as she approached it, trying to recall if Deodan had mentioned commissioning a new build during one of their many meetings. For the life of her she couldn't remember. It was entirely possible, but since the coronation, she'd been in hundreds of meetings, all which seemed to blur into one after a time.

Fascinated, she reached the construction site, trying to picture it as a finished design. It was similar to the quadrangle, with double-storey buildings on all four sides, numerous rooms within, still in their early framework stages. But at the far end was a stage and beneath a brilliant lattice archway was the piano she and Odi had built together in the second trial of the Queen's Tournament.

She had asked Deodan to have it transported here, believing that their friend would have preferred his work to be away from the confines and bad memories of the lair.

'Harlyn gave you my message, then?' Deodan's voice sounded from behind her.

Roh embraced the Warlock Supreme when he reached her, breathing in his familiar scent and finding comfort in the strength of his arms. Though, she still didn't care for the giant eagle that watched on from nearby.

'She did,' Roh replied. 'But before I forget,' she pulled a heavy volume from her satchel. 'Here.'

'What's this?' He took the book, turning it over.

'The seventh volume of Killian's journals,' Roh told him. 'Delja stole it in Csilla, it seems. I found it on the bookshelf in my residences.'

'You read it?'

Roh nodded. 'It details how Killian extracted her essence from the Pool of Weeping … He also writes of how she had linked and extended all their lives with dark, foreign magic.'

'Does he say why?'

'He only guesses … At first, he thought it was to ensure that she and Cerys had all the time in the world together, to prepare for The Dawning, and then to reign for longer than any other cyren ruler before them …'

'And after?'

'After it was to keep control over them all, to maintain power … To have their lives in her talons forever. It's no wonder she didn't want us to have it.'

'No wonder,' Deodan agreed, holding the book to his chest. 'Thank you for returning it.'

'Of course. It belongs here,' she said. 'Now, what is this place?' she asked, gesturing to the maze of timber around them.

Deodan smiled. 'See for yourself.' He pointed to a sign that rested against the foot of the stage. 'We're not ready to hang it yet, but I wanted everyone to know …'

Roh crossed the open space and stared at the sign, painted in beautiful script.

The Odalis Arrowood Academy of Music.

'Deodan …' Roh breathed, unable to take her eyes off the words. 'It's …' Emotion overwhelmed her for a moment and she fought back tears, wishing with all her heart that Odi could be there to see this, to witness the change he had wrought on the world.

'I did mention doing something like this a while back,' Deodan was saying. 'Though perhaps not on this scale … Do you like it?'

Roh swallowed the lump in her throat. 'Yes,' she told him. 'Odi would have too.'

Deodan nodded. 'I thought so as well.'

Together they stared at what would become the home for a new generation of musicians, Roh still in disbelief.

'There's one more thing,' Deodan said.

Roh choked out a laugh. 'Something else? Should I be sitting down?'

Deodan smiled. 'You'll want to stand for this.'

Roh shot him a questioning look, but Deodan gestured to someone Roh couldn't see beyond the stage wings. A small human girl took to the stage, and Roh felt her brows furrow as she combed her memories. She looked oddly familiar.

'You recognise her,' Deodan said.

'I do, but … from where?'

'From Serratega,' Deodan replied. 'She played the fiddle in the tavern, the night Odi —'

'The night Odi played for me.'

'Yes.'

'What's she doing here?' Roh asked, confused.

The girl seemed to be waiting for Deodan's instruction, and at his nod, she sat down at the piano.

'It turns out that the fiddle was not her first instrument of choice …'

Roh exhaled through her nose, not taking her eyes off the girl who sat straight-backed on the stool, her hands in her lap.

'We took the liberty of replacing the bone keys with a type of coral that the Eery Brothers deemed suitable,' Deodan told her. 'We figured Odi would want that …'

'Deodan,' Roh warned, suddenly feeling a fresh wave of grief coming on. 'Where are you going with all this?'

The Warlock Supreme reached out, his hand dipping into the pocket where he knew she kept Odi's music. She had told him and the others about it months ago after one of their family dinners.

'What are you doing?' she hissed, making a grab for the parchment.

Deodan held it out of her grasp. 'Trust me,' he said and went to the stage, handing it to the girl who waited there.

Roh's entire body was on edge. 'Deodan … The Eery Brothers said to wait —'

'Trust me,' he repeated and gave the girl a nod of encouragement. 'Go ahead, Hannah.'

With permission granted, Hannah unfolded the parchment with the greatest care, her eyes scanning the contents eagerly.

In the breath of silence before the music began, Roh recalled the only word she had understood written at the top in Old Saddorien by Odi's hand …

Ramehra.

Chosen Majesty.

Hannah set the pages on the little shelf before her and lifted her small hands to the keys.

At the sound of the first notes, Roh's knees buckled. At the next, goosebumps rushed across her skin in a tidal wave. A soft melody began, weaving through the timber structures around them, full of mournful echoes and considered pauses, only to begin to build, the rich sound flourishing beneath Hannah's touch. A graceful song began to unfold, intensifying with each chord, each press of the pedal. Roh's magic awakened within, stirring beneath her veins and rising to the surface, escaping through her talons in delicate gold ribbons. Her power drifted into the air around them, as though playing with the notes of the song, as it had back in Serratega all that time ago.

Roh knew deep in her heart that Odi had somehow guided Hannah, for her hands moved as his had across the keys, a graceful dance, an elegant offering. He had known it would be her to play *Ramehra* to Roh, he had somehow made sure the next master musician was within their reach.

Roh rocked on her heels to the melody, allowing it to sink into her soul and take hold of her. It was as though Odi was here again by her side. She didn't need the ability to read music to understand this: this was their story; hers and Odi's, from that first frightened moment to the last. An epic journey across unknown lands, brimming with crests and falls and vibrant crescendos. The melody shifted effortlessly from sorrow to joy, as they all had throughout the quest they'd taken together. By the second chorus, tears were streaming freely down Roh's face and she clutched her hand to her chest, as though it would somehow relieve the pressure on her heart. But it did not. That was the power of Odi's music, even as it flowed through the fingertips of someone else.

It transcended time and place, life and death.

It took everything and gave more than everything back.

Suddenly, she became aware of others having joined her and Deodan. She didn't know how they'd got there, but as Hannah played, Yrsa, Finn and Harlyn came to stand by them. Finn's fingers laced through Roh's and Harlyn draped an arm around her shoulders, tears tracking down her face as well.

As the final notes of the piece began to build, each more powerful than the last, Roh realised what they sounded like …

Hope.

Later, with Odi's song echoing in their minds and hearts, Roh and Harlyn stood upon the shores of Lamaka's Basin, waiting.

'You're sure she's out there?' Roh asked, scanning the skies.

'I'm sure,' Harlyn told her, adjusting her pack for the dozenth time.

'And we're *absolutely sure* the note is true?'

Harlyn smiled, a smile that lifted the months of grief from her face. 'We're sure.'

Upon having obtained Roh's permission to follow the persistent voice in her head, Harlyn and Orson's mother had been led to their old bone-cleaner quarters in the Lower Sector of

Saddoriel. Beneath her pillow, Harlyn had found a slip of parchment written in a familiar hand …

R & H,

They mean to sabotage the second challenge. They mean to lead you to your deaths. I convinced them of my jealousy, my rage at being cheated and left behind. I played my role well. They told me three answers to three riddles. I will use only one.

Here's to a better Saddoriel and a better realm, with a new queen.

Love always, your sister,

O

'Echo magic,' Marlow had explained to them when they had shown him the note. 'An ancient warlock spell created by none other than Killian, whose journals you've read. That's how you heard her voice, Harlyn. That's how she led you to this letter.'

Roh and Harlyn had gaped at their former mentor.

Marlow had simply smiled. 'She asked me about the technique, soon after your victory in the Rite of Strothos, Roh … I thought it had been a curious scholarly interest … I didn't realise she had meant to have the spell performed …'

'But *how*?' Roh had pressed.

'And *who*?' Harlyn had added. 'Who could have done such a spell in Saddoriel? And why me? Why could no one else hear her?'

'That, I'm afraid, is something you'll need to ask her yourselves,' Marlow replied. 'But my guess is that she knew Roh's state of mind would be called into question after being subjected to the vine of Strothos. And that you were her best chance, Harlyn …'

. . .

Now, great golden wings came into view and Valli flew towards the two friends. He landed effortlessly on the stony beach and nuzzled Roh's neck with his giant head.

'I missed you, too,' she told him softly, stroking his snout.

'I hope he's ready for an adventure,' Harlyn quipped, tucking in her wings and hoisting her pack high on her squared shoulders.

'We'll soon see.' Roh smiled, drawing back to gaze into his molten eyes. 'Are you ready to show Harlyn the true power of a sea drake?'

Valli huffed and lowered his belly to the ground, allowing both cyrens to climb across his broad back.

'Alright, then,' Roh said. 'Let's bring Orson home.'

Without warning, the mighty sea drake launched himself skyward and soared through the clouds. Roh and Harlyn let out shrieks of joy and hung on for dear life, as they set out to find their sister.

ACKNOWLEDGEMENTS

It feels incredibly surreal to be at this point yet again; not only at the end of another book, but at the end of another series. Neither would have been possible were it not for the help and support of some incredibly fine people …

First, to Aleesha and Claire, my wonderful beta readers of many years, to whom this book is dedicated … I cannot thank you enough for the time and care you've given me and my stories, and for championing this quartet from the very beginning.

Next, to my partner Gary, thank you for doing everything in your power to make life easier for an often weary author and for making me laugh until I cry.

Thank you to Sacha Black, for your constant support via voice memos and for providing me with a never-ending source of inspiration.

My eternal gratitude goes to my editor, Alexandra Nahlous, whose kindness and support have helped see this series to its conclusion.

For making this job far less lonely with conversation and community, thank you to Jenna, Katlyn and Dan.

A massive thank you to all my wonderful patrons for your ongoing support and updates in the HS Universe on Discord.

As always, thank you to my oldest friends: Lisy, Eva, Fay, Natalia and Erin for all your support and love over the years, and of course, to my family back home, who continue to show their support from across the pond.

Thank you to the usual suspects: Hannah Jermyn, Benjamin Stevenson, Margot Butler, the O'shea family, the Mulhollands, the Zapperts and Delzoppos, Emily-May Norman, Jordan Meek, Padraic Prendergast, Danielle Noah, Phoebe Woodward, Maria Carroll and fellow author Nattie Kate Mason.

More special thankyous to these incredible bookstagram friends: itsmejayse, thebooktweeter, bookbookowl, apapergarden, bookscandlescats, bookishbron, leezland, elle.cheshire, emilyandherbooks, just_perfiction, queenof_midnight, labsandliterature, missdysfunktion, readingmadly, catsandpaperbacks, zanybibliophile, books.and.hangovers, clareapediabooks, coffeebooksandmagic, devoured_pages, read.and.wander and readthewriteact.

And last, but never least … Thank YOU, dear reader, for sticking with me through thick and thin. I found it harder to say goodbye this time, but I hope Roh and her unlikely companions stay in your hearts as they will mine, and I hope you join me on whatever adventure comes next …

Much love,

Helen

ABOUT THE AUTHOR

Helen Scheuerer is the YA fantasy author of the bestselling trilogy, *The Oremere Chronicles,* and the *Curse of the Cyren Queen* quartet. Often likened to the popular series *Throne of Glass* and *Game of Thrones,* her work has been highly praised for its strong, flawed female characters and its action-packed plots.

Helen's love of writing and books led her to pursue a Bachelor of Creative Writing at the University of Wollongong and a Masters of Publishing at the University of Sydney. Now a full-time author, Helen lives amidst the mountains in Central Otago, New Zealand and is constantly dreaming up new stories. You can find out more via her website: www.helenscheuerer.com

ALSO BY HELEN SCHEUERER

The Oremere Chronicles:

Heart of Mist

Reign of Mist

War of Mist

Dawn of Mist

Cyren Queen Origins (novellas):

A Song in the Deep

The Law of the Lair

The Tides of War

Curse of the Cyren Queen:

A Lair of Bones

With Dagger and Song

The Fabric of Chaos

To Wield a Crown

The Legends of Thezmarr:

Blood & Steel (2023)

WHAT'S NEXT?

MORE ADVENTURES AWAIT...

With her death carved into a fate stone, Althea Zoltaire only has three years to become what she has always dreamed of – a legend.

Having spent her whole life spying and training in secret, she now fights to secure her place in an elite guild charged with the protection of the midrealms.

The sparring and hazing of the new cohort are near deadly, but even more dangerous is her growing fascination with her brooding warrior chaperon, Wilder...

Join Althea and her band of unlikely companions in *Blood & Steel,* the first book in the epic romantic fantasy adventure, *The Legends of Thezmarr.*

Coming soon.

www.ingramcontent.com/pod-product-compliance
Lightning Source LLC
Chambersburg PA
CBHW021957040826
48979CB00046B/2624/J
* 9 7 8 1 9 2 2 9 0 3 0 1 3 *